THE RING OF BELLS

The King of Bells

The Ring of Bells

Barbara Whitnell

Myriad Books Ltd
35 Bishopsthorpe Road
London SE26 4PA

ISBN 1 904154 12 3

Printed and bound in Great Britain

For Bill, with love

Contents

Prologue

London: 1887

"Oh, the foolish, foolish maid," my grandfather said in his soft, countryman's voice which seemed so familiar to me. "Oh, the foolish girl! Why didn't she tell us?"

He was sitting on the sagging chair after the funeral, staring miserably at the bare oil-cloth—a bulky, florid man, very close to tears.

"We thought she was doing well," he went on. "We never heard, no more than a line at Christmas. We thought she was too grand for the likes of us. Why didn't she come home?"

For a while I was silent, considering her reasons. Ultimately there was only one.

"She was too proud," I said.

"Aye, that's right. Eleanor was always a proud one, with fancy ideas." His sadness lightened a little and he smiled puckishly at me, looking up with one bushy eyebrow raised. "Like naming a little maid Genevieve! Now what sort of a name is that?"

"I'm never called anything but Jenny, Grandfather."

"And a good thing too, I daresay—not but what you're not a grand little maid, pretty as a picture." He sighed heavily, his sadness returning. "But it wasn't fair of her not to let us know how bad things were – not to you, nor to Sarah and me. We should have welcomed you both. Still, what's done is done; it's too late for Eleanor to come home. But you'll come, lass? You'll come home, won't you?"

Home!

It was a thought that had always haunted me. Sometimes when I was walking in the drab, endless streets of London, a

9

shaft of longing would pierce me, so acute that I would almost cry out with the pain of it.

"Oh, I want to go *home*!" my heart would weep—yet I hardly knew what I meant by it. For the two back rooms in Ackerly Street were my home, weren't they? I could hardly mean Collingford, for I had never seen it. Only in my dreams had I walked in its sunlit meadows and heard the liquid murmuring of the river.

We had lived at 32 Ackerly Street for ten years. It had been our home ever since I was seven, when my father had clapped his hat jauntily on the side of his handsome head, picked up his silver-topped cane, smiled his charming Irish smile, and disappeared out of our lives for ever.

Now I was to leave that hated house. I was conscious of a feeling of guilt—for was this not a kind of betrayal? My mother had set her face so sternly against going back. Yet even she would surely understand how I longed for a new beginning, how I yearned to close the door once and for all on this last dreadful week and to forget all the doubts and fears and confusion.

Never to see Bella again! Never to hear Mrs Blewett's voice raised in gin-soaked song or smell the damp, stale stench that rose from their rooms downstairs.

The smell had been the first thing I noticed when, as a little girl of seven, I had stepped over the threshold of the house for the first time.

"It's horrid, Mama," I had announced very clearly in my piping treble.

Embarrassed in the presence of our landlady, Mrs Blewett, my mother had frowned at me. Bella had been there too, I remembered, lurking in the background.

"There's a girl there of about your own age," my mother had told me on her return from seeing the rooms for the first time. "She'll be a little friend for you."

She spoke with determined brightness. I was too young at the time to appreciate her problems or to take note of the white, desperate look she wore habitually now that she was the sole breadwinner. Life for us had never been luxurious. My father's acting roles had always been spasmodic and we were accustomed to living on roast beef one week, bread and dripping the next. Our days had been dogged by irate land-ladies and tradesmen waving unpaid bills, but even so there had been compensations. Life was never dull with Gerald Fitzgerald. He was the sort of man who raised the temperature of a room the moment he entered it. My memory of those days was of warmth and colour and laughter. He may have been a bad husband, but he was an affectionate father and I adored him. Now I felt puzzled and confused by his absence, and could not understand why we had to live in this hateful place, while my mother had to strain her eyes over her dressmaking night after night.

Mrs Blewett was a vast, raddled woman, oozing with good nature, or so she appeared on first acquaintance. It soon became apparent, however, that this depended largely on the quantity of gin she had consumed at the Barley Mow, the public house on the corner. There were nights when my mother and I lay in bed unable to sleep for the drunken quarrels that went on beneath us.

She revised her opinion of Bella as a suitable friend for me, which I did not mind in the least. Bella was two years older than I and considerably larger—a big, hulking girl with wiry hair and highly-coloured cheeks, whom I found physically repulsive. It was her way to grip me by the arm when engaging me in conversation, and standing very close, to thrust her face into mine so that I was distastefully aware of her spittle spraying me. Her loudness and strength frightened me, poor timid little mouse that I was.

"She smells," I complained to my mother. "I don't think she ever washes."

"Just ignore her, dear," my mother advised loftily.

Bella was hard to ignore and rapidly turned into an implacable enemy.

Could it have been different? We were chalk and cheese, of course, and perhaps could never have been friends. Her grossness brought out my shyness and reserve: my reserve drove her to greater excesses of bullying. As I thought over our years in Ackerly Street it suddenly seemed to me as if Bella and I had been on a treadmill—a vicious circle which neither of us was capable of breaking, and now never could. We were enemies, and I was content to leave it at that; for the very next day I would be leaving London and would never see her again.

And yet a sudden memory flashed into my mind.

It was a winter's evening and the lamplighter was making his rounds. A cold wind was gusting round the corner of Ackerly Street where it joined Loft Street by the Barley Mow. My mother was click-clicking rapidly along the pavement with me, aged eight or nine, hugging her arm close to me for warmth.

We were laughing.

We had walked from Chelsea where my mother had been measuring a grand lady for a ball dress and to pass the journey more quickly and to keep up my spirits we had been playing singing games. I was being a horse.

"One more mile, my bonnie Black Bess," my mother was singing, adopting a sinister highwayman's croak. "And we'll gallop and gallop and gallop away."

Engrossed in our game we skirted the pathetic group of children who waited for their parents outside the Barley Mow. Poor things, I thought pityingly. How awful to have a mother who kept one waiting outside public houses on cold evenings like this.

I looked at the group in passing. There were two urchins in hand-me-down trousers and tattered jackets, scuffling over possession of some marbles. There was a thin, pale girl of about ten with a shawl over her head and a baby in her arms. And there was Bella, fat and untidy with a rent in her skirt and her hands tucked under her armpits against the cold. She was making an ugly face in my direction and instinctively I pulled even closer to my mother, scowling back at her.

I had forgotten the incident as soon as it happened. Why, I asked myself, should it come back to me after so many years? Why should I suddenly have this uneasy feeling that Bella had been crying out for something?

It was that night, or one very like it, on which my mother had spoken for the first time of the Ring of Bells and I learned that she had been brought up in an inn.

"Not like the Barley Mow!" I said in horror.

"Of course not." She went on stitching at the dress in her hands and said no more.

"What *was* it like?" I asked.

"Oh, it's all in the past. You don't want to know."

"But I do, Mother!"

Her hands were still, her eyes looking far away at something invisible to me, and when she spoke her voice was dreamy.

"It's all so different in the country," she said. "Life in London is so horrible that people drink to blot it out. But in Collingford—that's the village I lived in—men go to have a quiet beer and a yarn together, and I'll tell you something, Jenny, if your grandmother thinks they're spending too much time away from home or getting through money they can't afford, she soon gives them their marching orders. You don't find them arguing, not with your grandmother."

"Don't people get drunk, then?" Drink was a perennial problem in the streets where we lived.

She laughed shortly in reply to my question.

"I'd like to see your grandmother's face if they did," she said. "She won't allow drunkenness at the Ring of Bells. It's a respectable sort of place."

"Is life easier in the country?" I asked.

"Life's hard anywhere. There's poverty in the country the same as anywhere else, but there isn't the misery. And you can't class the Ring of Bells with your common ale house. It always was an inn right back to the time when there was a Priory in Collingford. It was opened as a sort of guest house for folks visiting the Priory, and then Oliver Cromwell burnt it down—"

"Burnt the inn down?"

"No, the Priory, of course. The Ring of Bells kept on going through the years. It became a coaching inn. Those were busy times for the whole of Collingford. Now there aren't any coaches any more and most other houses are going through a lean time, but not the Ring of Bells."

She resumed her stitching with a sigh that seemed to me to have an element of longing in it.

"It sounds so lovely," I ventured at last. "Can't we go back there, Mother?"

She was silent for a long while.

"When I married your father," she said at last, "I had the

13

most terrible argument with your grandmother. I fell out that bad with her that I can't ever go back, not now that he's left us and proved her right."

"That was all such a long time ago!"

"I can't help remembering—and she'd remember, too. She's not the forgiving sort, your grandmother."

It was then, I think, that I started to dream. I plagued her with questions about Collingford until she spoke sharply, regretting that she had ever mentioned it and telling me to speak of it no more. It was better forgotten, she said. We should never go back.

"But *why* didn't they want you to marry papa?" I asked.

"She said he was no good. My father didn't care for him either, but it was my mother I quarrelled with. He was an actor—well, you know that! He'd been acting at the theatre in Oxford and then somehow found his way to Collingford when the show closed down. He and another man, they gave concerts at the parish hall. He had a lovely singing voice as well as being a good actor. All the girls thought he was wonderful—such a gentleman! You must always remember that, Jenny, no matter what. He was always the gentleman."

I kept my silence. The gentlemanly status of my father had been impressed upon me for as long as I could remember and although very young, I was apt to regard it with a considerable degree of cynicism, remembering the callous way we had been left to fend for ourselves. Memories of the good times he had generated had grown dim, overlaid by the grim fact that life was hard and that my mother worked long hours for little reward.

Often we were cold. Sometimes we were hungry, though I was never allowed to go without food even if it meant my mother making do with nothing but bread and tea. But appearances were maintained at all times. I was never allowed to play in the streets like the other children. With all the skill she possessed, she saw that I was decently dressed. She herself never lost the Oxfordshire burr in her voice, but she rigorously corrected me every time she detected the faintest Cockney phrase or intonation in my speech. I noticed that hers grew appreciably more upper class when she spoke to the ladies for whom she made dresses, and she was

14

determined that nothing of back-street Fulham should cling to me in after life.

Not surprisingly, this hardly made for popularity with my peers. I was branded a snob and left to play by myself. I used to look longingly at the singing and skipping games that went on in the school playground, but no one ever chose me when picking sides and I turned more and more to the books that had been my solace for as long as I could remember.

I could never recall a time when I could not read. I imagine that my mother had taught me my letters, for by the time I went to school reading was as natural to me as breathing, and just as essential. Perhaps because of this facility I excelled at school work and when I was nine I jumped a class. I felt pleased with myself—until I realised that because Bella's work was poor and her intelligence limited, she was being held down a year. My pleasure evaporated as if it had never been, for she was a born bully, and I a born victim. I had Bella at home and Bella in the street, but at least the classroom had been a temporary haven. Now even that was to be taken from me—and worse, I became, in Bella's parlance, the teacher's pet.

Little did Miss Baker, our teacher, realise how I was made to pay for the fact that she singled out my work for praise while Bella received only scorn and punishment at her hands.

"Teacher's pet—Lady Muck," Bella would spit at me venomously. " 'Oo the 'ell do you think you are? Too good for the rest of us, you are."

I said nothing of all this at home, not from any lofty motive but simply because Bella threatened me with un-named miseries if I did and I knew her too well by this time to doubt that she would be true to her word. I merely withdrew into my shell a little further and tried to do nothing to draw attention to myself, ignoring as far as possible the Blewett family.

At the age of twelve Bella left school, as ignorant and unlettered as the day she started, and went into service in Chiswick. I had come to loathe her, and it was the happiest day of my life when she drove away on one of her brother-in-law's carts, her tin trunk beside her. Relieved of her malevolent presence, the whole house seemed brighter; the walk to school was no longer an ordeal and I was able to enjoy earning good marks instead of dreading the price I would have to pay afterwards.

I was fourteen when I left school—considerably older than most girls at that time, and I became an assistant in Gilroys, one of the new department stores in Oxford Street. I travelled there each day by omnibus and worked long, hard hours, always arriving home exhausted.

In my second winter at Gilroys, my mother fell ill. She insisted that a doctor was unnecessary—that she would pick up once spring came; but when it was obvious that she only grew worse I persuaded her to visit the doctor in the next street.

"Waste of money," she said when she returned, leaning over our meagre fire and rubbing her hands together to restore her circulation. "They don't know anything, doctors don't. And all those people, coughing and wheezing! If you haven't anything wrong with you when you go, you're bound to have caught something by the time you leave. All I need is a tonic, and I don't need a doctor to tell me that!"

Mrs Blewett waylaid me in the passage a day or two later.

"I don't like the look of your ma," she said, in her gravelly, wheezing voice. "She looks proper poorly to me."

"She's seen a doctor," I said.

" 'Oo? Which one did she go to?"

"The one in the next street. Dr Lawley."

" 'E ain't no good. Take my word for it, dear, I know them all around 'ere. She ought to see Dr Rodgers round at Parsons Green. 'E'd see 'er right."

I mentioned Dr Rodgers to my mother, but she dismissed the whole idea out of hand.

"It's a waste of money, Jenny. I don't believe in doctors."

" 'As she been yet?" Mrs Blewett asked me, buttonholing me some days later.

"I'm afraid not," I said. "I can't persuade her."

Mrs Blewett shook her head mournfully.

"I don't like the looks of 'er, I can tell you dear. I seen that look before. I'll go and 'ave a word with 'er."

But Mrs Blewett's words were no more effective than mine. My mother still refused to have any truck with doctors, though it was alarming how rapidly her illness seemed to devour her. The flesh fell off her bones and her skin had a greyish tinge. When summer came and went with no improvement in her condition, I grew frightened. I knew that she was in pain. She became difficult to live with, goaded by suffering into making cruel, hurtful remarks; then she would be overcome with remorse and would beg me to forgive her, tears pouring down her cheeks.

One night she was worse than ever, crying with pain, unable to rest. I was desperate, not knowing what I could do to help her, and in my desperation I thought of Mrs Blewett.

Illness was her speciality. Her eyes glowed with a kind of mournful joy as she described other people's operations and gruesome complications of childbirth, and while I had in the past been both repelled and amused in turns by this, there was no doubt that it invested her with authority of a kind. And so it was to Mrs Blewett I turned now. She would surely know what to do, I thought.

I ran downstairs, hesitating only momentarily with my hand raised to knock at her living-room door as I heard Bella's voice within. I had not known she was home that evening. No matter—I was beyond caring about her. Rapidly I told Mrs Blewett of my mother's condition.

"Don't you worry, dear," she said, taking charge with gusto. "I know where I can get something as'll dull the pain for the poor soul." She was already reaching for her coat and skewering her shapeless hat on her head. "You stay and 'ave a cuppa tea with Bella and 'er young man. I expect you've got a lot to talk about, being at school together like what you was."

Full of consequence she bustled off and Bella and I were left looking at each other.

" 'Oo's this, then?" asked Bella's unknown friend.

I turned my gaze to the young man who was sitting in a broken-springed armchair close to the fire. He was broad and swarthy with tight black curls, hot little eyes and a bad case of acne.

"This is Jenny Fitzgerald from the rooms upstairs," Bella said. " 'Er ma's dying of cancer—"

"No!"

My horrified voice cut her off in mid-sentence and she turned to give me a scornful look.

"No? You always was a bit simple, Jenny Fitzgerald, for all your 'igh and mighty ways. Don't know nothing, you don't—never did, never will."

"But she saw a doctor! He said she needed a tonic!"

"There's no tonic to cure your ma."

"Come on, Bella!" the young man was attempting to sound as if nothing had been said of any importance. To my amazement he even winked at me and looked me up and down with a leer. "What about that cuppa tea? The young lady would like one and so would I. Draw up a chair, love. Take the weight orf yer feet."

Bella went over to him and leaned against him possessively, lest I should make any mistake about his status.

"This 'ere is Albert," she said. "We're walking out."

"Congratulations," I said, through stiff lips.

He shoved her with his elbow.

"Get the tea, for Gawd's sake,"

"Not for me," I said, backing out of the room hastily. "Thank you just the same. I must get back to my mother."

I ran up the stairs, pausing on the half-landing to cling on to the newel post, suddenly weak with grief and fear and the certainty that Bella was telling me the truth. I heard a cry from the room above me. I knew I had to go in and face my mother. It was the hardest thing I had ever done in my life.

Mrs Blewett was as good as her word and it was less than thirty minutes before she was back with a small, green bottle. By this time my mother was glazed with pain, whimpering weakly. Mrs Blewett came into the room and looked at her.

"Lor', she's failing," she said. "I 'aven't clapped eyes on 'er for a week, so I notice the difference. Pounds, she's lost. She's nothing but skin and bone."

"Should I get the doctor to come here?" I asked.

"No!" my mother's reaction was fast enough at this suggestion. "There's no point, Jenny. We haven't money to waste."

I looked at Mrs Blewett, biting my lip with anxiety and indecision.

18

"I'd give 'er a spoonful of this," she said. "It'll give 'er a good night's rest.'

"What is it?" I asked.

Mrs Blewett shrugged. "Lord knows! Laudanum and other stuff."

"Where did you get it?"

"I got friends, dear. Don't ask questions. And don't give 'er too much—just a teaspoonful every four hours, my friend says."

I wasted no time in giving my mother a dose of the syrup and miraculously it brought an easement of the pain. She even managed to smile at me.

"You know, don't you?"

"Know what?" I asked.

"What's wrong with me."

"I know you ought to see a doctor," I said. "And what's more, tomorrow I'm going to make sure you do, whatever you say."

"Jenny, I've seen a doctor. More than one."

"And what do they say?"

"They say there's no hope. It's just a question of time—a few months, perhaps. We've got to face it."

"Oh, Mother!"

I ran to her and held her in my arms, feeling the stick-like body straining against me.

"You've got to be brave, Jenny. You've got to trust in God."

I could not answer her.

Later, before the four hours were up, the pain returned and she pleaded with me to give her another dose. I held out for a while, but eventually I gave in. It was more than I could stand, to hear her crying. Again the pain eased, and this time she seemed to fall asleep.

I pulled aside the curtains and looked down into the street. It had been raining and the lamplight gleamed on the shiny pavement. Almost opposite, I could see the church we attended every Sunday—a bulky, substantial building with a spire that rose so high I could not from this angle see the top of it. Suddenly I wanted more than anything to go there. It was not enough, I felt, to pray in this room; I needed to be closer to God than I could ever be in a house owned and occupied by the Blewett family.

I put on my coat and hat and eased myself out of the room quietly, careful not to disturb my mother.

There were other people in the church. A week-night service was just finishing when I arrived, and people looked at me with some curiosity as they rose from their knees and turned to leave the church. I suppose I must have presented an odd appearance—I was distraught and untidy. But I ignored their unspoken speculations and fell to my knees in a back pew, burying my face in my hands.

I prayed for a miracle. I promised that my entire life should be given to the service of God, if only my mother should be made well again.

I prayed for courage and for comfort—for myself and for my mother. It was only when I heard a deprecating cough, repeated several times, that I came to myself and looked up to find the verger standing close beside me.

"Er—excuse me, Miss," he said apologetically. "Do you think you'll be much longer?"

I stood up hastily and smoothed my skirt.

"No. I'm sorry—"

"It's me who should be sorry, Miss. I wouldn't want to hurry you, it's just that I've got to lock up. I promised my wife I'd take her to see her mother, see. She's feeling poorly—"

"I'm going now. Really, it's all right. I have to go."

"It's the wife's mother, see. Otherwise, I wouldn't dream—"

"Please," I said. "There's no need to apologise."

I smiled at him mechanically and left the church, his explanations still echoing after me.

As I crossed the street I could see a small group of people approaching the house from the direction of the Barley Mow, and not only could I see them, I could also hear them very plainly. Mrs Blewett, in the maudlin state that was common for her at this time of night, was lurching along singing a mournful song, while Bella and Albert supported each other up to the door. It was my misfortune that our separate arrivals coincided.

"It's the little tart from upstairs," Albert said, reaching out for me with his free arm. "Pretty, ain't yer, darlin'? Come on, give us a kiss."

"Give over, Albert—you don't want her with me about," said Bella, putting both her arms around his neck.

Albert was not to be deflected from his purpose. He held Bella off with one hand and with the other pulled me to him and landed a hot, moist kiss in the direction of my left ear.

I gave him a hefty shove in Bella's direction. "Oh, take your young man and keep him away from me," I said wearily. "I'm sure I don't want him."

"Not good enough, eh?"

Angry that Albert had wanted me, she was now furious that I did not want Albert, and stood like some avenging angel between me and the door, her hands on her hips. "None of us 'ave ever been good enough for you, 'ave we, Miss 'Igh and Mighty?"

"I just want to get back to my mother," I said. "Please open the door."

"Yeah—open the door, Bella." Mrs Blewett's voice was slurred and she staggered against me, breathing gin fumes into my face. "There's a bottle in there somewhere—"

"Makes me sick, she does with 'er airs and graces—oh, give *over*, Albert!" Bella's voice rose to a shriek of rage as once more Albert lunged towards me. "She won't 'ave any truck with the likes of you, you great booby! Too bloody 'igh and mighty. Leave *off*, I say."

Angrily she pulled his hand away from the front of my bodice, while Mrs Blewett pushed past her and managed to open the door. Somehow I wriggled away from the lot of them and ran inside. I could still hear their voices uplifted in anger as I went swiftly up the stairs. I was frightened that they would disturb my mother, but to my relief she was still sleeping.

I slept too. I thought that I would not be able to, but I was worn out. I had worked hard at the shop all day and on top of that had come the shock of finding out the true state of my mother's health.

When I awoke it was morning, and a leaden grey sky hung low over London. My mother was dead in the bed beside

21

me. I could not believe it. She was cold—quite cold, and hastily I scrambled from the bed, dragging on my clothes before running downstairs to hammer on Mrs Blewett's door.

It took me some time to rouse her which hardly surprised me when I remembered the condition in which I had left her the previous night. But finally she, too, pulled on a coat over her nightgown and plodded up the stairs behind me, grumbling and wheezing.

"What's going on?"

Bella, wrapped in a faded dressing gown, had emerged from another room and was standing at the foot of the stairs.

"Mrs F.'s gorn and kicked the bucket," Mrs Blewett said.

"Go on!"

I looked over my shoulder to see her standing there, an expression of dawning excitement on her face. Sudden death was the breath of life to her and her mother. She had not come up to our floor for years, but now she began to climb the stairs after us.

"She's gorn, all right," Mrs Blewett pronounced.

"I know that. What should I do?"

I felt numb. I could not cry—could not even believe this turn of events. A few months, my mother had said. This must be a mistake, I felt sure. It must be happening to someone else.

While Mrs Blewett was looking at my mother, Bella had been sniffing curiously around the room. She found the green bottle on the mantelpiece.

"'Ere," she said suspiciously. "'Ow much did you give 'er of this?"

The fact that I had given my mother a further teaspoon a little before the four hours had expired had worried me, but I had forgotten it in the light of events.

"Not enough to hurt her, I'm sure," I said. "A little more than you told me—well, she was in such pain, I couldn't keep it from her—"

"A little more!" Bella said. "A *little* more! The 'ole bleedin' bottle's gone, all but the dregs."

Mrs Blewett looked first at her daughter and then at me, her mouth slackly open.

22

"You never gave 'er all of it! I told you 'ow much."

"No," I said hastily. "Not all of it. Just a teaspoonful, like you told me."

It was as if I had not spoken.

"I *told* you!" Mrs Blewett sounded frightened. "You knew full well not to give 'er more."

"Mrs Blewett, you must believe me—"

"You said you did give 'er more," Bella said accusingly. "You said she was in pain and you couldn't keep it from 'er."

"I only meant that I gave her a dose before the four hours were up, that's all."

"Huh!"

Plainly Bella did not believe me—or chose to pretend that she did not. She was glorying in this situation, practically smacking her lips over having me at such a disadvantage.

"Never mind all this," Mrs Blewett said. "There's things as must be done. You run for Dr Lawley, Bella—'e'll give a certificate. 'E knew what was wrong with 'er. We don't want questions asked, do we? I mustn't get my friend into trouble."

"Why can't she go?" Bella asked.

"I've got things to say to 'er. Go on—get moving, girl."

Bella gave me an ugly look, but did as her mother told her. Once she was out of the room Mrs Blewett subsided into a chair and looked at me measuringly.

"Well, well," she said. "'Oo'd o' thought it?"

"Mrs. Blewett, I *didn't*—"

"Leave it," she said. "Your mother's dead, that's all that matters. Maybe you give 'er the stuff, maybe you didn't. Maybe she took it 'erself. What's the difference? She knew she was going to die. The main thing is to get 'er planted with no questions asked."

The awful coldness and loneliness hit me then with all the force of an avalanche. I hated her—hated them both; Mrs Blewett with her unfeeling crudeness, Bella with her pretended suspicions.

I was alone. There was nobody I could turn to for support. My mother had been all too expert at keeping herself to herself.

Then I remembered that I had grandparents. It surely was my duty to let them know of their daughter's death.

"I must tell her mother and father," I said.

Mrs Blewett gaped at me.

"I didn't know as she 'ad kinsfolk," she said.

"Oh yes! Her father is landlord of an inn in Oxfordshire."

"Then why would she live like this—slavin' at 'er sewin', workin' 'er fingers to the bone? It don't make sense!"

I made no reply. I would not confess to Mrs Blewett that it made no sense to me either.

" 'Ere," she said, a sudden urgency in her voice. "D'you think they'll come to the funeral?"

"I—I don't know," I said, with some hesitation. I had never been able to picture them, those unknown grandparents of mine. Would they remain hard and unforgiving? I had no way of knowing.

She got to her feet and came over to where I stood by the window looking miserably down on the rows of rooftops and tiny, cat-fouled backyards. She fondled my shoulder, pulling me closer to her so that I could smell her stale breath and the rancid odour of her unwashed clothes.

"Look, dearie," she said, her voice suddenly oily with assumed concern for me. "Don't brood, there's a good girl. You didn't mean no 'arm, we know that. You acted for the best."

"But Mrs Blewett, I didn't—"

"We'll say no more. That's the best thing—it's what *she* would 'ave wanted, look at it that way. All you did was save 'er a few weeks' sufferin'."

"I only gave her—"

"So she took it 'erself! Wot's the point in raisin' a rumpus, dearie? Suicide's an ugly word. The vicar wouldn't like it. 'Er parents wouldn't like it. It'd be kinder all round ter forget it, dearie—specially when splittin' might get my friend into trouble, what did 'er very best to 'elp you in your hour of need."

"But won't the doctor—?"

"Dr Lawley? Not 'im! 'E won't want no trouble either, just so long as 'e can get to the boozer before dinner time. Sides, 'e knew your ma. 'E won't be surprised."

24

He was not surprised. He wrote the certificate without doing more than give her a cursory glance and I felt heavy with misery that this bedraggled, seedy little man was the best that my mother could afford.

I did not know what to think about the medicine.

It was true that I had exceeded the strict dose that Mrs Blewett had mentioned, but only by anticipating by half an hour the time of the next dose. Yet—yet—I remembered my desperation and tears when she begged me for more. Had I become confused and given her too much? Or had she not been as peacefully asleep as I thought when I slipped out to the church? Had she got up and taken it herself in my absence? I should never have left her, not for any reason. For that I would always feel guilty, to the end of my life.

A narrow truckle-bed was lent to me by Mrs Blewett so that I could sleep in the living room until after the day of the funeral, but I lay upon it sleepless, night after night, going over and over the events of that night. There were times when I did not care whether I had been guilty or not; times when I felt glad that her suffering had been brought to a conclusion, no matter by whom.

But there were other times when I blamed myself bitterly, not only for leaving her but also for not realising the hopelessness of her condition months before. I should have written to my grandparents earlier, while there was still a chance that they could help her.

They would have responded generously, I knew that now. For my grandfather had come to London for the funeral immediately upon receipt of my letter and had proved himself to be the kindest and dearest of men. It seemed more incomprehensible to me than ever that she should have refused to go home for so many years.

They wanted me! I could hardly believe it, but my grandfather assured me that it was so.

"You're quite sure that grandmother will welcome me?" I asked diffidently.

"Her own flesh and blood? Of course she will!" He smiled at me. "She'll be glad to have you. There's always use for an extra pair of hands at an inn, and Sarah's not so young as she was. It's coming up Christmas, too, which always means a lot of work. So you come home with me, lass—home to the Ring of Bells."

He held out his arms to me and I flung myself into them, able at last to cry for my mother. As my tears flowed, they seemed to heal something of the hurt of the past few days, and hidden deep beneath my emotion I recognised the re-emergence of that old dream.

I was going home.

Book I

1887–1889

1

"Genevieve!"

My grandmother spoke my name lingeringly as if she were trying to extract the last drop of savour from it. I could see from her expression that she did not approve.

"That's what I call a hoity-toity name to call a girl. Your father's choice, I make no doubt."

I looked nervously at the small, black-clad figure standing in the inn doorway, the sign with its circle of bells creaking in the wind over her head, and my heart sank a little. I could not, in all fairness, claim to be unprepared for my grandmother. I knew that she was the type of woman who made girls leave home and strong men leave their pints, but still I had hoped for a warmer welcome.

By the time we arrived in Collingford I had established a very easy relationship with my grandfather. He was the kindest of men. All my life I had suffered from acute shyness and timidity, but with him I was completely at ease.

One look at my grandmother and I realised that this was, so to speak, a horse of an entirely different colour. Her expression was one of severity, as if she felt certain I would do something to merit her disapproval. She regarded me with a look which seemed to see through to my very soul and I was uncomfortably aware of all my deficiencies.

"I'm always called Jenny," I said in a nervous whisper.

"Well, speak up, Jenny! Are you used to hard work? Can you clean and polish and cook and sew?"

"Sarah, Sarah," my grandfather remonstrated softly. "That can wait, can't it? She's been through a bad time."

"Hard work never hurt anyone!"

"Still and all, Sarah, let the lass get inside the door."

He picked up my bags and nodded for me to go in. My grandmother turned and led the way.

"You'd best go up to your room," she said. "You'll be

wanting a wash after the journey. Nasty, dirty things, trains are. You'll have to share with Annie—go right to the top, up two flights, the door on the left."

She was leading the way to the foot of the stairs as she spoke and did not look round to see if her orders were being carried out. She had the supreme confidence of complete authority.

I followed after, looking curiously about me. We passed through a stone-flagged room with low beams where chairs were set around the walls and a fire smouldered in an inglenook fireplace.

"This is where the gentry take their drinks," she said. "The rest come to the kitchen."

"I see," I said.

This was only partially true. I had not somehow imagined 'gentry' taking their drinks anywhere; the public houses around our home in Fulham had only catered for the lowest of orders and though my mother's brief description had prepared me for something better than a common ale house, I had not imagined such a rambling building, while the thought of men drinking in the kitchen presented an unexpectedly cosy and domestic picture.

"If you see Annie upstairs"—my grandmother went on—"tell her to hurry up with her work and come downstairs. She's wanted in the kitchen. There's no call for her to take all night to turn a few beds down. You can come down for your tea as soon as you're ready."

She bustled off towards the kitchen and I made my way up the shadowy staircase. It was narrow and twisting. There was a small light coming from the room downstairs, but once I had turned the bend in the stairs I almost had to feel my way. Just as I reached the top, one of the doors opened on to the landing and light spilled out, revealing a girl of about my own age dressed in dark blue with a white apron, frilled on the shoulders, holding a lamp in her hand. She jumped with fright as she caught sight of me in the shadows.

"Ooh," she said, laughing and holding a hand to her heart in exaggerated terror. "Ooh, you did give me a start! you must be Mrs Austin's granddaughter—pleased to meet you, I'm sure. Here, wait till I light this lamp."

She set down the one she was carrying and turned to light a larger one that stood on a chest by the wall.

"There, that's better."

She turned to look at me and seemed to approve of what she saw as she smiled with considerably more warmth than I had encountered from my grandmother. Her fair hair was scraped back in a plait of hair that was folded up and tied with a blue ribbon, and she was pretty in a rosy, rounded, slightly buck-toothed way.

"I'm Annie," she said. "You're going to be in my room."

"I hope you don't mind."

She laughed. "Not if you don't snore."

"I don't think so. Do you?"

"Never had no complaints so far. Come on, I'll show you our *boodwar*."

She led the way to the far end of the landing where the narrow staircase continued upwards.

"I hope you're going to like it here," she said. "I was sorry about your mother."

"Thank you."

"You'll find it quiet, though, won't you? London sounds lovely—all those shops and music halls and *restrongs*! Different to Collingford, I can tell you. Have you ever seen the Queen?"

"No, I'm afraid not." I was conscious of her disappointment and hastened to make some sort of recompense. "I saw the Prince of Wales once, riding in the park."

"Did he have Mrs Langtry with him?"

"I'm not really sure. There were several ladies in the party."

Annie giggled. "He's a lad, isn't he? Well, here we are. Mind you don't bump your head."

It was hard to see where a second bed could possibly be fitted into this tiny attic room with its sloping ceiling and eaves window, but somehow it was managed and Annie and I settled down to sharing the limited space more amicably than might have been considered possible.

Annie fairly bubbled with good spirits. I had never before met anyone like her, and her company, coupled with the hard work into which I was immediately plunged, were just

31

what I needed to banish the gloom caused by my mother's death and the disquieting circumstances surrounding it.

Christmas was upon us soon after my arrival and my grandfather had spoken nothing but the truth when he said that an extra pair of hands would be welcome.

There were four letting bedrooms at the inn and these were filled every Christmas by the same family—Mr and Mrs Castle, their married son and his wife with their two small children, two unmarried daughters and a son of fourteen. Evidently it had become a family tradition for them to come to the Ring of Bells. Christmas seemed to have a special significance in the country, they said, and besides this they enjoyed the Hunt which took place each year on the day after Boxing Day.

My grandmother, of course, had been preparing for weeks. The puddings had been made as far back as October, but there was still a mad flurry of activity in the week preceding Christmas. There were the rooms to prepare, the decorations of holly, ivy and mistletoe to be festooned around the parlour and dining room, the tree to be set up and hung about with tinsel and presents for the children of anyone who had ever worked at the inn—sweets and oranges and bags of nuts. More substantial gifts of beef and sacks of potatoes had been given to their elders.

I flew through it all on wings of excitement. Never had I known a Christmas like it.

I had been in the kitchen all day on 23rd December and had just gone up to my room in the evening to wash and change my dress, for that night I was needed to help serve drinks in the parlour, when I heard the sound of the carol singers. I leaned out of the little window to see a motley assortment of carollers in flat wool caps or bowler hats, all muffled to their eyebrows, lanterns in their hands. It was bitterly cold and they were stamping and shuffling their feet until suddenly, at a signal, all their rough, inharmonious voices were raised to sing of the miracle, 'Once in Royal David's City'. Afterwards there was laughter as they came inside for mulled ale and mince pies before setting off on their round of the village.

The next day, Christmas Eve, was equally busy. Early in

the evening I stepped outside to sniff the air to see if we had any chance of a white Christmas, after a day spent running from one chore to another. It was a moment of peace. The stars were thick and bright above me, and across the village green which reached to the very door of the inn I could see the grey stone bulk of the church with its castellated tower. Suddenly, without warning, the bells rang out, their chimes cascading like chips of crystal through the frosty darkness. I was so happy I wanted to cry.

We all went to morning service on Christmas Day and returned to vast quantities of food which we ate after we had served the Castles amid much good humour. Boxing Day was mercifully restful, and the following day there was the Meet, a sight the like of which I never could have imagined.

The Hunt gathered outside the inn for the stirrup-cup, the men in their scarlet coats—gay and dashing and romantic, quite unlike their workaday selves—and the ladies more restrainedly elegant in their black flowing habits. They leaned gracefully from their saddles to accept their glasses. They laughed and joked and gestured with their riding crops, murmuring soothing words to their fidgeting horses who seemed anxious to be off, galloping over the frost-rimed countryside.

Oh, it was glorious, I thought. Just like a stage play—and a comedy at that, for just as the Hunt had gathered and the traps and donkey-carts and farm-wagons full of spectators had jockeyed themselves into position, there was a whoop and a holler and along the lane came three extraordinary figures, conventionally enough dressed from the shoulders down, but on their heads were head-dresses of feathers, just like the Red Indians that I had seen in my illustrated geography reader at school.

Most people laughed and cheered, though some of the older members of the Hunt frowned their disapproval of such levity in the context of so traditional an occasion.

"It's the Leytons," Annie giggled. "Oh, aren't they lads? Isn't it just like them? Honest, you never know what they'll be getting up to next."

The leader of the trio rode up to the Master of the Hunt with hand raised.

"I come in peace, O Big White Chief," he proclaimed in ringing tones.

"That's Mr Roger," Annie whispered in my ear. "Isn't he a lovely lad? I'll lay the colonel doesn't think so, though."

Colonel Farquarson, the Master of the Hunt, looked outraged. He spluttered a little. Then his neighbour, an elderly but still imposing gentleman on an enormous grey, tossed off his drink and guffawed loudly. It was, it seemed, a signal for general laughter and a nod of amused acknowledgment from the colonel.

"That's Lord Bollinger," Annie said. "That big man on the grey horse. Fancy him riding again! Everyone said last year that it was bound to be the last time, but he'll keep on till he drops, I reckon. Grand old man, he is." She giggled again. "Everyone says he was a real lad in his day, and I believe it. He might be old, but he looks at you in a way that makes you think he wishes he wasn't, if you know what I mean."

"Who are the Leytons?" I asked, much more interested in the three dashing young men who had caused such a stir.

"Their father owns Priors, a big farm in the valley not far along the road. Mr Roger's only just come back from America. Some said he was going to stay there, but it seems they were wrong. The dark one is Mr Mark. He's a caution, he really is. Then John is the youngest one. He's still at school studying for Oxford college."

They were an arresting looking trio, even without the flamboyant head-dresses which they changed for more conventional wear, having made their dramatic entrance. Roger rode over in our direction and I thought for one breathless moment that he was going to join us, but he reined in his horse beside a raven-haired beauty, smiling down at her in a way that aroused a twinge of envy in me. I felt I would have given anything in the world to be in the saddle, in well-cut riding clothes, my hair in a neat snood under a black topper.

"Roger, you idiotic boy," the beauty said, slapping him lightly on the arm with her riding crop. "What on earth will you think of next? Where did you get such things?"

"A souvenir of North America."

He looks like a prince, I thought. A well-travelled prince, too. To one who had so far considered a day on Wimbledon Common or in Richmond Park the height of adventure, his glamour knew no bounds.

2

Inevitably the grey weeks of early January seemed something of an anti-climax. The frosty weather turned to rain which fell in an interminable grey, dismal blanket. One forgot that the sun had ever shone and doubted if it ever would again. No one ventured further than absolutely necessary. We walked into the village for our essential shopping but nine-tenths of the time was spent within the four walls of the inn. It was a settling-in time for me—a time when I learned the routine that kept the Ring of Bells running on oiled wheels and began to feel part of it.

My grandmother proved to be less formidable than I had feared. Annie assured me, the first night I arrived, that her bark was a lot worse than her bite, and although I was terrified of her in the beginning, I found that as long as she felt I was making every effort to learn and to work hard, and as long as I spoke up and did not appear to be too meek, she improved immeasurably on acquaintance. She was just and considerate in small ways and she fed us like kings.

She was a hard taskmaster, a perfectionist. She organised Annie and me and Susan, the other maid who came in daily, so that we each knew exactly what duties were expected of us. She organised Jim Parkes who looked after the stables and the outside work, and the boy, Dick, who helped him and who scrubbed the seats of the earth closets snowy white every morning and did everything that no one else wanted to do. She organised the pot-boys who came in every evening, and she organised my sweet, slow-spoken grandfather to the point where sly jokes were made about which one of them wore the trousers.

He seemed more than content with the arrangement. He grew fresh vegetables in the garden, saw to the stocks of liquor, reigned supreme in the parlour bar in the evening, and when the constant stream of orders from his wife began to get a little too much for him, he would suddenly feel it his duty to go and see his widowed sister Millie, 'poor, dear soul that she is', and off he would go, whistling, for a quiet hour or so undisturbed by fresh directives.

The better class guests who came for the fishing put up with grandmother's sternness since her reputation as a cook was unparalleled in the county. She practised her art with the secrecy of a necromancer, keeping all her best recipes (receipts, she called them) locked away in the recesses of her mind or kept under lock and key in the bureau in her sitting room. I learned that many years before she had worked under a great cook in the kitchen of Watersmeet, the manor house occupied by the Bollingers, and she had obviously learned her lessons well. She took enormous pride in the excellence of her table and the reputation of the inn.

Rain or shine, we all trooped across the green each Sunday to the church of St Peter, sitting in a pew reserved for the Ring of Bells. There was a long-standing relationship between the inn and the church, going back to the Priory about which my mother had spoken. These days it was maintained by the bellringers' annual supper and the Harvest Home supper, both of which took place in the big upstairs dining room of the Ring of Bells, with its heavy mahogany sideboard and the table which it became part of my duties to see was kept polished like glass.

Grandmother cherished this connection and the respectability it bestowed on the inn. She was, I thought, the very epitome of Victorian rectitude. She would have made the Queen herself feel like a wanton.

After several weeks of attendance at St Peter's I began to be able to put names to the faces I saw there: the tradespeople; various customers of the inn; the doctor who attended Jim after a horse had given him a vicious kick; and of course, Lord and Lady Bollinger, the squire and his lady.

Lady Bollinger was a sweet-faced woman who gave the impression of vague kindliness. She seemed to have an other-worldly air as she smiled right and left at the village women, who respectfully bobbed curtsies as she and her husband left the church after the service to walk to their carriage which waited for them at the lych-gate.

Grandmother would smile in a superior and rather pitying way if ever her name came up in conversation. Lady Bollinger was too soft, she said. People took advantage. It was not, I felt, a fate that anyone could remotely imagine happening to her.

Lord Bollinger was a large, impressive man with a swagger in his walk and an arrogance that nobody objected to. He had every right to be arrogant, was the general view; and there was no one like him if you were in trouble. You felt that he really cared, people said. And laugh!—Why, he could swap stories with the best. I noticed that on the walk to his carriage his eyes would rest appreciatively on a pretty girl, and he knew everyone by name. His eyes smiled lazily under heavy lids, and though his beard was white, it revealed lips that curved in a devil-may-care grin that belonged to a much younger man.

I was fascinated by their presence and the power they wielded, but grandmother, for reasons of her own, always kept well in the background as they passed. I guessed that this was because she had once worked in the kitchen at Watersmeet and now felt herself unwilling to be reminded of it. She was far too stiff-necked, I thought, to drop a curtsy along with the rest of the women of Collingford.

The Leytons did not come to church every Sunday, much to my regret. I had thought about their dramatic appearance at the Meet many times and longed to see them again, but while Annie pointed out their parents to me, I had to wait several weeks before I saw the sons again. It did nothing for my powers of concentration to have them sitting in a pew well within my line of vision.

Reverend Thorogood went in for hour-long sermons; good, meaty, hell-and-damnation harangues they were. As my grandfather said, you felt you'd had your money's worth with Mr Thorogood.

This particular Sunday his sermon was concerned with the sanctity of the home—a favourite topic to which the reverend gentleman was inclined to return, time and time again—and the inestimable influence of a God-fearing wife and mother. Unfortunately, as an attraction to two silly girls of seventeen, it came a very poor second to the combined forces of the Leytons, sitting opposite.

John looked as if he were reading something under the cover of the shelf which held his prayer book. I found Mark, with his dark good looks and bold eyes, looking on me with interest—or so I fondly thought. I looked away quickly, but it was hard to prevent my eyes from returning in his direction. Roger seemed more interested in the colourful east window and the graceful arches of the transept. His expression was remote, slightly amused; he looked as if he were thinking of something else, far removed from the subject of Reverend Thorogood's oratory.

They were a good-looking family, no doubt about it. Mrs Leyton was a statuesque woman whose figure showed itself to advantage in the fashionable bustle which she wore. Her husband looked considerably older than she. He was a tall man, thin and stooped, with a look of haggard distinction. I should not have guessed him to be a farmer had I not known him to be the owner of Priors.

"Those Leytons!" Annie said to me on the way home. "Did you see Mark wink at me? Limbs of Satan, they are—but lovely boys, all of them."

"They're grand lads," my grandfather echoed a little later as he carved the Sunday roast. It was beef sirloin with roast potatoes, roast parsnips, Yorkshire pudding and sweet, nutty brussels sprouts. The sight and smell of it had my mouth watering in anticipation. I was still unused to meals of such proportions, but my delight in the thought of the apple tart liberally stuffed with cloves which was to follow was in no way diminished by this gargantuan first course.

We had no resident guests as the weather was too bad to tempt even the most avid sportsman from town. Great-Aunt Millie was with us. She was an amiably vacuous woman, well-intentioned but invariably disparaged by my grandmother.

"Millie," she said upon many occasions, "simply has no idea."

She did not elaborate, nor did she need to. Everyone knew exactly what she meant.

Annie was not present on that occasion. She was helping one of the pot-boys to cope with the lunchtime custom downstairs (out of the church and into the Ring of Bells was a routine with many of the village men) and would eat later. For once I was glad of her absence. I was determined to find out a little more about the Leytons without incurring the risk of teasing comments from Annie.

"Mr Leyton's a farmer, isn't he?" I asked casually. "Are they big landowners?"

"Not as big as Mrs Leyton would like to be," my grandmother said. "She thinks a lot of herself, that one. Two generations ago they were nothing but tenants of the Bollingers, the Leytons were, but somehow they managed to scrape up the money for Priors when it came on the market."

"She's a good woman, Sarah, say what you like," Aunt Millie said. "Always ready to help with food and blankets for the poor, if needed."

"Charitable, yes," grandmother agreed regally. "But quality, no."

Joe masticated thoughtfully.

"I've always liked Priors," he said, ignoring the issue of the Leytons' status. "It's the nicest farm in Collingford, to my mind."

"But they're not quality," grandmother insisted. "Not to say quality."

"Depends what you mean," grandfather replied, after a considerable pause for thought.

"You know full well what I mean!"

"They're fine, solid sort of people. The backbone of England, you might say. I mind when the old lord sold Priors to this Mr Leyton's father. Just a little lad I was at the time. You see, Jenny," he went on stabbing a laden fork in my direction, "Priors used to be the manor house, but it wasn't big enough nor grand enough for the old lord. Old Samuel Leyton was only a tenant farmer at the time—lived over where the Morrisons farm now—but when the old lord built his new place at Watersmeet, somehow the Leytons managed to scrape up enough to buy Priors."

"Since when," grandmother said, "they've carried on like they were quality."

"Well, that's the way it goes," grandfather said philosophically, resuming his meal. "Some go up and some go down."

"Mrs Leyton's the hoity-toity sort," grandmother said. "She likes to rule the roost."

I was amazed that neither grandfather nor Aunt Millie seemed to find nothing amusing in this criticism issuing from my grandmother's lips.

"She can't get over the fact that her father had money—not born to it, mind, but made out of wool. He was the one that sent the boys to their fancy boarding school. The Leytons were just like you and me; village people, till she hauled them up in the world. More potatoes, Joe? Millie? This is a lovely joint, though I do say it!" She looked in my direction. "Remember, slow and steady, Jenny, that's the way to do it. Slow and steady and plenty of basting. And never skimp. Poor quality meat is a waste of time and money and fuel for the cooking. You remember that."

I promised that I would and was wondering how to return the conversation to the subject of the Leytons when grandfather performed the task for me.

"Times aren't good for farmers," he said. "I wonder what those boys intend to do. I did hear tell that Roger isn't so keen on the land as he should be."

"I thought he was going to his uncle in America," Millie said. She lived in a little world of her own, did Millie. She never seemed aware of events until long after they had happened.

Grandmother snorted. "He went *and* came back again. Nothing better to do with his time and money than go back and forth across the Atlantic Ocean." She made it sound as if he went several times a week. "It's time that young man settled down to do an honest day's work."

"He's only young, Sarah," grandfather said mildly.

"Twenty-four," she said. "I know that for certain. He was born the year Dr Linley came to the village."

"That'll make Mark twenty-two and John eighteen. Sarah, you've surpassed yourself with this pie. The pastry fair melts in the mouth."

Grandmother inclined her head as a monarch might accept homage. She fixed her eyes on me with a speculative glance and inwardly I quailed. It was not that I had anything particular on my conscience, merely that grandmother possessed the sort of expression that immediately made me examine myself for flaws.

"I've been thinking," she said, "I might teach you to cook, Jenny. *Try* to teach you," she added, lest I get too swollen headed. "I'm pleased with the way you're shaping. You're a good little worker."

No knight receiving an accolade could have been prouder than I.

"She's Eleanor all over again," Millie said fondly.

Grandmother folded her lips and said nothing.

Since being in Collingford I had learned little more of my mother's childhood than she had been prepared to tell me. It seemed that grandmother had still not forgiven her for leaving home; or was it, I wondered, that she felt guilty that she had not made more effort over the years to find out how her daughter was faring? For whatever reason, it was clear to me that she did not want to talk about my mother.

Grandfather had been a little more forthcoming. He had pointed out to me a patch of the garden which she had regarded as her own; had shown me the apple tree from which she used to swing.

"Fell down such a crack, she did," he said. "But never a tear. Not our Eleanor. She was always one to put a brave face on things. Should've been a boy, I reckon."

"Were you sorry not to have a son?" I asked.

"God's will be done," he said. "We were lucky to have Eleanor. She were born nearly two months early—premature, like—and I was fearful that we'd never rear her. We were never blessed again."

It seemed unbearably sad to me that he should have lost his only child in the way he did.

On Sunday afternoons, Annie and I were free. It was our only official time off during the week, though grandmother turned a blind eye to the odd moments we snatched during the day to rest our legs and drink a cup of tea.

"Let's go for a walk," I said on this particular Sunday.

Annie looked without enthusiasm out of the window.

"It'll rain before long," she said.

"But I'm so tired of being cooped up! Come on, Annie—a breath of air will do us good. Besides, I want to explore. I've seen nothing of Collingford except the village street, the weather's been so bad."

"Well, if you're set on it . . ."

She grumbled a little as we put on our coats and pulled our tam o' shanters down over our ears, but she happily tucked her hand through my arm once we were outside, and we set off along the lane which led away from the village. The road bordered the green then took us past the church with its lych-gate and sagging gravestones. Almost immediately we were out in open country. On one hand the fields sloped gently upward towards a thicket, the trees now stark and black and bare of leaves; and on the other side, the ground fell away towards a valley. Beyond it rose hills, brushed here and there with snow. For the most part the hills were smooth and treeless, though here and there were isolated clumps. It seemed as if even the trees were huddling together for warmth on that wintry day. There was no colour anywhere. Everything was painted in shades of grey.

Then suddenly we rounded a bend and there before us was a fold in the hills and in the fold was a house. It was built of Cotswold stone, four-square, gabled, enduring, with tall windows set on each side of the porch. From a wide, ornate chimney-stack smoke gusted, hanging and drifting in the damp air. I stopped in my tracks, drawing in my breath sharply.

"That's Priors," Annie said.

I stepped up on to the bank at the side of the lane and leant against the grey stone wall, the better to see the house.

"It's lovely," I said softly.

Annie joined me by the wall.

"It used to belong to the Bollingers, years ago, but they built Watersmeet. You should see it! I went to a Primrose League fete there last summer, and ooh, Jenny, it's ever so lovely, it is honest. It's got towers at each end, round towers like you see in story books, and a terrace with urns full of flowers, and a huge flight of steps up to the front door, and pillars all along the front. And the garden's all laid out with a lake and ornamental beds with fountains, and there's an island in the middle of the lake with a summer house, and a little boat to take you there, and—"

"It doesn't sound nearly so nice as Priors." I was gazing at the house in the valley as if I had seen a vision.

"What?" Annie turned to look at me as if I had given her reason to doubt my sanity. "You should just *see* Watersmeet, Jenny! It's like a palace. Priors is all right, I suppose, but it's nothing special."

She shivered as I continued to gaze at the house.

"Come on, Jenny. I'm freezing! Let's go."

"In a minute," I said.

For some reason I could not bear to leave it. There was the strangest sensation of peace in my heart. *This* is what I meant, I said to myself. All those times when my very soul cried out for home, this is what I longed for.

"I think," I said, "that it's about the most beautiful house I have ever seen. It's absolutely—absolutely—" Frustrated, I stopped and shook my head. It was impossible to find the apt word to describe it's total *rightness*.

The stone had once been honey-coloured, I imagined, like the newer buildings I had seen in parts of the village. Perhaps it would look honey-coloured again with the sun on it. Now it was grey, but a warm grey, a weathered, mellow grey. The symmetrical gables, the mullioned windows, delighted my eye. The farm buildings stood to one side, in total harmony with the house, creating a picture of perfect proportions, of abiding stability.

I could be safe there, I thought. Secure. It was the summation of every longing I had ever experienced; the very essence of home.

And the Leytons lived there: Roger, Mark and John.

Where else, I asked myself? Where else?

"You look proper star-struck," Annie laughed, digging me in the ribs. "What's the matter with you? Come on, let's keep walking—I don't want to freeze to death, even if you do. There's a track down the lane that will take us close to the house if you want to have a better look."

But when we reached the top of the track it was ankle deep in mud and looked far from inviting.

I readily agreed to abandon the idea of walking closer to Priors. Although the house fascinated me, something within me baulked at the idea of sauntering past with Annie, half-hoping, half-fearing that one or other of the Leytons would emerge. It was, I felt, beneath my dignity.

But oh—what must it be like to live in a place like that, I wondered? For someone brought up in two back rooms in Ackerly Street, Fulham, it had the appeal of some distant, sun-filled country.

It was quite incomprehensible to me that it should look so familiar.

3

The kitchen at the Ring of Bells was large and warm and smelled of baking. Hams and strings of onions hung from the rafters and in its centre was a wooden table, scrubbed white. One side of the room was almost wholly taken up by the huge cooking range and at the far end was a tall dresser where shining copper pans were kept. Beside it stood the barrel horses on which rested the casks of ale, delivered regularly from the local brewery and quaffed by the men who occupied the settles at the other end of the kitchen. A door led through the wash house, which housed the deep porcelain sink and pump and the copper which gave us a constant supply of hot water, to the stable yard outside. All this became my domain.

True to her word, grandmother took my education in hand. At first I was nervous, frightened of disappointing her by showing no apititude for the culinary arts, but thankfully

I seemed to possess a natural talent and before long she was entrusting simple things, like bread and pastry, almost entirely to me.

All my life I had felt so insecure and unsure of myself that I can hardly find words to express the pleasure it gave me to know that she had such confidence in me. I was still shy when it came to talking to strangers, but I no longer crept round doors as if apologising for my existence. There was a place for me now at the Ring of Bells. I was working my passage; I belonged.

Life that winter was not all work. There was a bazaar in the parish rooms, and Penny Readings in the school hall, with Mr Greenwood, a schoolmaster from Witney, ploughing through highlights of Dickens in weekly instalments. There were devotional week-night meetings where the eyes of boys and girls would meet blushingly over the hymn books. Best of all, there was the annual parish concert.

The success of the entire evening was, without one dissenting vote, Roger and Mark Leyton. Annie had previously told me that they could be relied upon to produce a little light relief and I had been eagerly awaiting their turn on the platform. I was not disappointed. Mark was dressed as a villainous-looking village yokel and stood with assumed dignity and a solemn expression, one hand on the back of a chair on which Roger, rouged and grotesque in shawl, skirts and a bonnet, sat simpering up at him. The audience laughed at the very sight of them and settled down to listen to them full of amused expectancy.

With an earnest air, Mark sang:

> On yonder hill there sits a creature
> Who she is I do not know.
> I'll go and court her, for her beauty,
> She must answer Yes or No.

at which point Roger shot to his feet, and standing half a head taller than his brother screeched in a piercing falsetto:

> Oh *no*, John, *no*, John, *no*, John NO!

The whole hall rocked with laughter as verse succeeded verse, and applauded until their hands were sore.

"Oh, they're such *lads*," Annie said, wiping tears of mirth from her eyes. "Oh really, they are so comical, I could almost die laughing."

I could only agree with her—though dying was not something that the Leytons brought to mind. Rather, they made me want to live. Life was made to enjoy, they seemed to say; come on, everyone, laugh with us.

There were times when I felt a sudden pang of conscience. Perhaps I was enjoying life too much! I was forgetting to grieve for my mother. I did not miss her in the same way that I had done at first, and while common sense told me that this was only natural, a feeling of disloyalty still lurked somewhere below the surface of my consciousness. It was less than three months since she had died; surely she would have expected me to mourn longer than that?

I confided my guilt to Annie.

"She'd 've wanted you to be happy," she said. "No one can't go round with a long face for ever, stands to reason."

"I hope she knows I haven't really forgotten her," I said.

"If she's in heaven, she'll know," Annie said, with great conviction.

Snow fell again that February and seemed to hang around for weeks and weeks. The water in the pitcher on the washstand had ice on it every morning and our breath fogged the chilly air as reluctantly we poked our heads out from beneath the blankets. But eventually the worst of the dismal weather passed as it must do even in the bleakest of winters. It had been a hard time for farmers who lost countless sheep in the blizzards that swept the hillsides; but life went on. The first celandines showed in the hedgerows and bare twigs were touched with green.

By the time the chestnut trees were heavy with pink and white candles and the may-fly were rising in the stream, I had achieved the status of understudy to my grandmother, working almost solely in the kitchen. The inn was full of fishermen all as hungry as the trout who were lured by the insects to the surface of the water, and it pleased me to know that she was beginning to depend on me more and more.

Privacy was the one thing that was seldom available to me, and I craved it like an alcoholic craves the bottle. I knew that I was happy—happier than I had ever been before—but oh, how I longed sometimes to be by myself. I was fortunate that on many of those occasions I was able to find something very pressing to do in the linen cupboard and was able to make my escape.

But was this to be my life? I asked myself sometimes. Happy though I acknowledged myself to be, I felt certain that it would not satisfy me for ever. I wanted a house of my own. A home just for me, not for the whole village of Collingford. Then the vision of Priors would swim between my eyes and the sheet I was darning and I would think: *that's* what I want! That's the sort of place I ought to live in. After all, my father was a gentleman.

Thankfully, this echo from the past (how well I could hear my mother saying the words!) usually made me smile, for I well recognised the hollowness of that particular claim. Yet I could not deny my longing for the kind of stability which in moments of introspection continued to elude me at the Ring of Bells, contented though I was for the greater part of the time. There were times when I envied Annie. She seemed able to sail through her hard-working days with never-flagging high spirits, able to exchange quip for quip with the customers.

It was not often that I served in the parlour, since my grandparents considered it unseemly for me to work in the public rooms, although on particularly busy occasions they forgot their scruples.

There were always plenty of young men there, some more friendly than others, and I learned to unbend a little. It was always easy to tell when the Leytons were present. They seemed to possess a superabundance of high spirits; a vitality that made everyone sit up and take notice whenever they came in. Even the oldest labourer seemed to square his shoulders at the sight of them and bring out his most outrageous reminiscence to claim their attention.

They were always referred to, collectively, as the Leytons and at first I regarded them like that; almost interchangeable. But as time went on I realised that they were all totally different. Mark was a handsome extrovert who loved to laugh and who revelled in being the centre of attention. He paid me extravagant compliments, but I knew they meant nothing. He laughed at me when I blushed and I felt uneasily aware that underneath all the bonhomie and jocularity there was quite another Mark Leyton whom no one knew at all. I had the feeling that if it suited him he could be quite ruthless. There was something about him that made me uneasy in his presence.

Roger was quieter, more watchful, and much more sensitive to the feelings of others. I noticed the kind way he listened with every appearance of attention to boring anecdotes he must have heard a hundred times before, and his punctilious politeness to the humblest farm labourer. He was, however, just as ready as Mark was for a joke.

I hardly knew John since he spent most of the time away at school. He came to the inn with the others when he was at home, however, and seemed agreeable enough. He had, I decided, no small opinion of his academic abilities and was for ever repeating Latin tags and obscure quotations, which I felt sure were expressly designed to impress poor, uneducated village wenches such as Annie and myself. It was one of the most triumphant days of my life when I was able to cap one of his quotations from *Pickwick Papers*, which I happened to know almost by heart, especially when I knew the exchange had been overheard by Roger.

All the brothers and many others came regularly to the Ring of Bells during the summer months. Collingford was cricket mad and the team gathered on the green to practise during the long evenings, usually coming into the inn to slake their thirsts when the practice was over. It was at such times that the lines of demarcation between the classes seemed to blur a little, though on most occasions they were clearly defined.

Lord and Lady Bollinger were at the head of our particular pyramid, which broadened slightly to include other, lesser landowners such as the Leytons, with the vicar and other professional people like the local solicitor and the doctor on roughly the same level. Then came the more prosperous tradespeople, the skilled artisans, and so on, down to the broad base of the pyramid which consisted of the unskilled workers and the labourers who lived a hand-to-mouth existence only a little above subsistence level.

In this hierarchy, we at the Ring of Bells ranked equal with shop owners. I suppose I recognised this fact, but I did not wholly appreciate its significance until the day that grandmother announced to me that, having given the matter much thought, she had decided that Percy Wisden would be an excellent match for me.

We were in the garden picking raspberries at the time, and I almost dropped my bowl in alarm and horror. Grandmother stolidly picked on, apparently unaware of my reaction.

"They've a good, sound business," she said. "There's been a Wisden's Butchery here as long as I can remember. And they're going to set up young Percy with his own shop in Witney, I'm told, so you'd be doing very well for yourself. I've seen the way he looks at you. He won't need much encouragement to come to the point, I can tell that."

I was so horrified that I could not find the words to express my feelings and merely muttered that I was perfectly happy the way things were.

"Just so long as you don't get ideas above your station," grandmother said sternly. "No making sheep's eyes at the gentry, do you hear?"

I heard—but it did not stop me weaving fantasies. My thoughts had become almost exclusively occupied by dreams of Roger Leyton—dreams in which the unromantic figure of Percy Wisden, with his fleshy face and his eyes like stewed gooseberries, found no place at all.

One Sunday afternoon in July, Annie went home to see her family in a nearby hamlet and I went for a solitary walk by the river. Some way out of the village I realised that the most extravagant of my dreams was about to come true, for Roger was ahead of me, sitting on a fallen tree and gazing somewhat moodily into the river. The path I was taking led within three feet of him. I prayed earnestly that he would speak to me and that I would be able to answer without blushing.

He did speak and I did not blush—or at least, even if I did, he did not make me conscious of it. He seemed as glad to see me as I was to see him. It was incomparably easy to find things to say to him and the most natural thing in the world that he should fall into step beside me.

I spoke to him of Priors.

"It's the most beautiful house I've ever seen," I said. "Is it true there was a Priory on the spot at one time?"

"So we're led to believe. You're right, of course. It's a lovely house, but it feels more and more like a millstone to me."

"A millstone? What on earth can you mean?"

He shrugged. "Just that. I'm the eldest son and I'm supposed to want to live there and farm the land. The only snag is that I'm not at all sure I want to be a farmer. I'm not at all sure *what* I want to be."

"You went to America once, didn't you?"

"Yes. I have an uncle with banking interests in New York and everyone thought it a frightfully good idea for me to try my hand in Wall Street, as I didn't take too kindly to the idea of farming. But it wasn't any good. I hated banking and I hated the city. To my amazement, I was homesick for Collingford."

"So what do you want to do? You have had a good education—there must be a thousand things."

We were leaning against a small stone bridge at the time. Roger picked up a handful of pebbles and threw them one by one into the water, trying in a half-hearted sort of way to hit a tree stump that protruded from the water.

"I can only think of a thousand things I don't want to do," he said at last. "Isn't that terrible? Twenty-four years old and no idea in what direction I should go."

"What does your mother think?"

He laughed. "Oh, my mother has but one remedy for all restless males. She is quite sure that the love of a good woman will turn me into a worthy, conventional, hard-working, stay-at-home farmer. Preferably, of course, a good woman with a sizeable fortune."

He was joking, I told myself, and smiled dutifully. It hurt, though. I longed for a fortune to lay at his feet.

"And do you intend to do as she wishes?" I asked.

"Oh, my intentions are always of the best," he said. "But often my performance doesn't measure up to them. I just don't seem to be able to fit into the mould that's made for me, I suppose. It's annoying for my parents and uncomfortable for me." He stared across the water, smiling no longer, his expression one of perplexity. "I know I have it in me to be successful," he said after a moment. "But at what?" He looked down at me suddenly. "I'm sorry," he said. "It's too bad of me to bother you with all my doubts and frustrations."

"I don't mind," I said, truthfully. "I only wish I had some brilliant suggestion to make."

He studied me for a moment, smiling. "Your're nice," he said at last. "I've been a selfish brute, talking of nothing but my affairs. Do tell me about yourself; how are you adjusting to life in Collingford?"

He was, as I had suspected, an exceptionally good listener, and I found myself unusually loquacious. His interest in the behind-the-scenes-life at the inn seemed genuine and I was able to make him laugh with observations of village life seen from my own unique angle.

"And you enjoy Mr Greenwood's readings?" he asked, after I had told him about the entire roomful of people snuffling into their handkerchiefs after the schoolmaster's dramatic rendition of the death of Little Nell.

"Well enough," I said. "But not so much as reading things for myself, if I am to be honest. I love Dickens, don't you? And Thomas Hardy. Perhaps Hardy best of all."

From that point on, conversation was easier than ever. He was a reader too, and we continued our stroll along the river path exchanging opinions and observations in a way that was new and wholly delightful to me.

Eventually we came to the end of the path. Now there was a stile and a choice of routes—one through the water meadows and another that led through a small wood.

"Which way are you going?" Roger asked.

"I thought to turn back just here," I replied.

"Oh no, not on such a lovely afternoon! Let's sit on this bank for a while."

I pretended to think it over, but was honest enough to admit to myself that the question was never seriously in the balance. I was having the time of my life. It had somehow never occurred to me that one could actually *talk* to a man with any pleasure. Conversing with Roger was as easy as chatting to Annie, only considerably more interesting and exciting. Even now I have only to smell warm grass and honeysuckle and hear the murmur of bees to be back there on the river bank, seventeen-years-old and on the brink of falling in love.

That afternoon did not signal any dramatic change in my everyday life, however. Roger was captain of the cricket team and so I saw him frequently at the inn. I liked to think that he smiled more warmly at me than at Annie, but our walk was not repeated and from odd remarks I heard from others it seemed that there was still talk of his going away.

We watched many a cricket match that summer, Annie and I. Anyone could have been forgiven for thinking we were ardent devotees of the game, along with most of the other inhabitants of Collingford from Lord Bollinger downward; but in fact it was only the game as played by Roger that interested me.

Lord Bollinger often rode down from Watersmeet in a dogcart and stationed himself by the side of the green, loudly cheering on the Collingford side and damning their opponents in language that would have been frowned upon had it emanated from a lesser mortal.

He wore a panama hat on those summer days, and one day the breeze whipped it from his head and carried it almost to my feet. I picked it up and walked over to the cart.

"Your hat, my lord," I said.

"Thank 'ee, thank 'ee." He reached down to take it from me. "What a civil child you are, to be sure." He smiled at me, and I could see exactly the look that Annie had described: a look that said 'by Gad, young lady, you should have seen me forty years ago!'

He took his hat from me, but before I could withdraw, he grasped my hand in his.

"Wait," he said. "You're new to Collingford, I believe."

"I'm Jenny Fitzgerald, my lord," I said. "Mrs Austin's granddaughter from the Ring of Bells."

He dropped my hand but continued to look at me.

"Well, I'm damned," he said.

I bit the inside of my cheek to keep from laughing.

"It's as well my grandmother can't hear you, my lord," I said. "She turns men out of her kitchen for less."

He laughed outright at that, his blue eyes sparkling with life under bushy white brows. He had a weather-beaten face with a jutting, aristocratic, high-bridged nose. How strange, I thought, that such a very old man—why, he must be sixty or sixty-five—could create the impression of such exuberant *maleness*! I felt a heady feeling of power that I had amused him.

"I believe you," he said. "Can you wonder that I never go in there? The lady disapproves of me."

"Oh, I'm sure you're wrong, my lord," I said demurely, as if butter wouldn't melt in my mouth. But I was smiling too, half-shocked at myself because I knew that I was flirting with him. The words that passed between us hardly mattered. Somehow I knew that we were experiencing an instantaneous recognition of each other as people in our own right—not merely the squire and the village girl.

"You must be Eleanor's daughter," he said.

"Yes, my lord. She died last December."

"I had heard so. A sad business."

"Did you know her?" I asked.

"I know everyone in Collingford," he said, smiling again. "My flock. My children."

I had run out of things to say, had come to the end of my audacity.

"If you'll excuse me, my lord," I said, bobbing a curtsy.

He inclined his head.

"Your servant, ma'am," he said teasingly.

Self-consciously I walked back to where Annie was sitting on the grass, feeling certain that his eyes were upon me, but when I settled myself again and turned to look in his direction his attention was once more on the game.

"What was all that about?" Annie asked.

"He asked me who I was."

She giggled. "He's a lad, isn't he? My mother says he was ever so handsome when he was young."

"I can believe it," I said. "Has he any sons like him?"

"Not a one, poor gentleman—leastways, there was one, but he went into the Army and was killed in India. He has a daughter, but she married a Yankee and went to live in America."

Summer passed and the next big excitement came at harvest time. The Leytons always gave a supper for their workers when the last sheaf of corn had been brought into the barn and this, I was told, was a merry free-for-all, with the wives and families of all connected with the farm eating and drinking their fill, dancing until late to the music of a fiddler.

We at the Ring of Bells were responsible for the traditional Church Supper some evenings later. I knew that Mr and Mrs Leyton, because of their standing in the community, were bound to be there. I prayed earnestly that their sons would accompany them and took great pains with my appearance that night, hoping that I would catch Roger's eye.

I was busy in the kitchen as voices and laughter and the tramp of feet upstairs told me that the guests were beginning to arrive, and I had to rely on Annie who was dashing in and out to inform me who was there and who was still to come.

"Have the Leytons come?" I asked at last, when she had mentioned every name but the one I was waiting for.

"Haven't seen them," she called over her shoulder, cap ribbons flying. But a little later she was back again. "Mr and Mrs Leyton have come, but not the boys. I must say she looks a real picture, considering she's forty-five if a day. And guess what! Molly Johnson says it looks like Mr Roger and Miss Dodwell are going to make a match. Her dad's got a big farm over Standlake way, so it suits very well."

"The soup's already in the tureen," I said. "You'd better take it up."

She left without a backward glance and I gripped the edge of the table tightly. Around me surged all the activity that a meal for thirty demanded, but for the moment I was incapable of taking any part in it.

"Stop wool-gathering, girl," grandmother said, swooping down on me with a pile of plates. "What are you thinking of? They'll be needing these upstairs."

I took the plates upstairs. I brought them down again

once they were empty. I smiled and said "Won't you have a little more," and "Yes indeed, it *is* very warm in here."

I felt as if I had been kicked by a mule and could not wait to escape to my room after the party was over. Annie and I had worked hard and were both tired, so I needed no excuse to shirk the gossip we normally indulged in before we fell asleep. Long after I could hear the deep, even breathing that told me she had fallen into her accustomed untroubled slumber, I stared into the darkness, wakeful and miserable.

Fool, I berated myself. Idiot! Did you really expect anything different? Did you honestly think that one magical afternoon would change anything? He had been friendly because he was lonely and bored, that was all. Tears trickled down my cheeks and into my ears, and earnestly I wished I was dead.

My broken heart passed unnoticed, even by Annie, and the reason for this was that she, too, was in love. In her case all was progressing as merrily as the proverbial marriage bell.

Jed Stephens was an under-gardener at Watersmeet, the Bollingers' estate, a member of the cricket team and a regular customer at the Ring of Bells, though he did little more than nurse his half-pint of ale and gaze at Annie.

I marvelled, as I listened to Annie's outpourings concerning him, at this strange and inexplicable thing known as love. Never had there lived, according to Annie, a man so handsome and so kind as Jed.

To me he seemed a very ordinary young man—his looks were unremarkable and he was below average height. As for his character, I felt sure that Annie was endowing him with all kinds of imaginary qualities, for to my knowledge they had had only brief periods alone together and could not possibly know each other well. In fact her choice surprised me, for on the few occasions he opened his mouth in company he seemed dour and serious, speaking bitterly about the class system which others took for granted.

Although she and Jed had been intensely aware of each other that entire summer, it was not until the day of the annual Hiring Fair that things came to a head. Booths and stalls were set up outside the Ring of Bells on the green.

There were shooting galleries, swing-boats, a merry-go-round, and devices to test a man's strength. There were sweetmeat stalls and hoop-la stalls, a coconut shy, a fortune teller, an itinerant dentist, card-sharps and strong men.

My grandmother disapproved strongly. It attracted the rougher element from miles around, she said. Did you see the gentry there? No, you did not! And for why? Because they had better sense, that's why.

But the band was playing, vying with the music of the hurdy-gurdy, and girls in their summer dresses and flower-wreathed hats strolled with the young men in their best suits. The autumn sun might have lost some of its warmth, but it shone from a cloudless sky and you might as well have asked a stream to flow uphill as to expect Annie and me to keep away from the fair.

Thanks to grandfather's intervention, we were allowed an hour to visit it, on the strict understanding that we stayed together at all times. We met Jed by the coconut-shy, and the three of us tried our luck unsuccessfully to the accompaniment of gales of giggles from Annie.

We went on the swing-boats and sat side-saddle on adjoining horses on the merry-go-round. I had never seen Jed in such high spirits. For the first time I acknowledged that he had an attractive smile which lit up his otherwise sombre brown eyes.

Neither he nor Annie could have been more friendly to me, yet I was uncomfortably conscious that both would have preferred to be without my company. Couples were dancing to the music of the brass band, and Annie looked longingly in their direction.

"Go on," I said. "I'll be all right, really. I'll wait for you."

I was watching them twirl to the music of a Viennese waltz, with far more enthusiasm than skill, and was wallowing in a little pleasurable self-pity, when I heard someone speak my name. It was Roger surely—no one else had a voice like his. I whipped joyously around, and sagged a little with disappointment when I realised that it was John Leyton and not his elder brother who was standing close beside me.

"All alone?" he asked.

"Only temporarily. Annie's dancing with Jed."

"Care for a turn?"

I smiled at him cheekily, feeling no awe of this young man who was still a schoolboy.

"That's no way to ask a lady to dance!"

"I beg your pardon!" He bowed. "Madam, may I have the honour?"

I curtsied and he led me, laughing, to the makeshift dance floor.

"I'm not very good," I admitted, after he had fallen over my feet several times. "As a matter of fact, I've never danced before."

"You couldn't have chosen a better teacher, even if I say so myself. It's really perfectly simple." He gave me a few instructions and soon I was able to twirl almost as expertly as everyone else; at least, John seemed able to avoid my feet.

"Come on, I'll buy you a lemonade," he said, when the dance was over. I looked around for Annie and Jed. They were standing with both of her hands tightly clasped in his, smiling into each other's eyes, oblivious to my or anyone else's presence.

"It will have to be very quick," I said. "Annie and I should have been back at the inn ten minutes ago."

"Oh, nobody takes any account of time on a fair day," he said, easily.

"I doubt whether my grandmother would agree with you," I said. But it was a token resistance. I went with him to the stall next to the coconut-shy and accepted the bilious, fizzy liquid that he bought for me. John wrinkled his nose.

"It's not nearly so good as the lemonade you serve at the inn."

"That's my grandmother's secret recipe. By the way, she said that none of the gentry came here."

"We Leytons are a law unto ourselves!"

"Are your brothers here too?" I asked casually. I had been trying to work this question into the conversation ever since John had first spoken my name, but the result, when it came, was hardly cheering.

"Mark's here somewhere, but Roger stayed on the farm. I don't know what's the matter with him these days. He's no fun any more."

Very deliberately I ran my finger round the rim of my glass.

"Perhaps his attachment to Miss Dodwell has sobered him up a little."

If I was hoping for a denial that Roger was in any way attached to Miss Dodwell, I was to be disappointed.

"Oh, I don't think it's that," John said. "She's a cheerful enough girl. I should think she would do him the world of good."

"When are they to be married?" I asked.

John shrugged. "Roger doesn't confide in me. From what my mother was saying the other day, I think he's dragging his feet a bit."

"Do you think he's in love with her?"

"Heaven knows. Somehow I don't think so."

I could have hugged him.

"Of course," he went on, "she does have sizeable expectations, I understand, which in my experience makes a considerable difference to the ease with which a man might fall in love with a woman—"

"How cynical you are, for a schoolboy," I said, less pleased with him.

"A schoolboy no longer. I go up to Oxford at the end of the month."

"Congratulations." My voice was distant.

"You're angry with me!"

I hastened to deny it. "No, of course I'm not—why should you think that? It's just that I'm foolishly sensitive when it comes to talk of fortunes. It makes me wonder what I would ever have to offer a man."

I looked up in astonishment as he began to laugh.

"What have I said that is so amusing?" I asked.

"May I suggest you look in your mirror?" he said. "I think it will become immediately obvious what you have to offer a man. I happen to know that my brothers both admire you greatly."

My heart began to beat thickly; I almost expected the pounding of it to be visible through the thin stuff of my dress.

"I find that hard to believe," I managed to say. "Mark

flirts a little as he does with every other girl who crosses his path—much as you do yourself," I added severely. "And Roger—Roger is engaged to Miss Dodwell."

"Not yet," he said. "There's no official engagement. Roger is going away shortly to Hereford, to take over my uncle's farm while he and my aunt go to visit our relations in America, and I do not imagine there will be any definite commitment to Miss Dodwell until he gets back."

It was a small crumb of comfort and I grasped it tenaciously.

"Oh Jenny, *there* you are! I was that worried—I thought you'd gone back without me, and then the fat would have been in the fire!"

Annie's voice recalled me to the fact that we should have been back at the inn long before, and hastily I downed the last of my lemonade.

We were in luck. Grandmother for once seemed to disregard our transgressions, merely telling us sharply to get on with our work as far too much time had been wasted that day, and feeling we had got off lightly, we exchanged relieved glances as we donned our aprons, ready to deal with the increased flood of business caused by the fair.

I knew I was being illogical, but could not deny that my heart was lighter since my talk with John. Common sense dictated that nothing had altered and that my cause was as hopeless as ever; but really, common sense had nothing to do with it. While there was life there was hope, and I would continue to hope, however illogically, until the knot was actually tied between Roger and his bride.

Winter closed in on us again, colder even than the year that went before. Christmas brought the usual rush of activity and the Castle family arrived on Christmas Eve, just as they had done the previous year. I could hardly believe that I had been at the Ring of Bells for twelve whole months, although in some ways it seemed a lifetime.

Collingford had drawn me into its warm heart and the years that had preceded my mother's death seemed to recede. It was a different world. I was a different person.

Though not, perhaps, as totally, childishly happy as I had been the year before. I felt restless. Annie and Jed were now officially walking out and were full of happiness. Couldn't anyone see that I was suffering from a broken heart, I asked myself, full of self-pity? Roger stayed away from Collingford and I began to wonder if he would ever come back. Perhaps he had come to some decision about his future that necessitated his going abroad again. Perhaps I should never see him again.

Annie's wedding was to take place in early June. A cottage at a little hamlet called Berry Cross which belonged to the Watersmeet estate was falling vacant, and Jed had spoken for it. Lord Bollinger's agent had agreed that Jed should have it, and Annie sighed with excitement and impatience every night, complaining that June would never come. But to me, heavy hearted though I was, the weeks passed quickly, filled as they were with duties that kept us on the run from morning until night.

We talked a lot in those weeks before the wedding, tucked up in our beds in that attic room. We talked about men in general and Jed in particular; about people in the village, and clothes and hairstyles and marriage and babies and life and death. It was after Annie had said that in her opinion, six children were more than enough (her mother had nine), that I was silent for a while, wondering how best to frame the question that I had been longing to ask her these many nights.

"Annie," I said diffidently at last. "What do people actually *do*?"

"What do you mean?" she asked.

"You know. How do they actually get babies?"

I could hear the rustle of the bedclothes as she raised her head to look at me.

"You mean," she asked in astonishment, "you really don't know?"

"I wouldn't ask if I did," I replied with some asperity, feeling more foolish by the moment.

"You'd think with all your reading—"

"But books don't *say*! Ladies melt into gentlemen's arms, or else there's a row of asterisks. In the Bible they talk about 'knowing' a man, or 'going unto' him. There must be more to it than that! How can I know? My mother never told me and I've never before had a friend as close as you."

Very simply, Annie told me. I greeted the information with a stunned silence.

"I shouldn't worry about it," she said comfortably. "It can't be bad, or people wouldn't do it so often."

"It's seems so—well, so *extraordinary*!" I said. "I mean, you'd think God could have thought of something a little less embarrassing, wouldn't you?" The more I thought about it, the more astounding it seemed. "Just imagine," I said, "The Reverend and Mrs Thorogood! And Lord and Lady Bollinger! Even *grandmother*!"

"Even the dear Queen," Annie added, deferentially.

This last thought silenced me altogether for several moments, until a further observation occurred to me.

"Mercy me, Annie," I said faintly. "Your mother's done it *nine times*!"

I could not understand why this remark should be the cause of such hilarity on Annie's part.

4

The cricket season started and once more the inn was full in the evenings as the team came in after their practices to drink their ale and talk of batting averages and maiden overs. The first few matches were played without Roger who was still, as far as I knew, taking care of his uncle's farm in Hereford, but one evening in late May I was asked by my grandfather to bring another bottle of brandy into the parlour, and was suddenly confronted by the sight of Roger leaning against the door jamb, pewter tankard in his hand, just as if he had never been away.

My heart was banging away inside my rib-cage and suddenly it was very difficult to breathe. I gave the bottle to my grandfather, searching desperately for a reason to stay in the room, but there was none. It was impossible to leave, however, without one more look at Roger.

This time he was looking at me, and he smiled, his grey eyes crinkling at the corners in the way I had imagined so often during the long winter without him. I smiled back, for once careless that I was showing my feelings so openly. Life was suddenly painted in brighter colours. I was standing in the place occupied by the Christmas tree every year at the appropriate season and I felt just as incandescent.

As, reluctantly, I turned to leave, he pushed himself away from the door post and followed me, out into the dark no-man's-land where the staircase began. I was already climbing the stairs when I heard him call my name, and I turned to see him standing at the bottom, still holding his tankard, one hand on the newel-post.

I came down towards him.

"So you're back," I said inanely.

"Yes—and glad to be so. How are you, Jenny?"

"I'm well, thank you."

"You look different."

"It's my hair." I hardly knew what I was saying, my heart was beating so and my voice sounded strange in my ears. "Annie curled my fringe. It's supposed to be very fashionable, but I don't know that I care for it."

"You look very pretty. Jenny—I've thought about you so much while I've been away. Do you remember the walk we had by the river?"

Did I remember! I nodded, dumbly.

"I've thought about that—often and often. I almost wrote, but then I thought—" he broke off, and shook his head. "I've been at sixes and sevens with myself, not knowing what to do for the best. One hates to disappoint—to let people down. Perhaps we could—" he stopped again and looked further up to the top of the stairs. I knew without turning round that my grandmother had appeared. Sure enough, she was making her way down, towards us.

"Good evening, Mr Leyton," she said. "Jenny, I've been looking for you. That brown dress you said you would alter for me—can you come and look at it? I'm afraid there may not be enough to spare in the seam to make a great deal of difference."

My grandmother was growing stouter and I had said that I

would try to let out one of her favourite dresses. I never minded sewing, but on this one occasion I wished her and her entire wardrobe in the next county.

I looked back towards Roger. He bowed formally towards my grandmother, then smiled at me.

"Please excuse me," he said. "I will leave you two ladies to your work." For a moment his eyes held mine, and then he left us.

"Come along, Jenny," grandmother said, and turning, led the way to her room upstairs.

Once there she regarded me severely.

"I hope," she said, "that you do not intend to behave foolishly."

"What do you mean, Grandmother?" I asked innocently.

"Mr Roger Leyton is what I mean, and well you know it. And you can stop looking at me with those big blue eyes as if butter wouldn't melt in your mouth, my girl."

"We were only passing the time of day, Grandmother. He's just arrived back in Collingford."

"I'm fully aware of that. I'm also aware that you look like a cat that's swallowed the canary—and if you know what's good for you, you'll listen to me and take note of what I say. Know your place and stick to it, my girl. There's no happiness to be found in doing anything else."

I abandoned my protestations of innocence.

"Sometimes," I said slowly, "I don't feel very sure where my place is."

"Talk sense, Jenny! It's here, with us, until such time as you meet a nice, steady young man. Leave the gentry alone."

"But the Fitzgeralds were gentry!"

"We only have your father's word for that and I spotted him for a liar the first time I clapped eyes on him. Just mark my words, girl. That Roger Leyton is a rackety sort of a fellow; I've always said so. He can't settle to anything bar riding over the country to race meetings or playing cricket on the village green. There'll be nothing but unhappiness for you if you look in his direction. Oh, he'll smile at you, like enough, and talk you into giving him kisses and the Lord alone knows what else, him with his silver tongue! But he'll never do right by you. Take it from one who has more experience of the world than you have."

I longed to contradict her. Rebellion welled up inside me, but I controlled myself and said nothing, merely picking up the brown dress and forcing myself to study the seam.

"I think I can give you an extra inch," I said, deliberately closing the door on further discussion.

"I'd be grateful if you could." She had dismissed the subject, too. She had spoken, and to her mind that was enough. "I'd like to wear that dress at Annie's wedding."

It was only a week later that the bells pealed out over the village green, for Annie had elected to be married from the Ring of Bells rather than from her home. Annie wore a white muslin dress with a wide blue sash that I had made for her and Jed had bought a new black suit for the occasion. He looked ill at ease, and kept running a finger round his winged collar to relieve his neck from its unaccustomed stiffness.

My grandparents were giving the feast as part of their wedding present. A huge spread had been prepared in the kitchen, and even though the crowd of invited guests and other well-wishers that gathered there exceeded expectations, there was plenty of food for all. The ale flowed freely for those who wanted it. The ladies more delicately sipped sherry or the home-made lemonade for which my grandmother was famous.

Grandfather was normally an abstemious man. As he was fond of saying, it's a poor landlord who drinks his own profits; but the joyful nature of this occasion had tempted him to forget his principles for one day and I could see grandmother eyeing him with disapproval as his colour rose and his laugh grew louder.

"Now it's my turn to propose a toast," he announced, rising to his feet and waving his tankard in the air. "Pray silence, ladies and gentlemen." He beamed round at all the guests, bowing acknowledgment of the applause, cheers and whistles that greeted him. He gestured for silence.

"Now then," he said, having made sure of everyone's attention. "We have this lovely young couple here, Annie and Jed, just entered the blessed state of matrim—matrim—" The word was too much for him, and he paused, grinning broadly. "Well, dang it, I don't have to tell you what they've done, do I? They've been and got wed, haven't they?"

"Joe!" My grandmother, sitting next to him, tugged on his coat-tails. "Joe, sit down. Are you drunk?"

"We don't have weddings every day, do we? And I want to say to them, and *you* want to say to them, and we *all* want to say to them—"

"Well, get on and say it, then!" came a shout from across the table.

"Aye, get on with it, Joe." The company cheered.

"Well, you all know what we want to say to them. We want to wish them the best of health and wealth and happiness and—" here he winked and his grin grew broader. "May all their troubles be little ones."

"That'll *do*, Joe! That's enough! Sit down, do."

He brushed his wife's hand away from his coat-tails.

"Give over, Sarah, I haven't finished yet. I want everyone to be upstanding—now come on, everybody, on your feet!—and we'll drink to Annie and Jed. Charge your glasses, ladies and gentlemen, and raise them one and all, to Annie and Jed."

"Annie and Jed!" Friends and relations struggled to their feet, and in the resulting mêlée I was delighted to find that Roger had found his way to my side.

There was a small commotion in the corner of the room near the door. The fiddler had taken up his bow and started to play, and like a latter-day Pied Piper, he turned and led the way out to the green through the inn, the wedding guests spilling out of the door behind him.

"Come on!" said Roger, taking me firmly by the hand. "There's going to be dancing."

We followed the laughing, jostling mob outside, leaving the older folk and the wreck of the meal behind us. Outside help had been engaged. Today, Annie and I had nothing to do but enjoy ourselves.

I was wearing a cream-coloured muslin dress embroidered with yellow and blue flowers, and it billowed this way and that as I twirled with Roger on the grass in time to the fiddle, until breathlessly we collapsed, laughing with sheer pleasure.

"You know," Roger said, his grey eyes warm. "I used to think you a very prim and proper miss."

"So I am, Sir." I tossed my head in a parody of prudishness, and he laughed at me, leaning back on his elbows and crossing his long legs in front of him.

"It didn't look like it just now when you were cavorting around the green."

"I wonder where my grandmother is?" I asked, suddenly anxious. 'Cavorting' didn't sound the sort of activity that would meet with her approval, particularly in company with Roger Leyton.

"Too busy with Joe to worry about you, I'd say. I think the dear old boy had a drop or two too much, don't you? She's probably marched him off to bed in disgrace. Anyway, she surely wouldn't object to your dancing at Annie's wedding, would she?"

I could hardly tell him that it was he she objected to.

"She values dignity a great deal," I said.

Roger laughed. "I know just what you mean. She looks so like our gracious Queen that she strikes terror into my heart."

"She's been very good to me."

"And why wouldn't she be? Quite apart from discovering a granddaughter as lovely as you, you've proved to be the most enormous help to them. You've developed into her right-hand woman, haven't you?"

"I'd like to think so."

"It's true—the whole village knows it. They both rely on you a great deal. They're beginning to show their age, I think."

"Perhaps you're right. I've thought once or twice recently that grandmother is slowing down a little. Oh!" I sat up and hugged my knees. "How horrid old age is!"

"There's a year or two yet before you have to worry about it on your own account." He nodded smilingly in the direction of Jed and Annie who were hopping happily together, far too absorbed in each other to listen to the beat of the music. "Look at those two, bless their hearts. I've never seen Jed look so happy. He's always seemed on the dour side. It's impossible not to think this day marks a sort of peak for them, don't you agree?"

"What on earth can you mean?"

"Well, it won't be roses all the way for them, will it? By this time next year they will have a child, with probably another on the way. Annie will be a sober matron. She will have lost all of that delightful bounce that makes her so—so *Annie-ish*, and Jed will be worried about making ends meet."

"Oh, don't talk like that!" Suddenly I felt as if the whole fabric of life was threatened. Surely their happiness couldn't be as fleeting a thing as all that? "They're going to be happy, I'm sure of it," I said. "They love each other."

"And love conquers all?"

His voice was mocking and I frowned, disliking the feeling that he was laughing at me—dismissing me as a brainless ninny.

"No, I don't mean that, exactly. A successful marriage needs liking and respect too."

"You've thought it all out."

"Well, yes. Marriage is something a woman is bound to think about, don't you agree? There's so little else she can do. I mean," I went on, floundering a little as he continued to regard me with amusement. "It's an unfair world, for women. A man can marry, or he can decide not to; the choice is his. Whereas a woman merely has to wait and hope that the right man will ask her. And should she decide not to marry at all, then the world regards her as a freak. Don't laugh at me," I finished, fiercely.

"I'm not laughing at you, honestly." He sobered instantly. "I think you're absolutely right—it *is* an unfair world; it's just that your earnestness is very appealing." He smiled at me again. "Forgive me, won't you? I'm well aware that on the whole, we men get the best of it. There are many laws that discriminate against women. In theory, they are undoubtedly the most persecuted of people—but in practice, my dear Jenny—" he broke off, throwing back his head to laugh unrestrainedly.

"Pray tell me the joke!"

"In practice it isn't always so. I was thinking of my own mother and your grandmother, too. Not, perhaps, two typical examples of downtrodden womanhood."

I had to smile at that.

"I don't know your mother," I said, "though I've always admired her looks from afar. But you're right about my grandmother. Downtrodden is not the word to describe her."

"You see?" he said. "It's a joke, isn't it? There's something irresistibly comic about a hen-pecked husband."

"I can't imagine you in that role."

"I should hope not." He spoke lightly, but I knew his eyes were on me and was infuriated to feel my cheeks warming with one of the blushes I had hoped were a thing of the past.

"Just look at that brother of yours," I said, pretending interest in the dancing that was still in progress. "I declare he's trying to dance with at least three girls at once."

"Oh, a devil with the women is Mark," Roger said. "Or at least, he likes to think so. He and John are as madcap as each other."

"And you're the sober one?"

He laughed. "I don't think that 'sober' is quite the word to use—not today, at any rate. Or any other day, according to my parents," he added, half to himself.

"Have you decided to stay in Collingford?"

"Heaven knows!" His laughter died and he was quiet for a moment before jumping to his feet.

"Come on! This is no day for gloomy introspection. Let's have another dance."

There was to be no honeymoon for Annie and Jed. After I had helped her change from her wedding dress into the dark blue silk she wore for summer Sundays, she stood looking for a moment at the cramped little room we had shared for over a year.

"I'll miss you, Jenny," she said.

We hugged each other, for a moment too choked with emotion to speak.

"You are a goose," I said, half-laughing. "Anyone would think you were moving to Timbuctoo instead of just up the road to Berry Cross."

"It won't be the same, though," she said.

Her few possessions were loaded on to a cart borrowed from Watersmeet, and followed by cheers and waves from the wedding guests, they drove off to start life in their little cottage.

"I ought to get back," Roger said when they had gone. "Will you walk with me as far as the track?"

I looked around. My grandmother had emerged to say goodbye to Annie and Jed but had disappeared inside the inn again. People were drifting away in small groups, but there was still a hard core of revellers, Mark included, grouped round the seats outside the inn.

"Come on," Roger urged. "You're not going to be missed for a few minutes."

"Just as far as the track, then," I said.

We walked across the green and along the lane past the church, saying very little. I could think of nothing except how quickly the walk would be over. Suddenly I felt that it would be quite unendurable to come to the end of this afternoon without knowing Roger's feelings towards Miss Dodwell.

I decided to tackle the subject head on, and took a deep breath.

"I did hear it said," I began, "that you are to marry a lady from Standlake way—a Miss Dodwell, I believe?"

"Oh, you did, did you? Then you were misinformed."

"I *was*?" I stopped in my tracks. Until that point I felt that I had behaved with faultless restraint. I had been friendly, but thoroughly ladylike. Now I knew that joy was spilling unguardedly from my face and my eyes and my lips, but I cared not a jot, for Roger was smiling down at me, his hands on my shoulders.

"You're the sweetest girl, Jenny," he said. "The very sweetest."

He bent and kissed me lightly, then put his arm around my waist as we continued our walk.

"About the lady from Standlake," he said. "My family thought it a good idea, not I. She has money and land—the most important things in the world to a farmer. But she was one of those poor, downtrodden creatures we were talking about earlier. Oh, she's a nice enough girl, I suppose, but not for me. 'When it comes to choosing a wife,' I told my parents, 'I'll make my own selection, thank you very much!' "

"I said much the same about Percy Wisden."

"Percy Wisden!" He stopped short and looked down at me in horror. "You and Percy Wisden! How absolutely monstrous! He looks just like one of his own sides of bacon."

"That's very unkind," I said, laughing nonetheless.

"You know something?" he asked, going off at a tangent. "I don't think you've once called me by name. It's Roger, in case it had escaped your notice."

We had almost reached the point where the farm track to Priors joined the lane. I could see it clearly, its entry marked by a clump of elder trees. I wished the lane could have been ten times as long.

"Annie calls you Mr Roger," I said. "And grandmother calls you Mr Leyton. I have been wondering which is more appropriate in my case."

"How about Roger, plain and simple? You call John by his Christian name, I'm sure."

"John's just a boy!"

"And I'm a man?"

We had reached the elders by this time, and Roger stopped within their shade, holding me once more by my shoulders.

"Say after me," he instructed with mock severity. "From this day forward I shall call you Roger."

"From this day forward I shall call you Roger."

"And I shall be your true, good friend."

"And I shall be your true, good friend."

My voice was a whisper, a thread of sound in the scented summer air. His hands tightened. His eyes, serious now, seemed to encompass me. Suddenly he grinned and gave me a shake.

"Percy Wisden, indeed!"

I laughed up at him and all at once his lips were on mine, warm and searching, and his arms were round me and the tumble of responses within me was something I had never known before. We clung together, kissing and murmuring foolish things.

"Could you love me?" he said at last.

I leant my head against his shoulder. I was not restrained or guarded or ladylike.

"I do love you," I said. "For so long, I've loved you. I thought I would die, all last winter when you were away."

"I was the same. I went away because of you. I was beginning to feel—I mean, I knew there would be difficulties. I thought I owed it to my parents to try to be 'sensible' as they call it."

I put my finger on his lips.

"Don't say any more." I couldn't bear to hear it, not just then. He had no need to explain to me the way his parents would view his love for the girl from the Ring of Bells.

"I love you," he said in a firmer voice. "That's what matters. And they'll love you too, Jenny, when they know you better."

"Don't rush things." I was suddenly fearful, intimidated by the thought of the prosperous, self-assured Leytons.

"When can I see you again?"

"You know where to find me. I'm always at the Ring of Bells."

"I mean like this—alone."

"My only free day is Sunday."

"Tomorrow? We can meet tomorrow? I'm not going until you say you'll meet me."

"Of course I'll meet you. Where?"

"Here. At two thirty?"

We said a long and reluctant goodbye and I watched him go down the track towards Priors. I waited until he was out of sight and I could hear the dogs barking to welcome him before I slowly began my walk back along the lane.

Inevitably, when I came to the place where Priors was revealed in all its gracious loveliness, I stopped as I had done many times before, and leaning on the wall I gazed towards the house. Strangely, I had forgotten it in the overwhelming torrent of emotion that had been unleashed by Roger.

Now, the thought that it could one day belong to me made me gasp, as if someone had struck me a blow just beneath my heart. Again I marvelled at the feeling of homecoming that I had experienced the first time I had seen it. Was it some sort of foreknowledge? Was I predestined to live within those mellow walls—was my fate written long before I came to Collingford or met Roger Leyton?

"Admiring the family home?" a voice behind me asked. I

had been deaf to Mark's approaching footsteps, so rapt was I in my study of Priors.

"It's beautiful," I said, turning to smile at him over my shoulder.

Both his brothers admired me, John had said. I still doubted this statement, where Mark was concerned, and did not feel easy in his presence. For some time I could not quite understand why this should be; but then the explanation came to me. To Mark, I was not a real person at all, but merely a decorative shell whom he could smile at, flirt with, or ignore, whichever suited his whim of the moment. It seemed that on this occasion he had decided to converse with me, and he joined me by the wall.

For a moment he said nothing. I gave him a quick glance sideways. He was handsome, no doubt about it. There was a crisp vitality in his dark hair, and his smooth, brown skin bore the sheen of good health. He was a little shorter and stockier than Roger, but had a well-knit, athletic bearing.

"Thou shalt not covet thy neighbour's house," he said.

I flushed scarlet.

"It's not that I—believe me, I find it so beautiful—I wouldn't dream—" I floundered in a morass of half-truths. He smiled.

"My brother is safe at home, I take it?"

"I left him at the end of the track not five minutes ago."

"Delightful chap, isn't he? A little soft in the head, of course, but delightful."

"I find him so," I said. "Delightful that is."

"I'm sure you do." He turned so that his back was against the wall. Thoughtfully he eyed me through narrowed lids.

"I've seen you here before," he said. "It's as though Priors holds some sort of fascination for you."

"As I said, I find it beautiful."

"Just so long as you're not too ambitious."

"I don't know what you mean?"

"Don't you?" His voice was still pleasant, still deceptively friendly. "I think you do, Jenny dear. I dislike intensely the thought of a common little social-climber using my wide-eyed and innocent brother to haul herself up the ladder.

72

Find someone else, Jenny. Keep away from the Leyton family and keep away from Priors."

I stared at him with my mouth open, so taken aback that I could find no expression for the rage that was boiling within me. I swallowed convulsively and at last found a few incoherent words.

"How dare you! What I feel for Roger and he for me has nothing whatever to do with you. You speak of him as if he has no mind of his own, no feelings, no heart."

"On the contrary, Roger is all feelings and heart. If he used his mind a little, he might just possibly see you for what you are—a pretty enough little thing, but a nobody."

"My grandparents are the salt of the earth!"

"And your father? Who was he? Nobody knows!"

"I am *me*! And Roger loves me."

Mark laughed.

"You hope to marry him—and one day be the mistress of that house down there? Forget it, Jenny. Go away. Think it over sensibly. If you did marry Roger, he would take you to live at Priors, because that's where he belongs. And do you really imagine that you would be mistress there? With my mother still comparatively young and vigorous?" He laughed again. "I assure you, your life would be hell! My mother would make your life a misery. She knows exactly the sort of girl that Roger should marry, and believe me, you don't measure up in the slightest particular."

He looked at me again, still smiling, his eyes cold.

"I happen to be fond of my brother," he said. "And I'd like to give you my assurance that I'll do everything in my power to keep you out of the family. Priors isn't for you."

He pushed himself away from the wall, sketched a salute, and went on his way, leaving me with tears of impotent fury in my eyes. How could he—how *could* he! I beat the wall with my fists in frustration. There was so much I ought to have said! Why had I been struck so dumb—so totally unable to defend myself or my motives?

The worst thing of all was that such a perfect day should suddenly have become so ugly. I walked back towards the Ring of Bells. It was all so monstrously unfair. I loved

73

Priors, it was true. I craved for its grace and stability and style. But the afternoon had left me in no doubt that I loved Roger more.

5

There was a strange sense of desolation and anti-climax back at the inn. My grandfather had emerged rather tousled and bleary-eyed from his nap and was going about his business checking bottles in the parlour, his air far more subdued than was customary.

In the kitchen, the two women who had been engaged to help with the clearing up still lingered, gossiping with Susan who was putting the piles of plates away in the large cupboard that occupied the whole of one wall. They looked up as I went in.

"Your granny wants you," Susan said, a trace of virtuous reproach in her voice. "She's upstairs in her sitting room."

"I'd better get out of all this finery," I said.

"I'd see her first, if I was you," chipped in Mrs Tomkins. She had a little, sharp nose that seemed to quiver with excitement. "She was right put out."

I didn't need to ask why, and my heart sank still further. She must have seen my departure with Roger—or perhaps someone had kindly informed her of it. Whatever the case, it seemed certain that I was in for yet another tongue-lashing. Delay would only make it worse. Resignedly, I made my way upstairs.

My grandmother was sitting in the straight-backed chair she had made particularly her own, reading the local paper. She lowered it as I entered, regarding me severely over the top, her steely eyes glaring at me from behind round, gold-rimmed spectacles.

"What did I tell you?" she asked, without preamble.

I closed the door behind me and stood there dumbly, not knowing quite what to say to this opening gambit.

"I asked you what I told you," she said again.

"About what, Grandmother?" I asked.

"About what! About Mr Roger Leyton, that's what! I saw you out of this very window, skulking across the green."

I denied the charge hotly.

"There was no skulking about it. He asked me to walk with him and I did so gladly."

"Then you should be ashamed of yourself for an ungrateful, disobedient girl. Didn't I tell you not to behave foolish with him?"

"What's so foolish about walking along the lane?"

"I will not have disobedience!" She slapped the folded paper down on the table beside her. "If you're to live under my roof, you'll do what you're told." She put a hand to her head and closed her eyes. "Quite upset me, you have. I feel that queer."

I looked at her coldly, unwilling to be blackmailed by any pretence of frailty.

"You don't understand," I said, "I love him, and he loves me."

"Poppycock!" She opened her eyes and glared at me. "I can see your mother standing there, defying me just as you're defying me. She went her own way—did just as she thought best, and look what happened to her!"

"But my case is different," I said, tears of frustration welling in my eyes. "Why are you so set against Roger?"

"The Leytons consider themselves gentry, whatever my views on their origins. I've seen those boys down there, smiling and flirting with the village girls, meaning nothing. Roger Leyton is like the others. He won't do right by you, and then where will you be?"

"He isn't like the others. He loves me!"

"Poppycock," she said again.

"You don't know him as I know him, Grandmother!"

"Now listen to me, Jenny!" She wagged a finger at me. "And listen carefully because I mean what I say. If you want to stay here, you'll promise never to see Roger Leyton again—not alone, that is. I'll not have defiance! I know what's best for you."

"You don't, you don't!" I was openly crying now. This, coming on top of Mark's tirade, was just too much; it was more than I could bear. "You can't rule my life, Grandmother. I like it here. I don't want to leave. But nothing is going to make me agree not to see Roger again—nothing, nothing."

She rose to her feet with her fists clenched and her jaw set, but the furious words she was about to utter died as the door behind me opened and Susan put her head into the room.

"Mrs Tomkins and Mrs Dean want to be off now, ma'am," she said. "They want to know should they come back tomorrow for their money?"

"Tell them to come back," grandmother said. "Well, go on girl—don't stand there gawping."

Susan's expression was one of horror not untinged with delight as she looked at my grandmother's expression of rage and my tearstained face. I imagined that the account of this would lose nothing in the telling. Hastily she scuttled from the room back to the two women in the kitchen.

I turned to follow her.

"I've got more to say," my grandmother said. "You're a fool if you think any good will come from this. He won't marry you. His sort never marries girls like you."

I fumbled for the door handle. I could not stay to hear more. Already I was beginning to believe her—she was so sure of her ground, so certain that she was right. She raised her voice to call after me.

"I'll go to his mother—tell her what I think—" But I had had enough and fled from the room, down the stairs and out through the front, only dimly aware of my grandfather calling after me.

My every instinct made me long to run to Roger, but I knew this to be impossible. I lifted my skirts and ran across the green, not towards Priors but to the little lane which ran on the other side of the church and led to fields belonging to the Goodsons, another family who owned much of the land in Collingford. I climbed a stile, hardly noticing that I had snagged my lovely new embroidered dress on a

76

bramble, and panting now, my running steps slowing to a walk, clambered up a grassy hill to the shelter of a grove of hawthorne trees.

Face down I flung myself on the grass, sobbing against the welcoming earth.

I would defy her. I would *have* to defy her. I was grateful to her and I hated to think of leaving the Ring of Bells, but it would not be the end of the world. I now had skills that were a saleable asset. It would be easy to find employment, somewhere near where Roger would be able to visit me.

Miserably I turned over on to my back and gazed up at the cloudless sky, a more faded blue now that the afternoon was over.

"Could she possibly be right?" I whispered to a blackbird that was sitting on a branch close beside me, cocking his head this way and that as he regarded me with his beady eye.

I needed Roger's reassurance so much. My grandmother was a forceful woman and for the first time I appreciated my mother's reasons for staying away from Collingford. Suddenly the memory of her was more vivid than it had been for months. I remembered her courage and her determination to remain independent. I remembered the resolute way she had brought me up to appreciate a better life than that offered by the dismal area in which we lived.

She must have been strong, I thought; strong to have a disagreement of this magnitude with her mother and still pursue her own course of action, even if in the end events had proved her mistaken. Sarah Austin was a hard woman to defy. She was an autocrat—a despot. It would be all too easy to give in to her, to admit that her way was best.

And thinking of my mother, I suddenly remembered the manner of her death. It was as if I had blotted the memory out, just as Mrs Blewett had said that I should.

It was months since I had thought of the medicine that had so mysteriously disappeared, and of my own confusion. I still felt guilty about having left her alone, however worthy my motives had been, but I knew now without any doubt that my mother had been as strong in death as she had been in life. She had made the decision that she had suffered enough, and she had acted on it. The relief that this certainty brought me was indescribable.

I sat up, feeling calmer. I was my mother's daughter and could be no less brave than she had been when placed, all those years ago, in a situation similar to my own. It grieved me to leave my grandfather and the inn, but leave them I would if Roger was the price I had to pay for staying.

I stood up and brushed grass and pieces of twig from my skirts. I would go back now. I would avoid further arguments, I resolved, until I had had a chance to talk to Roger the following day. Then if grandmother still insisted on it, I would go. I smiled a little wryly, wondering where she would be able to find anyone else who would cook and sew and clean for as little money as I received.

I was so wrapped up in my own thoughts and emotions that I failed at first to notice the small knot of people standing outside the Ring of Bells.

It was, after all, not particularly unusual on a summer's evening for the men to sit outside to drink their beer, and there was always a certain amount of activity on the green. What suddenly struck me was not the activity, but the lack of it. There was a strange stillness about the group, and when I looked more closely I saw that it was made up of women in their aprons with babies in their arms and children round their skirts, as if they had lately run out from the cottages that surrounded the green.

Somebody noticed my approach and called out to me, and I stopped, blinked, and managed to get the picture into focus. Something was wrong. The dogcart that was outside, a small boy holding the horse's head, belonged to Dr Linley. I picked up my flowered skirts and ran across the green.

It happened not half an hour before, someone told me.

"Must've been just as you ran out," a woman from across the green put in. "I seed you, runnin' like the devil was at your heels."

"But *what* happened?" I asked urgently.

"Lucky Dr Linley was nearby, a-deliver'n of Mrs Meachem's twins, so he was on the spot, like, in no time at all."

"What *happened*?" I demanded.

"It's the old lady—old Sarah."

"She fell. Awful dark, those stairs are."

"She had her hands full, they say. Cup and saucer in one hand, paper in the other. She must've slipped. No way to put out a hand to save herself, poor soul."

Susan, Mrs Tomkins and Mrs Dean were still in the kitchen, huddled together whispering in a group at the end of the room. They turned to look at me as I went in, their tongues suddenly stilled.

"What happened?" I asked them. "How bad is she?"

"Much you care," Mrs Tomkins muttered under her breath, turning away from me.

"We don't know how bad she is," Susan said, more kindly. "No one's told us. She fell, that's all we know."

"Must have been just as you ran out—or just before," Mrs Tomkins said.

"Don't say such things, Mary," Mrs Dean said.

Mrs Tomkins was quick to take offence.

"I s'pose *you* didn't say anything of the sort, did you?" she asked sarcastically. "I beg your pardon, I'm sure. My ears must've deceived me. I thought it was you said she could've run out after Mrs Austin fell."

I couldn't take in the full meaning of their words. Impatiently I left them in mid-argument, sickened by the underlying pleasure they seemed to be extracting from the drama.

Grandmother had suffered a stroke, the doctor told us when he finally came from her room. It was this that had caused her to fall, not the dimly-lit stairs which she must have known with her eyes shut. It was just the worst of misfortunes that she had happened to be in such a dangerous position when the stroke occurred.

She lived for four days. Straw was put down on the road outside the inn to muffle the noise of the cartwheels and there seemed a strangely breathless atmosphere about the Ring of Bells.

My grandfather was inconsolable. Whenever I went up-stairs, I found him standing about, looming helplessly and miserably in the shadows on the landing, or sitting by his wife's bedside trying to be inconspicuous as I or one of the neighbours ministered to her.

What impressed me most was the kindness that was shown to us. In spite of the insinuations made by Mrs Tomkins, I noticed no lack of warmth in the attitude of other women who called at the inn to offer their help. Our neighbour, Mrs Oliver, who lived in the little cottage that was attached to the Ring of Bells, was particularly comforting when I confessed to her that I was troubled by the fact that on the last day of my grandmother's conscious life I had parted from her in anger.

"She wasn't an easy woman to like," she said. "And I should know. I've known her since we were children at school together. There's hardly a soul in Collingford that hasn't felt the rough side of her tongue, for one reason or another."

"She was very angry with me."

"She thought the world of you! It's just that she was born with a sharp tongue and Joe's never been strong enough to gainsay her."

In spite of this judgment, it seemed that Collingford regarded her as an institution and disliked the thought that she had gone. We were besieged with queries regarding our welfare. Lord Bollinger wrote with a strangely touching tribute to the pretty young girl he had known when she worked at Watersmeet. Roger visited me constantly. He helped me with menial chores and tried to cheer Aunt Millie who had taken up temporary residence, and my grandfather was so distraught that he appeared not to notice that Roger was behaving exactly like one of the family.

I had, of course, been unable to meet Roger on the Sunday as we had arranged. I knew that, Collingford being what it was, the news of grandmother's fall would have reached him; sure enough, it was earlier than the time we had arranged for our meeting that he came to the Ring of Bells to offer what support he could.

I had left Mark on the day of Annie's wedding with rage and fury in my heart, and this had only been increased by the quarrel with my grandmother. I had been determined to tell Roger everything. Now it all seemed irrelevant. In the face of this tragedy Mark's hurtful words had lost their significance. After all, Roger had not yet asked me to marry him, not in so many words. There would be time enough to worry about his family's reaction when things between us were more settled.

A hundred or more mourners followed my grandmother's bier over the green to the church where she was laid to rest in the shade of a sycamore tree. My grandfather was lost and disorientated and Aunt Millie, herself sodden with tears, was no help to him at all. I found myself thrust in the position of head of the house, a role I devoutly hoped I would not have to maintain for long. There were too many far-reaching decisions to be made.

When I thought of the future, I assumed that for the time being grandfather and I would go on running the Ring of Bells between us, until such time as Roger and I were married, for although the words had not been spoken he had told me many times that he loved me and I never for one moment doubted his intentions. This was a thought that filled me with joyous anticipation. I loved to think of running my own household and employing my skills for the comfort and convenience of Roger and our family, rather than for any Tom, Dick or Harry who chose to pay the price of a room.

It was Aunt Millie who unwittingly brought things to a head. She lived in a small house set in the middle of two acres of land up on the Oxford road and was for ever bemoaning the fact that since the death of her husband she had no one to work the garden or look after the pigs and chickens she kept there.

"Couldn't you come and live with me, Joe?" she asked plaintively. "Seems daft to keep two households going."

"I've thought about it," he admitted. "Somehow the heart's gone out of me for keeping on the Ring of Bells. But what about my little maid here?" He looked at me as he spoke. "I'm not leaving her high and dry."

"I expect I would be all right, Grandfather," I said. My heart began to race. Surely Roger would speak under these circumstances? "You could sell the inn and invest the money to give you a small income."

"My, my—will you listen to her, Millie?" My grandfather's voice was full of admiration. "Such a business head as she has on her! She's full of ideas, our Jenny."

And you don't know the half of them, I thought, as I raced down the lane to meet Roger at the end of the track. Oh please, please God, I prayed incoherently as I ran. Please make him strong too. I was sure that it was the thought of opposition from his family that was holding him back.

I could see him waiting for me. As soon as I came into his view he came striding down the lane and I stopped my headlong flight, slowing my steps to a more dignified walk just to prolong the pleasure of seeing him coming towards me. Our hands reached out to touch, and he pulled me into the shadow of the hedge where he held me and kissed me.

"Is there something wrong?" Roger asked, drawing away from me and looking down into my face. "You're very quiet."

"I'm worried," I said. "I don't know what's going to happen to me. Grandfather wants to sell the inn."

"I see." Roger looked away from me as if in thought, chewing his lip. "Come on," he said abruptly. "Let's walk."

We took a favourite path which led along the side of a field where the sheep eyed us incuriously, through a gate and across another meadow starry with wildflowers, and with Roger's arm around my waist, I told him Aunt Millie's problems and grandfather's desire to leave the Ring of Bells.

"And what is to become of you?" he asked.

I did not reply and the silence lengthened between us. He stopped and swung round to face me, his hands on my shoulders and his expression serious.

"Oh Jenny, I love you and I do want to marry you. It's just this awful indecision about my future that's prevented me from asking you. I just don't want to farm. I've tried to conform, but it's no use. So really I have nothing to offer you, you see—not yet. Not until I can see my way clearly."

I had stopped listening. He had said it! He wanted to marry me! Nothing else had any significance for me at that moment.

Still, a warning voice told me, in spite of Roger's intentions,

82

it would not do to dismiss the objections his family would raise. Mark's outburst on the day of Annie's wedding had been ominous enough. I sighed heavily.

"We'll find a way," Roger said, his gloom lightening a little. "We love each other, that's the main thing."

We walked on to the bottom of the field and took the path which led through the barley field and up to the bare hillside above Priors. It was higher here and the barley rippled and soughed in the breeze.

One more gate and we were out on springy turf looking down on the roof of the house and its clustered outbuildings. Roger sat down and held up a hand to pull me down beside him.

"I'll give up Priors," he said after a moment. "I think it's the only way. Mark made it clear—" he broke off.

"I know what Mark made clear," I said bitterly. "He made it clear to me, too. I wouldn't be welcome at Priors."

"I have some money in my own right. Not much—just a small inheritance from my grandfather. My father may be prepared to give me more, if I agree to give up any claim to Priors."

"But Roger, why *should* you? You're the eldest son—"

"And Mark's the farmer of the family. We should have been born the other way round. Priors means much more to him than it does to me. I'll do something else."

"Do you have something in mind?"

"Not immediately." His face was set, his expression troubled. "What a useless fellow I am!" he went on. "Good for nothing. I did think of the stage—"

"Oh, never that!" I interjected hurriedly. "It's a dreadful life."

"Well, a business of some kind. A shop, perhaps? Oh, there never was anyone with as few talents as I! Whereas you—you're as competent as a woman twice your—"

He broke off without completing the sentence, staring at me.

"I wonder," he said, as if inspiration had suddenly struck him. "I just wonder!"

"What?" I asked curiously, smiling since he was smiling too. "What do you wonder?"

He slapped the turf beside him with the flat of his hand.

"Jenny, I've had the most wonderful idea! It's the answer to everything."

"*What*? Roger, you really are the most infuriating—"

"The inn! The Ring of Bells! You say old Joe wants to sell it—well, I'll buy it and we'll run it between us. You know the ropes and I'll soon learn. I'm not afraid of hard work. If I can just raise enough to buy it—how much does Joe want for it, do you know?—I can get a loan from the bank to make alterations. We can enlarge it. Build a whole new wing on part of the garden. Take in the next-door cottage eventually."

I don't know when he realised that my silence was one of horror rather than delighted surprise.

"What is it, Jenny?" he asked at last. "Don't you think it a wonderful idea?"

I got to my feet and looked down on Priors.

"You don't know," I said. "You have no idea what it's like. There's never any end to the work. And there's never any peace or privacy."

I turned round to face him.

"You've always had a home to call your own. You've always had four walls and a good stout door you can shut against the rest of the world. Have you any idea what it's like in an inn? It's home to the whole village. Anyone can walk in there at any time, and sit down and demand to be served. Oh, I never expected a home like Priors, not really—that would be just too good to be true. But I do want a home of my own. Not a big one, or a grand one. Just somewhere with room enough for us and our children, and a garden they can play in. Somewhere we can be safe, with the rest of the world shut out."

"An ivory tower? You can't shut life out, Jenny."

"You don't know how it is when you've never had a home," I said. "Mother and I—we had two rooms, with shouting and quarrelling and other people's troubles going on just outside our door. The Ring of Bells is better than that, but it still isn't *home*!"

He stood up beside me and held me close, his arms tight around me.

"We could make it home, Jenny. Wherever we're together, that would be home." He rubbed his cheek against my hair. "You're so good at it—so efficient—"

"Stop trying to butter me up."

"But it's true! And you'd find it much more fun working with me than with your grandmother. My resemblance to Queen Victoria isn't at all striking."

"Oh Roger!" I laughed, in spite of myself. "Whatever would your parents say? They'd be horrified."

"Then they'd have to get over it. I'll enlarge it and improve it and we'll call it the Ring of Bells Hotel—it won't be an inn any more. And people will come from far and wide to sample the best food in the country."

"But I don't want to spend my life in the kitchen!"

"You won't have to, I swear it. We'll become so successful that we'll employ a French chef direct from Paris, and I'll buy you a house with any number of doors that you can shut to your heart's content."

"I can't bear to think of your losing Priors."

"Darling, I'm thrilled to the skies with this idea! I'm sure it's the perfect solution for me and I'm only amazed that I didn't think of it before. I like people. I like the thought of making them comfortable. I know I'm hopelessly ignorant, but I can't think of a more able teacher than you." He drew away from me and indicated the countryside before us with an expansive gesture of his arm. "Just look at all this—did you ever see such beautiful country? Now we have the railways, it's within everyone's reach. People think nothing of coming out from Oxford for a day's fishing. And mark my words, the bicycle is the thing of the future. It's being improved all the time and sooner or later someone will invent something less unwieldy than the penny-farthing and everyone will be dashing around the country on two wheels. We'll just have to make sure that they dash straight to the Ring of Bells."

It was impossible not to be affected by his enthusiasm.

"If I agreed," I said. "*If*, mind you, I'd want the drinkers out of the kitchen. Could we make a separate tap-room, somehow? I'd want the kitchen to myself."

"Sweetheart, it's yours!"

85

"Oh, Roger!" Half angry, half laughing, I pushed myself away from him again. "I'm still not convinced that you know what you're doing. You still have to raise the money. And I only said that grandfather was *thinking* of selling—there's nothing settled."

"I can't see him coping without your grandmother."

"No," I admitted. "Nor can I."

"I'll talk to him—and my father—tomorrow."

I walked a few steps away from him and looked down once again on Priors. Surely, I asked myself, I hadn't really expected to live there? Life was real, not a fairy tale.

Being with Roger was what counted, even if it meant that my life was to be spent, just as my grandmother's life was spent, between the kitchen, the bar and the bedrooms of the inn, planning meals and welcoming strangers, never with a moment to call my own.

Roger came over to me and turned me to face him.

"We can try it," he said seriously, not laughing now. "If it doesn't work out, we can sell up and do something else. It doesn't have to be for ever."

"Whatever you say," I agreed, reaching up to kiss him, quelling my doubts.

We were walking back through the meadow when a collie dog came bounding towards us, leaping up at Roger, his tail waving like a banner. We looked up to see Mark approaching us. My instinct was to turn and run, but Roger stopped and waited for his brother to join us.

"Of all the ill-trained animals—" he began.

"He's only a pup," Mark said easily. "He'll be all right, given time. Pedigree will out." I did not look at him, but felt sure that this shaft was meant for me. "What's got into you, old boy?" he went on. "You're looking mighty pleased with yourself."

"I confess I'm feeling it," Roger said. The three of us turned and began to walk slowly up the meadow together. "Mark, how would you like Priors?"

Mark stopped and looked at his brother with a puzzled expression.

"How would I—are you mad, old chap?"

"Not in the least." Roger made a sweeping gesture in

the general direction of the house. "There you are—it's yours."

"Don't be ridiculous! It's hardly yours to give."

"No, not yet, I admit, but in the normal course of events I might expect it to be eventually. However, events aren't going to take their normal course. I'm backing out, Mark. Retiring gracefully. I'm hoping that the old man will give me my portion and let me get on with my own life."

"Doing what, for heaven's sake?"

Roger blinked uncertainly and I could see that now it had come to the point of putting his idea into words, he was going to need a considerable amount of courage.

"I propose to buy the Ring of Bells. Jenny and I are going to get married and run it between us."

"Buy the—my dear chap, are you *quite* mad?"

"I'm not mad at all." Roger put his arm round my shoulders. "I've never been more in possession of my senses. For the first time in months I feel really happy."

"Did you talk him into this?" Mark ignored his brother and addressed me, but Roger did not give me the chance to answer.

"Jenny didn't like the idea of my sacrificing Priors," he said, in what I recognised as an unfortunate choice of words. "And she had her doubts about the inn, but I've succeeded in talking her out of them. You might have the grace to welcome her into the family, Mark."

Mark began to laugh softly, his dark, arrogant face alight with sardonic amusement.

"I'm sure she had her doubts," he said. "And even more sure that she hated the idea of your sacrificing Priors. That must have been quite a blow!"

His laughter grew louder and seemed to fill my ears, until suddenly I could stand it no longer and turned to walk away.

6

All Roger's indecision fell away from him. He now seemed
certain of the direction in which his life was going, and in all
fairness to his parents, I have to admit that once they were
convinced that nothing would deflect him from his purpose,
they accepted the situation, if not with unbounded joy, then
with resignation. Basically they were loving parents and had
been troubled by his obvious dissatisfaction with the role
they felt life had ordained for him. I was thankful, though,
that I was not destined to share a house with Mrs Leyton.
She reminded me of two lines from the tag-end of some
half-forgotten verse which my mother used sometimes to
repeat when she felt I was being unreasonable:

> Oh dear me, no, I'm not conceited;
> It's just that *my* way is always best!

I did not underestimate Mark's part in their eventual capitu-
lation to Roger's proposals. I could hardly blame him for
wanting Priors. Yet I could not help resenting the triumphant
mockery I felt I could see in his eyes every time he looked in
my direction.

My first sight of its interior was something of a disappointment. Mrs Leyton always presented such a well
turned-out appearance. The little trap in which she trotted
about the village on her various errands was smart and
freshly painted. I had expected at least as much order in the
house, but instead found that the beautifully proportioned
rooms were shabby and over-furnished, and smelled of dogs.
The furniture and silver were dull and there were piles of
newspapers and farming journals scattered everywhere. A
box of seedlings stood on the floor in a corner of the sitting
room, the folds of the velvet curtains were faded and there
were cobwebs suspended from the ceiling. I could imagine

only too well what my grandmother's reaction would have been to such disorder.

In spite of it all, Mrs Leyton possessed a grand manner, and I was totally intimidated on our first meeting. She poured tea from a beautiful Georgian teapot, criminally tarnished, sitting erect on a horsehair sofa, and handed the cup to me with a bright, social smile.

"Do you ride, Miss Fitzgerald?" she asked.

"N—no," I stammered.

"Jenny has hardly had the chance, Mother," Roger said.

"No, of course not." She smiled again. "Stupid of me to ask! What do you do with your time, Miss Fitzgerald?"

My mind went totally blank and I swallowed nervously. Did she really want to know about the cooking and sewing and cleaning?

"Jenny likes to read," Roger prompted gently, with an encouraging smile at me.

"*Really?*" It was as if he had announced that a South Sea Islander was fond of petit-point. She looked at me with raised eyebrows, her cup halfway to her mouth. "How very nice!"

For a few moments there was an awkward silence.

"Since Roger seems set on this marriage," she said at last, a note of distaste creeping into her voice, "I suppose we should discuss plans."

"We only want a quiet wedding, Mother."

"So that the entire county will wonder what we have to be ashamed of?"

"No!" Roger banged his cup down on his saucer and glared at his mother. "Because that is what Jenny and I would prefer, and the entire county can go hang. Remember, Jenny's grandmother died little more than a month ago. A large wedding would be entirely out of place."

"Then wait six months." Mrs Leyton's voice was all sweet reasonableness. She leant over and patted me on the arm. "No girl likes to be rushed, Roger. You must give Miss Fitzgerald a chance to gather a trousseau together."

And give yourself a chance to think again, she might well have said. I could read her mind like a book.

"Mother," Roger said, with an air of patient exasperation.

"We have been over this a dozen times. I've discussed it all with Joe Austin. He wants to be out of the inn as soon as possible, and we want to take over on the first date that the sale is legal. And *surely*, now that Jenny is to be part of the family, you could call her by her first name?"

"Certainly, if that is what she would like. But Roger, I can't bear the thought of a hole-in-the-corner affair. You must see that it wouldn't do at all!"

I sat silent as the argument raged around me. Whatever Roger decided would be all right as far as I was concerned, but when he leapt to his feet and strode about the room talking of Gretna Green I decided that it was time to conquer my natural diffidence and take a part in the conversation.

"Would not a quiet, simple church ceremony be acceptable?" I asked meekly.

Mrs Leyton regarded me thoughtfully.

"I think I have the answer," she said. "We could, perhaps, restrict the list of guests to a hundred or so without causing comment if we ask the bishop of the diocese to officiate. That will give an air of respectability to the whole thing. And as you say, your recent bereavement should be enough to explain why we have not invited the whole county."

"Mother, we don't *care*—"

I shook my head at him, begging him to be silent. Mrs Leyton seemed happy now, or at least as happy as she was ever likely to be, with her eldest son about to make such a misalliance. She got to her feet immediately and began rummaging through the papers that littered an escritoire which stood close to the windows.

"I'll write to the bishop at once," she said. "I know the dear man will be only too pleased to agree. He's some sort of distant connection by marriage, you know—cousin of the man your Aunt Augusta married. I'll invite him to stay the night."

Dear heaven, I thought. What can the bedrooms be like? He'd be better off at the Ring of Bells.

It was, in the end, the bishop who set the date of the wedding. Roger and I had hoped for the last Saturday in August, since the legal documents for the sale of the inn were due to be signed that week, but unfortunately the bishop was to be at a conference at Canterbury and would not be returning to Oxfordshire until Sunday, the first day of September. The following Wednesday he had arranged to go on holiday, so unless we cared to wait until the end of the month, he was very much afraid—

"It will have to be on Tuesday the third," Roger said.

"But nobody gets married on a Tuesday," his mother wailed.

"*We* do!" Roger's tone was firm and brooked no argument.

Mark smiled sardonically and said nothing, while his father said little more. I felt I knew Mr Leyton no better than the first time I had seen him in church. He was polite and pleasant and remote—silent in company and given to retreating to his study to read his farming journals; the result, perhaps, of living with Mrs Leyton whose tongue was hardly ever still. However, Roger reported to me that he had described me as a 'well-mannered, fetchin' little filly', and while I could not whole-heartedly approve of the description, I felt that his initial opposition to me and our entire venture was perhaps beginning to melt a little.

The Leytons' friends were drawn almost exclusively from the hunting, shooting, farming section of the community. Money not made from the land or inherited from past generations was, they seemed to feel, tainted in some way, and to engage in trade was unspeakable.

I knew that Roger was stepping out of his class to marry me, but even so I did not fully appreciate the effort Mrs Leyton was making to carry off the situation with panache until I overheard her one day talking to a group of her friends. She was unaware of the fact that Roger and I were sitting in the garden just outside the window and could hear every word.

"My dears," she was saying in her high, carrying voice. "I never have known what to expect from those sons of mine! They're such madcaps, all three of them. They inherit their spirit from my side of the family, of course! Really, we can do nothing but laugh. Roger regards the whole thing as the most enormous joke. I tell him he must go up to Saville Row to be measured for a leather jerkin. If he's going to be a landlord, then he must dress the part."

There were sounds of polite merriment from within, followed by words that were inaudible to me.

"Jenny?" Mrs Leyton's voice continued. "Oh, a sweet little thing—we've become simply devoted to her. Her father was very well-connected, you know. The Fitzgeralds are, of course, a well-known Irish family, and Jenny's father was quite famous in his own right. An excellent Shakespearian actor. Had he lived, he would have undoubtedly become another Henry Irving."

Roger and I turned to look at each other with amused amazement and had to run away quickly before our uncontrolled laughter gave our position away.

I still found it incredible that in a few short weeks I would be the chatelaine of the Ring of Bells—that Roger and I would occupy the bedroom where my grandparents had slept, and that for good or ill, the success or otherwise of the venture would be our responsibility and ours alone.

I still had reservations about the wisdom of it all. I felt that Roger had no idea of the work involved, but he himself seemed a changed man, brimming with ideas and energy. Already he had consulted with architects. There were to be four extra bedrooms and a new dining room downstairs, with small tables in place of the large one upstairs, though the old dining room was still to be kept for the meetings and private parties that we hoped would be held there. The new wing was also to hold a bathroom and an inside water closet.

There was to be a tap-room with an outside door so that muddy boots would no longer sully my kitchen. I was to have a new porcelain sink with a brass tap to replace the pump. In an era when most people still had the pump in the backyard, I think it was the tap that caused more open-mouthed astonishment in Collingford than anything else. Personally, it was the new kitchen range that pleased me most.

The parlour, Roger said, was to be completely refurbished. The paper on the walls was dark and discoloured with smoke from the fire and no one, he maintained, could possibly sit on the chairs provided without discomfort. That was to be my job, to choose new furnishings to make it warm and welcoming.

It was exciting, I had to admit, and when I wondered aloud how we were going to make enough money to justify these improvements, he waved my doubts aside.

"It's a question of getting known," he said. "I'll use every contact I can think of. We have everything to offer here—trout in the river and the best of hunting. We have a university town filled with enterprising young people less than twenty miles away. One thing I learned in my short stay in America—it pays to advertise, Jenny, and advertise we will. I'll see that posters are put up all over Oxford. We'll advertise in the local papers—even the London and Birmingham papers, why not? All right—I agree with all the Jonahs who tell me that it's a gamble, but what's wrong with that? I'm a gambling man! There's nothing I like better than a flutter on the gees or a game of cards; but they pale into insignificance beside all this!"

"Other inns are going out of business."

"We're not 'other inns'! We're the Ring of Bells Hotel. Pilgrims stopped here on their way to Canterbury. Passengers on the mail coaches stayed overnight. We're carrying on a long, long tradition Jenny, and people will come for miles when there's something worth coming for."

It was impossible to resist such enthusiasm. Almost in spite of myself I became infected with his optimism.

Mrs Leyton insisted on giving me my wedding dress. I had protested at first out of a sense of pride, but it would have taken a far stronger character than I to withstand her. I knew that her main object was to ensure that I did not disgrace the Leyton family when I walked down the aisle, and I burned a little with indignation to think that she distrusted my own taste; but once I had seen pictures of the dress she proposed for me and had fingered the material, I was lost.

I had never owned anything like it. It was high-necked and tucked, each tuck edged with lace. The front panel fell straight to the floor, but cunningly draped, lace-edged taffeta was caught behind in a graceful bustle. My only regret was that my mother was not alive to see it. How she would have loved it—and the whole idea of this marriage!

Mrs Leyton had engaged a dressmaker to make it for me and since the same lady was also concocting an elegant blue gown for Mrs Leyton, I dutifully turned up at Priors for my fittings.

The final fitting took place only a few days before the date of the wedding.

"*Very* nice," Mrs Leyton pronounced, walking round me and gazing at me with judiciously narrowed eyes. "I must say, Jenny, you pay for dressing."

"Thank you," I said humbly. It was the nearest thing to a compliment that had ever passed her lips.

"Yes," she went on. "I think we'll all be able to hold up our heads next Tuesday. You look most acceptable."

I said nothing.

Count ten, I told myself. Control your feelings. It's only natural she should feel this way. You're marrying Roger— that's what is important.

I knew that I should thank her for her generosity in providing such a beautiful dress for me, but somehow the words stuck in my throat. The dressmaker began to undo the row of buttons so that I could step out of it, and I did so in silence. Mrs Leyton noticed nothing.

"Mark is going into Collingford to the Post Office," she said. "I'm sure he will give you a ride back—he'll be leaving any moment."

"I should prefer to walk," I said.

Roger was in Oxford for the day, finalising the legal business in connection with the sale of the inn.

"Nonsense!" said Mrs Leyton, sure, as always, that she could organise everything better than anyone else. "I presume you'll be taking your dress back with you. It's quite unnecessary for you to walk carrying such a large box." She pressed a bell and a small, untidy maid appeared while I was still buttoning my skirt.

"Flossie, tell Mr Mark to wait for Miss Fitzgerald, will you? He's probably in the stable yard now."

Argument was useless. Besides, it was a big box and I did not particularly welcome the walk back to the Ring of Bells thus burdened. If it had been anyone but Mark, it would not have occurred to me to raise any objection at all.

"This is very kind of you," I said stiffly, when I had climbed up into the trap and was sitting beside him.

"My mother orders. I obey," he said, leaving me in no doubt that his own wishes had not been consulted in the matter.

We rode in silence until we reached the lane, a silence that seemed to me oppressive.

"I—I wish that we might call a truce," I said at last. "I know your opinion of me, but surely even you can see that Roger is happier now than he has been for a long time. You might wish us well."

He was silent for a long time.

"I wish I had not seen you looking at Priors so longingly," he said at last. "If I had not done so, I might more easily accept your devotion to Roger."

"You don't understand," I said. "I love Priors because it's beautiful, that's all."

"No," he said. "That's not all. I saw your face."

I looked away from him, staring unseeingly at the field at the side of the lane. I shook my head helplessly, biting my lip. It was impossible to put into words the longing for security that Priors had woken in me.

"I can't expect you to understand," I said.

"Oh, but I do—I do," he replied smoothly. "It's a house any girl would want to own, particularly a girl from nowhere."

"It's not like that!"

"You don't have to pretend with me. You're an ambitious little minx. I just wonder how long it will take my poor deluded brother to find you out."

"Please put me down here. I won't ride with you another yard."

"Don't be idiotic. I'll drop you at the door for appearance's sake, if nothing else."

I sat grinding my teeth with impotent rage, holding the dress box on my knee. My gaze was directed fixedly on the horse's ears.

"Hello!" We had turned into the road which led to the Ring of Bells and there was a change in Mark's tone. He spoke lightly, a note of amusement in his voice. "Who on earth is that frightful looking drab? She's a stranger to Collingford."

I looked towards the inn and the blood seemed to freeze in my veins. I recogised the shape of her even though her face was turned away. She was dressed in mauve, with torn frills stretched tightly across her billowing bosom. A black shawl, gaping with holes, was around her shoulders and she wore a black hat with a red ostrich feather. I drew in my breath sharply.

"You know her?" Mark asked.

He brought the trap to a standstill by the door and she swaggered over to us.

"'Ullo, Jenny," she said, grinning at me in the peculiarly mirthless way I always associated with her. "Ain't this a surprise, then? Ain't yer going to interduce me to yer swank feller?"

I sat perfectly still, unable to say a word. Mark, too, looked as if he could hardly believe his eyes.

"Cat got yer tongue?" she said jeeringly to me. "S'pose I'll 'ave to do the job meself. I'm Bella Blewett," she said, turning to Mark. "A friend of Jenny's from London. You must be the toff she's going to marry."

"I—er—haven't that privilege," Mark said drily.

Hastily I scrambled down from the trap, anxious only to get her away from him. He gave me a strange and mocking look as he turned the horse and drove away.

"What on earth have you come here for?" I asked angrily.

"That's not much of a welcome! I come ter see you, o' course," Bella said.

Desperately I tried to pull myself together, aware that at the first sight of her I was once again the mindlessly terrified little ninny of earlier years. I could not imagine what she was doing in Collingford.

"Ain't yer going to ask me in?" she said.

"I suppose so."

My lack of enthusiasm did nothing to discourage her and she followed me into the Ring of Bells.

"'Ere," she said, looking round at the parlour. "You done all right fer yerself, ain't yer? Nice place, this." She grinned at me slyly. "I stayed at the Nag's 'Ead last night.

'Eard quite a bit about you there, I did. Funny the way your granny died, wasn't it?"

I shut the door between the parlour and the kitchen where Susan was washing dishes and returned to where Bella stood, folding my shaking hands together.

"I asked you why you've come. You can hardly expect me to be glad to see you."

"I don't give a bugger whether you're glad to see me or not," she said. "I just need a bit of 'elp, that's all—and I thought, well, 'oo better to give it than Miss Genevieve Fitzgerald? After all," she added unctuously, "we was good to you in your time of need. We never said a word to a soul about the way yer ma died."

"Because it suited you!" I said quickly. "Your mother was afraid her friend would get into trouble."

"And now 'er friend's kicked the bucket so we don't 'ave to keep quiet no more. We've fallen on bad times, see," she went on, her voice taking on a whining note. "Me mum's sick and Vera's Wally upped and left 'er with all them brats and I lost me job."

"Well, you can't work here," I said. "I am to be married next week and the inn is being closed for alteration."

She laughed, rocking backwards and forwards and mopping her eyes.

"Ooh, you aren't arf a caution," she said at last. "Work for you? I'd need me bleedin' 'ead examined. Nah—I just come to ask you for a little contribution to tide me over."

"Contribution?" I echoed stupidly.

"Money," she said. "In consideration of us not spillin' the beans about what we know. Now don't tell me you ain't got none, 'cos I won't believe it. They tell me you're as good as running this place since your granny died—and there's some as say you might 'ave 'elped 'er on 'er way. Fell down the stairs, didn't she? Just after you and 'er 'ad an argument? Funny, ain't it, the way people just seem to peg out, right at the moment when it suits you best?"

"You're talking nonsense," I said, through stiff lips. "Nobody can believe that."

"Oh no? I heard a few rumours last night."

"There'll always be someone to gossip—"

"But they didn't know about your ma. And I didn't tell 'em," she added quickly. "I didn't tell 'em you slipped 'er an overdose—"

"I did no such thing!"

"But you admitted it, in front of witnesses. Me and me mum—both prepared to swear. And what's more, me mum's still got the bottle with the dregs in it, so it could be proved easy as wink that you give 'er too much." She laughed, completely at ease. "We don't want to go to the police," she said. "The less they know about anything the better, so far as I'm concerned. Still, we might 'ave to tell 'em, if you don't pay up. I don't suppose this toff you're going to marry would think much of it, do you?"

I got up from the straight-backed chair where I had been perched and went to the window, staring out unseeingly at the green with the church beyond—the church where in only a few days' time I was to become Roger's wife. I had nothing to fear, I told myself. My conscience was clear. I could tell Roger everything and he would get rid of Bella for me somehow, and I would never have to think of her again.

But it was so *ugly*—and it wasn't only Roger I had to consider. I remembered Mrs Leyton remarking that now she would be able to hold up her head on Tuesday, knowing I was decently dressed; and Mark—I baulked altogether at the thought of Mark. He, I felt certain, would be prepared to believe anything of me. I didn't want to start my life with Roger with this kind of cloud hanging over me. I had quite enough prejudice to contend with without that.

Bella came and joined me at the window and I edged away as she loomed over me, just as she had done in the past. Why did she always have to stand so close? I could smell her; that rank, musky, animal odour was unmistakable and I seemed to be back in the past again, a frightened schoolgirl, terrified out of my wits by the menace of her physical presence.

"It's not like I'm asking for much," she said. "Fifty quid would do."

"I haven't got fifty pounds."

"You expect me to believe that! Your young man would give it to you for dresses, if you arst 'im—and your old grandad trusts you with cash for the tradesmen, I expect."

"That's right. He *trusts* me!"

"Well, suit yourself, I'm sure."

I took a breath.

"I don't know how I'll find it, but just suppose that I manage it somehow. Do you promise to go away? You won't bother me again?"

She put her hand on my arm and I shuddered.

"Trust Bella, dearie," she said, laughing at me. "Why should I want to stay in this 'ole? I'll be off to the smoke in no time at all and you'll be left to live 'appy ever after."

"Do I have your word on that?"

"See this wet, see this dry," she said, drawing the edge of her hand across her throat.

It was easier than I imagined to amass the money. Grandfather had abdicated altogether from the business side of the inn. He had always been used to allowing grandmother to handle the cash transactions with local tradesmen, and although the sums now involved were far less than they had been when we had guests to cater for, he was sufficiently vague not to notice that the butcher's bill came to a good ten pounds more than he might have expected and that wages and other outgoings were considerably heavier than they had been the previous month.

I felt soiled and ashamed as I perpetrated this deception. I hated Bella more than ever for forcing me to do so and handed over the money to her with a bad grace when we met by arrangement on the Sunday evening.

"I never want to see you again," I said.

"You don't 'ave to worry," she assured me.

"I hope I can believe you."

I heard her laugh as I turned away from her and made my way back across the green to the Ring of Bells.

I must have seemed abstracted and unlike myself during those few days when I knew that Bella was in the village waiting for her money, but Roger made no comment. Perhaps he attributed it to last-minute nerves.

On Tuesday, Annie—already pregnant—came to help me dress.

"Oh, Jenny," she said, stepping back to look at me when I was ready, my veil in place. "You look a real dream!"

I realised, resignedly, that my idea of a small wedding and that of Mrs Leyton had little in common. The church was almost full. I was conscious of a blur of faces turned towards me, heads craned curiously over fashionably attired shoulders. No doubt they were anxious to see the little nobody that Roger Leyton was misguidedly making his wife, I thought. But I was in no mood to care, or to distinguish individuals. I was aware only of the long, stone-flagged aisle, worn and bumpy with the feet of generations of worshippers, and of the two men standing at the end of it; Roger, tall and erect, with Mark who was acting as his best man beside him.

Afterwards I could not remember feeling happy and excited. I was in a trance-like condition as slowly I advanced towards Roger, waiting for me at the altar beneath the blazing stained-glass east window, and my only lasting memory was his expression of wonder as he turned to me when I was just a few feet away from him.

We made our vows. The choir sang, and the bishop's sermon was mercifully short. The wedding party moved to the vestry for the signing of the register. People spoke to me and I smiled, but I had eyes for no one but Roger.

Triumphantly the organ burst into the strains of the Wedding March as we left the vestry and slowly we processed down the aisle. My hand was on Roger's arm. I could feel him beside me; slim and tall and beloved, and I knew that now my veil had been thrown back, my radiant happiness would be obvious to the whole world.

Let it, I thought. There was never a girl more fortunate than I. Let my happiness be seen by all these elegant people; all the aunts and cousins and life-long friends—even the Bollingers in their usual pew. I smiled joyously at the world, and the world smiled back. Perhaps they had come to scoff at me—to commiserate with the Leytons about the terrible mistake that their son was making, as I had imagined on my long walk down the aisle—but they did not look as if they were scoffing now.

And then I saw her, there in the back pew, and for a second my steps faltered. She had not left Collingford, as I imagined she would as soon as she received the money. Bella was still in the village. She was looking at me, a jeering smile pulling down the corners of her mouth, and I could read her mind as clearly as if she had spoken aloud. 'Oo the 'ell does she think she is? she was thinking, just as she always had.

Roger looked down at me as if conscious that something was wrong, his grey eyes questioning but full of reassurance. I smiled back at him; and in seconds we were past Bella and were in the church porch. Outside was a beribboned carriage waiting to take us to the wedding breakfast at Priors. Restrained though joyful dignity was to be the order of the day—or so we thought. We had reckoned without our friends of the inn and the cricket team, who had unhitched the horses from the shafts while the service was in progress and now, with the bells pealing and showers of rose-petals falling like rain from the cloudless sky, surrounded the carriage and pulled and pushed and cheered us all the way back to Priors.

"It was all most touching," Mark said to me after the speeches had been made and the cake cut, and Roger and I were mingling with the guests. I had become separated from him for a moment. An elderly aunt had restrained him in a claw-like grip while, unnoticing, I had moved on a few paces.

"I'm glad you found it so," I replied, knowing that he had found it nothing of the kind.

"The sound of muffled sobs of emotion practically drowned the words of 'Oh, Perfect Love'," he said. "There wasn't a dry eye in the house."

"Except yours," I said. "Don't tell me, brother dear, that *you* were overcome by tears."

"Far from it." He smiled at me coldly, his eyes hostile. "Hysterical laughter would have been more appropriate in my case. Doesn't it strike you as funny, sister dear, that with all your efforts to raise yourself in the social scale, you have merely succeeded in bringing my brother down to your level?"

"The most beautiful bride I've had the pleasure of seeing," said a voice behind me, and thankfully I turned away from Mark. It was Lord Bollinger who had spoken to me, and I smiled at him in relief.

"Thank you, my lord."

"Young Leyton's a lucky feller—oh, there you are, sir," he said, as Roger joined us. "I was just saying to your good lady here that you're a lucky feller. Tell you what, m'dear," he said, leaning towards me confidentially. "If he don't treat you right, you let me know about it, what? He'll have me to reckon with."

"I'll remember that, my lord," Roger said, smiling.

"God bless you, my dear children," the squire said, looking at us with what I could have sworn was real affection.

"He's rather a dear old boy, isn't he?' Roger said as we moved towards other guests. "No one can call *him* a snob." The implication was clear—there were others who could be so called, but I let it pass. This was too lovely a day to be spoiled by thoughts of Mark's contempt.

It had been arranged that we should spend that night in Cheltenham, travelling on the following day to South Wales where we were to spend our honeymoon.

It was a relief when we were at last alone in the railway carriage. We leaned from the window and waved as long as we could to the crowd of people who had escorted us to the station in their carriages, then collapsed comfortably with our heads close together and my hand tightly enfolded in Roger's. We put our feet up on the seat opposite and for a moment luxuriated in silence.

It was then that a small, niggling feeling of disquiet began to disturb my happiness. I only had Annie's information to prepare me for marriage, and suddenly it felt extremely inadequate. What *was* going to be expected of me? I looked out at the green countryside that was rolling past the carriage window and bit my lip nervously.

"I had this wonderful idea back at the house, when Lord Bollinger was speaking to us," Roger said.

I turned to look at him, resting my cheek against the back of the seat so that our eyes were only inches apart.

"What wonderful idea?"

"When we've finished the extension to the Ring of Bells we can have a Grand Opening, with Lady Bollinger to cut the ribbon and free champers all round."

I began to laugh.

"Oh darling, darling Roger! It's your wedding day, remember? Let's have a rest from the inn, just for today."

He laughed too, and leaned over to kiss me.

"I'm sorry," he said. "I do so want to make you happy, Jenny—and I will, I promise. I'll love you for ever."

"Even when we're old and grey?"

"Even when we're old and have no hair at all—*sans* teeth, *sans* eyes and *sans* everything. Even on our golden wedding day, I'll only love you more."

"Our golden wedding day! Merciful heavens!" I shut my eyes and tried to imagine it. "Whenever will that be, Roger?"

He did some rapid calculations.

"3rd September, 1939. I wonder how many grandchildren we'll have by then?"

"I wonder!"

I thought the question over. Grandchildren meant that first there would be children, and children meant that first— I caught my breath sharply, and Roger looked down at me questioningly.

"Is something wrong?"

I looked at him. I noted the strength and the kindness and smiled at his concern and my own foolish apprehensions.

"No," I said. "Nothing's wrong. Everything is going to be wonderful."

Book II

1889–1918

7

They stayed away from the Ring of Bells.

All those men who had sat so contentedly under old Sarah's authoritarian rule, who had supped their ale and puffed at their pipes, minded their manners and their language and gone home to their wives and families when she had given the word, objected strongly to the new tap-room that was speedily provided.

It had been an easy job to convert a store room that adjoined the main building. All it required was a window and a fireplace, a new floor and a great deal of paint. The old settles from the kitchen were fixed around the room; there was a hatchway through to the kitchen which made serving simple. The fire burned brightly and there was no reason on earth why our customers should not have felt as welcome and as comfortable as at any time during the past four hundred years, but for some reason they resented the change bitterly.

"Us do feel like monkeys in a cage," Goosey Parslow, one of the old regulars, complained. He had his head stuck through the hatch and looked to me less like a monkey than a tired old nag looking over a fence, and I could not help laughing.

"Ar," grumbled Noah Babcock from inside the tap-room. "Laugh away, missus, laugh away. We're not good enough for you, now."

I did my best to win them over. Would their wives like it? I asked. Just imagine the difficulties it presented, trying to prepare a meal for large numbers of people with the kitchen full of men.

They laughed in their turn. "What large numbers of people?" they asked mockingly. "We don't see no large numbers."

It didn't seem to affect Roger at all. We were blissfully happy. I had been taken by surprise to find that not only was his love-making positively enjoyable, but that in some strange way it brought us closer together mentally; an aspect for which Annie's clinical explanations had left me totally unprepared.

We had returned from our honeymoon full of joyful anticipation, and only a small and unspoken anxiety on my part that I should find Bella still in residence in Collingford. I did not really expect it. She was a Londoner through and through and I believed her to have been telling the truth when she said that she wanted to get back to 'the smoke'. To my relief there was no sign of her, and with a sigh of thanksgiving I relegated her once more to the past. She had only stayed on for the wedding out of sheer curiosity, I told myself. I shouldn't be seeing her again.

The only fly in our otherwise perfect ointment was that custom had fallen off so drastically.

"Never mind," I said to Roger—though in fact he appeared to mind very little. "The Castles will come at Christmas. They always do."

But the Castles did not come. I had written to them telling them of my grandmother's death and change in ownership of the Ring of Bells, assuring them that they would find no change in the quality of the service offered. However, in spite of my assurances, they replied saying they had this year made other arrangements.

The supper for the bellringers took place in January as usual and I took care to make it a truly sumptuous repast, since I wanted talk of it to spread throughout Collingford. Other functions followed. There were two smoking concerts during that winter and the annual Primrose League dinner. Roger insisted on regarding this as the beginning of better times and as soon as the weather improved in the spring he determinedly went ahead with the new building he had planned.

With the rooms we had still more than half empty, the Leyton family lost no time in telling us that we were fool-hardy to say the least.

"You're throwing good money after bad," Roger's father told him gloomily. "How can you squander your inheritance this way? You'll never see it back."

"We're building for the future," Roger said. "We have faith that things will get better."

"All your customers have gone to the Waggon and Horses and the Nag's Head," Mark said, with what I felt sure was unmistakable relish in his voice. "Jenny upset them, throwing them out of the kitchen."

"It was a perfectly reasonable decision, to build a tap-room," replied Roger, always quick to defend me. "You know what these country people are like. It always takes time for them to accept a new idea. They'll come back."

We could not have coped with many guests, that summer of 1890, since the inn was in a turmoil with builders every-where. We were forced to turn down many of the regular fishermen who did apply to us for accommodation, though we did so with as much tact as possible, writing to them and explaining that the following year we should be open with new and improved facilities for their delight.

Our old friends of the cricket team remained faithful, however, and on summer evenings with the parlour full of young men in open-necked shirts discussing tactics and the strengths and weaknesses of rival teams, it was almost like old times.

It was for this reason that we delayed our work on the parlour. We had intended to put up bright new paper and to replace the old furniture, but we decided not to do anything to risk upsetting the only customers who had demonstrated their continuing loyalty until after the end of the cricket season. It was thus not until the October of that year that Roger, picking away curiously to see what previous genera-tions had thought suitable to put upon the walls, found the beautiful, hidden panelling under the layers of cheap paper.

We were thrilled by the discovery and stripped all the paper off ourselves to make sure that the wood remained unscratched. Cleaned and polished, the full glory of the glowing, satiny texture was revealed and suddenly the modern furniture we had planned to buy seemed out of place. We decided to comb the countryside for good, solid pieces of a by-gone era—re-upholstered if necessary to conform to Roger's idea of comfort, but basically plain.

When it was finished, with the chair covers in dark red and shades of rose and copper ornaments glowing in the firelight, I thought it one of the most warm and delightful rooms I had ever seen, and I blessed the long ago monks who must have been responsible for the beautiful panelling.

It was quite impossible not to be optimistic, in spite of the dismal picture painted by the accounts. Gradually we were making the Ring of Bells into a place of comfort and beauty, and equally its reputation for good food spread throughout the surrounding country. Farmers in Collingford on market day began to drop in for their midday meal—a little tentatively at first, as if not knowing what to expect, but with growing regularity and appreciation. One or two of our old kitchen regulars trickled back and began to take their drink in the tap-room almost defiantly, as if daring us to make any comment. Best of all, we were together and I never stopped appreciating my good fortune.

Roger was such an unusual man. The majority of men seemed to assume that women had been put on earth for two reasons: the procreation of the species and the care of their menfolk.

Roger's attitude was, of necessity, quite different. He depended upon my expertise at the beginning of our occupancy of the Ring of Bells so that in some ways mine was the dominant role; but even if it had not been so, our relationship would never have been that of master and servant—a situation more than common between husbands and wives at the end of the nineteenth century.

Everything we did—every decision, every new venture, was shared and discussed between us. And always there was laughter. Sometimes no more than a gleam from one to the other of us across the heads of our customers. Always the quiet, shared intimate laughter of the bedroom. What was between us was tender, exciting, stimulating and joyful— and it was a state of affairs that I was not above flaunting before Mark.

He doubted my motives in marrying Roger, did he? He thought I was a social climber? Well, I would show him! I would prove to him that Roger had never been happier. One day he would be forced to admit it—that his brother had made a wise choice when he married me.

When I found that I was expecting a child, due to be born in October 1890, we were both delighted. Roger was protective and anxious about my health but I felt brimful of vigour and was determined to work as long as possible.

One job we carried out was the refurnishing of some of the bedrooms and this meant that chests of drawers, hitherto in the guest bedrooms, had been relegated to the attic where the servants would sleep once we had achieved the status of having living-in maids. To date our only help was Susan who came in daily. The old furniture that had been in the attic during Annie's occupancy was thus unwanted.

"Let's take it up to her," I suggested. "Heaven knows, she and Jed haven't got very much. I'm sure she'd be glad of the chest and washstand if nothing else."

I knew that Jed and Annie had few luxuries. Robbie, their first little boy, had arrived nine months after the wedding. Now Annie was pregnant again. Jed no longer played cricket. Roger suspected that this was because he could no longer afford the price of a half-pint afterwards at the Ring of Bells, and in as tactful a way as possible he had on one occasion tried to let him know that his bowling skills were sadly missed and that everyone would understand if he refused to drink after the match. Jed had merely scowled and hurried off without giving an answer.

Undoubtedly times were hard for him, as they were for many of the cottage folk. For the most part the mood was one of resignation. Few had known anything but long hours of toil for little reward and expected nothing more from cradle to grave; but there was nothing meek or resigned about Jed. I had heard it said that he was stirring up trouble among the Watersmeet estate workers, and while I sympathised with him I was a little fearful for Annie and the baby. The benevolent patronage of Lord Bollinger was all-important to them and I knew that Annie would merely be baffled by any questions of principle which might lead to the loss of even the small income Jed currently earned. She had married a young man who had appeared to be a little more politically aware than most of his friends but basically docile and hard-working. None of us had realised what fires burned beneath his rather inscrutable exterior.

It was a beautiful morning, that day we went up to Berry Cross. We took bread and cheese and a bottle of ale with us,

111

and we drove at a leisurely pace through the lanes where the early blackberries were beginning to show, still red and inedible, and the leaves were fading slightly from summer green to the first shimmering of gold.

There was a warm feeling of satisfaction, too, because we were taking a gift to Annie. How pleased she would be, I thought, to see her old familiar chest of drawers again! What laughs we had enjoyed together—heedless, careless girls that we were, quite unlike the settled matrons we had now become. Perhaps the sight of the furniture would bring those days back to her.

Jed opened the door to us, by sheer chance at home during the middle of the day as he had been working close to Berry Cross and had slipped home for his midday break instead of eating it under a tree in the garden as usual.

"You can take that away," he said, nodding contemptuously at the cart.

"Oh, Jed!" Annie was wiping her hands on her apron, and biting her lip in an agony of embarrassment. "That's rude, Jed. Jenny and Mr Roger only meant it as a kindness—heaven knows we haven't got much."

"I'm not having no man's charity," Jed said stubbornly.

I laughed at him.

"Come on, Jed! This isn't charity. Annie used these bits of furniture all the time she worked at the inn and rightly they belong to her more than anyone."

"Thank you kindly, I'm sure," he said woodenly. "But you'll do me the favour of taking it home with you."

"I thought we were friends, Jed," I said.

"And can be still, so long as charity don't come into it."

"Have some sense, man." There was a note of irritation in Roger's voice. "Charity has nothing to do with it. It's just plain common sense to ask you to give these things house-room. You'd be doing us a favour, taking them off our hands."

"We could do with them, Jed," Annie said longingly.

"You'll have what I provide."

We stood around, not knowing quite what to do with ourselves. I could see by Roger's face that he was angry and would like to leave, but Annie looked close to tears and I disliked the idea of abandoning her. Fortunately Jed solved the impasse by excusing himself unsmilingly, saying that he had to get back to work.

Annie asked us in for a cup of tea and we accepted. We sat stiffly on the bentwood chairs which, together with a plain deal table and an ancient coffer, were the only furnishings the room possessed. The usually easy relationship between Annie and myself was clouded by awkwardness.

On the last day of September our little boy was born, but lived only a few hours. He had a malfunction of the heart, Dr Linley said. Had he lived, he would have been an invalid; we should, perhaps, be thankful that he was spared much suffering.

It is hard to be thankful when one has lost something so precious, so excitedly waited for and lovingly welcomed. It was a bitter time for us. There are no words to describe it, except to say that a darkness seemed to have obliterated the sun that so far had shone upon our life together. It rained incessantly that autumn, as if the elements were in tune with us; but work was the panacea.

There was one other unexpected comfort.

My mother-in-law was a solid rock of dependability, seemingly more understanding than anyone, even Roger. She said little, but somehow I knew that for the first time she was totally in sympathy with me.

Life went on and trade grew better. There was no leisure to wallow in misery and before long I was able to look at the small gravestone in the churchyard each Sunday without fighting back tears, though I felt sure that the ache of loss would never be entirely healed however many more children I was fated to bring into the world in future years.

It was over a year before I found that I was pregnant again, and in spite of our natural anxieties, this time all went well. Our daughter, named Eleanor after my mother, was born in July 1892. She was under six pounds at birth, but perfectly formed with a mop of dark hair, and we both thought she was the most perfect thing ever created. She was a little under two when Lucy was born, and if either of us were at all disappointed about producing another daughter, it was quickly dispelled by the doll-like beauty of this second child.

Two years later, in 1896, I at last produced a lusty son for

113

Roger, and we called him Roger Benjamin—to be known as Ben. I was sad that my grandfather did not live to see his first great-grandson. He slipped quietly away during the winter of 1895 in his chair by the fireside, dying as quietly and undramatically as he had lived.

I missed him, but it was impossible to grieve for him too much as he had seemed lost ever since the death of my grandmother. There had been a perpetual question in his eyes, as if he were trying constantly to work out for what purpose he was continuing his days on earth without her.

It was seven years now since Bella's unwelcome visit to Collingford, and much had happened in the intervening time to quell the shock it had caused me. However, there were sometimes unpleasant reminders of the menace she seemed to pose.

One day John, now a junior partner in a law firm in Oxford and married to a plump and pretty girl called Angela, called into the inn at lunchtime, having been brought over to Collingford on business.

Over our meal, a current case was brought up in conversation concerning a woman accused of poisoning her husband in order to marry a lover. The aspect of the sordid affair that interested me was that the events which led to her prosecution had taken place five years before.

"Surely the long arm of the law isn't as long as all that?" I asked. "How could they prove something that happened so long ago?"

John pursed his lips in a knowing way. "The improvements made in forensic science recently are quite incredible," he said. "I don't think, on the evidence I've read, that the lady stands a chance."

"But with the husband dead and buried for five years, how did the police find out that there might have been dirty work anyway? How were their suspicions aroused?"

"Information received, I gather."

I said no more but merely prayed that no information would be received from Bella, now or at any time in the future, and that the past I had no wish to remember would also stay dead and buried. The Leytons accepted me now. Mr and Mrs Leyton were delighted with their grandchildren and even the dreadful fact that their son was the licensee of an inn seemed less horrendous to them now that it was called the Ring of Bells Hotel and was patronised by an impressive number of well-born visitors. They could see that Roger was happy, which was important to them. His life had changed out of all recognition, but there seemed little that he regretted from the past.

Racing, however, was the one legacy from his farming days that Roger had not abandoned. It was a part of his life which I could not share and did not much approve of. I considered myself of an optimistic temperament about most things, but when it came to gambling I was always certain that I would lose, and I usually did, to the point where the whole exercise had no enjoyment for me. Roger, on the other hand, loved the excitement. Win or lose, he never missed any of the race meetings that took place round about and I began to collect a few items of jewellery as a result. There was a seed-pearl brooch and a garnet pendant, even a diamond ring after a spectacularly successful bet at the Ascot Gold Cup—all, of course, intended to ward off my dismay at his recklessness. However, it was the sheer exhilaration he derived from these activities that finally made me accept them with equanimity. After all, he had gambled on the Ring of Bells and he had gambled on me; who was I to find fault with that aspect of his nature?

I extracted a great deal of quiet amusement from Mark's attitude towards me at this time. He sought Roger's company, for in spite of the differences in their characters they had always got on well. With his parents having warmed towards me and the children running in and out of Priors as if it was their second home, it was difficult for him to maintain any form of open hostility and he was never anything but meticulously polite to me; it was an icy form of politeness, however, and I knew that underneath nothing had changed.

One evening Mark was dining with friends and I happened to pass through the room just as they had finished their meal and were dawdling over their port, preparatory to retiring to our sitting room to play bridge with Roger—an occupation he enjoyed greatly. I smiled at them and bade them good evening and would have passed on, but one of the friends who was unknown to me detained me and congratulated me at length on the excellence of the meal.

"I envy you your cook," he said, being a stranger to Collingford. "I wish we had as good in Oxford."

"Most of the cooking I do myself," I said.

"By George! The devil you do! Well ma'am, there's many an hotel in London or Paris would be the better for your services."

I thanked him, only afterwards registering the fact that Mark had sat silent throughout the exchange and had not introduced me as his sister-in-law. I felt it told me quite a lot about Mark. He was still ashamed of me, even though he and his friends were about to take over my sitting room for the rest of the evening.

It was about this time that Catherine Godfrey came to stay with relatives in Collingford. She had been brought up in the neighbouring county of Gloucestershire by her father, a prosperous landowner who had recently died, leaving her with a large property and a considerable amount of money.

In all fairness to Mark, I do not think that it was only her position and wealth that attracted him. Catherine, even without a penny, was a sight that would have made most men's eyes light up. She was an exquisite creature with a pink and white fragility about her that made men—all men, even Roger—want to protect her from life's slings and arrows, and this frail look was accentuated by the severe riding habit which she wore almost constantly since horses were an obsession with her.

Mark, it seemed, was totally enslaved. He had sown many a wild oat in and around Collingford during the years since I had known him. I still retained the feeling that he considered women had been put on this earth for his pleasure and had no right to be anything other than decorative and agreeable objects. Now it seemed that he was ready to put aside his philandering and he set himself, with all the charm of which he was capable, to woo and win Catherine.

It was not long before she was a constant visitor to Priors, with her name linked to Mark's by everyone in the village. I need hardly say that the difference between the way Mr and Mrs Leyton welcomed Catherine into the bosom of the family differed very markedly from my own introduction. Indeed, this courtship was greeted with such approval that the silver was polished and the house cleaned from attic to cellar before her visit.

Again, I sensed that Roger and I were something of an embarrassment to Mark. We were part of the family, and there was little he could do but try to carry off our introduction to Catherine with self-confidence, as if it were quite common for wealthy farmers to spawn sons who became landlords.

"How very quaint!" Catherine said when she was told of our occupation. She had a high, little-girlish voice which privately I thought silly and affected, a first impression which time did nothing to change.

Their courtship was not without its problems. The uncle with whom Catherine had come to stay was an erudite gentleman, lately of Oxford University, who had retired to the quiet of Collingford; his wife was a remote but stylish woman who had been one of the very first students at Lady Margaret Hall, Oxford—a fact which for me made her a figure of some awe. To this learned pair, Mark seemed woefully lacking in academic ability. He enjoyed hunting and fishing and excelled at shooting. He liked the company of other similarly minded young men and was, in short, a fairly typical example of his time and class. The Godfreys were not impressed.

But Catherine had independent means, was very wilful, and absolutely determined to marry Mark. Their objections crumbled before her tantrums or—as Roger suggested to me privately—they merely decided that no man with a very acute brain would want to marry her anyway. My husband had soon become disenchanted with the fascinating Miss Godfrey.

A grand and costly wedding was planned and Catherine proceeded to drive everyone remotely connected with her to distraction with her insistence on the best of everything. The dress was to be made in Paris; nowhere nearer than London could produce shoes or gloves of the right quality; the bridesmaids were to wear dresses of such a rare shade of amethyst that the material had to be tracked down with as much devotion as if it had been the Holy Grail.

Roger rapidly lost patience with her. "She'd drive any man to drink," he muttered darkly.

"How do you think your mother will stand having her in the house all the time?" I asked.

"Heaven knows! I should think she'll go mad."

Would I have liked Catherine better, I wonder, if she had liked me more? From the moment of our first meeting she had made it clear that she considered me beneath her socially. To Roger she would occasionally address a remark, but I could have been invisible for all the notice she took of me—though in this I was not so very different from most others who came within her orbit. She loved to hold the centre of the stage, and while the subject under discussion was exclusively concerned with her doings, her clothes, her hopes for the future, her past conquests, she was animated and vivacious and one could understand Mark's captivation. Without this exclusive attention she grew captious and bored.

She seemed baffled by my role in life. On one occasion I ventured to remark, in relation to her aunt's career, how unfair it seemed that the women students at Oxford and Cambridge were not granted degrees, however high their examination results. She turned to look at me, her lovely eyes wide with amazement.

"It is a mystery to me why any woman should care to fill her mind with such useless knowledge," she said. "Men don't care for it, you know. Women should remain women, in my view—not try to ape their menfolk."

"I doubt if your aunt would agree," I said.

"Oh, Aunt Florence is a little like you, Jenny. Very strong-minded."

She made it sound like a certifiable condition.

"Better than being feeble-minded, anyway," I said to Roger on the way home. "My goodness! If only I had her chances and her money!"

"Why?" he asked, smiling down at me. "What would you have done?"

I thought longingly of the books I would never read, all the learning to which I could never have access. I thought of the new colleges for women—oh, *how* I should have loved to go to Oxford! I thought of the way women were exploited,

118

and of those who had worked to redress the wrongs. I thought of Florence Nightingale and Elizabeth Garrett Anderson and Josephine Butler; good women, all of them. Strong-minded women, as Catherine would say disdainfully.

There was something in me that longed to be of their number, pioneering a world in which there were equal rights and opportunities for women.

Then I looked at Roger and thought of my three babies at home.

"Do you know?" I said. "I expect I would have married you."

He laughed, shook the reins, clucked at old Brownie, and with his arm around me we drove back contentedly to the Ring of Bells.

8

Ben was an active, merry little boy who began to talk at an early age and from then on, never stopped. Ellie and Lucy adored him and vied for his favours. Carrie, his nursemaid, was a kind creature but began to look exhausted with the effort of coping with his high spirits. By the time he was two, I felt unhappy about leaving him to the ministrations of this rather dull girl, whose sole criterion of good behaviour seemed to be that he should 'sit still, like a good boy'—an instruction he was totally incapable of obeying.

I needed to spend more time with Ellie and Lucy, too. They were now attending the little church school in Collingford, and were thus occupied during the day, but by the very nature of my work it always seemed that I became busiest just as they returned from school. We were now on a better basis financially and we therefore decided to try to recruit someone who could take over the cooking from me, though I would, of course, retain the ultimate responsibility.

Mrs Kingsley was the first applicant for the position that I interviewed. I was so nervous that I had to clasp my hands together tightly to still their trembling. She was a black-haired, beetle-browed woman, thin as a board with hair peeled back from her forehead in a tight knot. Her references were impeccable and she succeeded in making it abundantly clear that I would be a fool not to snap her up before all the crowned heads of Europe engaged in pitched battle for her services. Intimidating was the word for her, and almost in spite of my better judgment I found myself agreeing meekly that she could start immediately—one month's trial on both sides, I added hastily, gathering a few tattered shreds of authority.

By the time the month was over I was fully prepared to fight off all the crowned heads of Europe and every eastern potentate besides. We wondered how we had ever managed without her. I discovered that she was not nearly as formidable as she looked and that her brusque manner was largely due to shyness—an emotion with which I could readily sympathise. We developed a healthy respect for each other, both ready to learn from the other's experience, and it was a wonderful feeling to know that the reputation of the Ring of Bells was safe in her hands. We consulted over menus, and living on the premises as we did, I was still able to oversee the cleaning and general care of the hotel. I was a part of it, but became more of a full-time mother. For the first time in ten years, I felt able to relax my constant vigilance and to enjoy my children.

I was sitting in the garden one morning in June of the year 1899 shelling peas, feeling contented and at peace. The sun was warm, the may-fly had risen, the inn was full. Ben was happily occupied digging in a small bed that had been set aside for the purpose, busily filling a number of small containers with earth.

I heard the click of the latch on the garden gate and turned to look over my shoulder with a smile, knowing that Roger had gone to the village and expecting that he had come back through the garden.

It was Bella.

She had grown fatter during the ten years that had passed

since I had seen her, but I recognised her instantly and the smile froze on my face.

"Aren't you going to say 'ello, then?" she asked, swaggering up to me. "It's been a long time, 'asn't it?"

"You said you wouldn't bother me again," I said.

"Well, there's a fine thing! An old friend comes all the way from London just to say 'ello, and that's all you can say!"

"What do you want from me? You'll not intimidate me again, Bella."

"Nark it, dearie!" She sat down beside me on the seat, far closer than necessary, and leant towards me. "It's not money I want."

Oh, that smell, I thought. I'd recognise it anywhere. In spite of my defiant words I was conscious already of the helpless distaste that Bella always provoked in me.

"Why have you come here?" I asked, edging away from her so that I was on the extreme limit of the seat.

"I remembered what a nice place it was," she said.

"That's not what you said before!"

She laughed, her mouth now full of blackened stumps.

"Well, we all change when we get a bit older, don't we? I 'ad to get out of London for me 'ealth." She dug me in the ribs with her elbow. "Tell you the truth, it was a brush with the law. 'Oo should I turn to but you, dearie? You done right by me the last time—"

"But you swore you wouldn't come again!"

"Well, I changed me mind, didn't I?"

"Bella, what do you want?" I asked.

Ben left his digging and trotted over to us, resting his body against my knee and looking up at Bella curiously.

"Mama," he said. "Who is this lady?"

"I'm an old friend of your ma's," Bella said, while I was still searching for an answer.

"Ben, go back and do some more digging, there's a good boy," I told him.

He gave Bella a long and puzzled stare, but returned to his occupation.

"Your little boy?" she asked. "Nice little chap, bless 'is 'eart. Wonder what 'e would think, to grow up and find 'is ma was a murderess?"

121

"Bella," I said softly, my voice tight with anger. "I said you couldn't intimidate me, and I meant it. My conscience is perfectly clear. You can do your worst—I've done nothing to be ashamed of."

A look of amazed innocence appeared on her face.

"What 'ave I done? What 'ave I said?" she demanded of heaven. "I told you I don't want money."

"Then what's the purpose of this visit?" I asked.

"I need a reference."

I was so taken aback that I laughed.

"*A reference*! And you come to me! What do you expect me to say, Bella? That you make an excellent blackmailer?"

She said nothing, just looked at me with her unpleasant features folded into the sneer I remembered so well from my schooldays, her eyes boring into mine.

"A reference," she said again, after a long pause. "I need a job and there's one going at the Nag's 'Ead."

"I'll do nothing to help you to stay in Collingford."

"Oh yes you will," she said.

I fought down the feeling of panic, the awful swamping, helpless feeling that eventually I would end by doing just as she wanted.

"I refuse," I said. "I utterly refuse. And if you continue to bother me, I shall—I shall—" For a moment I floundered. What could I do? So far she had done nothing but ask me for a recommendation for a job.

"You'll do as I say," she said. "Because if you don't, I'll blacken your name so bad you won't get anyone coming to your pub no more. I know what you're thinking," she went on. "You're thinking you'll tell your 'usband everything, and he's rich and powerful enough to get rid of the likes of me. All right, dearie—try it! That's all I can say—try it! Maybe it'll work, and maybe it won't. Whatever happens there'll be a lot of mud stirred up from the past, and a lot of talk in the village. Those little girls of yours would hear about it—stands to reason, don't it? They're bigger than the little nipper there—they'd understand that it ain't quite the thing for a girl to polish off 'er mother, to say nothing of pushing 'er granny down the stairs."

"Those lies don't scare me," I said. But I could not look at her. There was silence between us for a moment, and I could hear her wheezy breathing. "Why Collingford?" I went on at last. "Why on earth do you want to stay in Collingford?"

"It's as good as anywhere else, ain't it? Nice friendly lot, I thought, down at the Nag's 'Ead. And then there's you, dearie. I know you'll always do right by me."

"No," I said. "No, Bella. I won't do it."

"Me mum's still alive and well," she said, seemingly at random. "Still got a good memory, she 'as. And that little bottle."

"I have nothing to be afraid of!"

"Be a pity to lose your customers, wouldn't it? After all the 'ard work you and your old man 'ave put in. Funny things, 'otels. People don't like 'aving meals somewhere they think they might get poisoned."

I stood up and immediately she stood too, hugely fat and still conveying the aura of menace which to me was almost tangible.

"Bella," I said. "You're being ridiculous! Don't you see you're overplaying your hand? I wouldn't have minded too much giving you a note to say that I've known you for many years, if that's what you want. I utterly refuse to perjure myself by saying you're a good worker, though. And after all these threats, I'm not even going to give you the time of day! After all, how do I know where it's going to end? You promised me before that you'd go away and never bother me again, yet here you are, ten years later, just as threatening as ever. I won't help you, Bella. And you can do just as you like."

She stood looking at me, a sneering smile on her face.

"So that's the way the wind blows, is it?" she said. "You'll be sorry, Lady-bloody-Leyton, you'll be sorry. Always thought yourself too good for the rest of the world, didn't you? You, with your prissy way of talking, your fancy duds—cor, strike a light, wot a sight you was tripping down Ackerly Street. And now look at you—enough to make a cat laugh, you are, with your airs and graces. Well, that won't last long, once the word gets out. Don't say I 'aven't warned you."

"I didn't like her," Ben said, sidling up to me when she had gone.

"No," I agreed. "I don't care for her myself."

Her threats were empty, I told myself. Our reputation was strong enough not to be damaged by slander or rumour. I would tell Roger everything when he came home.

Where *was* Roger? I knew he had gone into town on business, but that was much earlier. Normally he could be found somewhere about the hotel, checking the bar stocks or writing up accounts or doing maintenance jobs about the place. He could turn his hand to any practical task and was never happier than when a small carpentry or mechanical job demanded his attention. How annoying that he should be missing this day of all days! I felt quite sure that he had met some of his old cronies and was no doubt enjoying a pint with them at one of our rival establishments.

Much troubled by Bella's visit, I nevertheless sat down and finished the peas, taking them inside to Mrs Kingsley. By that time it was almost twelve o'clock, when Ellie and Lucy came home from school for their midday meal, and although they were perfectly capable of walking home across the green by themselves, I thought it would be an outing for Ben if we were to go and meet them.

We had gone a few yards when I saw the familiar bulky figure of Bella some way ahead of me, walking in the same direction. The little school lay close to the church, not on the front lane that led to Priors, but on the other side of the green, and quite unmistakably Bella was heading that way. Beyond the school there was nothing but fields and woodland.

What was her errand at the school? I wondered. Almost immediately the answer came to me. Ellie and Lucy, of course. Whether or not she proposed to brand me as a murderess at that moment seemed unimportant. What was important was that she should not be given the chance to make their lives as unhappy as she had made mine.

I took Ben by the hand and made him run, urging him along faster and faster until what had started as a joke ended with him almost in tears.

I caught her within inches of the school gate. The children had not yet emerged from the school, but a bell sounding from within indicated that they would soon be pouring out.

"What are you doing here?" I asked her, short of breath from my dash across the green.

She stopped, turned, and smiled her slow, jeering smile.

"Come to see your little 'uns dearie, that's all. No 'arm in that, eh?"

"Don't you dare speak to them!"

"Well, I told you, didn't I?" Her tone was one of sweet reasonableness. "Anyone would think I 'adn't warned you."

"Bella, you're to leave my children alone."

"Tell you what," she said, coming up close as if to confide a secret to me. "I'll scratch your back, you scratch mine. You give me a nice reference, and I'll keep away from your bleedin' brats—'ow's that for a bargain?"

For a few moments I was silent, staring at her helplessly, my jaw clenched with rage.

"You ain't got a lot of choice, dearie," she said.

"I'll think it over," I said at last.

"I'll come and see you tomorrow," she said. "About the same time."

The children were streaming from the school now, in a noisy, chattering crowd, and Ellie and Lucy bounded up to us, delighted that Ben and I had come to meet them.

Without a word to Bella I turned, and the four of us walked back across the green. Thank God I had been in time, I thought, and that I had taken it into my head to meet them that day. What on earth was I to do about her? I would have to talk it over with Roger.

He was waiting for us when we got back to the Ring of Bells, an air of suppressed excitement about him.

He kissed the children and despatched them all upstairs, with instructions to Ellie and Lucy to wash themselves and Ben before their meal, then when we were alone, he kissed me too.

"What," he asked, "would you like most in all the world?"

"Hmm, let me see," I said. "I think, perhaps, a husband who doesn't waste his time gallivanting around the town with his disreputable friends. Roger, I really needed you here this morning!"

Before I could launch into my account of the visit from Bella, he lifted me from my feet and twirled me round.

"You'll forgive me when you hear what I have to say. Now, come on—what do you want most?"

Priors! The thought dropped into my mind with no hesitation at all, and it came as almost a surprise to me since I had long since stopped yearning for it in the way that I had when I first saw it. The sight of it as I walked or drove along the top lane still gave me a warm feeling of pleasure. But I was now so familiar with its shabby interior and the people who lived within its walls—the initial cleaning-up process, designed to impress Catherine, had been a once-and-for-all operation, and it remained as cluttered and unkempt and dog-filled as ever—that the long-distance view merely pleased my senses in much the same way as a beautiful picture in an art gallery. I enjoyed it, but did not long to possess it. My life was too full and too happy to covet something I knew I could not have for myself.

Nevertheless it was Priors I thought of now, although that was something I would not confess, not even to Roger. I would feel too predatory, too much like the ambitious social-climber that Mark still believed me to be.

I thought very hard.

"New curtains for our sitting room?" I suggested. "No— a new sewing machine. Have you bought me one, Roger?"

He grinned down at me, hugging his secret. He had grown a moustache in the years since our wedding in an effort to look more dignified, but apart from that, to my eyes he had changed little. I still thought his quite the nicest face I had ever seen.

"I seem to recall," he said, "that once upon a time you made great play of wanting your own front door—"

"You've bought a *house*!" I flung my arms around his neck. "Oh Roger, is that it? Which house—where? I am right, aren't I? It is a house?"

He was laughing down at me, his eyes sparkling with an excitement every bit as great as mine.

"Steady on! I haven't exactly bought it yet, not without your approval."

"Which house, Roger?"

"Miss Truscott's old place. Her estate has been cleared up now and the trustees want to sell it."

126

"Bridge House? Oh Roger, I've always loved it! Next to Priors it's the best house in Collingford."

"Somewhat smaller, I believe."

"Oh, but a *pretty* house! I know I'll love it."

It was situated at the end of the High Street where the road narrowed and crossed a humped-back-bridge, and I had passed by it many times, though I had never been inside. It was a flat-fronted Georgian house with elegant windows on each side of the door, which had in its centre a large brass knocker. In Miss Truscott's time it had always been kept bright, shining on the darkest day against the plain wooden door, but since her death it had tarnished and shone no longer. I could hardly wait to make it bright again. It was not Priors, but it was a house to love. I hugged Roger again in an ecstasy of excitement.

"It might be disappointing inside," he said warningly.

"Oh, we'll make it beautiful. Can we afford it, Roger?"

"I think so, provided we go on as we are doing at the moment. I shall have to raise a loan—that's what I've been consulting with the bank about this morning—but I see no reason why business shouldn't be just as good this year as last, do you?"

Was this the time to tell him about Bella? Would she— *could* she—really affect the business with her lies?

Roger looked at me narrowly.

"You are pleased, aren't you?"

"Oh darling, you know I am!"

We went to Bridge House that afternoon, and although, as Roger had suspected, much redecoration needed to be done, it was a roomy, well-proportioned house and just as attractive on the inside as I had been led to believe from the outside appearance.

"And once we're living here," Roger said, "you're not to concern yourself with the Ring. I made you a promise when we were married that you wouldn't work all your life and I mean to stick by it. You shan't be confined to the kitchen any more."

"You can hardly say that of me now," I said. "Mrs Kingsley would take a very poor view if she could hear that remark."

"You'll always find something to keep you busy while we live on the premises And if you want to have Aunt Millie here, I'm sure we can find a corner for her."

"That would be a relief!" Aunt Millie was a great worry to us. Since grandfather's death she had lived on in her little house, more vague and forgetful, it seemed, with every passing week. I visited her regularly but it was all too plain that the time was rapidly approaching when visits would not be enough to ensure that she was properly fed and cared for. We had talked of having her at the Ring of Bells, but I had felt that the number of strangers who were in and out of the place would have confused her and made her utterly miserable. Bridge House would be a completely different matter.

"Everything seems to point towards making the move, doesn't it?" I said, as we stood in the empty front room.

Roger frowned.

"Do I detect a trace of doubt in your voice?"

"No—no, not at all," I said hastily. "As long as we can afford it."

"Darling, why so cautious? We've steadily increased our trade over the last few years. Why should anything change?"

Why, indeed?

I couldn't tell him, I decided. Not yet, anyway. I would talk to Bella again the next day—give her the letter, if that truly was all she wanted, make her swear to leave the children alone and to keep her mouth shut. On calm reflection, it seemed a fairly small thing for her to ask of me.

If only she had not wanted to stay in Collingford! I would cheerfully state that she was the most amiable, competent, trustworthy woman alive if only she would seek employment in the north of Scotland or anywhere other than Collingford.

She refused to be moved from her purpose. The Nag's Head needed a barmaid, and the Nag's Head was where she wanted to work.

"It's quite useless my saying you have worked for me," I said. "This is only a small village, after all. Mr Jackson will know perfectly well that you have not."

"You'll think of something," she said comfortably. "You always was good at Composition. Teacher's little pet, you was."

"How can I know that you won't continue to make demands on me?" I said.

"You can't dearie," she said. "'Ow can you? You got a bad conscience, after all! All I can say is—I won't be unreasonable. Can't say fairer than that, can I? After all, I only troubled you twice in ten years. 'Ow can you complain about that?"

"If you go anywhere near my children—"

"Oh, leave off about your bleedin' brats! I'm sick and tired of hearing you whine about them. Just give me the letter."

I took the sheet of paper from the drawer of my writing desk, wrote the address and the date and sat irresolutely looking at the blank sheet in front of me.

"Get on with it," Bella said, contemptuously.

I wrote a few lines.

"I think that will do," I said.

"Read it to me."

I picked up the sheet of paper and turned towards her.

"Miss Bella Blewett has been known to me for the past twenty years," I read tonelessly. "She has held domestic situations and to the best of my knowledge has always given satisfaction. I consider that she would be suited to the position of barmaid."

"There," Bella said when I had finished. "Didn't I say you'd think of something? Proper little Shakespeare, you are."

She took the paper from me and folded it, thrusting it into some hidden pocket in her skirt.

"I won't be bothering you no more then," she said.

"I sincerely hope not."

My hope was not entirely justified, for although the Nag's Head was a small and inferior public house in a back lane at the other end of the village and I had few occasions to walk near it, there were many times when I caught a glimpse of Bella doing her shopping or strolling on the green. Her very appearance bothered me and I never felt entirely sure in my mind that, through sheer love of mischief-making, she would not say or do something to upset the children. The weeks passed, however, and she did not approach me again.

Plans for our move to Bridge House moved forward.

Roger and I were there one afternoon discussing the work we required from the carpenter who was due to present himself the following day.

"I'd like plenty of shelves for books," I said. "Do you think, perhaps, those alcoves on each side of the fireplace could be utilised?"

"I was going to suggest the same!"

"Oh Roger, this is such fun!" In an excess of high spirits, I put an arm around his neck and reached up on tip-toe to kiss him. We had not heard Mark walk in at the front door which was standing open, an invitation to all intruders.

"How very touching," he said, catching me in the act. "How many years have you been married?"

"Ten years, all but three months." Roger smiled down at me.

I gave Mark one of the bright, meaningless smiles I kept especially for him.

"It seems like only yesterday, doesn't it, Mark? Well, what do you think of our new house?"

He turned his back on me and walked to the window, stooping to look critically at the skirting board beneath it. Roger and I exchanged an amused glance, knowing that whatever he said was likely to be gloomy.

"Could be a bit of dry-rot here, old chap."

Roger winked at me.

"You're perfectly right, old chap. I've already arranged to have it seen to."

"Hm." Mark straightened up and stood rocking from his heels to his toes, hands in his pockets, craning his neck and looking about him as if desperately seeking for some other fault to bring to our attention.

"Hm," he said again. "Not bad, I suppose. Not bad at all."

"Praise, indeed," murmured Roger.

"Though of course you're very near the river. It will probably be damp."

"Dear Mark," I said brightly. "You're always so encouragingly optimistic!"

"No point in closing your eyes to the things that need doing."

"I hadn't intended to," Roger said drily. "What brings you here, Mark?"

"Catherine wanted to go to the drapers, so I thought I'd take the chance of dropping in to see this new venture of yours. You're splashing out a bit, aren't you?"

"Why not? The business is going well and this will release four more letting bedrooms at the Ring. It'll give the family room to spread themselves, too."

"Yes," Mark said heavily.

I had been examining the moulding on the fireplace, but there was something in his tone that made me turn to look at him closely—not as my brother-in-law, my old adversary, but as a man who, one would have thought, enjoyed many of the privileges of life. Farmers had been going through a bad time, but sheep farmers had suffered less than most, and surely Catherine's money must have made a difference.

Yet there was something defeated about him, as if much of his arrogant vitality had been quenched. A button hung from his jacket by a thread. There was a crumpled look about his shirt collar. He's not cared for; I thought—and I was not merely referring to his clothes. A wholly unworthy feeling of triumph shot through me. At that moment it seemed to me no more than poetic justice that Mark, who had grudged Roger to me and gloated over his ability to deprive me of Priors, should somehow have missed happiness along the way.

I did not see him again for some weeks. We visited Priors but he and Catherine were away for the weekend, and at least a month had elapsed since that occasion at Bridge House when I saw him come into the Ring of Bells one evening.

We were still living there, though the time was rapidly approaching when we were to leave. The inn was still full of fishermen. It was high summer, and we also had several families taking a country holiday.

I was making my usual evening appearance after dinner, exchanging polite conversation with the guests, when there was a sudden flurry of activity over by the bar and I looked across to see that Mark had arrived and was greeting friend and stranger alike with much of his old éclat. There was an undeniable ripple of interest among the ladies, albeit decorous and well-concealed.

How very strange, I thought. The other day I would have said that all his old, youthful attraction had somehow drained away, but suddenly there was the dashing, high-spirited young man of yore, and I could tell from the heightened tempo of the voices and the laughter of the gentlemen that he could still exert much of his old magnetism.

I was curious. Something had happened—he had news to impart, of that I felt sure, and when he and Roger left the guests and went towards the stairs leading to our own sitting room, I allowed them a decent interval, said good night to the ladies, and followed them.

I found them raising their glasses in what was obviously a celebration.

"To the son and heir," Roger was saying.

"Catherine is to have a baby? That's wonderful news," I said, with the instinctive pleasure that one feels on these occasions. "Do congratulate her for us, won't you? You must both be so pleased. When do you expect the birth?"

"About Christmas time." He smiled at me, open and happy as a boy, and for once there seemed no undertones of antagonism between us.

Over the next week or so I spent as much time as possible at Bridge House with samples of paper and swatches of furnishing material, determined that this—my first real home—should be everything I had dreamed of.

The Ring of Bells rumbled with rumours of events in South Africa. Around the bar and in the parlour, Chamberlain's attitude to Kruger and Kruger's attitude to Sir Alfred Milner were discussed and dissected, with the weight of public opinion coming down heavily on the side of the Uitlanders.

For some reason not at all clear to me, Mark took a great interest in the progress of the renovations at Bridge House. He dropped in frequently, invariably managing to find some evidence of a grievous imperfection which, he seemed to want us to believe, could easily cause the entire house to collapse into a heap of rubble. I grew very tired of his relentless pessimism.

It was on one of these visits—an occasion to which he found quite definite traces of serious subsidence which he pointed out to us with gloomy satisfaction—that he suddenly abandoned his concern for our pocket and engaged Roger in a long harangue concerning the rights and wrongs of the South African situation.

I grew impatient. There were things concerning the house that we needed to discuss and Roger's time was limited. Concerned though I was about South Africa, it seemed to me at that moment that we had more pressing problems, and that Joseph Chamberlain's conciliatory attitude towards the Boers was something of an irrelevance.

"It's strange," I said, as Mark paused to draw breath, "the furore that a few disenfranchised Uitlanders make in Parliament, when women have been disenfranchised since the world began without anyone turning a hair."

The remark was designed to irritate Mark, and it succeeded. He turned to look at me with amazement.

"You're surely not one of these weird females who demands the vote?"

In truth it was not a question on which I had, at that time, thought very deeply, but my hackles rose at his tone.

"I've never heard any argument that convinces me that a woman is less able to vote than a man."

"And what, may I ask, does Roger have to say to that?" He looked towards his brother who was listening to the exchange between us with considerable amusement.

"I have faith in Jenny's good sense," he said. "I have no reason to suppose that the vote wouldn't be as safe in her hands as in those of many men of my acquaintance."

"You always have been a little soft in the head," Mark retorted. "And Jenny, of course, was always full of ambition."

My God, I thought, meeting his cold eyes. How I would love to see that man brought low! Why on earth wouldn't he leave us alone? He gave the impression of hating to see us happy, yet being unable to ignore us.

"It's an excellent thing that we shall have more room at the inn," Roger said as we drove back there. "The bookings are well up this year." He sat looking at the inn meditatively as

133

he brought the trap to a halt outside it, studying it through narrowed eyes. "In fact," he said, "it's about time we managed to get our hands on the cottage."

The fact that the cottage adjoining the inn did not belong to us was a constant source of annoyance to him and it remained his ambition to buy the lease and incorporate it into the Ring of Bells.

"You'll never get it in Mrs Oliver's lifetime," I told him. "Nor should you! She's lived there the whole of her married life, and since she went to school with my grandmother, that must make her all of seventy-nine. It wouldn't be fair to expect her to move."

"There are other cottages just across the green where she'd be equally comfortable."

"That's not the point, Roger. That one has been her home for over fifty years."

He sighed. "Unfortunately Lord Bollinger agrees with you. I heard that her lease with the Watersmeet estate comes up for renewal next year and I asked him about letting me have it on its expiry, but he wouldn't hear of it. He says that I can buy it on her death, but not before."

"He's a nice man," I said. "Besides, we have enough to think about with the move to Bridge House. You'll just have to be patient."

The girls were ecstatic at the thought of the move and all the extra room it would give us. Aunt Millie, too, expressed herself delighted with the thought of a future home with us, but not unnaturally she wanted to hang on to her independence as long as possible and we did not commit her or ourselves to a definite date on which she would take up residence.

It was that summer, I remember, that I went up to see Annie, taking with me several outgrown dresses that I thought might be useful for her little daughters. By this time I was sufficiently tactful not to thrust them at her before we had had time for a cup of tea and a chat.

The room was hardly better supplied with furniture than the time Roger and I had made our abortive trip there during the eary days of our marriage, but it was spotlessly clean and there were a few homely touches—a bright red and blue rag rug on the floor, some patchwork cushions on two wheel-back chairs, and a geranium in a pot on the window-sill. A pan simmered on the fire, giving off a wonderfully savoury smell and I sniffed it appreciatively.

"Mm. That smells good! Something nice for supper tonight?"

"Oh, nothing special," Annie said, brushing the comment aside. "Onions do make everything tasty, don't they? Oh Jenny, it's really grand to see you, it is that. Lucky the children are out playing. We can have a nice peaceful cup together."

She bustled about the small room, setting cups on the table, taking the brown earthenware pot over to the kettle which was boiling on the hob. I looked at her with some dismay. Her waistline looked considerably less trim than the last time I had seen her.

"Annie," I said. "Are you expecting again?"

She looked at me over her shoulder and pulled a face, half-rueful, half-resigned.

"Men!" she said. "There wouldn't be so many children about if they had to have some of them, would there?" She sighed heavily. "I can't pretend I'm pleased, though Jed's found Robbie a place over at Lord Havering's come the spring, so at least that'll be one less mouth to feed."

"Good heavens," I said faintly, appalled by the way the years were flying past. "Is he old enough for that?"

"He'll be eleven by then."

"So he will! It hardly seems possible, does it, Annie? It's no time at all since those days when we were two giggling girls, sharing a bedroom. That means Rosie is ten?"

"That's right. Not too many years before she can go into service." She sat wearily down at the table. "It's a good thing we can't tell what the future holds for us, isn't it? Women have a hard life, that's what I think." Even as she spoke the dismal words she began to laugh. "You were a caution!" she said. "Do you mind the time—"

I nodded, laughing with her, knowing that she was referring to the night she had instructed me in the facts of life, appreciating the joke now that I had been married for ten years.

"Nine times!" Annie giggled. "You didn't have no idea, did you?"

"You're feeling well?"

"Tired, sometimes, but well enough. We'll manage somehow, I expect. After all, it's God's will, isn't it?"

"Have you heard that Mark and Catherine are expecting a child?"

"Well, that is good news," she said. "It's been long enough, goodness knows."

I thought there was a note of reserve in her voice—a lack of enthusiasm that was unlike her.

"What's wrong, Annie?" I asked.

She pursed her lips.

"I'm not one to gossip, Jenny you know that. Not malicious, anyhow."

I waited.

"Still, some people aren't fit to have children, if you'll pardon me speaking so blunt."

"Annie, what are you talking about?"

"Mrs Mark Leyton, that's what."

"Come on, out with it. What has she been up to?"

Annie hesitated a moment longer, her expression one of outrage. Then she leaned forward and lowered her voice to a confidential whisper.

"Last week, it was," she said. "Mrs Leyton was riding through Halfacre Field towards the spinney. As you know, there's a five-barred gate between the field and the spinney, so she calls out to little Willy Smith to open it for her. He was catching butterflies along the hedge, see, all taken up with what he was doing, and he didn't quite understand what she wanted him to do. Well, none of those Smiths are what you'd call bright, and Willy's the worst of the lot. Even so, there was no call to beat him the way she did."

"*Beat* him!"

"With her riding crop. Crying his little eyes out, he was, when he came back home. He's not above six, you know.'

"Annie, this is terrible! Was he badly hurt?"

"Bruises all over, his mother said, and a nasty cut above one eye and on his neck."

"Did anyone tell Mark?"

"Oh yes! Willy's dad went down to see him and threatened to have the law on them, but Mr Mark gave him a couple of sovereigns so he said no more. But Jenny, it's not right, is it? I mean, no decent woman would do such a thing."

"I find it incredible. Are you sure the boy did nothing else? He didn't throw a stone at the horse, or anything like that?"

"Jenny, true as I'm here, that boy wouldn't hurt a fly."

"Catherine does have a quick temper," I admitted. I had seen it in action more than once. But to beat a child! I shook my head in disbelief.

Before either of us could say more we heard the sound of children approaching the cottage; a baby crying, a dog barking, voices raised in altercation.

"Oh, dearie me," Annie said resignedly. "That's the end of our peace for today."

Her family appeared at the door. Robbie was not with the rest, but even so the influx was more than enough to fill the room. There was the eldest girl, Rosie, staggering under the burden of Eddie, a round-faced bawling two-year-old. Tommy was four, thin and dark like his father. Lizzie and Katie must have been about five and seven, and the three-year gap between Katie and Rosie was explained by the tiny grave in Collingford churchyard, only a few feet away from my own firstborn.

I stayed long enough to have a word with them all, but as Annie had said, the peace was shattered and any further conversation impossible. I could see that they were hungry and that she was anxious to give them their tea, so I prepared to leave.

"Whatever is in that pot smells so good, you're lucky I haven't eaten it myself," I told them.

I had driven myself up in the trap and Annie walked out with me to where Brownie, our old and gentle horse, was cropping the grass outside her sagging gate. The black lurcher dog followed us out, as if to see me off the premises.

"That dog!" I exclaimed, pulling my skirt away from him. "He's had a wonderful afternoon in the mud, somewhere. What a knowing expression he has, Annie."

Annie laughed. "That dog's the wiliest creature ever born."

"Why do lurchers always make me think of poachers?" I asked lightly, my attention on the buttons of my glove.

There was silence from Annie and I looked up to find her eyes wide with horror, her face frozen into an expression of guilt.

"Annie? Is something wrong?" I asked. But, of course, I had already guessed it. The savoury smell, so hurriedly dismissed by Annie, must have had its origins in a rabbit or a hare poached by Jed with the able assistance of the dog.

"You won't tell, will you?"

"Annie, for goodness sake! Of course I won't. There's been a lot of talk of poachers lately, though, and I'd hate Jed to get caught. Lord Bollinger is on the Bench, isn't he? It could be the end of Jed's job, and then what would you do?"

Annie shrugged, her face tight with worry.

"I don't know, Jenny—I don't know at all. That's what I say to him. But God's truth, I don't know how we'd manage without it. It makes all the difference, with all those mouths to feed, having a rabbit or a pheasant sometimes. Jed don't make above sixteen shillings a week, and we pay three for the cottage. By the time I've fed and clothed the eight of us—"

"I know, Annie, I know—you don't need to tell me. But Mr Bainbridge was in the Ring of Bells the other night complaining about the number of pheasants they lost last year." Hugh Bainbridge was Lord Bollinger's agent, a good friend of Roger's and normally a mild-mannered man, but he had waxed hotly indignant on the subject. "They're doubling the number of gamekeepers, he said, so for heaven's sake tell Jed to be careful."

I left with her assurances ringing in my ears. She would warn Jed. She was always warning Jed.

I had plenty to occupy my thoughts during my drive home. Annie's plight, for one thing. How right Roger had been when he prophesied that life would be hard for her, and what a strange man Jed had proved to be. I found it hard to understand the thought processes of a man who could reject as charity a few sticks of furniture given to his wife in friendship, yet place his whole family's future in jeopardy by stealing from his employer.

Then there was Catherine. Did she really set about a small boy with her riding crop in cold blood? What sort of a woman could do such a thing? And what sort of a life did Mark have with her? How blissful my life was in comparison with others, I thought in gratitude.

9

By the time we moved into Bridge House all doubts about events in South Africa were resolved and Britain was at war with the Boers. A number of men from Collingford volunteered to join the Army and were seen off at Witney station with a great deal of flag-waving and cheering, and the town band played 'Soldiers of the Queen'.

I took the children to see the spectacle in a rush of patriotic fervour, but could not help wondering if the cause were great enough to warrant the probable sacrifice of these men's lives. It was not a point of view to be stated out loud, not in October 1899.

We went back to Priors after the outing. Grandfather Leyton had not been well, but was now pronounced to be on the mend and had been asking to see the children. I was shocked at his appearance and felt guilty that it was some time since we had visited him. The move to Bridge House had been excuse enough, I suppose, but I had postponed taking the children to Priors for quite another reason.

Catherine was insisting on being treated like an invalid now that she was pregnant and on our two previous visits had made so much fuss about the noise made by the children—even though they had played only in the garden and in my view had behaved impeccably—I had vowed that it would be a long time before we went there again.

"Nobody—but *nobody*," Catherine told us when we were gathered round for tea, the children sitting like a row of little mice on a long stool, "can possibly know how I feel. It's always been my misfortune to be more delicate than most. Dr Linley doesn't understand me. I shall insist on a specialist from London for my confinement."

"Lot of damned fuss," Mr Leyton muttered. He was sitting in a chair by the fire with a tartan rug over his knees in spite of the mildness of the weather. "Jenny never made such a fuss. Dr Linley was good enough for Roger's children."

"Well, he's *not* good enough for *mine*!" Catherine set her tea cup down with a crash and her cheeks grew scarlet. "Why does everyone in this house insist that they know better than I?"

Ellie, Lucy and Ben looked at her with round, astonished eyes. They regarded Mr Leyton with a respect which amounted to awe and they were horrified by this display of temper and defiance. Mrs Leyton pressed Catherine back in her chair, patting her shoulder in a soothing manner.

"There, there, don't upset yourself," she said. "Of course everything must be just as you and Mark think best." She turned to me and resolutely changed the subject. "I hear the girls have a new teacher," she went on. "Is she as satisfactory as Miss Allday?"

"Miss Hodgson is very nice," I said brightly, entirely for the girls' benefit. Ellie looked at me coldly, as if I had betrayed her. She mourned the departure of her old teacher who had run the village school with warmth and understanding, and had taken an instant dislike to the newcomer. I knew that she saw my defence of her as an unfair alliance between adults, but at that moment I was concerned more with my mother-in-law than with Ellie.

To my amazement, I felt heartily sorry for her. It was obvious that scenes with Catherine were not uncommon, and with Mr Leyton in such a frail and peevish condition I could readily see that her life must be difficult. Yet she seemed in good spirits. There was no doubt that she could be infuriating, but for all that I had a great respect for her.

It was to be our first Christmas in Bridge House, which gave an added dimension of excitement as far as the children were concerned. The news from South Africa could hardly have been worse, but in spite of our anxiety over the British soldiers—more particularly those from Collingford who were known to us—we were determined to make this occasion a time of joy for the children.

The season was made even more thrilling for them by the fact that Catherine gave birth to a baby boy on Christmas Eve, and on Christmas morning when the whole family was gathered at Priors for the turkey and plum pudding, they were allowed to see him and even hold him for a second.

Catherine looked pale and pretty in pink silk and swansdown as she reclined against her pillows to receive the homage of the Leyton clan. In view of the fact that Dr Linley had taken on a new assistant—a rather handsome, blue-eyed man called Richard Fenwick—she had revised her demand for a London specialist and had agreed to accept Dr Fenwick's ministrations. Needless to say, she had had a perfectly *dreadful* time. No one else had ever suffered quite like she had suffered, though I gathered from Mrs Leyton that there had been no particular complications and all had gone smoothly and relatively speedily.

An excellent woman from the village had been brought in to sit with Catherine, and Mark made frequent trips upstairs during the day to ensure that she wanted for nothing. He was on top of the world, delighted with his son and heir and pleased to be with his brothers again.

It was several months since the three brothers had been together and now they clowned quite in the way of times gone by—'for the sake of the children', they said—though they extracted so much pleasure out of it themselves that I felt it fortunate that the children were present to provide the excuse for it all.

With Angela at the piano they sang 'Three Little Maids from School' in high falsetto voices, fluttering fans made from newspapers, as well as a melodramatic and hysterically funny version of 'Oh Father, Dear Father, Come Home to Me Now'. The children laughed as if they would never stop and even Mr Leyton shook soundlessly and was forced to mop his eyes.

'For the sake of the children' we played guessing games and charades and Hunt the Thimble, until Mark and John left to attend to the horses, most of the farm workers having been given a day's holiday.

It was at this time, just after tea, that one of the young maids whose name I did not know, edged her way into the room. There was always a great coming and going of maids at Priors. None of them could get on with Dora, the old harridan who ruled the roost in the kitchen there, and it seemed that no sooner had I become used to seeing one girl about the place than she was gone, to be replaced by another, even less efficient and more untidy.

I became aware of the girl now, thin and pale, twisting her hands as she tried to pluck up courage to interrupt the festivities. As the one nearest to her, I asked what was wrong.

"It's Mrs Mark," she said. "She wants to speak to Mr Mark, if you please, m'm."

"He's gone to the stables for a moment," I said. "Isn't Mrs Myers with Mrs Mark?"

"She's just gone to the kitchen for her tea, m'm."

"I see. Well, I'll go up to her."

The girl bobbed nervously and scurried off.

I went up the stairs—the beautiful, sweeping stairs where the carpet was threadbare and the carving on the banisters blurred with grime—and along the passage at the top to Catherine's room. I found her in tears.

"Where's Mark?" she demanded as soon as I entered the room. "How dare he send you! I want my husband. Where is he? Doesn't he care that I'm alone—all alone after the most dreadful experience of my life?"

"He looked in only half an hour ago," I said. "He said that you were asleep."

"Asleep? What nonsense! How could I sleep with all that noise going on. It's monstrously selfish of everyone, especially you—bringing your noisy children here, just when I need peace and quiet and attention." She snuffled mournfully into her handkerchief and I sat on the bed beside her, patting her shoulder and trying very hard to feel sympathetic. By dint of straining I could hear, very faintly, the sound of a child's laughter.

"Mark doesn't care," she sobbed. "Not one bit! How can a man know what it's like—how much I've suffered?"

"He does care," I assured her. "I've never seen him so happy and proud."

142

"You're wrong, I know you're wrong! He doesn't care a bit. He should be with me."

"He will be, in a moment. He only went to see to the horses."

"*Horses*! On a day like this, all he thinks of is *horses*! Of course, *your* husband couldn't go, could he? I don't suppose you would let him." I could hear rapid footsteps approaching and looked round in relief as Mark entered the room, only too happy to relinquish my role of comforter.

"What's wrong?" he asked, looking concerned.

"*You're* what's wrong," Catherine shrieked, ugly in her rage. "You're a brute, a brute! How could you leave me all alone? I hate you—don't touch me, don't ever come near me!"

She reached for the nearest object to hand which chanced to be a vase of carnations sent from the Watersmeet hothouse. She hurled it in Mark's direction, missing him by yards but covering the bed with flowers and greenery and water. She flung herself across the pillows, moaning and sobbing like a wild thing.

'Catherine, you mustn't—please stop!" I entreated her. "Don't upset yourself this way. Think of the baby!" I knew I was being totally ineffectual as I tried to pick up the flowers and to remove the wet eiderdown.

"Leave it," Mark said curtly, his face white and set. "Please go. Get my mother, will you? She knows how to deal with this sort of thing."

He was looking at Catherine, not meeting my eye or going to comfort her. How he must hate my presence, I thought. Me of all people.

I left the room in search of Mrs Leyton and signalled to Roger that it was time for us to be going home. The festivities were over.

Mrs Leyton came downstairs just as we were leaving and kissed me as we left—an event so unusual that I was taken by surprise.

It wasn't until later that evening after the children had been put to bed that I had a chance to dwell on events that afternoon at Priors and discuss them with Roger.

"Roger," I said, "there was something really frightening about Catherine today." He knew what had occurred in her bedroom. "I can't help wondering if she's not a little unbalanced. It made Annie's tale about the beating of Willy Smith quite believable. I've never seen such an ungovernable temper."

"Poor Mark."

"And poor baby."

"Perhaps it was just the usual sort of depression that women suffer after giving birth. You were inclined to be tearful yourself, if you remember. I can clearly recall you sobbing over a broken teapot after Ben was born."

I looked up at him indignantly.

"It was Crown Derby—enough to make anyone weep! At least I didn't shout and scream and throw things at you. There was something truly vicious about her, Roger."

Catherine's baby, christened Peter, did not thrive. Not surprisingly, she found herself unable to feed him. Cows' milk and various patent foods were tried to no avail, and finally a mixture of goat's milk, sugar and water was found to suit him and he began to put on weight.

My admiration for Mrs Leyton knew no bounds. She seemed to cope magnificently with all problems, even though the nursemaid who was engaged to care for Peter walked out, true to Prior's tradition. As usual, Dora upset her and she left to find work in Oxford.

It was the beginning of a dismal period. Roger's father died at the end of February after a short illness; I was unable to go to the funeral as we were still in the thick of nursing the children, who had come down with measles. Roger came home from it chilled and depressed. It had been a bleak, windy day with sleet in the air—the sort of winter's day which makes spring seem an impossible dream.

"Was it dreadful, darling?" I asked.

He nodded. "Yes. A miserable affair."

"How is your mother taking it?"

He took a sip of brandy, a frown on his face.

"I'm worried about her, Jenny. She looks—worn, I suppose is the word I'm looking for. I rather think that Catherine has abdicated all responsibility for the baby—as far as I can make out she spends most of her time in bed."

"She's not ill, is she?"

"I don't exactly know. There seems to be a conspiracy of silence about her."

"Haven't they engaged another nursemaid?"

"They did, but she proved unsuitable and left last week. Peter still cries a lot, Mark says."

"Poor little scrap! Your mother ought to go away, Roger. She's had a terrible winter. She needs a complete break."

"I'll try to persuade her, when the better weather comes." He shivered. "It's terribly cold in here, Jenny."

I looked at him suspiciously.

"It's not, you know. I've had the fire banked up all afternoon, just so that it would be nice and warm for you to come home to. Are your feeling well, darling?"

He poured himself one more brandy and moved closer to the fire. "Oh, I expect I'm just a bit down. There's something exhausting about funerals. Poor old boy. I wonder what he really thought about things. He never said, you know. We none of us knew him."

I put my arms around him and held him close. He had been fond of his father in an undemonstrative way and I had never seen him looking so depressed.

The following day he, too, went down with measles.

If I'd thought life was difficult before, it became doubly so now. I took on another maid, Mary Anne, to assist Carrie and it seemed to me as if the three of us were up and downstairs all day long.

Roger was very ill indeed. He worried constantly about the hotel, and this was yet another task that fell to my lot. I was the only person able to attend to the various bits of business that were outstanding, so was compelled to abandon the invalids to the care of Carrie and Mary Anne, wrap myself against the bitter wind, and battle my way to the Ring of Bells, there to check the stocks and pay the wages and the tradesmen's bills and organise the various functions which were an important source of our income during the winter months.

Late one afternoon I was sitting at the desk in the upstairs sitting room which also did duty as an office, wearily making out bills for several guests who were leaving the following day, trying hard to emulate the immaculate copperplate handwriting which made Roger's bills look like works of art. The children had been impossibly fractious all morning, and I was very worried about Roger, who showed little signs of improvement. In fact I could cheerfully have laid down and died, I felt so tired and overwrought.

I heard footsteps coming down the passage and looked up as one of the kitchen maids knocked at the door and put her head into the room.

"If you please, m'm," she said. "There's a person to see you."

Before she could say more she was roughly pushed aside. The figure of Bella filled the doorway.

"Thank you, Fanny," I managed to say. "That will be all."

Bella stood looking at me, grinning. I could feel my fingers tensing around the pen I was holding, and my left hand gripped the table.

"'Evening, my lady," she said at last, sketching a grotesque curtsy. "And 'ow is your ladyship this evening? Still as bloody 'igh and mighty as ever?"

"What do you want, Bella?" I asked evenly.

She walked towards me. Oh God, I thought—not too close; don't let her come too close. I just can't bear it—not the feel nor the smell, nor yet the *idea* of her!

She towered over me. I could feel the pressure of her body against my thigh.

"Money," she said. "I need money."

"What for?" I asked foolishly, fighting for control of myself, wanting to be sick.

"It don't signify what for!" She was angry, suddenly. "I need it, that's enough. And you're going to give it to me."

"No," I said.

"And I say yes! You're going to give me the money, Mrs-bleedin'-Leyton, because if you don't you know full well what I'll do. In front of witnesses, dearie—that's 'ow you confessed. In front of witnesses."

"And how would you explain the fact that you've kept silence all these years? Twelve years, Bella. How would you explain that?"

She smiled and crouched over me, and I steeled myself not to recoil, to stand my ground and stare her straight in the

146

eye. With both hands flat on the desk she leered into my face, and I could smell her fetid breath.

"It's not me that would 'ave to do the explaining, dearie—it's you. I been tortured by my conscience all these years, see. Suddenly I can't stand the strain no more. Gawd love us—you'd be up there before the beak before you could say 'knife'."

"Bella," I said. "Go and sit in that chair—that one, across the room."

She straightened up and looked at me as if suspecting my motives.

"Why should I?"

"Because I can't think straight with you looming over me like that. Go and sit down." I was delighted that my voice sounded sharp and authoritative, without a trace of the revulsion I felt for her. Amazingly, she did as she was told.

I rested my head on my hand and closed my eyes.

It was wrong to give in to her. If I gave her money, she would be back; there was no trusting her.

Yet our business rested on goodwill. No smoke without a fire, people would say. That's the hotel where the owner was suspected—no, it was no good, I dared not risk it.

I was tired—so tired.

"I 'aven't got all night," Bella said, from across the room.

How terrible it would be for the children! Their school-mates wouldn't care whether I was guilty or innocent—it would make no difference to the names they would call. Up before the beak, Bella said. How on earth would a child cope with that? How, physically, would the business cope with that, just at the moment with Roger so ill and my presence at the hotel absolutely vital?

"'Urry it up, do," Bella said, getting to her feet again.

I stood up, too.

"Fifty pounds?" I said.

She laughed coarsely.

"That's a joke, that is. Fifty pounds? That's what you give me when you was young. Now business is booming, any fool can see that. I want an 'undred."

"I haven't got a hundred."

"Expect me to believe that, do you?"

147

"It's true. I don't keep that much in cash." I knew to the last penny how much I had in the drawer of the desk. "I've got seventy-eight pounds, nine shillings," I said, opening the drawer as I spoke. "Take it or leave it."

She licked her lips, weighing the alternatives.

"I'll take it," she said. "Give it 'ere."

I put my hand over the notes that I had laid on the desk, preventing her from picking them up.

"Bella, this can't go on," I said.

"Course not, dearie." She was all smiles now that she was assured of a happy outcome to the encounter. "It's only that I need the cash, special. I wouldn't dream of troubling you otherwise—not a fine, 'igh-and-mighty lady like you."

"I'll stand only so much," I said. "Next time I'll tell you to say what you like, and be damned to you."

"Course you will, dearie."

She took the money, stuffed it into the bag she carried and made for the door where she stopped with her hand on the knob, looking back at me.

"Your girls are growing up lovely, ain't they? I go past the school sometimes, just to keep an eye on 'em, like."

"Don't you ever speak to them!"

She chuckled, and left the room. I heard her going down the passage towards the stairs and found that I was trembling.

It was the worst thing, knowing that her shadow was over Ellie's and Lucy's life, just as it had been over mine at much the same age. She had not reached out to touch them yet; but she could do—at any time, she could do.

I had been weak and foolish to give her the money—I was convinced of that now. For a long time I sat, staring blankly at the unfinished bill I had been making out when Bella had interrupted me, the figures a meaningless jumble. Impulsively I gathered up the papers and stuffed them all in the drawer. They would have to wait until morning. I had had more than enough to cope with for one day.

Dick was waiting in the yard with the trap to take me home, much to my relief. It was a comfort to feel him solicitously tucking the blanket around me.

"You look tired, m'm," he said, speaking freely on the strength of our long acquaintance.

"Oh Dick, I *am* tired!"

I closed my eyes as he clucked at the horse and drove out of the yard, skirting the green in silence.

He cleared his throat and I sensed him moving awkwardly in his seat. I opened my eyes and saw that he was glancing at me sideways.

"Is something bothering you, Dick?" I asked.

"Well, it ain't none of my business, m'm, I know that. But seeing as we've known each other a long time—"

"Out with it," I said wearily.

"That woman a-coming out, just afore you, the one as works at the Nag's Head. She ain't no good, m'm."

"I know that, Dick."

He relaxed visibly.

"Oh well then, I've got no call to worry, m'm. I was afraid you might have taken her on, like. It's said that Mr Jackson thought she was dipping her hand in the till and he's given her the sack, so I thought maybe she was trying her luck with you and that you wouldn't know what a nasty, foul-mouthed object she is."

"I know that, too," I said drily.

So that's why she needed the money—she had lost her job. Dare I hope that she would now leave Collingford? Perhaps. But Collingford was growing. There was a factory on the outskirts now for the manufacture of army uniforms and another that made blankets. The old brewery had been considerably enlarged. No doubt Bella would be able to find employment in the area if she really looked for it, though I doubted whether she would be able to extract a recommendation from Mr Jackson as easily as she had done from me.

Roger struggled back to health and was champing at the bit to get back to work long before he was fit to do so. I wished that we could take a holiday, but that was out of the question. What a way to start a new century, I thought dismally.

Eventually, of course, spring came, and our spirits rose along with the temperature, especially when the news from South Africa showed an improvement. Ladysmith was relieved and suddenly there was a feeling of optimism in the air.

Roger must have been aware of it even more than I, for he amazed me one day by announcing that what he would like more than anything would be to buy another inn.

"What's wrong with the Ring of Bells?" I asked.

"Nothing, you goose. I mean I'd like to have two—and eventually three or four or five. I'd like to find somewhere that's been neglected, something I could really get my teeth into that needs to be brought up to our standards."

"You *must* be feeling better!"

To me it seemed too much to contemplate. The winter must have taken more out of me than even I realised, and I almost found it in my heart to envy Mrs Leyton when she departed for Hereford to stay with her late husband's brother and his wife.

Her trip was made possible by the fact that Catherine had taken more of a grip on life and that Peter was sleeping at nights. It was some time since I had been at Priors owing to the illness of the children and of Roger, but Mark reported that all was now going swimmingly and that they had even found an excellent nurserymaid. I was therefore unprepared for the urgent message that one of the farm workers brought me one morning. It was a day when Roger and Hugh Bainbridge had taken themselves to Ascot for the races. Mark had gone to Witney market to look for a new horse, and Catherine was therefore alone at Priors.

"Dora's been took poorly," the man from Priors told me. "And Daisy upped and left. Seems the mistress threw a pitcher at her. There's a proper to-do up at the house, missus. Reckon you'd better come."

On the way to Priors I tried to elicit more information but without success. He merely muttered, over and over, that there had been a right to-do, with the mistress screaming blue murder and the baby crying and the maid leaving.

"Bloody blue murder, missus," he repeated. "Bloody blue murder, that's what 'twas."

In view of this I was fully prepared to find bodies strewn in all directions, but on entering the kitchen found instead a clutter of dirty dishes and a pile of soiled baby napkins in a corner. On the table a cat chewed furtively at the contents of a saucepan. Honey, Mark's golden labrador, lay with her muzzle resting on her forepaws, her cocked eyebrows asking with mild curiosity for my reaction to the mess. I looked aghast at the disorder. There was a dirty, long-term look about it.

"How long has this been going on?" I asked. "Surely there is someone who could at least have come in and cleaned up a little. Isn't there a kitchen maid?"

"Aye, m'm, there is; but she's up tending the baby."

He gave a jerk of his head towards the ceiling. Peter was lifting up his voice in howls of rage or hunger or both, and shooing Honey out of the way. I abandoned the mess and ran upstairs.

I discovered the poor girl, who could not have been above twelve or thirteen, doing her best to clean up the baby who had all too obviously just vomited his last feed. She was close to tears herself and looked at me with dazed relief as I appeared in the doorway.

"Oh, thank God, m'm! I'm that glad you've come."

"Where is your mistress?" I asked, coming into the room and taking Peter from her.

"She's locked herself in her bedroom, m'm. She's crying and carrying on in there—says the baby cries too much, poor little fellow. I think he was hungry. I tried to feed him, but he threw it all back."

"What did you give him?"

"His special milk, m'm. Goat's milk, it is."

"Did you add water to it? I believe it has to be diluted . . . I don't know much about such things, I'm afraid. Didn't Mrs Leyton give you instructions?"

"There's no talking to her, m'm," the poor girl said, looking more worried than ever. "I tried—I did, honest!"

"I'm sure you did. What about Dora?"

"She's got a fever, m'm. I tried—"

She broke off, listening, just as I was, to the hysterical cries that could be heard coming from the direction of Catherine's room. I thrust the baby at the kitchen maid and rang along the passage. As she had told me, Catherine's door was locked and although I called to her I could get no response. There was nothing now but a low keening, interrupted from time to time by a noisier outburst of sobbing.

I went back to the nursery.

"Go down and tell the man who came for me to go and fetch Dr Fenwick or Dr Linley," I said. "Preferably Dr Fenwick. And please tell him to hurry."

I took the baby back from her and only too grateful to be away, she ran downstairs.

I turned my attention to Peter, ignoring the noise from the bedroom. I washed and changed him, debating as I did so what to do about feeding him. I was totally ignorant of artificial means of feeding babies, but it was obvious that the milk given to him by the little maid was too rich. It was equally obvious that the poor mite was ravenous and that I should have to give him something. Going downstairs I decided on a half-and-half mixture with a little sugar. Better, I thought, to err on the weaker side rather than to risk making him sick again.

Poor scrap, I thought once more. He was a dear baby— red in the face now, but rapidly calming as he took the bottle I gave him. He was asleep before he had finished, worn out with crying. I sat down in one of the arm chairs in the hall where a few logs smouldered in the fireplace, holding him close, rubbing my cheek softly against his hair, conscious of the warm, powdery, baby smell of him.

It was thus that Mark found me as he stood in the doorway, his expression one of astonishment. I had been alerted to his approach by the way the dogs bounded out to the stable yard, but nothing had prepared him for the sight of me sitting in the chair by the fire, holding his son. He looked at me with a frown of bewilderment, his gaze taking in the more than usually unkempt room; then he looked upward as he heard the noise from Catherine's room.

"Catherine," he said flatly. It was a statement, not a question.

"I think she must be ill," I said. "I've sent for the doctor."

He ran up the stairs two at a time, and I could hear him knocking at the bedroom door calling urgently to his wife. Richard Fenwick arrived at that moment, and met Mark as he came back down the stairs.

"I'll have to break in through the window," Mark said. "I'll get a ladder. Fenwick, would you be good enough to go upstairs and wait outside the door? It shouldn't take more than a moment."

I stayed where I was, quite still, holding the baby. I felt strangely frightened; sick, almost. I had no idea what was wrong with Catherine; no doubt she could not help whatever ailed her. But I hated the thought that it was this tiny, defenceless baby in my arms that would be affected by her.

In moments Mark had broken into the room by way of the window and had opened the door to admit Dr Fenwick. I could hear their soothing voices talking to Catherine. For a while her cries seemed to intensify, but at last she was silent—the result, I afterwards learned, of a draught administered by the doctor. I could hear the maid clearing up in the nursery and soon she came downstairs to the kitchen and began the cleaning up process there. Mark came down, saw Richard Fenwick out, and slumped heavily into a chair opposite me.

We sat in silence for a few minutes.

"We—we thought she was better," Mark said at last. He looked tired, grey and drawn and old.

"This has happened before?"

"On and off ever since Peter was born. She seems quite unable to cope with him—or with life in general."

He got to his feet and going to a table at the side of the room poured himself a glass of whisky.

"I don't know what to do, where to turn," he said.

"If I can help—keep the baby for a while, perhaps—"

He interrupted me with a harsh, mirthless laugh.

"My God! How you must be loving this. I hope you're savouring your moment of triumph!"

"Mark, it's not like that!" I spoke softly, mindful of the sleeping baby, but there was no lack of intensity in my voice.

"Don't pretend, Jenny," he said bitterly. "You've hated me for years, ever since I warned you away from Roger."

"Any girl would have resented the things you said—the names you called me. Yes, I suppose I did hate you Mark, but that doesn't mean that all this makes me happy. I'm sorry, that's all, and worried on Catherine's account. She needs more help than she's getting here. For too long we've all thought it was merely a case of persuading her to pull herself together, but I'm convinced now that she's incapable of doing so. She's not being capricious or trying to be difficult—"

"You're saying she's mad?"

"I'm saying she needs help."

He gave a long, shuddering sigh and walking over to the fireplace, he folded his arms on the mantelpiece and rested his chin on them.

"You're right, of course," he said at last, and was silent for a long time.

Then he raised his head and looked at me. "You'll never know how I've envied you." He was speaking quietly now, almost as if I was not meant to hear. "Every time I heard you and Roger laughing over some silly joke or saw you touch each other. I hated to see it, yet I kept putting myself in the way of it."

I remembered the number of times I had gloried in flaunting my happiness before him, and I felt ashamed.

"I admired you too, you know—all those years ago when you were a sweet, shy little girl. But you preferred Roger."

I smiled then.

"You would never have married me!"

"No. My intentions were strictly dishonourable."

"There's a thing to say!"

We laughed together, frankly and openly with shared amusement, but he sobered rapidly.

"What's to be done?" he asked me.

"What does Richard Fenwick say?"

"He considers that she was always unstable but that childbirth has made her more so. To me she seemed just spoilt and headstrong at first, but shortly after our marriage it became obvious that she had a violent temper. No one but my mother and myself know the half of it."

"Take her to a London doctor, Mark," I urged. "I'll keep Peter for the time being, until things are sorted out."

He looked at me for a long time, opened his mouth as if to speak, but finally turned his head away without saying anything. I thought I knew what was going through his mind.

154

"Mark, let's forget the past," I said. "After all, no one who can father a baby like this one can be wholly bad. If I try hard to search out the nugget of gold in your character, will you try equally hard with me?"

He looked at me again, this time with something resembling his old audacious grin.

"You reckon you have one to find?"

"If you dig deep enough."

We laughed again. How strange this is, I thought, wondering at the friendship that seemed to be coming to life after so many years of enmity. I'd miss it, in a way. Scoring points against Mark had added a certain spice to life—yet I felt relief that I could regard him affectionately at last. We had both changed since our respective marriages, and although apologies came hard to Mark, I had the feeling that he had long realised how wrong he had been in accusing me of wanting Roger for his worldly goods alone.

"I wonder when Dora will be on her feet again?" he said now.

"It would be the best thing for all of you if she never was." I spoke feelingly, convinced that Dora was at the root of many of Priors' domestic problems. "It's time she was put out to grass, Mark. It's entirely because of Dora that you can't keep any staff here and never have been able to. Just look at the state of this house! You can't possibly operate with only Dora in the kitchen driving off any other maid that comes near you."

"She's mother's concern."

"Well, talk her into pensioning Dora off when she comes back from Hereford."

He agreed to try, and left me to get Peter's clothes and equipment together while I looked down at the sleeping child in my arms, feeling oddly happy that once again there would be a baby in our nursery.

10

Peter's stay with us was far longer than we could possibly have foretold.

Dora quickly recovered from her bout of influenza but Catherine's condition did not improve and Mark, seeking the help of the Godfrey relatives who had moved from Collingford to London the previous year, found a nursing home in Wimbledon that was highly recommended by them. They assured him that they would visit her regularly and he was able to relax a little, feeling that she was receiving the expert attention she needed.

The summer term was a nightmare, with Ellie sobbing over her sums in bed and Lucy often physically sick before going off to school. When Ellie returned one day, white with misery, to say that she and Lucy had been castigated before the entire school because their father was a publican and sinner, Roger—equally white, but with rage, not misery—was moved to descend upon Miss Hodgson and to inform her exactly what he thought of her intelligence, her humanity and her teaching methods. The result of this was that we removed the girls from school forthwith and for the rest of the term they ran wild.

It was a joy to have them looking carefree again. Much as I wanted them to have a good education, I could still remember the blight that Bella's persecution had put upon my childhood and could not bear the thought that they, too, were being held up to ridicule. We made arrangements to send them in September to a little private school just outside Collingford which was known by the grand and totally unsuitable name of Balmoral Academy.

I was walking with the girls one gloriously sunny day in July along a leafy lane that bordered Hart's Spinney—a day for them made all the more glorious by the thought that their friends were bent over their desks—when we turned a bend in the road and came upon Lord Bollinger, a spaniel at his heels. He was leaning on a five-barred gate and had obviously been surveying his rolling acres that were clearly visible at that point, stretching before him as far as the eye could see. However, as we came into view his face was turned towards us and he was smiling.

"Heard your voice," he called to me. "Knew it was you. Would have laid any money."

"Good morning, my lord," I said more formally. "How nice to see you about! It's been a long time."

"Damned leg's been playin' me up," he said. "Keep thinkin' if I ignore it, it'll go away—but it don't seem to work any more. Age is a terrible thing, m'dear."

"You'll never grow old."

I had reached the gate by this time and halted beside him. A smile gleamed at me through the thicket of his white beard and his eyes were as bright as ever.

"The spirit's no more than twenty-five," he said. "Unfortunately, the flesh will be seventy-nine next birthday. These are your gels, eh? Good morning, young ladies. Eleanor, isn't it, after your—bless my soul, your grandmother! Where does the time go?"

"And I'm Lucy," said Lucy.

"Who could forget Lucy! Tell me, do you know the names of all those flowers you've picked?"

Lucy smiled up at him, her eyes demurely veiled by her enormous eyelashes.

"I know buttercups," she lisped engagingly.

"*Everybody* knows buttercups," Ellie said, irritated as she always was by this kind of display. She snatched a flower from the bunch that Lucy was holding and proffered it to Lord Bollinger.

"*That's* purple knapweed," she said authoritatively. "And *that's* scabious."

"A scholar!" Lord Bollinger's countenance expressed suitable deference. "A scholar, I declare! Well now, ladies; here's a competition for you. Somewhere in the hedge in this field before us I have spotted the meadow crane's-bill—some call it the blue geranium. It's a round, blue flower with ragged, drooping leaves. There's a sixpence for the botanist who finds it first."

They were off like a streak of light, and the old man watched them go, chuckling to himself.

"Fine gels," he said. "Fine gels, both of them. That Lucy, she'll break a few hearts before too long. Puts me in mind of your grandmother."

"My *grandmother*?" I turned to him in amazement. "You mean Mrs Austin?"

"Young Sarah was as pretty a wench as I ever saw," he said. "Time, like an ever-rolling stream, Jenny, bears all its sons away—aye, and daughters too. Tell me," he said, peering a little closer at me. "Treatin' you well, is he? That young man you married?"

I laughed.

"That was more than ten years ago, my lord, and that young man is now well into his thirties. Yes, he's treating me well."

He grunted.

"Glad to hear it. Don't see much of you, but I like to know you're well. See the partridges?' He pointed with his stick towards the field where a covey of birds had risen. "Enjoy yourselves," he called in the direction of the birds. "You haven't got long. It'll be time for the guns very soon."

"Poor things," I said. "Little do they know."

"Little do any of us know!" His voice had softened. In the distance I could hear the voices of the children and all about us were the sounds and scents of summer; birdsong and the murmuring of bees and unseen sheep bleating somewhere behind a hedge. There were no words between us for a few moments and I had time to reflect on the strangeness of this accord that had always existed.

We had never been on visiting terms. The only times I had been to Watersmeet were on occasions when the rest of the village was there too: the annual Primrose League fete, or a special cricket match. Lord Bollinger had only infrequently called at the Ring of Bells and had never visited us at home, though he always sent fruit and flowers when there was sickness in the house. There was no logical reason to feel that I was in any way singled out from any other woman in the village, yet for some reason I felt quite sure that I was. He's like God, I thought irreligiously, in that he's always *there*, a

He slapped his clenched fist into the palm of his other hand.

"Because it's the breath of life to me, Jenny—surely you know that by now!"

I shrugged. "No doubt you'll do what you think best," I said. "It's your decision."

I was glad, though, when for some reason the Angler's Rest was withdrawn from sale and so his mind was made up for him. Of the two, it seemed to me that the Red Lion Hotel in Long Branstead was more the calibre of place we should own, although I still could see no real need for buying anything.

My mother-in-law, meanwhile, was apparently enjoying her stay in Hereford and it seemed from her letters that she had entered upon a new lease of life, largely because of the ministrations of a doctor who had attended her on her arrival when she had all but collapsed through sheer exhaustion.

She wrote frequently, her firm dashing hand covering page after page with an account of her doings, but her return to Priors was mentioned only vaguely, while Dr Gough's name cropped up more and more.

"This man seems to have a great deal of influence on her," Roger said disapprovingly after reading one of her epistles. "It's time she came home."

"Roger, she is over twenty-one and she sounds very happy. Surely she can please herself."

"She talks of him wanting to open a private nursing home. I hope he doesn't imagine she's a wealthy woman, able to finance his schemes. He sounds a charlatan to me."

"I don't see your mother in the role of innocent dupe," I said with some amusement. "I imagine she's enjoying having his attention instead of having to deal with Catherine's tantrums. Which reminds me—has Mark said if he expects her home soon?"

"Not to me."

But letters had been passing to and from the Godfrey relations in London and arrangements were made at last for Catherine to return to Priors. She was, it seemed, much better, though not yet well enough to run her own home. A distant cousin was to accompany her and to stay with her as a sort of companion housekeeper. Evidently she was a widow whose husband had been killed at Spion Kop, and it occurred to me that this arrangement probably suited the Godfrey family admirably, killing two birds very neatly with one stone. It disposed both of the problem of Catherine and that of the unfortunate widow who, it appeared, had been left with very little means of support.

I would miss Peter—but not as much as I might have done, for I once again found myself pregnant, and both Roger and I were delighted at the prospect of adding to our family. All three of the others were now at school, and I felt that the nursery would seem strangely empty once Peter had gone.

The news of Catherine's imminent return accompanied by her cousin, which I communicated in a letter to Mrs Leyton, prompted a very rapid reply from her.

The news that you have imparted [she wrote], fills me with delight, since I feel it leaves me entirely free to follow my own inclinations. For some weeks now, Dr Gough has been anxious to obtain my consent to marriage, but I have refrained from giving it, feeling that my Christian duty lies at Priors with Mark, at least until we can be certain that Catherine is fully restored to health.

Now that I know she is to be accompanied by her cousin and that Mark and the dear baby will be suitably cared for, I feel I may give Dr Gough the answer that he assures me he desires above all things.

He is a dear man whom I hope to bring to meet you all before too long. I know only too well the long faces that you boys will pull! You will tell each other that there is no fool like an old fool, etc. etc., and I will waste no time here in recounting his many virtues for I am convinced that anything I may say will be counted as exaggeration! However, you may be assured that he is a good, kind man who regards me with love and respect, as I do him, and that upon your meeting him you will be able to do nothing but applaud my choice.

Roger snorted as he read the letter, passing each page across the breakfast table to me, his disquiet growing with every second.

"Applaud her choice, indeed! I can't think what my aunt and uncle can have been thinking of, allowing her to get into the clutches of a man like that."

"Oh Roger—a man like what? He is a doctor—an educated man. Your mother assures us he is good and kind. We ought to be rejoicing with her."

"Hmm." He continued to look sceptical as he picked up the letter once more. "I wonder what Mark will say."

"I know just what Mark will say! He will be his usual pessimistic self and prophesy all sorts of dire consequences, just as your mother foretold. You might at least wait until you've met this Dr Gough. It could be the beginning of a wonderful new life for her."

"But why should she want a new life? She has a comfortable home at Priors, surrounded by her family, with her dogs and horses."

"And she should be content to don a cap and sit by the fire and meditate on her past youth? What nonsense, Roger! She is what age? Fifty-three, fifty-four? Well, she looks ten years younger than that and has the energy of a twenty-year-old. Would a man be expected to regard his active life over at that age?"

Roger lifted an eyebrow at me in amusement and said no more.

A further letter announced that Mrs Leyton and her husband-to-be would be arriving for Christmas and would be married in Collingford, very quietly, on Christmas Eve.

As Catherine and her cousin, Mrs Charlotte Mannering, were also due to arrive shortly before Christmas, I decided to take Mark to task about the state of the house. Dora had been alone and unsupervised for weeks and I felt that the dismal air of neglect which hung over the place like a pall would be the worst possible welcome for the two newcomers, even though Mrs Leyton herself was not one to notice dog-hairs and untidiness.

"Do what you think best," Mark said. "Engage someone to help Dora. Talk severely to her."

I gave him an exasperated look. Many maids had been engaged and almost all had left. And as for talking severely to her, no Leyton had ever succeeded in doing that for the

163

past thirty years. However I began looking around for someone really competent—not a meek, untrained little girl, but a mature person who would be able to stand up to Dora, and meantime I embarked on cleaning up Priors myself.

Life was so full I wondered how I had ever had the time to work at the Ring of Bells. Aunt Millie had settled into our household and seemed happy, but she was vague and confused, needing help in dressing and undressing, otherwise she would leave buttons unfastened or put shoes on the wrong feet. Sometimes she would not know where she was. Our two maids were kind to her, but she disliked the company of strangers and more and more of my time seemed to be taken up with leading her back to her room and talking to her to allay the irrational fear she seemed to feel about everything. She was obsessed with the thought that she had lost something of importance. What this thing was, we were never to know, but poor Aunt Millie spent a great deal of time looking for it—in vases, behind cushions, under chairs.

Fortunately she rested in her room a great deal, and I was sitting sewing one afternoon when Annie was ushered in to see me. My cry of delight died when I saw that she was desperately upset.

"It's Jed," she said tearfully. "Caught poaching up in Hart's Spinney. It'll be jail this time, Jenny—Lord Bollinger's warned him often enough. He'll lose his job, for sure."

There was little I could say to comfort her, but I promised my support and looked forward to talking the matter over with Roger when he returned from Long Branstead, where he had spent the day at the Red Lion. Although these premises had not needed structural alterations as the Ring of Bells had done, the building was in a sad state of repair and I had found it hard to enthuse about it when he took me there to see it before finally committing himself to buying it.

"Are you sure we should?" I asked. "Suppose the cottage suddenly became available? You'd want to have the money ready for that, wouldn't you?"

He took no notice of my doubts and went ahead with completing the purchase and thereafter builders and decorators had been hard at work. I had not yet found time to go and see the changes he had made, what with Peter's needs and Aunt Millie to care for. It was even difficult to talk things over together without interruption, but I seized upon an unusually quiet moment before our evening meal to tell him about Annie's visit.

"We must help her somehow," I said. "I can't help agreeing that Jed will be dismissed."

"Of course he will!" Roger's voice was impatient. "Lord B. has warned him time after time. Nobody could have been more lenient."

"But it's so hard on Annie and all those children."

"My dear, good girl—Jed's responsible for his own family, and you well know how he'd resent it if anyone implied otherwise. Surely we have enough on our hands with Priors and Aunt Millie and little Peter, not to mention this new business venture of mine?"

His words struck a small chill in my heart, a chill that was tinged with guilt. I had shut him out, I knew. There were times when he had come back from Long Branstead alight with enthusiasm, burning with a need to talk things over with me, but more often than not Aunt Millie was indulging in some of her rambling reminiscences or one or other of the children was demanding my attention. And now Annie and her troubles; I had flung them at him before he had a chance to sit down and light his pipe.

"Of ours, Roger," I said. "This new venture of ours."

He smiled at me fleetingly, tamping down the tobacco. "Of course. Perhaps you'll be able to spare me a moment to tell you about it some time."

Aunt Millie opened the door and blundered into the room, looking about her vaguely. Her gaze fastened upon Roger and she approached him.

"Behind you, dear," she said. "I think it's behind the cushion."

Perhaps fortunately neither Aunt Millie nor I caught the exact wording of the expletive that issued from his lips as he impatiently got to his feet and strode from the room.

11

Out of several applicants for the position of housemaid at Priors, I chose Izzie Newton.

She was a woman in her late twenties who had worked for a rector's household in a neighbouring village, and it was known the length and breadth of Oxfordshire that her late employer was the sort of man who would measure the candles in the maid's bedroom to guard against waste, and would check the pantry to make sure just how many slices of a leg of mutton had been carved after the joint had left the dining room.

She had been there for five years and had left, she said, after a disagreement. She had no reference to show me and was reticent about what had caused the disagreement, but knowing the reverend gentlemen's reputation as I did, I was inclined to think that she probably had good reason to leave. Her reticence, I thought, was something in her favour. My instinct told me that she would be a hard and loyal worker and that she had sufficient strength of character to cope with both Dora and Catherine. She had a thin but pleasant face with a manner that was respectful without being subservient. She would do well at Priors, I thought.

Barely two weeks after her appointment I visited Priors, only to be cornered by a slyly triumphant Dora who told me that the girl was leaving. She had sent her packing, she said.

"She's in trouble," she told me gleefully. "Expecting. *That's* why she left the rectory. I'm not having that sort here, m'm, no matter what. I wouldn't lower myself. Out, I told her. Out this very day."

I looked around the kitchen which was cleaner than I had ever seen it before, no doubt attributable to Izzie's labours.

"Where is she now?" I asked.

"Upstairs, getting her traps together."

I turned and left her, making my way up the back stairs to

the servants' quarters. I found Izzie fastening a small tin trunk, tears slipping silently down her cheeks.

"Izzie," I said reproachfully. "You should have told me."

"Then you wouldn't have taken me on, m'm. I had to find a place to live. There wasn't nowhere else, bar the workhouse. I've got a good four months' work left in me, m'm—more, even. I'm strong. I could have kept on, almost to the end."

I sat down on the iron bed with its thin, hard mattress and looked at her.

"What about your parents, Izzie? Can't you go home?"

"There's only my dad, m'm, and he won't have nothing to do with me."

"And the father of the child?"

She sniffed away her tears and tossed her head.

"I wouldn't take nothing from him. I'll manage alone."

There was something about the set of her chin that made me believe her.

"When is the baby due?" I asked.

"The end of March, m'm. Five more months, near enough."

"Just about the same time as mine."

I got up and went to the window and stood for a moment, thoughtfully toying with the little wooden acorn on the end of the string attached to the blind. How could I possibly turn her out and condemn her to the workhouse when she was carrying a baby, just as I was myself? I sighed. Dora would undoubtedly make her life a misery and Mark would accuse me of being foolishly sentimental; but even so, I was going to let her stay.

"Take your hat and coat off. I'll speak to Dora. I don't know what arrangements we'll make when your time is near, but sufficient unto the day . . ."

"Oh, I don't know how to thank you, m'm"

The tears started to flow again and I patted her awkwardly on the shoulder, took a deep breath, and went to do battle with Dora.

The interview was by no means an easy one, but Mark, thoroughly tired of the whole domestic turmoil and impressed by the differences Izzie had already introduced into his household, upheld my decision, with the result that

Dora finally packed her own bags and departed muttering curses, looking like a malevolent witch.

I felt a twinge of compassion for her as I watched her thin, hunched backview retreat down the track on the way to the station in one of the farm carts. Priors had been her home for a long time. But Mark had given her a substantial present and Mrs Leyton, hastily contacted by telegram, had promised a small pension, so in fact she had been more fairly treated than she probably deserved.

It was easy to find a young kitchen maid once Dora had left and Izzie, filled with grateful zeal, set about scrubbing and polishing and preparing beds for Catherine and Mrs Mannering, whose arrival was now imminent. She also displayed a talent for plain cooking and Mark delightedly reported meals more satisfying than he had ever eaten before. I was relieved that my instinct regarding Izzie had not been wrong, and engaged yet another maid to help with the increased volume of work which would arise once the house was full and Peter back at Priors.

Catherine and Mrs Mannering arrived in the evening of a damp December day, after the early darkness had fallen. Mark had insisted that both Roger and I should be there with him to greet them; I imagine that he thought it would ease any tension that might be present, but personally I had my doubts as to the wisdom of it. Catherine had never liked me particularly and I did not feel that she would welcome my presence.

I was anxious to meet Mrs Mannering, however, and so complied with his request without raising too many objections. We had grown to love little Peter as if he were our own. He was now a sunny, engaging child with a fair mop of curls and an ability to crawl at tremendous speed. He could already take the odd hesitant step on his own before collapsing with a thump, and would be walking properly at any moment. I wanted to see the woman who would be taking over the responsibility for his welfare from me.

Much to my relief, I liked her immediately. She was tall with an air of well-bred authority and although she was soberly dressed in black, as befitted a widow, there was an indefinably dashing air about her. Perhaps it was the angle of her fashionable hat, or the fact that her hair was a bright auburn that glowed in defiant contrast to her widow's weeds. She was younger than I had imagined, too, and not sad and suffering as my fancy had painted her. She may well have been both of those things, but the impression she gave was that of eagerness to see what next life had to offer.

Catherine looked as lovely as ever and seemed quite unchanged by her spell in the nursing home, though I thought her manner a little subdued. She kissed Peter absently as if she could hardly remember him, then went off to her room with Mark, leaving me to do the honours with Mrs Mannering.

"I do hope you'll be happy here," I said politely, as we went upstairs together.

She smiled at me warmly, and I knew that I was going to get along well with her.

"I daresay I shall be as happy here as anywhere," she said. "I've—I've been in a sort of limbo recently, not quite knowing in what direction to go. Looking after Catherine seems a useful occupation, for the time being, anyway."

"You are fond of small children?"

We were by this time in the bedroom which was to be hers—a large, pleasant room overlooking the garden and rolling farmland. For a moment she did not reply. She unpinned her hat and placed it on the dressing table before turning to look at me.

"I love them dearly, though my experience with them has not been great. May I tell you this, Mrs Leyton, and then not mention it again? I lost my baby soon after I had the news that my husband had been killed. A miscarriage."

I stared at her, turned to stone by the horror of it.

"I'm so very sorry," I said inadequately at last.

She turned to the dressing table again, and looking in the mirror, patted her hair into place.

"Life goes on. I think that I am, perhaps, over the worst now. One thinks, when something like that happens, that one never will get over it—but really there are so many good things in life."

Life with Catherine, I thought?

"Collingford is a quiet place," I said. "I hope you won't find it dull."

"Oh, I can put up with that for a few months!"

"A few months!" I was horrified.

She turned to look at me again.

"Why yes—perhaps a year. I don't wish to commit myself to a longer period. We have every hope that Catherine will be fully recovered by then and that my presence won't be necessary."

"I see," I said, doubtfully.

"I was engaged in other work in London but put it to one side to come here."

"I see," I said again. 'What other work was that, Mrs Mannering?"

"Oh, please call me Charlotte! After all, we are practically related. I was helping Mrs Fawcett run the NUWSS."

I must have looked blank, for she laughed.

"The National Union of Women's Suffrage Societies," she explained. "Until recently there have been a number of different societies all working towards the same end, more or less. It seemed common sense to unite. We thought we would be more effective that way."

"You're a suffragist!"

She laughed again. "You make it sound as if I should be in a circus, or stuffed, inside a glass case."

I hastened to correct the impression.

"Oh no, I don't think that at all—quite the contrary. As Mark will tell you, I've always waved the suffrage banner myself, much to his disgust."

"Then he won't approve of me." She looked undismayed at the prospect, as if she had been eyed askance by better men than Mark Leyton.

"If his domestic affairs run smoothy, he will be happy," I said. "This past year has been a difficult one for him. But come—you must be gasping for some refreshment and I am sure tea will be ready downstairs. We must have a really long talk, for me to tell you about Peter and Izzie and the other servants and anything else you need to know—but that will keep until after tea. And then you must tell me about the— what is it? The NUWSS. It sounds quite fascinating!"

"What do you think of her?" Roger asked me when we were driving home.

"I like her," I said. "I like her very much. But Roger, she's no intention of staying very long. What on earth will happen when she goes?"

"For heaven's sake, the woman's only just arrived! Don't start worrying about this time next year."

"You're perfectly right, of course. We do have more immediate problems, like Jed and Annie."

Roger moved impatiently.

"Jenny, I am sorry about Jed and Annie—more sorry than I can say; but they are *not* our problem!"

As we had all feared, Lord Bollinger had both fined Jed and dismissed him from his service when he appeared before him on the Bench, but he was humane enough not to order the family's eviction before Christmas, although they were told they would have to leave by New Year, now only three weeks away. Annie was grateful for the breathing space thus provided, but Jed was bitter. He refused Roger's offer of a loan to pay his fine and instead sold the collection of gardening tools he had managed to build up over the years.

"I told him that was plumb foolish," Annie said to me. "Wherever we go, we'll need to grow vegetables. I can't think what's got into him, I can't really."

What had got into Jed was blind, helpless anger, and I felt I could easily understand his feelings. For too many years he had worked on the Watersmeet estate and witnessed the profligacy that ruled there, not only in the house but in the grounds surrounding it. To the cottage people, struggling to live on a few shillings a week, it all seemed little short of wicked. Lord Bollinger might be a kind, just man whose estate gave employment to hundreds of workers, but nothing he did could, I felt, justify the system.

"But where would Jed and the rest of Collingford be without Watersmeet?" Roger asked, giving the reins an irritated shake as on the way home I stated my views. "Lord B. is an excellent landlord. Everyone knows it."

"But why should people like Jed and Annie feel grateful because they're given a hamper for Christmas, and other people's cast-off clothing?" I demanded. "They work hard, long hours. They deserve enough pay to allow them to

171

retain their self-respect. People like you have no idea how the working classes feel."

"People like me?" Roger's voice, beside me in the darkness, was suddenly cold.

"Yes, people like you! You're blind and deaf to all the inequalities, just because you've never wanted for anything."

"When have I ever behaved in a way that justifies your saying that?"

"If you'd ever gone hungry—"

"Oh, for pity's sake! I apologise most humbly for having been born a Leyton; just spare me the tragic tale of your deprived childhood."

For a second or two I was speechless with rage, but then we were quarrelling as we had never quarrelled before, our tempers damped down as we drew up at home only by the need for an appearance of normality before the children and Aunt Millie. She, poor soul, was agitated because I had been out for several hours and she had been searching in every corner for the nameless thing but could not find it, not anywhere. And Ellie needed help with her arithmetic and Ben apologised for frightening me but was perfectly certain that there was a giant in the attic. By the time these problems were satisfactorily dealt with, Roger had gone back to the Ring of Bells to make sure that the Freemasons' Christmas banquet was going according to plan and the anger between us had cooled to a chilling formality.

I could not settle to anything. I tried to read but abandoned my novel because I could think of nothing but my fury with Roger. I stared at myself in the mirror over the mantelpiece and seemed to see the face of a stranger. I had *never* been so angry, I told myself. I had thought Roger sensitive and sympathetic; he had always appeared so. Now I hardly knew what to believe. Admittedly Jed had brought his difficulties upon himself, but anyone with an ounce of compassion could surely see how it had happened.

We seemed to have moved so far away from each other, I thought miserably. It was weeks now since I had heard what was happening at the Red Lion and even events at the Ring of Bells were hardly ever mentioned. Until recently we had been like a pair of well-trained carriage horses, pulling briskly in the same direction. Now, suddenly, the rhythm was broken.

It's not my fault, I raged, beating my clenched fists on the arm of the chair. I know I'm busy with the children and Aunt Millie and that Peter and Priors have been taking my attention; and it's not my fault that I'm huge with child so that even in bed we're denied the solace of physical harmony.

Perhaps that's the trouble, I thought. For some reason this pregnancy seemed to be taking years rather than months; I was far larger than I had ever been before and thought that I should give birth to twins at the very least, though Dr Fenwick assured me that this was unlikely. Still, I felt uncomfortable and immeasurably plain. Was that why I had provoked Roger to anger? Was it because I had needed to attract his attention in some way?

I sat quietly now gazing into space, my head against the wing of the chair.

It had been a stupid quarrel. I would apologise to Roger when he came home. He was a kind and thoughtful man, no more to blame for the way the system worked than I, and I couldn't bear to be at odds with him.

It was only two days later that Mrs Leyton and Dr Gough arrived at Priors. I had said to Roger on one occasion that she looked ten years younger than her actual age. Now I would have put the figure even higher for she was radiant in a new gown of French navy with a short, matching jacket with light blue facings and a high-necked blue blouse. She looked both youthful and elegant, and also extremely oppulent since the entire outfit was topped with a sable coat, a present from the bridegroom.

I lifted an eyebrow. A fortune-hunter, eh?

She embraced us all, including the dogs which leapt at her with their tails waving frantically, exclaimed at Peter's growth, at Catherine's appearance, at the joy of being home. She did not mention—probably did not even notice—the new sparkle that Priors had taken on since Izzie and Charlotte had taken up residence.

Dr Gough stood by and smiled at her exuberance, apparently oblivious to the fact that her sons' greeting had been polite but scarcely more. He seemed quiet and watchful, summing us all up. As one who had served her apprenticeship as a stranger, on the outside looking in, I thought that probably I could understand his feelings more than most.

As if conscious of my gaze, he looked across at me over Mrs Leyton's head and smiled, seemingly recognising our kinship. He was a tall man, dark of complexion, with deep brown eyes which looked as if they had seen much of the world and of human nature, yet still retained humour and compassion. There was strength in his face, but gentleness too. All this I seemed to read—yet so far he had said little.

He was not nearly so quiet at dinner, which took place a little later. In fact, his presence at the table led to a more stimulating evening of conversation than I had ever experienced at Priors, where farm prices, the desirability of early lambing, the increased use of farm machinery, and other such topics usually dominated the discussion. If politics were mentioned, the talk was likely to consist of Mark damning the Liberals and Roger supporting Chamberlain and his policy of Tariff Reform. For years the reactions to current events of both the brothers were so predictable that I was hard put to it to continue to look interested.

Now, listening to Charlotte and Dr Gough, the issues became infinitely more immediate and vital, mainly because both of them assumed that women's suffrage was inevitable, a question only of time. A whole new world seemed to open up before me, a world in which my opinions could be just as valuable as those of the men of my acquaintance.

"Even so," Dr Gough said, "I can't see the Liberals giving women the vote in a hurry, for all that many of them are in favour of it. They are too much afraid that women would use their vote in favour of the Conservatives."

"Then what is the answer?" Charlotte asked, leaning forward with sparkling eyes. "The Conservatives don't believe in it at all!"

"I should hope not," Mark said with a laugh as he raised his glass to his lips. "They have better sense."

"Just what is your objection, Mark?" I said, deliberately schooling myself to sound calm and friendly. It was on occasions like this that I tended to forget that Mark and I were no longer enemies.

He shrugged casually as if the whole subject was too trivial to occupy his attention.

"It's just so—so totally *superfluous*!"

"That's right," Catherine said, nodding emphatically. "It's just as Mark says."

No one took more than the politest notice of her.

"I mean," Mark went on, "most wives would vote as their husbands instructed them, surely."

"Not all women have husbands," said Charlotte.

"And some women have minds of their own," I added.

Mark contented himself with a superior smile as he reached for the decanter as if to take away the taste of our foolish words.

"In my view," said Dr Gough, "the new Independent Labour Party holds out the best hope for women. Keir Hardie and Philip Snowden have quite definitely spoken out in favour of women's suffrage."

I glanced a little fearfully at my mother-in-law, expecting the sky to fall. To my astonishment she merely gazed with fond reverence at her fiancé as if endorsing every word he uttered.

"The fellow's a damned Radical," Roger pronounced on the way home. "I'm amazed that mother takes it so calmly."

"He has great charm—and also I think it's his energy and ideas that appeal to her."

"I thought him likeable," Roger admitted. "Radical ideas notwithstanding. And he appears to have plenty of scratch, which is a load off my mind. He was left a considerable amount by his father, I understand, which he intends to use to finance this private nursing home he's so keen about. I feel a lot happier about mother marrying him now that I've met him."

"I think he's delightful," I enthused, going even further. "I do like people with ideas and opinions. How different life will be for her. He's not a bit like your father."

"My God—poor father must be spinning in his grave! Women's suffrage, indeed! And the Labour Party!"

"You don't oppose giving women the vote, do you Roger?" I asked anxiously. I felt I could not bear it if he dismissed the matter as Mark had done, as something totally irrelevant.

"Who am I to be against it?" he asked. "You know I have never been so. I've depended on you for so many things, all our married life, just as old Joe depended on your grandmother. Why should I hold the view that you and others like you are not capable of casting a vote?"

I tucked my hand in the crook of his elbow and leaned against him, feeling closer to him than for many weeks.

We all gathered together once more for the wedding on Christmas Eve.

"I didn't know grannies *could* get married like other people," Lucy said, when we were setting off for the church. She was six now, a pretty, pink and white little girl with her golden hair brushed into shining ringlets. Ellie was eight and vastly more mature, already an avid reader and inclined to boss her brother and sister unmercifully. Of the two, she had more affinity with Ben, even though he was only four.

All three were resplendent in new clothes, and Roger, too, looked elegant and distinguished in frock coat and top hat. I had bought a splendid new hat, very wide and swathed in draped velvet, which I hoped would counter-balance my ridiculous girth, but I was not in the least sanguine about the result of this stratagem. My last glimpse in the mirror before leaving home made me think more of a ship in full sail than anything else.

Roger, as the eldest son, was to give his mother away. No one, as they walked down the aisle together, could possibly have guessed at their relationship. The bride looked amazingly youthful in a coffee-coloured wool ensemble trimmed with fur, and a brown feathered hat even more spectacular than mine.

The reception at Priors was attended only by the family. John and Angela, of course, had come from Oxford and the aunt and uncle from Hereford, who were also close friends of Dr Gough, had travelled to Collingford for the ceremony, but because of the wintry weather and the nearness to Christmas it had been decided to make it a small affair. It was, nevertheless, a very joyous occasion. I was proud of Roger's speech of congratulation and good wishes which was both warm and witty. Dr Gough replied in a similar manner while his wife looked at him adoringly, and all agreed that they made a touching and charming couple.

At the New Year, Annie came to say goodbye. Jed had left Collingford several weeks before and had gone to Manchester where he had managed to find work in a factory, promising to send for Annie and the children as soon as he had found somewhere to live.

"He's managed to rent a little place," she said. "Not so big as the cottage, but we'll fit in somehow. Lord Havering said he would take Robbie now instead of April, so that's something. It'll make a difference, having him off our hands."

I agreed that it would and did not voice my consternation at the thought of the rest of them having to fit into accommodation smaller even than the cottage at Berry Cross. It was something hard to imagine.

"I hope the neighbours are friendly," she went on. "Jed says we're all in a row, like; a terrace, they call it, with another row built right behind, back to back. Jed was right, you see, about not needing his gardening tools."

"Oh Annie, I do hope you'll be happy," I said anxiously.

"We'll get along," she said.

"You will write?"

"I'm not much of a hand at it, Jenny, you know that; still, I'll do my best. *You'll* write, won't you? Let me know about the baby. I still think Dr Fenwick's wrong and you're having twins!"

We laughed and embraced, but I watched with foreboding Annie's family and chattels leave on the cart that Roger had provided.

Before the end of January of that year we heard the news of the death of Queen Victoria. It was the strangest feeling, knowing that she was gone—just as if we had thought she would live for ever. There was an undeniable feeling that England would never be the same without her. The Prince of Wales was regarded in Collingford as a middle-aged roué, and although quite a crowd gathered in the town to hear him proclaimed King Edward VII, I heard more than one person express the view that the Kaiser, the late Queen's grandson would make a better king than Edward. Nevertheless, his accession was the excuse for a grand celebration, with Lord

Bollinger donating an ox for roasting, while the band played, and everyone momentarily forgot that there was still a war raging in South Africa—all the might of the British Army had still not been able to put an end to the Boer guerrillas. It was not until the actual Coronation in August 1902, particularly as he had been seriously ill, that the nation truly took Edward VII to their hearts.

By this time I had produced my fourth baby—or rather my fifth, but no one except Roger and myself ever remembered our first little son. Richard Fenwick had been perfectly right; for all my size, I did not give birth to twins but to a fine, strong boy. We called him Philip John and the whole household doted upon him.

Aunt Millie had been ill with bronchitis during the winter and because of this and Philip's arrival I had not seen the Red Lion since the day that Roger had first taken me over to Long Branstead before he had made the final decision to buy it.

All winter he had been much occupied with it, but I had heard little about the progress of work there—partly, I was certain, because he was aware of my doubts about the wisdom of acquiring the place. I could see its possibilities as far as accommodation was concerned, but the necessary repairs were daunting to say the least. Another drawback to my mind was that Long Branstead was a sleepy little village, not a thriving centre like Collingford, which had grown so much over the past ten years that it was now more of a town than a village.

Where would our customers come from? I asked him.

From Oxford, was his reply, and from even farther afield. For there was a great movement towards the country these days now that the safety bicycle had revolutionised the life of the ordinary man—and woman too. It was certainly true that coveys of young people swarmed out from the towns at weekends. Perhaps he was right. He had nearly always been proved so in the past—yet somehow I could not feel convinced.

He was anxious that I should see the changes he had made and on a fine day at the beginning of June, with Philip in my arms, we drove over to Long Branstead in the trap. In spite of all my good resolutions, the opportunities for quiet conversation with Roger had continued to prove elusive. This day out would perhaps make up for a lot. I felt as if I were shedding ten years as we drove out of Collingford and into the open country. The sky was blue and the sun warm on our backs. There was the smell of meadow-sweet in the air and the hedgerow was dotted with elder-flower and the first of the wild roses.

"Glad you came?" Roger asked, smiling down at me.

"Oh, yes! I'd almost forgotten how lovely the country is, and how wonderful it is just to sit and enjoy it without feeling that there are a million things I ought to be doing."

"There's never enough time, is there?"

"Never! Sometimes I feel I shall be as old as Aunt Millie before there's time to turn round."

He laughed. "You look about eighteen at the moment, if that's any comfort."

"What nonsense you talk," I said, but lightly and gratefully. "Roger, we haven't talked much lately, have we —nonsense or otherwise?"

"Oh, I don't know. I distinctly remember asking you to pass me the salt the day before yesterday."

"Idiot!" I rested my head against his shoulder. "You know perfectly well what I mean."

"Well, now's your chance," he said.

We rode for a little in silence. There may not have been a word between us, but somehow I felt we were communicating in a way we had not done for months.

"Roger, I've been thinking," I said at last, one of the subjects I wanted to discuss suddenly striking me. I lifted my head from his shoulder and sat up straight. "I'm a little worried about Ellie."

Roger sighed. "I thought it was too good to last. What's wrong with Ellie? She seems happy enough at this new school."

"Well yes, she is—up to a point. She's not worried or harassed or miserable like she was with Miss Hodgson, but I don't think she's learning very much. She's a very bright little girl, Roger."

"I'm well aware of that, my dear."

"I've been talking to Charlotte," I went on, after a

moment's hesitation. "She went to Cheltenham Ladies College, you know. She speaks so highly of it, and of Miss Beale, the headmistress—and really, Charlotte is one of the most cultivated women I know." I held his arm tightly in my enthusiasm. "It's a simply splendid school, Roger—the very best in the country, I'm convinced. Wouldn't it be a perfectly wonderful thing to send Ellie there?"

His mouth tightened in exasperation.

"Can't we discuss anything rationally these days without bringing Charlotte into it? Jenny—the fact of the matter is this. Just at this moment I am more than a little strapped for cash. Perhaps by the time that Ellie is of an age to go on somewhere else things will be different, but just at present I have to confess that financially I am over-extended. Fancy boarding schools for my daughters are something I cannot possibly contemplate just now."

I stared at him in consternation.

"But what's gone wrong?" I asked.

He was silent for a moment.

"There was more construction work to be done at the Red Lion than I first thought," he said at last. "The drains had to be relaid and there was a great deal of dry-rot in the timbers." He stopped rather abruptly and I knew there was more to come. I waited without saying a word, looking at him with wary expectancy.

"Also," he said, staring at the road straight ahead of him, "you remember the Angler's Rest at Stavercote—the other inn I was interested in?"

"The one that was withdrawn from sale?"

"It came on the market again last month. I bought it. I knew it was a risk"—he went on, talking over my horrified gasp—"but it was a calculated one, Jenny; a gamble I simply couldn't resist. I just *know* it's a winner. I was sorry when I bought the Red Lion that I couldn't buy it and it was more than I could do to pass up the chance when it came round a second time."

"How could you possibly afford it?"

"I took out a mortgage on the Ring of Bells. You're not to worry. In a year or two we shall be reaping the harvest, you'll see."

"And meantime we're in debt up to our ears!"

"Taking out a mortgage isn't like being in debt. We're making enough at the Ring to keep up with repayments. If only the Red Lion hadn't proved so costly to repair—"

"How could you have gone ahead without discussing it with me?" I asked. It was this aspect of the affair that worried me more than anything else.

He sighed with exasperation.

"Because there's never any time or any opportunity and I knew anyway that you'd be too cautious."

"It's good of you to inform me at last," I said bitterly. "Is everything going well now that the Red Lion is open, or is there something I should know about that?"

"Business is slow," he admitted reluctantly. "I expected nothing else. You know how conservative these villages are. If a thing has been done in a certain way for the last four hundred years, any change is resented. It will improve."

"Is the staff good? Who have you in the kitchen?"

It was incredible, now that I came to think of it, how little I knew of this new business venture.

"I engaged a woman who was cook at Abingdon Hall for a while. She seems quite good."

I went into the kitchen of the Red Lion prepared to be critical. My pleasure in the day away from home had evaporated completely, leaving a small knot of misery behind. How had we come to be so far apart? It was worse, even, than I had thought. But even though my earlier mood had changed so drastically I had to admit that the kitchen seemed well run and clean and that Mrs Hardcastle was very anxious to please. The luncheon she placed before us was simple but good, though—as I mean-spiritedly observed—it is almost impossible to ruin a good trout.

What surprised me about the Red Lion was its cosy atmosphere, due almost entirely to the way Roger had decorated and furnished it. I had been responsible for the furnishings at the Ring of Bells and had waited, in vain, for Roger to seek my advice about the Red Lion. I was a little nettled—totally illogically, for where would I have found the time?—that not only had he managed very well without the benefit of my help, but that the rooms had a rustic charm

181

that I should not have thought of attempting. He had followed the trend begun by William Morris to romanticise cottage life of the past. The bedrooms were tastefully furnished and were eight in number. There had been ten, but two of the smaller ones had been converted to bathrooms.

"No wonder you're strapped for cash," I said at last. "This must have cost a fortune."

"One thing led to another," he replied defensively. "Besides, you have to speculate to accumulate."

"As any drunken costermonger on Epsom Downs can tell you each Derby day. I simply can't see how you hope to recoup. Who's going to come here, Roger?"

"You said exactly the same thing about the Ring of Bells," he said. "And look how busy we are there. Just wait till all the weekend cyclists discover it. They'll come streaming out."

"I certainly hope so," I said, with feeling. "I hope your Mrs Hardcastle in there is up to it."

"Oh, I'm sure she is."

We were on our way home by this time, with Philip fed and asleep.

"What are you going to do about the other one? The Angler's Rest?" I asked. "You surely can't intend to spend money on it to the same extent as you have done here?"

"There's no chance of that—I simply haven't got it to spend. It's ticking over quite nicely as it is—it's well run, with an excellent woman in charge. Any plans for improving it will have to wait for the time being."

"You took over the staff that was already there?"

"Yes. The woman who runs it is exceedingly capable and rules it with a rod of iron, rather like your grandmother did with the Ring. A Mrs Rose Burdett. I intend to introduce a more efficient method of bookkeeping, but apart from that I can safely leave things to her."

"And just suppose the cottage becomes vacant?" I said. "I thought that was the dream of your life—to buy that and make it part of the Ring."

"So I shall, one day. Meanwhile, I saw Mrs Oliver only yesterday and I swear she looks healthier than ever, so there's no immediate prospect of my having to find the cash for that." He narrowed his eyes thoughtfully. "I'd still like Lord B. to settle the matter now. I'll have another talk with him. I can't see why he won't agree to sell me the lease-hold—I'm not likely to turn Mrs Oliver out of house and home during her lifetime."

"But Roger, you haven't the money!"

"I'd find it from somewhere if the opportunity arose. I'd have to—it would be madness not to buy it, the costliest economy we ever made."

I sighed, not noticing the sunshine and the flowers any more. The old, simple days when we had both worked at the Ring of Bells in happy partnership seemed far distant. The worries were forgotten. I could only recall now the shared triumphs, the times when we would sit down at the scrubbed kitchen table to snatch a cup of tea and laugh together at some minor disaster.

We covered the rest of the way home in silence, but it was not the silence of companionship. I felt lost again; unsure of myself, unsure of Roger, bewildered by the way events seemed to be nudging us apart.

12

All through that summer Roger spent a great deal of time away from Collingford and there were times when I had no idea whether it was the Red Lion or the Angler's Rest that was claiming his attention. When I asked for information I was merely told, infuriatingly, not to worry my head about it.

I was about to leave Bridge House one morning by the front door to go shopping, when I realised that a cartful of timber had drawn up outside and that an elderly, grey-haired man was climbing down to speak to me. I did not know him and waited curiously to see what he wanted with me.

It was really Roger he wanted to speak to, but after much

embarrassed hesitation he revealed to me that he had done some contracting work for Roger six months before, for which he was owed fifty-seven pounds. I gave him all the money I had in my purse—fifteen pounds—and promised that he would be paid in full the next day. He took the money thankfully. After he had gone, I went back inside the house and took off my hat, my shopping trip abandoned. I was furiously angry.

"How much more?" I demanded, when Roger returned. Stony faced, I had summoned him to the bedroom where we could talk in peace. "Who else do you owe?"

He sat down on the side of the bed, his shoulders bowed. He made no attempt to excuse himself or bluster, as I had half-expected.

"There's quite a lot, actually," he said. "His is one of the smaller bills outstanding."

I sat down beside him, my anger evaporating now that I saw how worried he looked.

"What are we going to do?" I asked. "You can't make poor little tradesmen like that suffer because you've stretched yourself too thinly. I promised you'd pay him tomorrow."

"So I shall," Roger said. "I have money set aside for the mortgage repayment at the end of the month. I'll use that."

"But what happens at the end of the month?"

"There's still two weeks before then. I'll work something out."

"What other debts have we, Roger?"

"I owe the brewery two hundred pounds, but they're not pushing me. And there's another hundred or so owed to the warehouse that supplied the furniture for the Red Lion."

I was silent. It hardly seemed possible that our thriving little business of less than two years ago had come to this— that we were short even of the comparatively trifling amounts that were needed to pay our debts.

"And then there's the bank loan," Roger said.

My heart sank still further.

"Which bank loan is that?"

"I needed more for the Angler's than I could raise by a mortgage—it was only a couple of hundred."

"How *could* you?" I whispered.

"Jenny, ask yourself how I could *not*! I'd gone too far. What would have been the point in buying the Red Lion and not repairing it or furnishing it or stocking the bar? And as for the Angler's Rest, I know I've backed a winner there. It's only a question of keeping our heads above water—"

"And in the meantime?"

Roger sighed. "The bank has been indulgent up to now; I can always go and see Mr Bannister and ask him to extend my overdraft facilities."

"Whatever happens, you must pay the timber contractor and the furniture people."

"I will, I will. Don't worry about it."

How could I avoid it? I laughed shortly.

"I don't seem to have your gambling instincts," I said. "I can well do without this sort of excitement."

"Talking of excitement," Roger said, getting to his feet. "I have a small piece of news for you that may possibly divert you. Who should I see lunching at the Randolph but Lord Bollinger?"

"Don't say he's ready to sell the cottage!" I said. "That would be too much."

Roger laughed shortly.

"No, he didn't mention it and for once I was glad that he didn't. He did ask us to dinner, however."

"He did *what*?"

"He asked us to Watersmeet, Saturday night as ever was. It seems his nephew and wife are staying there and he appeared to think that we might prove lively company for them."

My heart plummeted.

"Oh Roger, no! I don't want to go."

"Lord B. was most particular that you should."

"But why, in heaven's name?"

My astonishment was, I felt, fully justified. Even the Leytons in their heyday were not normally entertained socially at Watersmeet.

"Why shouldn't he ask us?" Roger's voice was impatient. "We're hardly likely to commit some terrible solecism."

He was right, of course. However unused I was to great country houses, I had learned which knife and fork to use and probably appreciated good wine as well as anyone. Lord

Bollinger I knew to be well disposed towards me. It was the thought of the footmen and the butler and the grand people from London that filled me with disquiet.

"They'll know each other," I said miserably. "And they'll think I'm some sort of a freak because I worked at the inn. And I haven't anything fashionable to wear."

This last was true, for I had put on a little weight since Philip's birth and could now no longer wear several of my better dresses. I decided to consult Charlotte who had as good an eye for fashion as anyone I ever met.

She looked critically at the dresses I put out for her inspection and chose one of misty blue taffeta.

"A little more décolleté, I think," she said thoughtfully, her head on one side. "We can lower the neckline and trim it with lace. Lace is all the thing this season, I promise you, and it can hide a multitude of sins. You look very well in that shade of blue, Jenny. Truly, I don't know why you're so worried about Saturday night."

"It could have something to do with the fact that my grandmother once worked as a kitchen maid at Watersmeet," I said.

"Oh, rats to that!" Charlotte spoke breezily, secure in the knowledge that she came from solidly respectable upper middle-class stock and was a product of the most prestigious girls' school in Britain.

I had no such background to bolster me and what little self-confidence I did possess seemed to ebb away when I saw the expression with which the liveried footman greeted me. He was dressed in a royal blue jacket with a striped blue and gold waistcoat, white knee breeches and stockings and black shoes with gold buckles and for one second I did not recognise him; then I realised that he was none other than Tom Larkin who from time to time called in at the Ring of Bells. I had served him once or twice myself, and I could tell that he was appalled that Lord Bollinger had actually invited me to the house just as if I were one of the gentry. He took my wrap as if it was a garment I had salvaged from the local rubbish dump.

Tom disappeared with my wrap and it was left to the butler, clad not in livery but in a tail-coat, breeches and black stockings, to announce us. He was not a man I had ever met before, but I felt quite certain that he, too, despised us utterly.

I had hoped for a large party in which I could pass unnoticed, even though I knew that Lord Bollinger did not entertain now on the same scale as in the past. Certainly I hoped that Hugh Bainbridge would be present, for he at least was a friend whom I knew I could rely on, but I was to be disappointed. Besides Lord Bollinger, who was leaning even more heavily on his stick but insisted on limping forward to greet us, there were only four others in the room.

Lord Bollinger's nephew and heir, Mr Gerald Melville, was perhaps the thinnest man I had ever seen—narrow head with hair like black lacquer, a long thin nose, narrow shoulders. Even his lips were so thin that they were practically non-existent, and were fringed by a moustache that was waxed into thin points which curved upwards. His handshake was cold and limp and his strangely yellow eyes were devoid of warmth. They seemed to scrutinise me closely as if he were puzzled that Roger and I had been invited.

His wife, Lydia, was as smart as paint with a fashionable hour-glass figure. Her nose was too sharp for beauty, but both she and her friend, Lady Silcock, were possessed of great self-assurance and vivacity which silenced me even further.

Sir Montague Silcock, who evidently was a bosom friend of Mr Melville, was also slight with hair the colour of tow and a concave sort of face that made me think of a jam spoon. He laughed a great deal at very little and made a quantity of weak jokes and puns, looking at his friend whenever he did so, as if seeking his approval. It gave the effect of a conspiracy in which no others were invited to join; as if the two men belonged to an elite little club for two.

Lord Bollinger indicated a gilt love-seat and begged me to sit down, himself taking the place next to me. I had not seen him since that day in the lane and I was shocked by the change in him. I could not now say that he would never grow old; he looked already more frail than I could have believed possible. He asked about the children, complimented me on my appearance, flirted a little as he had always done; but whereas in July he had said that his spirit was only twenty-five, somehow I felt that now even that had aged.

Another liveried footman brought round sherry on a silver tray and we both took a glass.

"Only a small party," he said leaning towards me confidentially. "Wanted you to meet me nephew—after all, he'll rule the roost here when I'm gone."

"Oh, Uncle Arthur—*such* a way to talk!" Lydia Melville rustled over to us and perched on the arm of the settee by his side. "He's an old fraud," she said to me, speaking across him as if he were not there. She tapped him coquettishly on the shoulder. "He'll see us all out, mark my words. That is, if he does what his doctor tells him. He's such a naughty boy! Uncle, you really should not have taken that drink."

He ignored her and turned to me.

"Damned nonsense!" he said. "They say I can't have me drink. I tell them I'll do what I like." Defiantly he sipped his sherry. "It's me innards, you know. Refuse to pander to them, that's my attitude. Me innards will go down fighting, that's what I told that young Doctor Fenwick."

Mrs Melville gave him a melting look.

"You should think of those who love you."

Lord Bollinger said nothing but cast a somewhat jaundiced eye in her direction. I could not help reflecting that village gossip said that the Melvilles had been only a few times to Watersmeet, which seemed odd if her affection was as great as she implied.

I could hear Roger and the other members of the party talking of race meetings and horses and was gratified to note that he was more than upholding the honour of the family by speaking with a great deal of authority. Lydia Melville swept away to take her place closer to them, obviously feeling that she had done her duty by me.

"Humbug," Lord Bollinger confided to me as she left us, in a voice which I swear was capable of being heard in every corner of the vast room. "Can't wait to shovel me six feet down. I feel sorry for Collingford, not meself. I shan't know, shall I?"

"I wish you wouldn't talk like that," I said. "I can't imagine the village without you, and everyone else is the same."

"Wish you'd known me daughter," Lord Bollinger said.

188

"You'd have liked her. A spirited girl, she was—not like that milk and water miss over there. Upped and married a Yankee."

"Does she never come back to England?" I asked.

"She's been a couple of times over the years, but her husband suffers from poor health. It's not easy for them to get away. I've been to Boston, too. Whole bevy of grand-daughters I have over there, and great-grandchildren too. Lots and lots of little Yankees. There's Aileen and Marianne and Jessica and Sophy—bless my soul, I can't remember them all! Not a boy amongst 'em—would you believe it? That long streak of misery over there's me only male relative."

I was thankful that Mr Gerald Melville was in full spate, talking in a high, braying voice about the products of Lord Branstead's stable, and appeared unaware of his uncle's derogatory remarks.

"Me son was a fine young man," Lord Bollinger went on.

"So I've heard, my lord. His loss was a great tragedy."

The old man nodded sombrely.

"Never got over it," he said briefly. "People thought we did, but we didn't. Neither me nor me poor wife, rest her soul. Something I want to show you after dinner—been making up me mind to it for a long time. Suddenly thought, perhaps not much time left."

I looked at him enquiringly, but before I could ask him what he had in mind, the double doors were flung open and the resplendent Tom Larkin announced that dinner was served. With difficulty Lord Bollinger stood up.

Lady Silcock materialised by his side. She was a tall, willowy lady and was forced to bend her elegant neck to speak to him.

"Lydia tells me that I'm to have the honour of going in with you," she said, smiling widely and attempting to take his arm.

"Oh, does she?" Lord Bollinger moved irritably, jerking his arm away from her. "Then you have been misinformed. I'm taking Jenny in to dinner."

I have seldom been more embarrassed. Lady Silcock behaved impeccably, smiling graciously at me and retreating despite my protestations that really, I would not dream of usurping her proper place. By all laws of etiquette, as the highest ranking lady present there was no doubt that she was right to expect to be taken in by Lord Bollinger; but if I thought I was embarrassed at that point, it was as nothing compared with the fuss that was created at the table when Lord Bollinger discovered that I had been placed three seats removed from him, on Mr Melville's left hand.

"I want Jenny next to me," he said. "Here, on my right. Simmonds!" This to the butler. "What's the name on this card? Lady Silcock? Well, put her down there in place of Mrs Leyton. Well, put Mrs Melville down there, then. What does it matter if she's next to her own husband? Doesn't she like her own husband? Never could see the point of all this changing and chopping around, meself. Gerald, you change with Montague, and then we'll all be ship-shape."

He was, of course, behaving abominably—but it was his house, his title that would be coming to the Melvilles, and his privilege to behave exactly as he liked. We all played a sort of general post round the table.

"Just hope I find my place before the *plaice* arrives—haw, haw, haw," brayed Sir Montague.

There was polite laughter, but I was aware of hostile undercurrents.

Once settled, the meal began. Such quantity, I thought, as course followed course. Enough, surely, to feed not only Jed and his family but all the residents of Berry Cross for an entire week.

As the conversation was almost entirely monopolised by Lydia Melville and Lady Silcock talking non-stop about parties and plays in London, I was able to sit quietly and observe. Lord Bollinger was, I noticed, drinking quite as much wine as anyone else and made irritated gestures to the footman behind his chair whenever his glass was empty.

Mr Melville was applying himself to his food with great energy. When the ladies allowed him to insert a word or two into the conversation, I was diverted by the way he seemed able to speak at the same time as shovelling into his small mouth vast quantities of meat and vegetables. He managed, in some obscure way, to do this with no breach of good manners. Did he not have to masticate like everyone else, I wondered? Did he possess some strange, superhuman digestive processes?

"What'll you do when you live down here?" Lord Bollinger shot at Lydia Melville who was in the middle of describing a party given by Mrs Keppel at which King Edward had looked in for a few minutes. "None of that in Collingford, yer know. We live quietly in the country."

Mrs Melville again switched on her smile of loving solicitude.

"We don't even *think* about it," she said. "Dear Uncle Arthur, it will be many, many years before we come here. But when we do—why, I'm sure we shall find all sorts of diversions. How do you pass the time, Mrs Leyton?"

"I have my home and my children," I said.

She had been smiling as she turned to me, and at my reply the smile remained but her eyes flickered with something— ridicule? Bewilderment? I was not sure.

"How nice," she said, after a moment's pause.

Lord Bollinger lifted his glass to me.

"Tell yer something," he said. "Jenny's useful as well as ornamental, which is more than can be said for you London ladies. M'wife was the same. Always kept herself busy."

"How fascinating," Lady Silcock smiled, obviously finding the subject no such thing. "What a drone you make me feel, Mrs Leyton. May one ask in what direction you make yourself useful? I presume you are full of good works?"

I looked at her, aware that she was patronising me. Her immaculately-dressed blonde head was held enquiringly on one side, her smiling lips turned down at the corners in what seemed to me a faintly concealed sneer. A devil of perversity seemed to take hold of me.

"Until quite recently I worked in my husband's inn," I said. "The Ring of Bells, in the village. You may have seen it."

There was a moment of silence, then a few uncomfortable laughs.

"How very droll," Lydia remarked.

"We worked together," Roger said, coming to my rescue. I flashed him a look of gratitude. "And great fun it was, too. My wife is the best cook in Oxfordshire, I assure you." He

191

became aware that this was not the most tactful thing to say while sitting at another man's dinner table, and smilingly apologised to Lord Bollinger.

"It's true, it's true," the old man said. "No need to apologise, my boy. I know Jenny's worth."

"Above rubies," Gerald Melville murmured sardonically.

Lydia Melville was still struggling with the enormity of what Roger had said.

"You mean—you mean you actually *worked* in the inn?"

"Indeed I did," I replied.

"How very, very droll!"

"I enjoy cooking."

"I once knew a woman," said Sir Montague, "who actually enjoyed sweeping chimneys! I promise you, I'm not codding in the slightest. She was a bishop's wife, couldn't have been more respectable! She said there was nothing more satisfying than bringing the soot cascading down around her—she never went anywhere without the brushes tied to the back of her carriage, just in case her hostess needed her services."

"Oh, Monty!" his wife said. "I don't believe a word of it."

"Gospel, my dear—absolutely gospel!" He glanced over to catch Gerald's eye, and winked at him. "Often thought I'd like to be a landlord myself," he went on. "I can just see myself, dispensing drinks. One for you, one for you, one for you and two for me, eh what? Great stuff!"

"Just imagine your mother's face if you went into trade!"

There was a moment's pause which no one attempted to fill. Lord Bollinger was too busy arguing with the footman about the advisability or otherwise of refilling his glass while the Melvilles and the Silcocks were apparently struck dumb at the thought of anyone in their circle demeaning themselves to the extent that Roger and I had done. The two of us exchanged gleams of amusement across the table.

I dreaded the moment which I knew would come all too soon; the time when Lydia Melville would rise to her feet to lead me and Lady Silcock away from the dining room, leaving the men to their port.

It was every bit as bad as I expected. They talked of people

192

I had never heard of and plays I had never seen. Neither addressed me and I added nothing. I wondered afresh at the strange caprice that had prompted Lord Bollinger to include us in his party that night.

It seemed an eternity until the men joined us. When they did so, it was with an air of purpose. A game of baccarat had been proposed, a suggestion that was evidently much to Sir Montague's liking. He was rubbing his hands and exchanging meaningful smiles with Mr Melville with a kind of conspiratorial gleefulness as the card table was set up.

I knew nothing of the game and suspected that Roger knew little more—a fact which I felt sure would in no way deter him. If there was a game of chance in the offing, I knew my husband well enough by this time to be sure he would be all eagerness to join in. It was a prospect that filled me with unease. It seemed to me that these two worldly gentlemen had every intention of taking the shirt from his back, neither knowing nor caring that the garment was, at that moment, exceedingly threadbare.

Lord Bollinger hobbled to my side.

"Come, my dear," he said to me. "I told you there was something I wanted to show you. I know these two ladies will excuse us."

Mrs Melville and Lady Silcock looked at us strangely. He managed to make it clear that they were not invited to accompany us and I could feel their speculative gaze on my retreating backview. Did they imagine I had designs on the old gentleman, or he on me? Mentally I shrugged; let them think what they liked. It was none of their business.

Leaning heavily on my arm, he led me from the room and along a corridor lined with family portraits, stopping every now and then to point upwards with his stick.

"There's me grandmother," he said. "A beauty, she was. Toast of London and Bath, I'm told. And this feller here was her husband—my grandfather."

"You're like him."

"He was a hell-raiser, by all accounts, so perhaps you're right. I haven't led a blameless life, you know."

"Who of us has?"

He grunted at that but made no comment. We had reached

a door at the end of the corridor and through it we passed to his own private study. There was a large, roll-top desk in the window and deep leather chairs by the fireplace. The room had a comfortably used, shabby atmosphere, unlike the drawing room which was furnished purely for show.

"Sit ye down, sit ye down," he said, painfully making for the desk. A little puzzled, I did so.

"I wanted to show you this," he said, hobbling back with a photograph he had taken from a drawer. "It's more like him than the portrait upstairs. It's me son, James."

I took the sepia photograph from him and looked at it. I saw an alert, determined-looking man dressed in the uniform of a cavalry officer. His eyes, bright with intelligence and humour, looked straight at the camera and there was an amused quirk to his lips as if he was thinking of something that made him laugh. His hair was dark, his chin pointed with a slight cleft in it. I felt as I looked at it that somewhere I had seen this young man before.

"He's a fine man," I said. "I'm more than ever sorry that he was killed, my lord."

"Should never have gone," Lord Bollinger said. "Only son, heir to all of this, no business to be joining the Army at all. It was some foolish border skirmish in India, y'know. Such a waste—such wicked waste! Still, it was what he wanted. He was always a boy to get his own way."

"He certainly looks like a man who knew his own mind."

"Yes. It was always the Army with him. Remind you of anyone?"

He shot the last four words at me, taking me a little by surprise. I looked up at him, then back at the photograph.

"I—I don't know. I thought at first there was something familiar . . . he's not really like you, is he? Did he favour his mother?"

The old man laughed softly to himself.

"I wouldn't say that. Not surprised he looks familiar to you, though. It's the way the eyes are set and the shape of his chin. You see them every day."

I frowned at him in bewilderment.

"I'm sorry, my lord. I can't seem to think—"

"It's *you*, girl—*you*! Don't you see it?"

I looked again at the picture.

"I suppose there is a resemblance," I said at last. "How strange!"

"Noticed it the first time I saw you," he said. "Remember—it was on the green, and you returned my hat to me?"

"I remember it well. I told you that my grandmother would turn you out of her kitchen for using unseemly language."

"Such impudence!" He laughed as he spoke. "It was your smile that reminded me of James before anything else."

"What a strange coincidence," I said. "I hope it didn't add to your grief."

He said nothing for a few moments, looking at me with an unreadable expression.

"It was a joy to me," he said at last. "Always a joy, knowing you were about, seeing you married to young Leyton, seeing the business prosper."

He was sitting in the chair opposite mine, leaning forward, and at this he stretched out a hand towards me although I was far out of his reach.

Suddenly it seemed imperative for me to let him know what he had always meant to me. He was a lonely man and was ageing so fast. I moved over and sat on a stool close beside him, taking his hand.

"I've always felt something strange about you, just as if somehow I knew you in a previous existence." I smiled as I spoke, not wanting him to think that I held such eccentric views in reality but not knowing how else to explain the bond that I had always felt between us.

He grunted.

"I've no time for such poppycock," he said. "In my view, this existence is more than enough for anyone. So many years, so quickly gone. I can hardly believe . . ." His voice trailed away, but then gathered strength again.

"I made up my mind to tell you tonight," he said. "There have been times before when I've nearly come out with it; other times when I've thought, 'No, least said, soonest mended.' But somehow I can't stomach the thought that my line ends with that namby-pamby coxcomb out there and that empty-headed wife of his. They've no children, yer know."

I murmured sympathetically, even yet not aware of what he was about to tell me.

He cleared his throat as if, for all his resolution, he was finding it difficult to begin.

"Fifty years ago," he said, "your grandmother was a maid here in the kitchens."

"Yes?"

"She was a pretty girl, full of fire and spirit. And quick-witted, too! We used to laugh together . . ." His voice trailed away again.

"You and my grandmother?"

"We were both young. Hot-blooded. I was—I was very taken with her, and as for her—well, she fell deeply in love with me. She was a good girl, not light-minded in any way."

I stared at him silently.

"Are you trying to say that she had your child?" I asked at last.

He released my hand and leaned back into the depths of his armchair.

"I am," he said. "Your mother—Eleanor."

"But my grandfather—Joe Austin—he was my mother's father! There was never any doubt."

"Sarah had an understanding with Joe before she came here. Before she and I got to know each other. It was a simple enough matter for her to hasten the marriage."

I stood up and went back to my original chair like a sleepwalker, turning to stare once more at him in amazement before sinking down.

"No wonder she distrusted 'the gentry'," I said.

Everything became clear; her hostility to my father, to Roger. She had felt certain that I could only suffer from my passion for him, just as she had suffered.

"Wasn't there any talk?" I asked. "I never heard any gossip."

"She was a quick thinker and a quick talker."

"Of course! My grandfather—" I checked myself, but went on, for to me, old Joe would always be that—"My grandfather told me once that my mother was premature."

"It was all so long ago." He moved his head restlessly. "I thought you would want to know."

"I hardly know how I feel! My grandfather was the dearest of men. He loved my mother—"

"And never had another child, don't forget that!" From the depths of his armchair the old man grinned at me. "He should be grateful to me, perhaps."

"You made a fool of him, between you."

"Which is why this will stay our secret. You will promise me that, won't you, Jenny? My memory can take care of itself, but I don't want you to besmirch the memory of the worthy Austins."

"Roger and I have no secrets."

"That's a bold claim, my dear."

"A true one. I shall naturally tell him."

"Then swear him to secrecy, for your own sake and your grandmother's, if not for mine."

"Why should I want to tell anyone else?" I stood up and moved away from him.

"Oh, Jenny! Have I done wrong to tell you? Can't you see that it was I who was the proud one. I wanted to claim you!"

I looked at him and saw again that he looked frail and lonely and I went swiftly back to the stool by his knee.

"I'm sorry," I said. "I didn't mean it. It was old Joe I was thinking of—of course I'm proud to belong to you, too."

Before either of us could say more there was a tap on the door and Lydia Melville opened it.

"Oh, there you are!" she said. "We wondered where you had taken Mrs. Leyton. Are you not coming back to join the rest of us?"

Lord Bollinger flicked a brief glance at her but otherwise ignored her. "Will you come to Watersmeet again? You'll always be welcome," he said to me.

I nodded, conscious of Mrs Melville's curious glance. I rose to my feet, and laboriously Lord Bollinger did the same. She stood back by the open door as we went through it and I caught her cold, unsmiling eyes upon me, regarding me with a speculative expression.

My own thoughts were in chaos. It suddenly struck me as we passed the portraits on the walls that these were

197

my ancestors too, even if none but I knew it. I longed to tell Roger.

He, it seemed, had hardly noticed our absence from the drawing room, being engrossed in the game.

Lady Silcock was standing behind her husband biting the inside of her cheek nervously, but she forced a smile as we entered.

"You're missing all the fun," she said. "Mr Leyton seems to have found a winning streak."

I concentrated my attention on the game that was in progress. Roger, they told me, held the bank. I had no idea whether that boded good or ill, for his face was expressionless as he dealt, first to Gerald Melville on his right, then to Sir Montague on his left. Bets were then placed on the cards that were face down in front of them.

No money was in sight. Instead, Sir Montague was jotting down figures on a small pad by his side.

I could see at a glance that there was no skill involved. It was all pure chance. Still, it was the sort of entertainment that I knew Roger enjoyed and I smiled upon the group benevolently, glad to think that for a short time he was able to forget his troubles.

"Luck of the devil," Gerald Melville said shortly, throwing his hand of cards back at the banker.

"Shall we double up?" Roger asked.

I thought the look that Sir Montague flashed at Mr Melville expressed disquiet and for the first time I began to feel seriously worried. Just how much was being wagered? I had resigned myself to the loss, however unwelcome, of a few pounds, which was the sort of money involved in a game of cards with Mark and his friends, but there was something about the tenseness of the atmosphere and the way Lady Silcock was pleating the material of her skirt in her fingers that made me think that there was much more at stake this evening.

"Have you seen Lord Bollinger's collection of china?" Lydia Melville asked me. "There are some very interesting and rare pieces—"

Common courtesy forced me to follow her to the extreme end of the room where she stopped in front of a cabinet crammed with china. She opened it and withdrew a pottery figurine.

"Staffordshire," she said. "Beautiful, isn't it? But not as valuable as the Meissen and the Sèvres. It's all rather a mixture. I shall have to sort it out one day. I'm afraid poor Uncle Arthur is really not capable—really, he gets quite confused these days, the dear old thing. These figures are Bustelli, made at Nymphenburg; very rare. I understand . . ."

Desperately I was tuning my ears to hear what was going on at the card table. Surely there was some way I could get Roger to leave.

"We ought to go," I said abruptly in the middle of Lydia Melville's discourses. "The children—"

"But you can't remove your husband while he's winning!" she said, smiling in a superior way at my stupidity.

To me it seemed the best time to leave, but I subsided into silence.

"Your husband is a very attractive man," Mrs Melville said, pausing with her head on one side to consider the group at the end of the room. There was a faint note of surprise in her voice, as if landlords of inns had no business to be attractive.

I was hardly aware of her words, for there had been another explosion from the gaming table.

"Lord Bollinger is very tired. I feel sure we should go," I persisted.

"Did he seem tired to you? I always think of him as such a tough old man, though of course he's far from well. He's always so energetic and enthusiastic—no doubt you found that, in your talk with him." Carefully she replaced a piece of Crown Derby that she had taken from the cabinet. "What was it that he was so anxious to show you?"

"Merely an old photograph that he thought would interest me."

"I see."

"Lyd-ja," Lord Bollinger called from the other end of the room. "Ring for Simmonds to bring me another brandy, will you? These card-sharps are ready for another, too."

"We ought to go," I said, walking back towards him.

"Nonsense! Have a brandy yourself—you look a bit peaky."

I was not surprised. Time was passing and as far as I could make out, Roger was still winning; however I was by now feeling sick with worry that I should not get him out of that room before we had lost everything we possessed.

"To be honest," I said, "I'm feeling a little faint."

I sat down on the settee beside him and he patted my hand.

"Haven't upset you, have I?"

"Of course not. Far from it."

"Better friends than ever, eh? Bless my soul, you do look pale! It has been a shock for you, is that it? Or is the room too hot? Do you need some air?" He regarded me with a frown of concern. "Perhaps that husband of yours should take you home." He eased himself to his feet and limped over to the card table.

"Last hand, gentlemen; Mrs Leyton isn't well. Out with your cheque books and settle your debts."

"Oh, I *say*!" Sir Montague protested.

Roger looked up and caught my eye, permitting himself a small, self-congratulatory gleam in my direction. Lady Silcock was very still and watchful as if the suspense of knowing what her husband had lost was almost too much for her to bear. He retained his determinedly light-hearted air as he added up the bets. I had no idea what sort of sum was at stake.

"You were damned lucky tonight," Gerald Melville said as he shook Roger's hand. "We'll have a return game some time."

"I shall look forward to it," Roger replied.

All was politeness and affability as we took our leave. I thanked Lord Bollinger for an interesting evening—how interesting only he and I knew—and expressed the false hope that we should see both the Melvilles and the Silcocks again. I was heartily thankful when we could drive away into the night.

For the first few yards we were both silent; then as we drew well away from the house, Roger began to laugh. It was little more than a chuckle at first, but it grew and grew until his peals of mirth rang out into the night and he dropped

Brownie's reins to put both arms round me, squeezing me so hard that I thought my ribs would surely crack.

"Two thousand, five hundred pounds," he gasped at last. "Jenny, can you believe it? We're solvent! We're home and dry. Two thousand, five hundred—and that pair of smart-Alecs thought they'd be showing *me* a thing or two."

Stony faced, I pushed him away from me.

"Don't you ever do a thing like that again. I died a million deaths in there, once it dawned on me you were playing for high stakes."

"But it paid off! I can pay everyone now—the timber man, the brewery, the bank, everyone."

"And if you'd lost? Did it occur to you that it was at least a possibility?"

He grasped me by the shoulders and shook me.

"But I'm a winner, Jenny, not a loser! Come on, be happy—smile, for heaven sake. All life is a gamble. Surely you're pleased!"

"I don't know that I am. It frightens me, Roger, the thought that you'll think this is easy money so that you'll try it again. And next time you might not be a winner."

He picked up the reins almost sulkily.

"You're not turning into a killjoy, are you, Jenny?" he asked in a voice from which all laughter had fled.

"I'm a realist," I said. "Luck runs out. Suppose you lost the Ring of Bells?"

"Just as long as I don't lose you!"

"It's a possibility you should not ignore," I said coldly.

13

At least now I was not pregnant our differences could be resolved to some extent in bed. I said that I was sorry—that of course he would never lose me and that I was delighted that we could now pay our debts. And Roger assured me that he would never again gamble for such high stakes. On the surface all was well.

He was highly amused that my ultra-respectable grandmother had fallen victim to the squire's charms and given birth to his daughter.

"You won't tell anyone?" I begged. "Not Mark, or John or anyone?"

"I promise. Not even my mother, who would be delighted to know that her grandchildren were the descendants of a peer of the realm."

I saw a great deal of Charlotte. She was the first real woman friend I had ever made, in the sense that we shared ideas and understood each other's points of view. I had been fond of Annie and always would be, but we could never have the common interests that Charlotte and I shared.

It was one day when I was going to visit her that I stopped again by the wall and looked at Priors. A thought came to me with a stunning impact.

Priors was just as much my ancestral home as Roger's— more so, as it had been home to the Bollingers for hundreds of years before Watersmeet was built. Was it remotely possible that the almost mystical attraction that it had held for me from the very first moment that I had seen it had its roots in the fact that my forebears had lived there?

I laughed a little at my foolishness and went on my way, wondering how I should find Catherine that day.

She still had long periods of complete withdrawal when she refused to live any sort of a normal life, merely lying on a couch without bothering even to turn the pages of the magazines that lay beside her. Charlotte tried, with the utmost patience and good-humour, to stimulate her in all manner of things from the care of her own baby to painting watercolours, but nothing sustained her interest.

Mercifully, Charlotte appeared to grow very fond of Peter and she did not mention going away. He was growing into a sturdy, wilful boy, with a great deal of charm. Mark doted on him and if anything was too indulgent, as if to compensate for Catherine's indifference.

Izzie was a tower of strength. She had produced her

baby—a boy, whom she named Amos—three weeks before I gave birth to Philip, and he spent his time in a perambulator either outside the kitchen door or inside, according to the weather. Priors, always an unconventional household, seemed to absorb him without difficulty. The farm-hands who trooped into the kitchen for their breakfast made much of Amos and appeared to think no worse of Izzie for having produced him.

"First one as passes a remark to me," she said to me on one occasion, "knows as how he'd get the rough end of my tongue. I'd soon turn round and tell 'im it takes two to make a baby."

Izzie was always 'turning round and telling 'em'. If a shopkeeper attempted to fob her off with less than his best goods, she would 'turn round and tell 'im' not to waste his time or hers with his second-rate wares. And she was always quick to defend Priors against the least whisper of gossip.

"They were talking in the Post Office about Mrs Mark," she told me once. "Didn't see me come in, see. Said she was funny in the head and likely to turn violent. So 'course, I turned round and told 'em, she's sick, I said. Quiet as a mouse—wouldn't hurt a fly. That told 'em."

"If Izzie turned round as often as she says, she'd be spinning like a top," Charlotte remarked to me one day. We were enjoying a frivolous afternoon sitting on the river bank while the children made mud pies.

"There's no sign of Catherine becoming violent, is there?" I asked.

"Not so far. She's not happy though, Jenny. Not unhappy either, perhaps. Just strange and withdrawn."

"You're not thinking of going yet?" I had hardly dared to ask the question before.

Charlotte shook her head.

"No. I feel I'm performing a useful function here, and at the moment the cause seems to have entered a discouragingly quiet phase."

Since coming to Collingford, Charlotte had initiated a weekly meeting of ladies to discuss current works of literature. There were the two of us; Mrs Chalmers, wife of the new vicar; Mary Poulson, the solicitor's wife; and several others who liked to exercise their minds. Inevitably our discussions seemed to lead us towards examining one aspect or another of the position of women and I would come away from the meeting feeling stirred and restless, aware of my own helplessness. Time was going by, I felt. We were on the brink of a new era—but how long could one teeter on the brink?

For ever, it seemed. Christmas came round again, bringing the usual family gathering. Goffy and Granny (finally christened by Ben and thus universally known until the day they died) had bought a substantial house in the Pitville area of Cheltenham and the dream of the nursing home for lung disease was now a reality. Each Christmas now there were three events to celebrate: Yuletide itself, Peter's birthday, and Goffy and Granny's wedding anniversary.

I received a card from Annie which told me nothing, other than that she was still alive. Roger spent New Year's Eve away from home for the first time ever, saying that his presence was necessary at the Angler's Rest, to which I replied that of course I understood, and that I should be quite content to have an early night. But I was not content, and welcomed in 1902 with a flood of self-pity and a deep feeling of loss.

I was shopping in the High Street, on a day when spring suddenly seemed just around the corner, when I happened to meet Mrs Kingsley whom I had not seen for several months.

"Oh, Mrs Leyton!" she said. "I'm so glad to have seen you. I thought perhaps I might have to leave without saying goodbye."

I stared at her in bewilderment.

"What on earth do you mean?" I asked. "Surely you're not leaving the Ring of Bells?"

"Didn't Mr Leyton tell you?" She looked at me in surprise. "I'm moving over to Long Branstead, to the Red Lion. The cook's given notice and the barman's been dipping his hand in the till. Mr Leyton says I'm to be called a manager."

"Well!" I was flabbergasted that such things had been going on without Roger breathing a word to me. "What will the Ring of Bells do?"

"I've been training up a new girl—Florrie Masters. I expect you know her mother. She's only young, but seems quite bright—and, of course, Mr Leyton will be there to keep an eye on things."

"Of course. Do you mind going, Mrs Kingsley?"

"Not really. It's more money see, so how can I object to that? And manager! Just fancy! No, taken all in all, I don't mind going—and I'm glad to have seen you, Mrs Leyton."

"And I you," I said faintly. "And I do wish you the very best of luck, Mrs Kingsley. We are bound to meet again as I'm sure I shall be over at the Red Lion myself before too long."

We parted there on the pavement before the butcher's shop and for a moment I stared unseeingly at the rows of dangling, plucked poultry hanging outside, until an assistant in a blue-striped apron and straw hat approached and I returned to my senses. No, I told him, there was nothing I required, just at the moment.

Only information, I thought, as I continued up the street. Why hadn't Roger told me of these developments? He must surely know that the Ring of Bells was still very close to my heart and that I was vitally interested in everything concerning it.

He looked surprised when I asked him about it with an unmistakable note of reproach in my voice.

"There was no real problem," he said. "I didn't imagine you would want to be troubled, with so many other things to occupy you."

"But I'm always interested in the Ring, Roger. You must know that."

He smiled at me, as one humouring a child.

"Everything is perfectly all right, Jenny. And with Mrs Kingsley at the Red Lion I am relieved to think that things will improve there."

"And what about the Angler's Rest? Is everything well there?"

"Yes, thank heaven." He spoke absently, his attention on a magazine concerning the hotel trade which he had recently started taking regularly. "Thank God for Mrs Burdett. The woman's a tower of strength."

"She really does sound like grandmother," I said, wanting to hear more.

"Mm?" He looked up at me in vague enquiry, his finger marking his place on the printed page. "Yes, I suppose there is something of the same martinet-like quality about her. She's certainly efficient."

"I hope she's not as difficult to deal with."

"Oh no, not at all." His eyes wandered down to the magazine again.

"I'd like to meet her," I said, pursuing the subject relentlessly, determined that on this occasion I would not be accused of lack of interest.

"You wouldn't care for her," he said, not even bothering to look up.

Resignedly I abandoned the attempt to draw him out.

I had also reluctantly abandoned any idea of persuading Roger to send Ellie to Cheltenham Ladies' College, but we had succeeded in reaching an agreeable compromise. It had been decided that she would sit the entrance examination for the Oxford High School for Girls and, if successful, would go there at the beginning of the school year in September, by which time she would be ten years old. There was a boarding house attached to the school, but John and Angela had offered to have her during the week and we preferred the idea of her staying with them and returning to us at weekends. She was fond of them and of her little girl cousins, now four in number, and as they possessed a substantial house in Banbury Road not far from the school, it all seemed highly satisfactory.

Ellie herself was exhilarated by the prospect. She drew a chart of the months that were to elapse before she was due to burst like a meteor into the unsuspecting world of the High School, and much as I loved her and great as my hopes for her were, I could not avoid the thought that the stiffer competition that she was bound to find there could not fail to do her good. Not to put too fine a point upon it, Ellie was getting just a little too big for her boots.

Lucy was a happy, affectionate child who had long since decided that academic success was something she could do without. It was not that she was dull; her vocabulary was excellent and she was acute enough over practical matters, but school work was boring and the world was too full of other things to waste her efforts on sums and spelling. She liked to play with her dolls—an occupation which Ellie never cared for—and painted very detailed and highly coloured pictures, and knew that she had only to smile at her doting father for him to reach her down the top brick from the chimney.

Ben was as ebullient as ever and showed signs of being as bright as Ellie. He could read long before he went to Balmoral Academy. Philip continued to thrive and gave no cause for concern. He was a sunny, placid baby, surrounded by love.

I was lucky, I kept telling myself. I had four lovely children and a comfortable home, and a handsome husband who treated me with courteous consideration. Why, then, did everything feel out of joint? Why did I feel as if I had wandered into a trackless, empty desert—as if Roger and I were mouthing soundlessly to each other from a great distance?

To Ellie it seemed as if the day for the High School entrance examination would never come. She never doubted the outcome, and nor, in truth, did I, so that it was with an air of pleasurable expectancy that we rose early on the appointed day and took the train to Oxford.

I delivered her to the school in good time and then made my way to Elliston & Cavell to buy a few things that were unobtainable in Collingford, and to look at the latest fashions. I needed material for the girls' new summer dresses and some gloves for myself of a shade that the village shop did not stock.

And while I was there, I said to myself, I might buy a hat. It was not that I really needed one particularly, but something frivolous and fashionable for summer would be cheering. There would be no harm in looking . . .

It was on a stand, staring me in the face, the first thing I saw on entering the department. It was a veritable confection in cream straw and peachy-pink veiling, the exact colour of my new summer gown.

My reaction to the sight of it was noted at once. A young assistant left the lady she was serving to press me to try it on, and I needed little persuasion. I sat myself at a counter before a gilt mirror, removed my sensible, everyday navy blue hat and replaced it with the delightful piece of nonsense from the stand. It looked incongruous atop my tailored jacket, but even so I fell in love with it immediately. I turned my head this way and that, admiring myself unashamedly from all angles.

"It is rather nice, isn't it?" I asked the girl, smiling.

"Most becoming, modom. If I may say so, it's quite definitely modom's colour."

"I wonder if I should?" I mused. "How much is it?"

It was my own wish to be modest in my spending that held me back. Roger had never grudged me buying anything for myself and in fact was always urging me to do so.

"Would you mind serving me, dear?" the woman at the next mirror called to the assistant. "I think I've made up my mind now and I'm in a terrible hurry."

I glanced sideways at the same time as she looked at me, and we both laughed, for it was quite obvious that her hurry had not prevented her trying on what must have been the store's entire stock. The counter was littered with hats of every description.

"Spoilt for choice, I am," she said to me, and laughed again, the tip of her tongue protruding between her lips. I noted the faintly London intonation. Not quite a lady, I thought—and was amused at myself, for I could not believe that even the fact that my mother was Lord Bollinger's illegitimate daughter qualified me to make such judgments. Still, I was right, I thought. She wasn't a lady. She was, however, an attractive, glossy woman with a glorious complexion and a generous mouth.

"What do you think of this one?" she asked me.

"I think I preferred the one you were wearing before—the blue one," I said.

"Reely? This red one too bright, d'you think? Oh well, I expect you're right, though I like a bit of colour myself. Tell you what, dear," she said to the assistant, woman to woman. "I'll take them both. Put them down to my account, will you? The name's Burdett. Mrs Rose Burdett, Angler's Rest, Stavercote."

I stared at myself in the gilt mirror, not seeing the lovely hat any more.

Where, I asked myself, had I got the idea that she was like my grandmother? Had Roger actually said that, or had I imagined it? One thing was certain: Mrs Burdett bore no resemblance to the grandmother that I knew, not in any way, shape or form.

I sat in a kind of numb, mindless state of suspended animation, dimly conscious that she was getting up from her chair and gathering her parcels together. I could smell her musky perfume as she passed close beside me. She stopped to speak to me.

"That's reely lovely on you, dear," she said, bending down so that her warm, brown eyes met mine in the mirror. "You take it! It looks a picture. Your hubby will think it's money well spent, mark my words."

I sat for a moment or two longer after she had gone, then took off the peaches-and-cream hat and replaced it carefully on its stand.

"Has modom decided against it?" the girl assistant asked, her disappointment apparent. "It really was *most* becoming."

"Thank you—no. I think not."

I stood up, smiled meaninglessly at the girl, and somehow found myself going down the stairs and out into the street.

I passed the rest of the day in a strange state of mind, feeling as if I was standing outside myself and watching myself behave quite normally. I spoke to the headmistress of the school and was mildly surprised to hear myself discussing Ellie's abilities and interests in a perfectly natural way. We bought a new paint-box for Lucy and a book for Ben, and we reached the station in plenty of time to catch the train.

Ellie seemed happy and confident. She had loved what she had seen of the school and babbled cheerfully all the way home, and seemed not to notice that I smiled and smiled and said little.

I dined alone that evening as Roger was attending a meeting of local traders followed by dinner at the Ring of Bells. I was glad of it. Normally in such circumstances I would have had my meal with the children, but I pleaded a headache and banished them to their playroom. I desperately needed to be alone, to be quiet and have time to think.

And the more I thought, the more it seemed that Roger had deceived me. Perhaps my assessment of Mrs Burdett's age and appearance had arisen entirely in my imagination, but even so, Roger had been completely aware of it. I had compared her with my grandmother more than once and he had never in any way attempted to disabuse me. Why, I asked myself? Because of all the time he had been spending recently at the Angler's Rest? Surely that could only have one significance? He was having an affair with her—*her*, that common, overblown barmaid! I should never have thought it possible—never have believed it for one moment if he had been quite open with me about her attractions. But how could I interpret his secrecy any other way?

It would explain everything: the strangeness that had developed between us, the surface politeness and kindness that had taken the place of the unique camaraderie we had shared before. And how long was it since he had made love to me in more than a perfunctory way?

I was pouring myself a sherry with a shaking hand when Mark was shown into the room by Carrie. He raised a mocking eyebrow at me.

"So! A secret drinker, eh?"

"I felt the need," I said shortly. "You'll join me?"

"Thank you." He accepted the glass from me and looked at me curiously. "Is there something wrong? You're upset, aren't you? Where's Roger?"

"Which of those questions would you like me to answer first?" I asked lightly, struggling for composure. "Roger's gone to a meeting and out to dinner, and I'm quite exhausted after a day in Oxford with Ellie."

"Ah yes—the examination! Did she do well?"

"She seems to think so."

"With every reason, I'm sure."

He sipped his sherry in silence, still regarding me with a quizzical look.

"Did you want anything special?" I asked at last, breaking the silence.

"I was passing," he said, "and felt like some lively

beneficent presence in the background. Then I remembered the rumours I had been hearing recently about his new housekeeper and his past reputation as, in Annie's parlance, a bit of a lad, and mentally I apologised to God.

"Age is a terrible thing," he said again, meditatively. "They say there are compensations. Can't see any, meself. Hope I go quickly, when the time comes."

"Please don't," I said, genuinely distressed.

"Bound to happen. No runnin' away from it."

"No, but—I shall miss you. We'll all miss you."

He cleared his throat.

"Had a good innings. Enjoyed most of it." He turned and looked at me again and for a moment I thought he was about to say something of importance. But the girls were running towards us clutching a mixture of flowers in their hands and the moment was lost.

Neither had found the meadow crane's-bill but they both were awarded sixpences for trying, and after they had thanked him ecstatically we took our leave of him.

"Did you ask him about Mrs Oliver's cottage?" Roger asked me when I recounted what had happened.

"Oh Roger, really! I certainly did not."

"All I want is a promise in writing that will hold water after he's dead."

"And I was supposed to say, 'My husband doesn't think you'll last very long, so please get your affairs in order!' That was the last thing I could have said. Somehow he seemed a little sad and lonely."

Roger sighed lugubriously. "I can't help looking at Mrs Oliver and then looking at Lord B. and wondering just which one of them is going to win the race to the pearly gates. Perhaps I should open a book on it."

"Don't be so unfeeling! Anyway, you don't know that Lord Bollinger's nephew won't sell when he inherits, do you?"

"I don't know that he will, either. He's an unknown quantity as far as I'm concerned. I just want to be *sure*!"

There was nothing I could do but counsel patience and Roger went off looking irritated. That cottage was like a nagging tooth to him.

It was on the day that Aunt Millie moved into Bridge

House, that Roger came home looking unusually abstracted. It turned out that he had seen two inns during the course of the past few days, both of which seemed suitable for his next purchase.

"Where are they?" I asked.

"One's at Long Branstead. Quite a large place—an old coaching inn in terrible condition but beautifully sited in the High Street. It's a really historic place in the traditional style with a gateway through to a courtyard. It's been in Lord Branstead's family for generations but money's short and he wants to sell. It's going cheap because it needs so much renovation."

"And the other?"

"Quite a different proposition. Small—only two bedrooms, but a garden running down to the river just twenty minutes walk along the tow-path from Oxford. It's more expensive than the other because of its position and general condition, but I have the strong feeling that it could be a gold mine."

"It's sounds more like an ale-house than an inn."

"You sound disapproving!"

I *was* disapproving. I felt strongly that the Ring of Bells had long developed beyond this, if in fact it ever could have been so described, and I disliked the idea of lowering our standards.

"Think of all those undergraduates!" Roger said.

"And think of all the competition. Oxford is full of public houses."

"Not like this one. It's outside the city—just an easy afternoon's punt along the river. It's in a village called Stavercote; just a tiny place, no more than a cluster of cottages. We could hire out punts, perhaps. Introduce musical evenings. That would appeal to the students!"

"It doesn't sound our kind of place," I objected. "I thought we were trying to build up a reputation for good food and comfortable accommodation."

"I know, I know. This inn attracts me, though. The Angler's Rest, it's called."

"I can't see why you have to expand at all," I said. "We're doing well enough with the Ring of Bells. Why take risks when you don't have to?"

company. It seems, with my unerring knack of doing the wrong thing at the wrong time, that it would have been better if I'd just kept right on passing."

"Mark, I'm sorry. I really am very tired."

"You don't laugh much any more, Jenny. Had you noticed?"

"I can't say that I had." My voice sounded strange. Oh God, I thought, I musn't cry. Not in front of Mark.

"But there is something wrong, isn't there?"

I got up swiftly and went to the table in the corner of the room to refill my glass, but my hand was shaking so much that I spilt the sherry on the cream, lace-edged cloth. I stood as if mesmerised, watching the stain spread.

Mark was next to me in two strides and took the decanter from my hand, pouring the drink for me and propelling me to the sofa where he sat down beside me.

"It might be a good idea to tell me about it," he said gently.

His unaccustomed concern was almost the end of my control and for a few moments I hesitated.

"I don't know that there's anything to tell," I said at last. "At any rate, I hope there isn't."

"Is it the business? Has Roger over-extended himself?"

"No, no." I shook my head, dismissing such suggestions, forgetting how worried I had been over his reckless expansion until his win at cards. "Mark, do you know Mrs Burdett of the Angler's Rest?"

Mark's eyes shifted away from mine and very carefully he placed his glass down on the small table by his side. There was silence in the room and I was aware of the ticking of the clock.

"Yes," Mark said, his voice almost painfully hearty. "An excellent woman. Runs the Angler's Rest most efficiently."

"Roger is having an affair with her, isn't he?" I asked.

"What on earth gave you that idea?"

"I saw her in Oxford today. She was—very different from what Roger had led me to believe. Suddenly everything fell into place—the time he spends over there, the fact that we're not close any more."

Mark was looking at me warily, one finger thoughtfully

stroking his moustache as if he was choosing his words carefully.

"You should be asking Roger about this, not me," he said. "After all, I'm not my brother's keeper."

"Then it is true!"

I realised that I had been hoping for a vehement denial from Mark; that against all the evidence, he would be able by a few authoritative words to prove to me that my suspicions were groundless. The pain that shot through me was physical, more piercing than anything I had experienced before, even childbirth. I folded my arms over my stomach and bent forward, crying soundlessly in my agony.

"Don't, Jenny, don't," Mark murmured comfortingly, putting his arms around me. I clung to him for a few moments, then, unable to keep still, pushed myself away from him.

"Why? Why?" I asked, getting to my feet and walking distractedly about the room. "Has he stopped loving me? Does he want to leave me?"

I found myself close to the fireplace and stared at my ashen face in the mirror, my hands gripping the cold stone of the marble mantelpiece.

"It's not like that," Mark said.

I turned round to face him.

"That woman," I said. "She's nothing but a common barmaid."

Mark shook his head.

"No, Jenny. That's not true. She's warm and uncritical and sympathetic."

"So am I, so am I," I cried, knowing that Mark was seeing me in all the ugliness of my grief, and not caring.

"Once you were," he said. "But not, I think, any more."

"What do you *mean*?" Furiously I ran back to the sofa on which we had been sitting and shook him by the arm. "How can you say that? Roger means everything to me—he always has—"

Mark produced a handkerchief and mopped my eyes as one would have done for a child.

"Do you remember my saying once that I envied you?" he asked me in a gentle voice which had a stern edge to it. "I

212

have not envied you and Roger for some time. Whatever the secret was of your closeness, you seem to have lost it."

"It's not my fault," I said. "He keeps me at arms' length. He tells me nothing about the business. I don't know what's going on, whether we're making money or facing ruin. All he tells me is that I musn't worry—just as if I were a feather-brained idiot with no interest in the business at all! When I think how I worked in the early days! It's so *unfair*!"

"Jenny, Jenny! Hush now, calm down a little. Look, Roger hasn't stopped loving you, I'm certain of it, and any thought of his leaving you would fill him with horror. I'm not making excuses for him. I simply think you should ask yourself what he finds with Rose Burdett that he doesn't find at home."

"I can't help being abstracted," I said. "There's been so much to think about—the children and Aunt Millie—yes, and Priors."

"Yes, yes I know," Mark said quickly. "I know I'm partly to blame, and Peter too."

"I didn't mean that, we loved having—"

"Jenny, it's no good having a heart as big as the Albert Hall if you neglect the person who's closest to you."

"That's preposterous! I've never neglected him."

"Not his bodily needs, of course; but I've seen you quite obviously *not* listening when he's been trying to tell you something, and heard you criticise him in front of others in a way you never would have done a few years ago."

I knew he was right. I knew that I was far from blameless, yet the thought of him in Rose Burdett's arms filled me with outrage and anger. I could kill her, I thought. Kill them both.

"What shall I do?" I asked Mark miserably, knowing that whatever I did it was unlikely to be anything so dramatic.

"What do you want to do?"

"I want things to be as they were." My tears started to flow again, and I took Mark's handkerchief from him in an effort to stem them.

"I'm not sure I'm qualified to give anyone advice," Mark said. "But I think you should go back to work."

"What?" I was so astonished that I removed the

handkerchief from my eyes and stared at him. "How can I? Philip is only a baby still."

"So were Ellie and Lucy and Ben babies when you worked before. You can make arrangements—hire another nurse-maid if necessary."

"But I gave up work to be with my children!"

"And has it made you happy?"

My gaze faltered.

"Roger needs you," Mark went on. "He really does. How do the children benefit from having parents drawing further and further apart with each succeeding week? Before you left the Ring of Bells you were busy and contented. Together you and Roger had something wonderful—you were equal partners, sharing everything. Now things have changed. Of course I don't know why—what outsider can possibly know what goes on between a husband and wife when the bedroom door closes? But I feel absolutely sure of this, that Rose Burdett is only a very small part of what ails your marriage. It would be quite wrong for you to blame her for everything, when it's the way you conduct your entire life that's brought Roger and you to this pass."

"But other wives don't work! They stay at home and raise their families and are perfectly happy doing so. Nobody expects more of them."

"Who is to know whether they're happy or not? To listen to you and Charlotte, one might think that no woman on earth will be happy until she gets the vote—just as if that were the panacea for all the ills of womankind. But other women aren't the point at issue. It's *you* we're talking about—Jenny Leyton, a capable, efficient businesswoman with skills that are going to waste. Aren't you aware that Roger is worried to death because the standard of the Ring of Bells has dropped since Mrs Kingsley left? Don't you know he'd give his right arm to have you back there again?"

"How could I? He never tells me anything."

"You can't have tried very hard to find out. When did you last go there?"

"Not for a long time," I admitted. "But Mark, he doesn't want me there! Surely he would have asked—"

"That's the way you wanted it, Jenny."

I frowned at him, bewildered by his words.

"That's nonsense."

"You told Roger and Roger told me that the last thing you wanted was to spend your life in an inn. As I understand it he made you a promise—"

"But that was years ago, before we were married. Everything has changed since then."

Mark looked at me with an exasperated smile on his face.

"When," he asked me, "did you actually *talk* to Roger? You both seem to have been doing your best to make sure that one misunderstanding has led to another."

"Does he really need me at the Ring of Bells?"

"I'm sure of it! Young Florrie Masters does her best, but she's very inexperienced and inclined to panic. Nothing seems as well presented and organised as it once was."

"In a way," I said slowly, "I should like to go back. It's strange, isn't it? All the time I was working I thought that all I wanted was to have a real home, right away from the hotel. But I've missed the constant interest, I can't deny it."

"Then go back."

"That wouldn't make Rose Burdett disappear, would it?"

Talking to Mark I had forgotten her, but now the pain flooded through me afresh. I closed my eyes to hold it at bay. How could he? I asked myself. How could he?

"It might very well," Mark said. "Rose is a good-natured, generous—"

"I'm *sick* of hearing her good points!" I burst out.

"I was about to say," Mark continued, "that she is not over-endowed with grey matter and the way that she continually agrees with everything that anyone says becomes very cloying. If I had to put money on it, I'd back you as the winner every time."

"*If* I go back to work! The problems would be enormous, Mark."

"Perhaps, but not insoluble. Carrie is good with Philip, isn't she? And no doubt you could get extra help in the house."

"I should hate Lucy and Ben to feel neglected," I said. "Carrie is perfectly all right with small babies but not so good with children who have minds of their own. And then there's Aunt Millie to think of."

"Jenny, surely you've lived long enough to know that problems are like Boer guerrillas—no sooner do you polish off one lot than reinforcements take their place. All you can do is deal with the current set in the best possible way."

"And how do I deal with Rose Burdett? How can I be sure Roger doesn't keep on seeing her? He's bound to, anyway, if she continues to run the Angler's Rest."

Mark pursed his lips and raised his eyebrows.

"I can only suggest that you ensure he has neither the time nor the energy," he said. He got to his feet. "I really ought to go. Will you promise me not to dissolve into tears again the moment my back's turned? It's not like you, you know."

"I don't know what I am any more," I said, standing up too. I could not find the right words to express my true meaning. It was as if Roger's infidelity had diminished me to the point where nothing seemed real, myself least of all.

He took both of my hands in his.

"You want my advice? Forget Rose Burdett. Put her from your mind. I don't believe she's important to Roger, and if you've any sense at all you'll dry your tears, climb into bed and wait for him in your prettiest nightgown."

"Mark, *really*!" I snatched my hands away.

He laughed, quite unrepentant, as he said goodbye, and I was left to think about all he had said to me.

I thought desperately, sometimes weeping in abject misery, sometimes striding about the room blind with anger. But underneath it all I knew there was much truth in what Mark had said. I huddled in the armchair and sat looking into the fire, while small, niggling doubts emerged to plague my mind.

Roger had not changed. He had blazed with his old eagerness about expanding the business and I had reacted almost with boredom. I had known from the moment that he had stood with me on the hillside overlooking Priors before our marriage, thrilling to the challenge of taking over the Ring of Bells, that he was a man who took chances—a gambler, if you like. Well, he had acted true to form. He had gambled on buying the new inns at a time when more cautious men would have held back and even though his lucky win at Watersmeet had helped us immeasurably in those early stages, I knew now that he had been right to buy. Somehow we would have managed without that windfall. Already business was improving at the Red Lion.

Not that I had found time to show much interest. The Ring of Bells, I thought with a pang—what was happening at the Ring of Bells? I had been hurt and surprised that he had not told me Mrs Kingsley was leaving, yet it had not occurred to me to enquire how Florrie was managing, so swamped had I been with domesticity. And at night, I remembered, I had turned from him many times with murmured excuses. Was it any wonder that he found Rose Burdett's uncritical company preferable to mine?

Oh, how I hated to think of them together! My anger flared all over again, but somehow the quality of it had changed. The helpless feeling of misery had gone. Now I felt strong and determined, capable of almost anything.

I would go back. It was worth any amount of effort to try to recapture the harmonious partnership Roger and I had revelled in. Somehow I would manage—would see that the children did not suffer. Aunt Millie was now more used to our maids and they were very kind to her.

Roger needed me! I was certain of it—surely the very fact that the woman he had chosen to turn to was also associated with the business proved it beyond doubt. By God, I thought, I could beat her at her own game, if it was companionship she supplied. Whatever she shared with Roger, it must surely be as nothing compared with our early struggles.

And by God, I thought, my trembling fingers already dealing with the buttons that marched down the front of my dress, I could beat her in other fields too.

By the time Roger came I was dressed in the nightgown that I normally kept for visits to friends' houses or confinements—a fine, embroidered lawn with lacy inserts at the neck; a far cry from the more utilitarian garments which had become my habitual wear in Bridge House. I was sitting in front of the dressing table brushing my hair as I waited for him, turning over in my mind whether to let him know that I knew about Mrs Burdett.

I heard his step on the stair and my heart beat faster, like a young girl. I would not tell him, I decided; not yet, anyway. Perhaps not ever. Everything would depend on the happenings of this night.

He came in softly thinking that I might be asleep but began to speak when he saw me, something casual about thinking the speeches would never end. He stopped in mid-sentence, sensing that there was something strange about me.

"You look different," he said, sounding puzzled.

"I am different." I put down the brush and looked at him over my shoulder. Wonderingly he came over to the dressing table and put out a hand to touch my hair.

"What's happened?" he asked.

I stood up and turned to face him, reaching up to twine my arms about his neck.

"I love you," I said. "You and only you, for always and always. I thought it was time I reminded you."

His arms tightened round me and we kissed like the lovers we once had been, not the matter-of-fact husband and wife we had become. I yearned for him, pouring out my love for him in my hands and my lips and my murmured words, feeling him at last draw away from me.

"Don't go—don't go," I pleaded.

"I must, you sweet idiot," he said, both trembling and laughing. "I have far too many clothes on."

But the laughter was stilled when he came to me on the bed where we had shared much love but none quite like this. For it was as if we had returned to each other from a long separation, as if every kiss and touch was a renewal of vows.

And long after our passion was spent we lay in each other's arms and talked; reassessing, explaining, assuring—closer in spirit than we had been for months. But still I did not mention Mrs Rose Burdett.

He admitted that he needed me—both like this and in a purely practical way; that the past few months had seemed lonely and arid.

"But I promised that you shouldn't have to come back unless you wanted to," he said.

"I *do* want to," I assured him. "I want to share everything

218

with you, just as we did before. I couldn't love the children more, but they're not enough. It's us—you and me, our marriage, that's central to my life."

He held me close and made love to me again with infinite tenderness and I felt certain then that there never would be any need to mention Mrs Burdett. I was so happy I felt I would die from it.

In spite of a night spent doing almost anything other than sleeping, we were both remarkably bright-eyed and cheerful the next morning and breakfast was a light-hearted meal as we explained to the children that things were going to be different from now on, since I was going back to the Ring of Bells to help their papa.

"But first," Roger said, "your mother and I are going to have a holiday—just on our own. Much as we love you all, we feel the need for a little time to be together."

"Oh, darling, how would that be possible?" I asked, delighted at the prospect but unable to see how all our many responsibilities could be shelved.

"We could go to Priors," Lucy said helpfully.

"That would be for Uncle Mark to say. He and Aunt Catherine and Aunt Charlotte might not welcome the addition of four ruffians to their household."

"Three ruffians," said Ellie, neatly slicing the top from her boiled egg. "And me."

We decided on Switzerland, since Roger felt that we could combine business with pleasure by studying the way the Swiss ran their hotels. Ben was devastated that he was not to come with us, for he had seen pictures of snow-capped mountains.

"It will be wasted on mama," he said plaintively. "She is not at all good at making snowmen."

"We must all be profoundly thankful that she has other talents," Roger replied, straight-faced, catching my eye in a way that made me aware of the fact that it was not my skill with the needle or rolling pin that he was referring to.

"Could we really go?" I asked him after the children had left for school.

"I don't see why not. Do you fancy a second honeymoon?" He reached out and took my hand.

"More than anything in the world. Oh, darling, how lovely it would be! How long can we take?"

"How long would Charlotte stand? Or should we ask Angela and John?"

"I'll talk it over with Charlotte this very day."

"If you're going to Priors, call in and have lunch at the Ring of Bells on the way back."

He bent to kiss me as he left the dining room, a kiss that was protracted long after the husbandly peck of recent months would have ended.

Once he had gone I went to Aunt Millie's room where she invariably breakfasted in bed. She looked small and crumpled, and was now more confused than ever; but one advantage of her advanced senility was that she did not mind these days who ministered to her and did not cling to me as she had done earlier.

At Priors I found Charlotte looking tired. Catherine had taken to wandering in the night, growing violent and abusive when Mark tried to get her back to bed.

"Richard Fenwick advises that she goes back to the nursing home," Charlotte said. "So having your children when you go on holiday is a marvellous idea. You know Collingford! All the tongues will wag if Mark and I are left unchaperoned."

I laughed at this. I had never heard Mark address a word to Charlotte other than to make some request or remark concerning Peter and Catherine. As for her interest in the suffrage movement, Mark treated that as if it were of no consequence at all. I wondered that she stayed to run the household of a man who was so out of sympathy with all her ideals.

"What news of the cause?" I asked.

She shrugged. "It's stalemate at the moment."

"I shall miss our weekly meetings when I go back to work."

"What nonsense, Jenny! Talking about women's emancipation is small change compared to living it."

That Charlotte had been right about Collingford's reaction to her staying alone with Mark I came to accept from a remark made the following day by Ellie.

Ben's voice, plaguing her to play with him, begging for

her attention, floated to me through the open window of the sitting room where I was writing a letter.

"Ellie," he was saying. "Shall I tell you a most awfully good riddle?"

"No, thank you." As usual, Ellie was immersed in a book.

"Ellie, don't you want to amaze your friends? 'Cos I can tell you how. It says so in my *Little Folks*."

"Ben, I'm *reading*. Go away!"

Taking pity on her I leaned through the window and told him to run upstairs and tidy himself so that he could come with me to the post office.

"Thank heaven," Ellie said, turning round from the seat outside the window to smile at me.

"Is it a good book?"

"Mm, lovely. *Jane Eyre*."

"Oh, I loved that too. It's a bit gloomy, though."

"I like gloomy stories." She seemed to hesitate for a moment, then climbed up to sit on the back of the seat so that she was nearer my level.

"Something struck me about it."

"Oh?"

"It reminded me of Aunt Charlotte and Uncle Mark. I mean, Aunt Charlotte is rather like Jane Eyre, isn't she? She's come to look after Peter because Aunt Catherine is sick in the head. And somehow I imagine Mr Rochester looking a bit like Uncle Mark—sort of dark and handsome and rather sad."

"But Jane was a very young girl and Aunt Charlotte is a lady who was once married to someone she loved, and she's only staying at Priors out of the goodness of her heart until she can go back to London to live her own life."

"Oh, she's told me all about the cause," Ellie said eagerly. "It's awfully exciting, isn't it, Mama?"

I agreed that it was, and the subject was dropped as an unnaturally clean and tidy Ben presented himself, all ready to accompany me to the post office. The exchange with Ellie gave me food for thought, though. If the possibility of an attachment between Mark and Charlotte had occurred to someone as young and innocent as Ellie, the chances of the gossips of Collingford having overlooked the possibilities of the situation were non-existent. Only I, I thought, knowing them both as well as I did, could know how ridiculous such gossip would be.

During the next few days we talked constantly of the proposed holiday, but it was relegated to the back of our minds when Aunt Millie suffered a serious fall while negotiating the small step into the garden.

Her old, brittle bones were in no state to resist the impact of the flagstones and her hip was broken in two places. Richard Fenwick was on the spot quickly and insisted on her removal to the cottage hospital where the bones were set, but he emerged from the operating theatre looking grave.

"You must prepare for the worst," he said. "Quite honestly, I don't believe she will survive this. She's so very old and frail. I shall be surprised if pneumonia doesn't develop."

"Then let me take her home," I begged. "She'll hate to wake and find herself in a strange room."

"No, I can't allow you to move her. She'll be so confused anyway that I don't suppose the room will matter to her."

I was unhappy about it but felt I had no alternative but to accept his decision. I managed to spend a great deal of time with her. For much of it she was unconscious, breathing stertorously, but at others she seemed restless, moving her head on the pillow and muttering. At these times I held her hand and she clasped mine with a grip that was surprisingly tenacious. I felt certain that she was aware of my presence.

During the afternoon of the second day she opened her eyes and looked at me, smiling with apparent recognition.

"Well, if it isn't our Eleanor!" she said, quite clearly.

For a moment I thought she was referring to Ellie, but then realised that she was confusing me with my mother. I held her hand tightly and smiled at her.

"It's Jenny, Aunt Millie."

"Our Eleanor! Well I never!" Her expression was one of delight and I forebore to correct her again. She closed her eyes, a smile still on her lips, and I thought for a moment that she had slipped into unconsciousness. But after a few moments she looked at me once more.

"He's a lovely man, Eleanor. A lovely man. Never mind your mother."

The realisation that she was talking about my father, that forgotten man who had walked out of my life so many years before, was a shock that made me catch my breath. No one had ever talked of him. I had thought of him from time to time over the years but never as a real person. He was a fictitious character to me, totally insubstantial. But I remembered the words that my mother had drilled into me.

"A proper gentleman," I said softly.

"Oh yes, he is that. Always so good to me."

She closed her eyes and slept, and some time during the next hour while I continued to sit at her bedside, she fell into the deepest sleep of all.

How strange, I thought. How very strange. That Aunt Millie, whom everyone clearly recognised had no idea and never had, should have cherished this one through the years, so strongly that her last words should have concerned him. Gerald Fitzgerald, failed actor, failed husband, failed father; but a lovely man for all that.

Curiosity stirred within me. Would I ever know the end of his story, I wondered? What happened to him? Perhaps I had judged him too harshly over the years. Perhaps he had suffered an accident, been killed before he had been able to send for my mother and me. And even if he had not—even if he had coldbloodedly abandoned us, how could he possibly have known that my mother's pride would have kept her in London, living in poverty, when she could have returned to live in comfort with her parents?

I'll never know, I thought. Yet he made me, this shadowy figure, just as surely as did my mother. It takes two, as Izzie would have said. Did I get my love of books from him? The thrill of satisfaction at a well-turned phrase, the shaft of pleasure that poetry so often gave me? It seemed likely.

I laid my hand on Aunt Millie's cheek in a gesture of farewell and gratitude, and went outside to tell the nurse of her death.

223

14

Aunt Millie's funeral was well-attended. She had lived the whole of her unadventurous life in Collingford and had been regarded with affection, but in spite of the number of genuine friends who turned out to follow the hearse, the occasion could not have been described as a sad one.

She had lived a long and, in the main, a contented life, and at the end had departed it peacefully. I heard many of her remaining contemporaries express the pious hope that their end would come in the same way. And as if to lighten even the small amount of sadness we felt, the news had come only the day before that the long, costly war of attrition in South Africa was at last over.

Aunt Millie had gone, but the young men who had left so blithely to fight for their country would be back—or some of them would. Will Mather from the smithy would never come home. His bones were resting somewhere in the Transvaal, and Robert Brass had fallen to a Boer bullet at Ladysmith. Jesse Sanders who once worked in Wisden's butchery had died of enteric fever in a prison camp. But at least the war was over and spirits rose accordingly.

We were to go to Switzerland during the last two weeks in June and the first week in July. Catherine was being taken to the nursing home by Mark on the 13th June and I gathered from Charlotte that her behaviour was now so impossible that the arrival of my brood would seem like a rest cure.

There were last minute things to do before we left. I paid a farewell visit to Lord Bollinger, now very sick and confined to his room. The Melvilles were once more back in London and he was a lonely old man, though his pleasant-faced house-keeper looked after him well enough. Sometimes I wondered if he had confided the secret of our relationship to her, for she seemed to accept it as perfectly natural that I should call upon him from time to time; however, nothing was said.

On the night before our departure we took the children over to Priors and stayed there to dine. Mark reported that Catherine had settled into her old room in the nursing home in Wimbledon, apparently happy to be back there. He, poor fellow, looked as if he had shed ten years, and the atmosphere as the four of us sat round the dining table was relaxed and convivial.

There had been a moment before dinner when I'd had a chance of a quiet word with him. Roger had gone upstairs to kiss the children goodnight and Charlotte had absented herself momentarily to check with Izzie on the progress of our meal.

"I gather," Mark said, "that your problems have resolved themselves. You look happier than when we last had a tête à tête."

"Your advice was invaluable," I admitted. "May I suggest that you apply for a position on *Home Chat*? The lady who offers help to worried readers could learn a thing or two from you."

"Hm!" Mark leaned against the mantelpiece and looked thoughtfully into the glass he was holding. "Advice comes cheap. Why is it always easier to solve other people's problems than it is to solve your own?"

"Poor Mark," I said softly. "Life hasn't been particularly kind to you."

He flashed a grin at me.

"There are compensations. I still have Priors. I beat you there, my girl!"

"So you did."

He was certainly in excellent spirits, I thought, as later I studied him at the head of his own table. As always he was arguing with Charlotte, but teasingly, his eyes bright with humour. And his talk was not solely of agricultural matters any more, but of politics and South Africa and Cecil Rhodes who had died only a few months previously, even of the prospects for the tennis championships at Wimbledon, due to open a week or two hence. It was as if he had suddenly become aware that there was a large and diverse world outside Collingford, full of interesting happenings. Charlotte had done that for him, I thought.

I was so looking forward to our holiday in Switzerland. We travelled by train from Paris to Lucerne where we had booked into a hotel for two nights. Deliberately we had left future plans vague, preferring to go where the fancy took us rather than follow a pre-arranged itinerary, and we sought out the smaller, family-type hotels which we felt would compare with our own, rather than the larger and more luxurious places.

From Lucerne we went to Interlaken, then, after a few days, up to Grindelwald on the little railway. The hotels were universally clean and comfortable. We spent interesting evenings talking to their proprietors, most of whom spoke some sort of English. In Interlaken I was even shown the kitchen and introduced to the chef who was kind enough to give me recipes for several dishes I had admired. I had sufficient experience not to underestimate this privilege, we cooks being notoriously jealous of our own specialities.

But instructive and interesting though this aspect of our trip was, it was the scenery that we loved—the heart-stopping beauty of the lakes and the mountains, and the Alpine meadows with more species of wild flowers than I could count. I loved the chalets and the faint jangle of the cow bells that floated across the valleys, and the clarity of the air, and oh, I loved Roger!

We spent the days walking and talking, making plans and dreaming dreams. I was not to think of returning to the kitchen of the Ring of Bells simply to cook, he said. I knew the business through and through; it would be my place to teach and train and organise. I would cook when necessary, of course, and could certainly relieve Roger of everything that had to do with catering, the side of the business that he knew little about. As he elaborated on his plans, I realised what an oppressive burden this must have been to him.

We would be full, equal partners again! And Rose Burdett?

As I lay in his arms, night after night, I was certain that he had forgotten her, and while there were times when I longed to mention her name—there was still a small part of me that ached to hear him assure me that she meant nothing to him—something told me to let her stay forgotten. It was in a meadow on a hillside outside Grindewald that he mentioned her himself.

226

"You know," he said. "I've been thinking."

I was lying on my back with the sun warm on my face, my eyes closed.

"I read somewhere that that's the most ominous sentence in the English language," I said lazily.

"About the Angler's Rest."

I kept my eyes closed, but he had my full attention.

"I thought next winter I would close it down altogether so that we could get on with the renovations. I know that Mrs Burdett is anxious to get back to London so it would seem a good opportunity. We can spend the time recruiting staff we can trust."

I was silent for a moment as I digested this.

"What a very good idea," I said smoothly.

I opened my eyes fractionally just enough to see his face. He was looking down at the grass, plucking a few blades nervously as he spoke, his expression serious.

"You'll miss her," I said, wickedly.

He turned his head sharply and looked across the valley.

"No," he said. "Not in the least."

I closed my eyes again. Let it rest, I thought. She's served her purpose. Who knows, without her we could have stumbled along only half-living for the rest of our lives.

We sent home a volley of postcards to the children saying how much we were missing them, but they told something less than the truth for in fact we were conscious only of each other and were blissfully content, though, as the last week drew to its close, there was a tingling feeling of excitement at the thought of getting back home and starting work again with the old partnership restored.

There was nothing in my return to the Ring of Bells to remind me of the feeling I had experienced when we had gone to the Red Lion, that I was superfluous, my talents unsought and unnecessary. From the first moment I set foot in the kitchen which young Florrie had managed to reduce to chaos I was struck, first by a pang of conscience that I had stayed away for so long, and then by fury that it had been allowed to get into this state.

I did not blame Florrie. I am sure she had tried her best, but working under Mrs Kingsley's supervision had proved very different from taking the initiative and making decisions on her own account. She seemed to greet my appearance with relief and to feel no resentment when I immediately set her about a massive cleaning operation. There was a dank, sour smell about the place that had me sniffing like a bloodhound to track it to its source. Nothing shone any more and cobwebs festooned the corners. I soon had all the maids scrubbing and polishing and sweeping and gradually the place began to seem more like the hotel I had left.

It was cheering, too, to find that the tradesmen welcomed my return.

"We never did know where we was, like," the fishmonger said to me when he called on his weekly visit.

"You should have told me," I said reproachfully to Roger when we were talking over what had to be done. "I know—don't say it! You didn't want to bother me."

Our household arrangements seemed satisfactory, much to my relief. Carrie now concerned herself almost exclusively with Philip and we had engaged another girl, Daisy, to help Mary Anne in the kitchen.

During the school holidays, Ellie, Lucy and Ben were as likely to be found in the garden of the Ring of Bells as at Bridge House. They enjoyed the life that was to be found in the vicinity of the inn; the ever-changing cast of players who trod upon the stage of our hotel, the bustle as guests arrived and others left.

There were other diversions, too. A German band came to the village and played outside the hotel and once even a shabby looking creature with a dancing bear—a poor, mangy, dispirited beast. Ben hated to see it and rushed into the kitchen to find me, almost incoherent with misery, begging me to go and tell the man that his bear was old and unhappy and should not be made to dance; and I hugged him and loved him for his sensitivity.

Ellie went off to her new school in September, returning for her first weekend brimming with importance and talking incessantly of Miss This and Miss That and the *frightful* wigging that Lottie Carisbrooke got for talking in prayers. We took her to Witney in the trap on the Sunday afternoon to catch the train back to Oxford, putting her in the charge of the guard, and on our return it became very obvious to me that Lucy's nose had been well and truly put out of joint. I found her in her room playing hospitals.

"Good evening, Nurse," I said, peering with concern at the doll she was bandaging. "And how is your patient today?"

"She has an abhorred womb," Lucy said off-handedly.

I was silent for a moment as I digested this. Lucy was peeping up at me through her thick lashes, her eyes wary, waiting to see my reaction.

"A *what*?" I asked.

"Oh, you know, Mama. It's to do with having babies. It says in the carol, 'Lo, he abhorred not the Virgin's womb' and that's why Mary was all right after Jesus was born and able to go to Egypt and everything. I heard Carrie say that Mrs Irwin had trouble with hers and couldn't even travel to Oxford."

I bit my lip to keep from laughing and did my best to impart a little knowledge of anatomy as well as the meaning of the word 'abhorred'. One thing was certain, though, I reflected as I descended the stairs. Lucy had intended to shock me. Our cherished, pink-and-white little fairy child had been thoroughly offended by Ellie's air of consequence and her increased status.

The Ring of Bells provided a welcome change of pace for me. Mercifully, Florrie's régime had not continued long enough to affect our business too much and our dining room was well patronised, especially on market day. It was gratifying to see that even more people came once it became known that I was back in the kitchen.

That Christmas we tried a new venture. On the night following the Meet when the hotel and the larger houses of the district were full of visitors, we cleared the dining room, already festively decorated, and installed a rostrum for a visiting orchestra. The old upstairs dining room was used for a buffet supper. The result was an evening which everyone voted an enormous success, not least the joint proprietors since it netted a substantial profit.

"*Most* satisfying!" Roger said the following day, rubbing his hands with glee over the account book. "There were no less than four motor cars outside, did you see? Some of the best people in the county were here."

"Snob!" I teased him.

"Not at all. It's their pocket books I'm interested in, not their pedigree. Do you realise that our bank account is in the black at last?"

I went up and kissed him.

"That's to say thank you," I told him. "Thank you for not saying 'I told you so!' I'm sorry I was such a doubting Thomas when you wanted to expand."

"There were times when I doubted myself. Jenny, don't you think you could ask your illustrious grandfather about his cottage one of these days? Surely you can persuade him that we'd let Mrs Oliver continue to live in it for her lifetime?"

I sighed.

"I don't like to bother him, Roger. He's terribly old and frail these days. Far better if you tackled Hugh Bainbridge about it."

"He's got no authority to sell property, even though he runs everything else on the estate. I know exactly what will happen. Lord B. will die and that bastard Melville will refuse to sell to me, simply because I beat him at cards. Glad as I was of the money at the time, that win could prove the most unlucky thing that ever happened to me."

"I certainly don't suppose it endeared you to him," I agreed.

His mind had moved on to other matters.

"Did you see Major Bennett's motor car?" he asked me, full of eagerness. "It was the most splendid vehicle—a de Dion Voiturette."

"Really?" I could raise no enthusiasm for the wretched contraptions. "They're horrible things to my mind. Noisy and dirty and positively dangerous."

"Nevertheless, they're the coming thing, mark my words."

He began to spend considerable time poring over advertisements for the horseless carriages that were beginning to appear more and more frequently in towns. They were still a rarity in the country, but I knew from that moment that it was only a matter of time before Roger became the owner of the first one to grace Collingford.

Change was in the air everywhere. Our oil lamps had been replaced by gas and towards the end of 1903 we had some major construction work carried out at the Ring of Bells to enlarge the entrance hall, making a reception desk with an office behind it where we could keep our growing collection of visitors' registration books, account books, and all the other records and documents that were accumulating day by day. The office was small but accommodated a massive desk which contained all Roger's private papers and a table on which stood two new acquisitions of which he was inordinately proud—a typewriter to give our letters a more business-like appearance, and a telephone. This of course meant that we had to employ someone to operate them, and before long Violet Perkins, a rather prim spinster of uncertain years, was recruited.

New headed stationery arrived from the printers. Roger had ordered it without consulting me and he brought a sheet through to the kitchen to show me after he had unpacked it. I could tell from his air of boyish enthusiasm that he was delighted.

"The Ring of Bells Hotel, Collingford, Oxon," was engraved in elegant flowing script across the top of the paper, and underneath in smaller letters: 'A Leyton Hotel— Comfort and Good Food Guaranteed'. Then in smaller letters still at the right-hand side was written 'Mr and Mrs R. C. Leyton, Joint Props' and to the left was the telephone number—'Collingford 3'.

"Oh darling, it's lovely," I enthused. "Oh, I do love being a Joint Prop. It looks terribly business-like, doesn't it?"

"What do you think of this?"

He pointed to a very small line that ran across the bottom of the page which I had missed in my excitement at seeing my own name in print. It said:

'Other Leyton Hotels include the Red Lion Hotel, Long Branstead and the Angler's Rest, Stavercote."

"What do you mean—'include'? I asked. "You haven't any more tucked up your sleeve, have you?"

"One day I will have," he said. "The best hotel in Oxfordshire."

"How's the work at the Angler's Rest coming along?"

"Very well. When can you come and see the kitchen? I want to know where you think the sink should go."

Oh, lovely, lovely! I thought. Surely it's the most important thing in the world, to feel that someone needs you, if only to determine the position of a sink.

Catherine returned from the nursing home again and seemed a little better. We dined at Priors from time to time but it was a strange situation. In her absence, the four of us had taken to playing bridge in a very light-hearted way. Now that she was back it was impossible to do so without excluding her and the cards, therefore, were never produced. Conversation was difficult, too. It occurred to me on one occasion that it was almost as if she were a guest in her own home. Going to Priors to me meant going to see Charlotte and Mark. Catherine was someone we had of necessity to put up with.

Charlotte herself mentioned the difficulties to me.

"She's so—so *uninterested*!" she said. "We try so hard to involve her in the life of the house, but it's no use. It's as if she can't be bothered. She gets very angry with us."

"Poor Mark," I said. "One feels sorry for Catherine, of course, but what a life for him!"

Charlotte said nothing and I felt that perhaps I had been tactless for after all it was Charlotte herself who bore the brunt of Catherine's strange moods and was equally deserving of sympathy.

By the end of 1905, when Roger had finally persuaded me that a motor car was essential to our business, the effect of the combustion engine on country hotels had become very marked. Other inns in the district realised too late that weekends in the country had become a craze. We had a head start. We were already larger than any of our competitors, and while their untrained maids were still scurrying about with cans of water to fill basins in bedrooms and the only sanitation provided consisted of earth closets in the yard, we had bathrooms and running water and chains to pull. During the summer season we could have filled the Ring of Bells several times over. Roger's gamble in taking on the Red Lion and the Angler's Rest paid dividends, over and over—but the fact that Lord Bollinger was now in no fit state to make any disposition of his property plunged him in gloom.

"He'll have to give someone power of attorney very soon, and who but Melville?" Roger asked. "I'll never get hold of that cottage."

Mrs Oliver, on the other hand, flourished like the green bay tree. She must have been approaching ninety at that time but was still able to take care of herself and though she seemed to shrink with every year that passed, she was spry and energetic and could still read without glasses.

"I wish you wouldn't ask her how she is in that meaningful way," I said to Roger.

"Do you think you could contrive a little wax image for me to stick pins in?" he asked. "On the other hand, there seems little point. Even if the cottage were vacant, friend Melville is unlikely to sell."

"We'll simply have to manage without it," I said.

Our visitors seemed to have no complaints. "So very quaint," they exclaimed. "Straight out of Pickwick!" And they came again and again and again.

The Christmas of 1905 was shadowed for me by the news that Lord Bollinger was sinking fast, and in the middle of January, he died.

The whole village went into mourning. Like Queen Victoria, he was an institution—an all-powerful personage whom many of the villagers had known throughout the whole of their lives.

I felt I had lost a friend whom I had missed knowing as well as I should have liked, and now never would know. I treasured memories of him, however—odd things, like his sudden smile and his warmth and kindness. He'd had the failings of his class, of course. He had seen my grandmother and had lusted after her, not caring about the consequences for her, but for all that, he was a lovable man and I knew I should never forget him.

On the day of the funeral every shop in Collingford was shut and the whole population wore black arm-bands at the very least; many were wholly in black. The more extravagant ceremonial connected with Victorian funerals had largely fallen into disuse, but for Lord Bollinger there were black-plumed horses pulling a closed black carriage which bore his flower-decked coffin.

Behind it rolled carriage after carriage as all the great families of the county came to pay their last respects, and behind the wheeled vehicles came the mourners on foot—the estate workers, the tradespeople, the ordinary men and women of the village who were genuinely sad that the old squire had at last left them, even though he had lived in a mansion and had enjoyed great riches, while they worked hard, lived in small cottages and earned little.

The bell tolled its single, doleful note as we filed into church for his commital service, and I saw more than one handkerchief wipe away surreptitious tears as the vicar, Reverend Chalmers, spoke eloquently of Lord Bollinger's charity and his concern for those less fortunate than himself. He was a countryman, Reverend Chalmers said, who understood the problems of those who lived on his estate.

The Melvilles sat, solemn faced, in the front pew. Lord and Lady Bollinger, we should now have to call them. I saw the new first lady touch her eyes delicately with a lacy handkerchief from time to time, but her husband was without expression.

"He do look a bloodless, niminy-piminy little rat," I overheard one of the estate workers whisper to another behind me. I could not find it in my heart to disagree.

"Not a patch on the old lord," his friend said.

After the service was over, I walked back to Priors with Catherine who had attended with Mark, the men following behind us. Charlotte had stayed at home. She never went to church, describing herself as an agnostic, a very bold and emancipated stand in 1906. On this occasion her abstention from church-going had proved convenient as the children had walked over during the afternoon and we had arranged to meet them at Priors for tea.

After tea, which we took round the fire in the hall, Charlotte and I withdrew a little from the others. Lucy, now twelve years old, was developing into quite an accomplished pianist and began to play for her own entertainment, very quietly so as not to disturb the men who were involved in one of their interminable political wrangles involving the policies of the new Liberal administration, which Roger supported and Mark did not. Catherine and Ellie joined Lucy at the piano. Peter and Philip had gone off somewhere on their own devices, most likely in search of Amos, and Ben—as befitted one who was about to go to boarding school and considered himself above their childish games—found a book and retreated to the window seat. He had long ago given up plagueing Ellie for her company. Girls were not in favour with him just at present—a condition which I felt sure he would eventually outgrow.

"How pretty Ellie is getting," Charlotte said to me now, looking across at the group by the piano.

"Oh do you think so?" I was delighted by the compliment. "Most people seem to admire Lucy to the exclusion of poor Ellie."

"She has good bones and such beautifully marked brows—the sort of looks that will get better and better and last even until she is quite old. She's intelligent, too."

"What sort of a world will she grow up in, Charlotte?" I said. "Will things be different for her?"

She turned towards me eagerly, putting a hand on my arm.

"That reminds me, Jenny. Can you get away on the 16th February? There's going to be a meeting in Caxton Hall in London—Mrs Pankhurst herself is going to be there and lots of other influential people. I'm determined to go! Will you come with me?"

"Oh, I'd love to," I said, then hesitated a little.

"What's wrong? Do you think Roger will object?"

"No, it's not that." I spoke with assurance, but on reflection I was not sure that I spoke the truth. He had no objection to my support for the suffragist cause, I knew, but his antipathy to the methods adopted by Christabel Pankhurst and Annie Kenney at the meeting in Manchester, where both of them had ended in jail, had been very violent. He might well be worried to think of my getting involved in that sort of hooliganism. "I was thinking more of the hotel. We have several quite large functions coming up in February."

Well before then we received a piece of news that delighted Roger more than anything had done for a very long time. I was informed that Lord Bollinger (the old lord, as everyone now called him) had bequeathed me the cottage that was attached to the inn.

"Oh, the dear, sweet, kind man," I said. "You see, he knew all along that we wanted it!"

Roger had said once that he was a born winner. I was beginning to believe it. It was, I thought, quite amazing the way that everything seemed to go in his favour—mine, too, of course. I once had longed for a fortune to lay at his feet. Well, the cottage was hardly a fortune, but there was nothing at that moment more calculated to please him. Mrs Oliver was still in residence, but like everyone else she was mortal, whatever the evidence to the contrary. Eventually she would vacate it and we could then incorporate it, as Roger had planned to do from the moment he had decided to buy the inn.

"Doesn't she have any children anywhere?" he asked me. "I seem to remember a son, back in the dim and distant past."

"There was one, I believe," I said. "But she never speaks of him. I remember my grandmother telling me that he was a ne'er-do-well—a jailbird, she said, though that could have been her exaggeration. Anyway, it's quite useless to think of him coming to carry Mrs Oliver away from here. He hasn't been near the place in all the years I've known her. You'll just have to be patient, as I've said before and no doubt will do again."

He looked pensive, but said nothing.

The day of the meeting at Caxton Hall arrived, but in the event, Roger's approval or disapproval made no difference. The numbers of the staff at the Ring of Bells were decimated by influenza, both Florrie and Roger being among the victims, and there was no question of my being able to absent myself for an entire day. Truth to tell the weather was so vile, with the rain pouring down in torrents, that I felt a guilty sort of relief that I was to be spared the journey to London.

I was frantically busy as we had a Primrose League dinner in the evening, but I thought of Charlotte at intervals throughout the day and wondered how she was faring, hoping and praying that the meeting would pass off peacefully. I could not help agreeing with Roger's view, that brawling and shouting and spitting at policemen would do little to further the women's cause. Yet the blank wall of indifference that greeted women at every turn was more than enough to induce desperate remedies.

Charlotte had promised to come to Bridge House direct from the station to report the proceedings no matter at what time she arrived and the cab drew up long after darkness had fallen. She was soaked through and exhausted and I gave Daisy her coat and shoes to dry by the kitchen range while Charlotte hunched over the fire in the sitting room, wriggling her stockinged feet to the blaze. Roger had betaken himself and his influenza to bed, and we had the room to ourselves.

"Before you say a word, you're to have a brandy," I said. "For medicinal reasons! You look chilled to the bone."

"I feel it," she admitted.

She drank a little and lay back in her chair, her eyes closed, her face white and drained.

"Oh," she sighed. "That's better."

"Have you eaten?" I asked.

"Just a little, on the train. I didn't feel like much."

"What happened?" I asked, unable to contain my curiosity any longer. "Was the meeting a success?"

She was silent for a moment.

"I don't know that you'd call it that," she said at last, her voice weary. "There was a lot of shouting and rhetoric. The Union had brought in hundreds of women from the East End who didn't have the first idea what it was all about—I'm quite sure they were lured there with the promise of free tea and buns, just to prove that we have working-class support." She sighed again. "During the meeting the word came through that there'd been no mention of votes for women in the King's Speech so we broke up and a whole crowd of us marched to the Houses of Parliament in the pouring rain to lobby M.P.s."

"What was Mrs Pankhurst like?"

Charlotte pondered the question.

"Impressive," she said. "Such burning conviction and total commitment are very catching, but I'm told that Christabel is the better speaker."

"But wasn't it thrilling?" I was leaning forward in my chair, all eagerness.

"Oh, in a way, I suppose." I frowned in a puzzled way at her response. For one who was so passionately in favour of the cause, her half-heartedness was bewildering. "Jenny," she went on. "I met several friends from my London days."

I was suddenly apprehensive. It was not a casual statement.

"They want me to go back and work for them. There's so much to be done."

"What—what did you tell them?"

"Nothing definite. I said I would think it over."

I did my best to stifle the selfish objections that were already springing to mind; Catherine, Peter—were all those problems about to arise again, just when I was so involved at the hotel?

"It's your life, Charlotte," I said. "We'll manage here somehow. Peter's older now—not a baby any more, and you've already given the Leyton family far longer than you promised in the beginning. We all know how you feel about the cause."

"Do you?" She moved her head restlessly against the back of the chair. "Then it's more than I do."

"What on earth do you mean?"

She sighed and closed her eyes, as if she were deathly tired, and for a moment she said nothing.

"I've thought and thought," she said. "All the way back on the train I thought of nothing else. Yes, of course I care about the cause—I care most passionately. But I can't leave Priors, Jenny. I just can't."

"Izzie would look after Peter."

"It's not Peter I'm worried about—well, not primarily. I love him dearly but I know he would be all right. The point is, would I? Because passionately as I care for the cause, I care far more passionately for Mark."

I stared at her with my mouth open.

"Mark!" I said at last.

"Yes, Mark." She laughed, without humour. "Haven't I disguised it well? Haven't we been clever?"

"How does he feel?"

"The same. He loves me, he says. The only thing I'm sure of is that I'm nothing without him. I couldn't bear it, not seeing him every day."

I shook my head in amazed disbelief.

"I simply can't believe it, Charlotte! You're chalk and cheese! Never in a million years would I have thought him the sort of man who would appeal to you."

"Funny, isn't it? For a long time he didn't—or at least, I told myself he didn't. I suppose I always thought him physically attractive. How could I not? He's the most handsome man I ever saw, with such vitality and charm when he chose to exercise it. But intellectually he infuriated me, with his bland assurance of male superiority. We argued— my God, how we argued, the nights we were on our own when Catherine and the servants had gone to bed."

"But then you stopped arguing?"

"No—we've never done that! It was really because of an argument that everything changed. He made me so furious that I physically attacked him—rushed up and started pounding his chest with my fists! Then before I knew it, I was in his arms, and—" she waved a hand, dismissing the subject. "I don't have to go on, do I?"

"How long—?"

"Has this been going on? You sound like an outraged husband. Four years, give or take a month or so. My only feeling now is amazement that it didn't happen much sooner."

I sighed. "Oh, Charlotte! I'm not like an outraged husband—not, in a way, outraged at all; just very sad. It's such a mess, isn't it? Do the servants know?"

"I don't think so; Izzie, perhaps—though of course, she wouldn't say. We really have been very discreet."

"Jane Eyre and Mr Rochester," I mused.

"And poor Catherine taking the role of the poor mad woman in the locked wing. She hasn't suffered from this, Jenny. You must believe me."

"I know that. You've always been wonderful with her, and Mark too. But what's to come of it, Charlotte? There's no possible happy ending to this, is there?"

"No. I'm resigned to that. But I'm going to make sure that it lasts as long as humanly possible."

"Mark will never appreciate what you're giving up for him."

"That's hardly the point, is it? I'm doing it for selfish

reasons. He's a wonderful man, Jenny. Strange and complex and not a bit the way he appears at first."

I suppose it was naive of me to be so astonished. They were both attractive people who had lived under the same roof for years, inevitably drawn together not only by their own sexuality but by so many outside forces, such as their mutual care of Peter and Catherine's unpredictable behaviour. Yet astonished I was, and also shocked to the depths of my Victorian soul, though I hesitated to admit it to someone as liberated as Charlotte.

"Don't judge me too harshly, Jenny," Charlotte said softly, breaking in on my thoughts. "How could anyone, God included, condemn a man like Mark to a life of celibacy? Catherine's a child. She gives him nothing—not love nor companionship nor comfort nor care."

"Of course I don't judge you," I said, feeling ashamed that I, with my husband and family and happy life, had fallen into the trap of doing so. "It makes me sad, that's all. It's such a waste. You and Mark could have a good life together."

She sighed and shrugged.

"That's just a pipe-dream. Meanwhile, we go on as we are."

"Be careful, Charlotte," I urged, suddenly fearful for them. "People can be very cruel."

"We're perfectly well aware of that."

"What strange creatures we are," I said, after a few moments' silence. "I thought that the one thing I wanted was to stay at home, away from the hotel—but I was wrong. I hated it! And you—your ambition was to work for the cause. But given the chance, you throw it away. Don't you envy people like Roger who seem to know exactly what they want from life and are perfectly happy when they've attained it?"

She nodded, smiling.

"Mark knows what he wants too—but the poor man hasn't much chance of getting it. He loves farming and he loves Priors and he loves me. Oh well—perhaps a total of two out of three is more than most people attain in a lifetime. Jenny, I must go. Mark will be worried."

Long after she had gone I sat on by the fire thinking about her and Mark and Catherine, and how I wished things would come right for them, until the fire died down and the room grew cold.

Sadly, I turned out the lamps and went to bed.

15

Roger's plan was to have the Angler's Rest finished and opened by May Day.

By long tradition, students stayed up all night to join in the revelries and at daybreak to hear the singing from Magdalen Tower. Many thereafter punted up the river to the Trout at Godstow for breakfast, but Roger saw no reason why others should not punt in our direction. To this end he was planning a breakfast of gargantuan proportions with free champagne thrown in to mark the opening of the Angler's Rest, and had mounted a vast advertising campaign in the local paper and around the town.

Anxiously we scanned the sky on the evening of the last day of April, desperate that the next day should be fine. We were staying the night at the Rest, which is what Roger always called it. I had overseen the preparations for the breakfast. We had been lucky enough to engage the services of a couple who seemed suitable in every way to run the inn on normal occasions, but for this special day it seemed prudent to make certain that everything was as it should be.

They were a strangely assorted couple. Edward Jepson was a slow-moving countryman who gave the impression of dogged reliability. He had worked as gardener and handy-man in the home of a wealthy wine-importer at the beginning of his working life, but had graduated to indoor work, eventually reaching the position of valet. This had meant trips to France with his master, and it was on one of their periodic visits to the chateau of one of the biggest suppliers that Edward met Marie who had a place in the kitchen there. Marie was older than Edward by a good ten years and perhaps saw eternal spinsterhood as her fate since she lived in an isolated village and met few new people. I have no doubt that it was she who decided to marry Edward rather than the other way round, and she who persuaded him to abandon service and to make a start in the hotel business.

The garden of the Rest sloped down to the river but had been no amenity to the inn in the past since it had long been neglected. Roger was altering this. A lawn had already been laid and flower beds planted. There would be punts for hire and a tea-garden where students could bring their family and friends, and Marie was already talking of a vegetable garden where she would grow courgettes and fennel and artichokes as well as the more usual beans and peas and carrots.

The rain held off, but only just. The first spots fell as the punts began to arrive at our small and recently constructed jetty, but it made no difference. The gilded youths who spilled out of them were high-spirited, not to say euphoric, and totally impervious to a few drops of rain.

More than a few of our customers were clutching champagne bottles. Other empty ones were left rolling in the abandoned punts. Were they drunk? Well, maybe, but only in the happiest, most inoffensive way. As they poured into the inn and made for the breakfast table, I felt an amused affection for them mixed with envy. If I could choose to be anyone other than Jenny Leyton, I thought, I would be young and male and at Oxford University. For although there were now female students there, they were everywhere and at all times rigidly chaperoned, and would certainly never have been permitted to carouse as their male counterparts were doing on this occasion. Plates were piled high time and time again and glasses filled, and there seemed no loss of good humour or self-control, merely uproarious laughter at the esoteric jokes.

By this time Lucy had joined Ellie at the high school and was apparently enjoying life without exerting herself. She suffered a little by being compared in her studies, always unfavourably, with Ellie, only two years ahead of her, but being pretty and popular this did not seem to worry her unduly.

She was no more than thirteen when I became aware that heads turned as she passed in the street, and not very much older when she received through the post a very bad sonnet which ended:

> Thy loveliness lights up the dreary High
> And I will love thee, dear, until I die.

"Which just shows he must be stupid," Ellie pronounced scornfully, "because the High isn't dreary. No wonder he sent it anonymously. *Anyone* knows it's the most fascinating street in the whole world."

Both the girls were supposed to be working hard for examinations, Ellie for the Senior Oxford and Lucy for the Junior. It perhaps goes without saying that Ellie found it necessary to work throughout the holiday preceding the examinations, while Lucy tossed airily aside any suggestion that some extra effort might possibly prove beneficial. She received the news that she had done badly with her usual equanimity.

"It's not your fault, Mother," Ellie said to me, having found me cast down at Lucy's results and inclined to blame myself for not taking enough time from the affairs of the hotels to make sure she was working. "Lucy just doesn't care whether she does well or not."

"But what does she want to do with her life?"

"What all the other girls want, of course—or at least ninety per cent of them. They just want to get married and have babies."

"But you want something more, don't you?"

Ellie had done brilliantly in her examinations, with distinctions in almost all of the subjects she attempted except mathematics and science. She nodded at my question, her face lighting up.

"Oh, I do—so much!"

"Oxford?"

She grinned at me. "Where else? I think Somerville rather than St Hughs or Lady Margaret Hall, if they'll have me. Oh mother, I *wish* they gave degrees."

243

"Why not go to London where they do award them?" Roger suggested reasonably on another occasion when he was present and the same topic came up for discussion.

"Oh Daddy, I just couldn't! It has to be Oxford."

I knew exactly how she felt. Roger was intensely practical and seemed not to feel this strange affinity for places; witness the ease with which he was able to give up Priors, for example. I was thankful, more often than not, for this sane outlook which was more than balanced by my own often over-sentimental attachment to people and places. And thankful beyond all things that he was the kind of father who would not raise his hands in horror at the thought of a daughter of his going to any kind of university whatsoever, as many would have done.

The major preoccupation at Priors that summer of 1908 was Izzie's romance with Bert Noakes who had returned from sea, bringing with him a parrot, a concertina, and a burning desire to settle down in Collingford and work on the land. His old father, christened Herbert but never called anything but Woolly, had worked as a shepherd at Priors for more years than anyone could remember, and he put in a word for his son with Mark.

Thus Bert became part of the Priors work force, and a popular part too. He had what can only be described as a 'way' with him. The breakfasts in the kitchen at Priors took on a new and far more entertaining aspect with Bert to tell his tall stories or perform conjuring tricks, such as producing an egg from Amos's ear. And in the evening he would sometimes be prevailed upon to play his concertina, when everyone would join in and sing.

Izzie turned round and told him until she was blue in the face that she couldn't have a day out in Oxford with him—that she was too busy, that Mrs Leyton was having bad spells, that she didn't care for towns anyway. But Bert wouldn't take no for an answer, and privately I felt sure that Izzie wanted to go with him anyway. She was simply scared to death of being let down again, of caring too much and being forced to suffer.

"I'm too old to go through that again," she said to me once.

"Izzie!" She was several years younger than I, and I was certainly not too old to enjoy life. "Izzie, just you go," I said, persuasively. "You'll have a wonderful time with Bert."

And in the end she went, and she did have a wonderful time, so she went again, and by the time the summer had come to an end she had promised to marry Bert and they were looking for a cottage.

"You ought to build some new ones, Mark," Charlotte said. There was now no pretence about the true nature of their relationship when the four of us were together. Catherine's condition had deteriorated to the point where she would never have bothered to get out of bed and dress unless Charlotte helped and encouraged her. This withdrawal was only interrupted from time to time by furious outbursts of violent temper. It was an impossibly difficult situation for them, made bearable by the fact that on occasions they could behave like the married couple that, for all practical purposes, they had become.

"I know," Mark admitted. "I've been thinking of it. They could be built up at the top of the track by the road, which would make it easier for services—water and electricity and so on." For now it was unrealistic to contemplate building a house that would have to rely on oil lamps, even though by far the largest proportion of people in Collingford would probably never use anything else in their lifetime. Mark's new cottages would not be wired for electricity at first, but they would be ready to receive it one day.

Two pairs were built up by the road and Bert and Izzie were married and moved into one of them. From that time on, it was no uncommon sight to see Bert and Amos plodding off to fish together or taking an omnibus into Witney to watch a football match. Izzie still worked daily at Priors, though one of the other maids now provided the breakfast for the farm-hands.

I was pleased for Amos's sake, for he had grown into a delightful boy and a great friend for Philip, and for Peter too. In fact the three of them were inseparable and roamed the countryside together, often on mysterious excursions that always seemed to involve quantities of mud, scratched knees and torn jerseys. They spent a great deal of time at

Bridge House, consuming vast amounts of food to appease the appetites caused by their tree-climbing, stream-damming activities. They knew just where to find the juiciest blackberries, the sweetest hazelnuts, the very first primroses.

Peter was a year older and a head taller than either of the others and naturally assumed leadership. He was a blond, good-looking boy with a great deal of self-assurance and charm, but there were times when his flashes of temper reminded me uncomfortably of Catherine. Philip admired him greatly, but in fact was able mentally to run rings round him.

We enjoyed a happy relationship with the Goughs. Roger's mother was by this time over sixty, but her health and vitality was still that of a much younger woman and although she had in some ways reverted to the forceful and autocratic manner that had so characterised her back in the days when I first knew her, her husband was always able, by a word or laugh, to cut through her pretensions and bring her down to earth. They often came to stay in Collingford, dividing their time between Priors and Bridge House. Sometimes I thought they suspected the true state of affairs at Priors, but it was not a subject that was ever raised between us.

They were both present one day when the subject of Lucy's future was being discussed. She had been causing us a considerable number of headaches recently. She had quite obviously come to the end of her useful life at the high school, though we had arranged for her to stay on one more year.

And then what? She herself would have liked nothing better than to be the daughter-at-home, occupying herself with all the frivolous, time-wasting things that most girls indulged in while waiting for a suitable husband to present himself. I had set my face against this. I was determined that she should be trained for *something*.

Then Roger's mother volunteered a suggestion. A friend of hers in Cheltenham had recently opened a kind of finishing school for young ladies which in addition to classes in deportment, musical appreciation and the like, also offered a course in commercial subjects. I thought it sounded interesting but Roger blanched at the cost of it.

His reaction was instinctive but not strictly necessary,

even though he had once again stretched our finances to the limit by the acquisition of another inn in the village of West Harley. This was an attractive place called the Rose Revived and West Harley itself was a picture-book village, with thatched-roof cottages set round a village green.

Now we had four inns under our control and staffing problems were multiplied, but all of our carefully selected managers seemed happy with the way we worked. They could never feel that they were on their own with a boss who did not care about their day-to-day worries. Roger visited each one of them frequently, never stinting his praise when he saw things that pleased him, always ready to listen to constructive ideas for improvement. Equally, he could be stern if the occasion demanded.

My function had changed considerably over the years. I had trained a cook—a young man called Alfred—who now reigned supreme in the kitchen at the Ring of Bells, but it was I who ordered the food in bulk, checked on its quality and price and arranged for its delivery to the different hotels. The furnishings were also my responsibility.

For several years we had taken a house somewhere by the sea during the summer holidays—sometimes Wales, once Torquay, and several times on the south coast in Sussex. But in the summer of 1910 Roger decided that it was time for something quite different. The Edwardian era had come to an end and we had a new king on the throne. The Liberals were back in power in a government which included four Labour Members of Parliament. Times were changing, Roger said, and it was high time for us to become more adventurous. He proposed that he should drive to Cornwall in the car, taking Ben, Philip and Peter with him, while the girls and I took the train.

"I never heard the like of it," Mrs Oliver said to me when I was telling her of the proposal. "That Mr Roger, he always was a reckless boy. Where was it you said you was going?"

"Cornwall," I told her.

She shook her head, her wizened nutcracker little face a network of lines.

"That's a powerful long way away, I reckon. Further than London, is it?"

247

"Quite a bit," I said.

"Never been further than Oxford m'self," she said. "Nor never felt the lack of it. Still, times are changing. You young people are all alike—gadding here and gadding there. What your grandmother would say, I can't imagine."

"I can," I said, and we both laughed, for although Mrs Oliver was ancient she had all her wits about her.

It was a major operation to organise the packing and the distribution of the luggage. Roger was unable to take much in the motor car with him as it was necessary to take a large supply of petrol as well as every conceivable spare part. They were to take three days over the journey, and Scott of the Antarctic could not have taken more time in planning it. Needless to say the boys were wildly excited, while I was full of foreboding. Cornwall seemed such a great distance to drive and the perils of motoring no less frightening for being incalculable.

We were woken early on the morning before the day they were due to leave by a thunderous knocking on our front door. It was the village policeman, Noah Dandridge—a plump man with a fringe of ginger whiskers framing his round face.

"In a terrible state," Mary Anne told us, rushing upstairs to summon Roger to go and speak to him.

It could only be some disaster at the Ring of Bells, we thought, and Roger was halfway down the stairs before she had finished speaking, pulling on his dressing gown as he ran.

Collingford was a law-abiding village. Noah rode slowly and majestically around the lanes on his bicycle and never found much in the way of crime to disturb the even tenor of his ways. Never before had he encountered a crime such as the one he was describing in detail to Roger. He was halfway through his story by the time I joined them downstairs.

"It's Mrs Oliver," Roger said to me, interrupting him. "You'd better put some clothes on and go up there."

"What's happened?"

"There's been a breakin' and a henterin'," Noah said. "No call for Mrs Leyton to go up there—she can't do nothing for Mrs Oliver. Stone cold dead, she is. The doctor's there now."

I gasped in horror.

248

"Noah, how dreadful! What happened?"

"Looks like some ruffian broke her back window and got in that way. The whole house was ransacked."

"And he *killed* her?"

Collingford had never known anything like this before.

"Stone cold dead," Noah repeated, with a certain grim satisfaction. "What we was wondering, Sir, is whether you'd come up and see if the thief got into the Ring of Bells at the same time. Seems strange, like, bothering to go into a poor old lady's cottage, and leaving the hotel. She couldn't have had much in the way of savings."

Roger could find no sign of illicit entry at the Ring of Bells and there was nothing missing, as far as we could see. In the cottage next door it was a different story. Stuffing had been pulled out of an armchair that was overturned and the contents of drawers were scattered over the room. While we were there poor Mrs Oliver's body was removed to the cottage hospital for a post-mortem.

Richard Fenwick came into the Ring of Bells for a cup of coffee before proceeding on his way, so angry that he found it impossible to keep still.

"Of all the miserable, petty, pointless crimes," he said. "What could she have had there? A few pounds, perhaps? Something tucked away under the mattress?"

"How did he kill her?" I asked. "Would she have suffered?"

"There weren't any visible marks. Of course we won't know for sure until after the post-mortem, but it's my guess that she was literally frightened to death. A little old lady like that—she must have been terrified out of her wits to find a stranger had broken in."

"It's horrible," Roger said. "Horrible! But *why*? Why Mrs Oliver? It wouldn't have been any more difficult to break into the Ring and he'd have been more likely to find something worth stealing there."

Richard shook his head.

"It's beyond me," he said. "Absolutely incomprehensible. You'd better make sure that Noah keeps a watchful eye on this place while you're away, Roger."

He finished his coffee and left us.

"That's a good point," Roger said. "I hardly like to leave at all if there's a maniac like that in the village. Are there strangers about, do you know? Any travelling tinkers?"

I shook my head.

"I haven't seen any. What can Noah do all on his own? Roger, perhaps we shouldn't go."

"The boys would die of disappointment!"

And so would you, I thought.

It was a perfect holiday. I loved walking with Roger, as always planning and dreaming. Shocked as we had been by Mrs Oliver's death, it was impossible not to welcome the thought that the cottage was now empty and that at last Roger could implement his plan of incorporating it into the Ring of Bells. But also I revelled unashamedly in the rare luxury of being alone occasionally with nothing to do except relax and enjoy the sight of the sun glinting on the waves, listening to the cry of the gulls and the humming of the bees among the lavender bushes close by the little terrace.

You're a fortunate woman, I told myself, as I sat and basked in the sun. I knew I was smiling for I was thinking of Roger and Ellie and Lucy and Ben and Philip; and the Ring and the Rest and the Rose and the Lion. Fortunate, indeed! What else was there in life to wish for?

Priors!

No! My eyes flew open. That was a mistake—a mental aberration. I did *not* want Priors. I had long ago got over my longing for it. I had more than enough for any woman and it was wicked even to harbour the thought unconsciously. No good would come of a thought like that. Please God, I thought, forgive me. I didn't mean it—I was half-asleep, not responsible. I got up and went in search of tea. Idleness obviously did me no good at all.

By the end of the fourth week we were all ready to go home, much as we had enjoyed our stay in Cornwall. Ellie was looking forward eagerly to Somerville. Lucy faced her return to school for one last year with resignation. Ben would be going into the sixth form at Glenthorne, his public school, and Philip would be going away for the first time to the same preparatory school that Ben had enjoyed and where Peter had already been for the past year. They were hardly children any more. And there was a sprinkling of silver in Roger's hair. Where were the years going to? I wanted to put the break on—to catch them as they flew.

Our respective arrivals had been carefully orchestrated to coincide and miraculously both parties returned to Bridge House within an hour of each other. It was good to be back again—to smell the unique atmosphere compounded of pot-pourri and beeswax and leather that added up to home. But there was, I thought, something a little guarded about the way Mary Anne greeted me.

"Is everything all right?" I asked her. "What's the news of Collingford? I feel as if I've been away for years."

"Everything's much as usual, m'm," she said, her eyes lowered.

I looked at her, a little puzzled.

"Are you sure there's nothing wrong?" She was normally a cheerful creature and her manner was strangely remote.

"Quite sure, m'm," she said.

"Have they found the man that broke into Mrs Oliver's cottage?"

"No, m'm. Nothing's been heard."

"And there have been no other incidents?"

"No, m'm."

She spoke politely enough but there was something in her manner that I could not account for. Probably some kitchen quarrel, I thought. She had no doubt had some sort of disagreement with Daisy or Carrie. It would blow over.

I was anxious to contact Charlotte again after such a long absence and to hear the news of Catherine. I was thankful that they had at last installed a telephone at Priors and I put through a call as soon as I had finished in the kitchen.

Charlotte answered the telephone, sounding distracted.

"Thank heaven you're back," she said. "Jenny, we must talk—the sooner the better. Can you possibly come over this morning? I don't like to leave Catherine."

"What's the trouble? Is she giving you a bad time?"

There was a pause before Charlotte answered me, during which I could distinctly hear the heavy breathing of Mrs Harmsworth who operated the local telephone exchange, no doubt hanging on our every word. It was quite impossible to have a confidential chat under the circumstances.

"Never mind," I said. "I'll call in later and you can tell me then."

Charlotte thanked me and rang off.

I walked up the High Street in the sunshine feeling a joyful sense of homecoming in spite of being slightly apprehensive at what Charlotte had said.

For almost thirty years now I had felt a shaft of pleasure at the sight of the stone gables and eaves, the funny crooked windows that made up Collingford. There were alleyways down which it was possible to catch a glimpse of a cottage garden blazing with flowers. There were swinging inn signs and a barber's pole. It was good to exchange greetings with people I had known for years and to catch up with the news of the village—to hear of a new grandchild for Mrs Barlow and to see Mrs Archer's son home from the Navy. And if people seemed less inclined for gossip, more in a hurry to pass on than they sometimes did, I thought nothing of it. It was Monday morning, after all—washing day for most, with more than enough work to occupy anybody.

I turned into the grocer's shop and handed Mr Reid my list, agreed that it was a lovely day but that the gardens could do with some rain, and was about to leave when I came face to face with Miss Parsons—a thin, dried-up little body who had on several occasions made dresses for me and also for Charlotte. She was a pillar of the Methodist Church, but not the kind of Christian whose faith appeared to fill her with joy.

I greeted her civilly and said that I hoped she would be free to make me some new clothes before the autumn.

"I'm too busy to oblige," she said sourly, and turned her back on me.

The rebuff left me with my mouth open in amazement, for I knew that she depended on her dressmaking for a living and until that point had been most eager to work for us. Mr Reid, obviously embarrassed, turned away to wrap butter with a great deal of energy and attention.

I left the shop and ran slap into the arms of Mrs Chalmers, the vicar's wife and one of the members of the Ladies' Literary

Society. She was large and overpowering; a lady given to flowing dresses and gushing speech, but one who possessed a heart of gold.

"My *dear* Mrs Leyton," she said, almost embracing me there on the pavement. "How lovely to see you home again."

"Thank you," I said, a little overwhelmed by the warmth of her greeting and the throbbing, meaningful way it was delivered. "It's always wonderful to be back, however pleasant the holiday."

"I want you to know," she said, lowering her tone to a more intimate level and looking intently into my eyes, "that if there's anything I can do, you have only to ask. Life is difficult, we all know that, and there is more than one side to every question. Far be it from me to cast the first stone." She lowered her voice still further before she continued. "And as for the question of Mrs Oliver—well, of course, it's all quite unthinkable. My husband was moved to preach on the subject of malicious slander last Sunday."

I looked at her in total bewilderment, and as she billowed away, I went on my way towards Priors deep in thought.

Roger was being blamed for Mrs Oliver death, I felt quite sure of it. He had never made any secret of the fact that he hoped one day to get his hands on the cottage; even if he had never mentioned it, it would have been obvious to anyone that the inn would benefit by incorporating it as part of the hotel. But surely no one in his right mind could possibly think that he would break into an old lady's home and frighten her to death? It simply did not make sense. No one who knew him could give any credence to such a preposterous idea.

"What *is* going on?" I greeted Charlotte. "Why am I being treated like some social leper? Is it about Mrs Oliver?"

"I have heard talk," Charlotte said guardedly. "But I think there's a little more to it than that. Our secret's out, Jenny—Mark's and mine."

"How?" I asked.

"Izzie."

"*Izzie*? I don't believe it! She wouldn't gossip."

"Oh, she didn't mean to. She just got angry and turned round and told 'em." Charlotte tried to laugh, but there was little humour in it.

"What happened exactly?"

"Mark took on a man from over Banbury way who turned out to be a cousin of your Mary Anne. He was a lazy, good-for-nothing creature—a work-shy sort of man, not in the least like Mary Anne—and after several warnings, Mark dismissed him a couple of weeks ago.

"It seems he went straight round to see Mary Anne to vent his spleen against Mark and evidently made some very foul accusations against Mark and me, not only alleging that we were lovers but that we treated Catherine cruelly and had driven her mad between us. You can imagine it, perhaps. Well, who should walk into the kitchen at the crucial moment but Izzie, returning a pair of Philip's gum boots he had left here, and she happened to overhear part of this conversation. She was incensed, of course, and leapt to our defence. But you know Izzie—she managed to say just that little bit too much! Lovers we might be, she said, but Catherine had never had anything but kindness from either of us."

"Oh dear!"

"Exactly. The poor woman's distraught about it, of course, but as you can imagine the fat is in the fire with a vengeance. Collingford is now sitting in judgment in no uncertain way."

"Oh Charlotte, I'm so terribly sorry."

She laughed a little.

"It's all so stupid," she said. "Why should any third person excite themselves about the relations between a dull, middle-aged couple like us? Seven years ago we might perhaps have been juicy subjects for scandal—but now? Well, even illicit passion cools just a little! We're a settled, unexciting married couple in everything but law."

I lifted my shoulders helplessly.

"I'm so sorry," I said again. "Does it make life difficult for you?"

"Very. I try not to mind, but I can't walk into the village now without being conscious of faces peering at me from behind curtains, just as if I'd suddenly sprouted two heads. Of course, it's only what people expect, isn't it? I'm a suffragist, an agnostic and an adultress."

"What does Mark say?"

"Can't you guess? To hell with the lot of them, of course. Let them say what they like, he says. But he doesn't have to shop in the village. It's Peter I'm worried about, Jenny. I should hate him to hear the gossip—he's far too young to understand. He adores Mark and I couldn't bear to be the one to come between them."

"He'll be back at school in under a week. What about Catherine?"

"Oh yes—Catherine! What a way to welcome you back, Jenny. Nothing but bad news and miseries. Catherine suddenly seems to have started drinking. We have very little in the house and anything we do possess is under lock and key, but she's getting it from somewhere."

"I feel so helpless! There doesn't seem to be anything I can do or say."

Before either of us could say more there was a tap on the door and a little maid brought in the midday post. Frowning, Charlotte studied the envelope that was offered to her.

"How odd," she said. "Who on earth can this be from? The writing is practically illegible."

She was slitting it open with a paper knife as she spoke, and as she read it, her expression changed from one of mild interest to sheer horror.

"Oh God," she whispered, grasping the flimsy sheet of paper until her knuckles showed white. "Oh God, how horrible."

She passed the letter across to me. In uneven capitals was written:

A hundred years ago you would of been burned for the evil witch you are driving a poor woman out of her mind and fornicating with her husband God will surely smite you.

There was, naturally, no signature. All colour had drained from her face. She looked sick, physically ill. I threw the letter down on the table between us.

"It's horrible! Ignore it, Charlotte. No one who really knows you can believe such a thing."

With shaking hands she took it up and read it again, then

255

tore it into small, confetti-like pieces, her mouth twisted with distaste.

"You should have shown it to Mark," I said.

"Never—I couldn't. Not such an ugly, horrible thing—not after all he has done for Catherine."

She got to her feet and began to walk restlessly about the room, twisting her hands. "There's only one thing for it, Jenny," she said. "I'll have to leave. Catherine will have to go back to the nursing home. Peter doesn't need me any more."

"And Mark? Doesn't he need you?"

She said nothing for a moment but leaned by the window looking out at the green fields in front of us.

"Perhaps he needs Priors more," she said at last.

We were both silent for a few moments. Suddenly I recalled the cryptic words of Mrs Chalmers.

"Charlotte, you say you've heard talk about Mrs Oliver's death. In heaven's name, what? I quite clearly got the impression from Mrs Chalmers that somehow people are connecting us with that."

Charlotte sighed heavily.

"Villages!" she said. "Are they all the same, or is Collingford worse than most? People are so ready to believe the worst. One of your customers—heaven alone knows which one—suddenly remembered that Roger was making a few enquiries about the whereabouts of Mrs Oliver's son a while back, just after you inherited the cottage. He was asked why, and Roger replied that he'd give a lot if she could be persuaded to vacate the place, and surely at her time of life her son should be prepared to give her a home."

"And that's all?"

"Well evidently the cricket team was present at the time and a few stupid jokes were made about ways of making her move. Someone suggested putting a sheet over his head and haunting her, and someone else thought that burying a dead cat under a floorboard might make her leave. All in the worst possible taste as things turned out, of course, but humorously meant at the time."

I closed my eyes in exasperated resignation. I could see it all. I had heard the cricket team—yes, Roger as well as the others—making silly jokes, outdoing each other, always someone ready to cap another's witticism.

"So Roger's cast as the villain of the piece, is he?" I said wearily. "Who could really think that he broke into the cottage?"

"I don't think anyone thinks that he did it himself. He is supposed to have incited a person or persons unknown. And Jenny—you might as well have it all. After all, things could hardly be blacker all round. There's talk about you, too."

"Me?"

"You and Lord Bollinger. It's said that you wormed your way into his affections, just so that he'd leave you the cottage. His housekeeper has been proving herself far from the pleasant creature that everyone thought."

I had been standing up preparatory to leaving, but at this I sat down again.

"Will you take it amiss," I said faintly, "if I head straight back to Cornwall?"

16

Roger, of course, said exactly the same thing. No one who knew either of us could believe such lies, he said, and the only course of action was to ignore them.

I dismissed Mary Anne. She had been with us a long time, but I could not forgive her for spreading the wicked gossip about Mark's and Charlotte's treatment of Catherine, when she knew full well that the problems suffered by Catherine had begun long before Charlotte had appeared on the scene.

Roger said it was the wrong thing to do and as usual he was proved right. Public opinion swung against us and there were many in the village who spoke coldly to me or refused to speak at all. We appeared to change overnight from the popular licensees of the best hotel in Collingford to social pariahs, and trade suffered accordingly.

I was able to bear it for those who were our true friends remained so, and I cherished the hope that sooner or later the mystery surrounding Mrs Oliver's death would be cleared up, and that Roger would be vindicated. For Charlotte things were far worse. As she had said, she had always been regarded with suspicion and Collingford seemed only too ready to believe any enormity.

The mother of Molly, the little maid at Priors, marched up to the back door in a positive fury of self-righteousness to snatch her daughter away from this den of iniquity, and Meg, who had taken over the provision of the farm breakfasts, gave notice that she was leaving at the end of the month. Charlotte found it impossible to replace them.

Should she go into a crowded shop, silence fell. Cold, inimical stares followed her down the High Street. Worst of all, the letters continued, the abuse growing more virulent on every occasion.

In November of that year a tragedy occurred which shocked us all.

Only a few miles from Collingford was a small hamlet called Little Tissington, unremarkable except in one particular. It possessed a truly magnificent church dating back to Norman times. It was not large, but was of considerable historic interest with unusually decorative panelling. We awoke one morning to hear the appalling news that it had been razed to the ground and that militant suffragettes in the area had been responsible.

At first I refused to believe it. It was too monstrous, too pointless; there had to be some other explanation. But little by little the indisputable facts emerged. Canvas and tow soaked with paraffin had been placed at strategic points around the church; under the organ, in the bell-tower, under the ancient carved pews. Securely fastened to a gravestone in the churchyard was the message:

To the Government Hirelings and Women Torturers.

Let the Church follow its own precepts before it is too late. Blessed are those who suffer persecution for the sake of justice, for theirs is the Kingdom of Heaven. No surrender!

Tied around the stone was a length of material in the colours of the Women's Social and Political Union.

"How could they, how could they?" I demanded of Roger, moved almost to tears by this wanton desecration. "What on earth could they hope to gain? It was a wicked, wicked thing."

My opinion was, of course, echoed in all quarters, and even Charlotte who had been so sunk in her own problems that those of the outside world seemed remote, was roused to fury.

"It's those *damned* Pankhursts, inciting violence the way they do," she raged. "We'll *never* get the vote this way! This has probably set us back years."

But of course, in the eyes of Collingford the whole incident was Charlotte's fault—for had she not preached women's suffrage at open-air meetings on the green? Had she not distributed its literature, walking miles to stick copies of the latest pamphlets through every letter box in Collingford? What did the ordinary countryman know of the difference between the militant tactics of the WSPU and the more pacific approach of the NUWSS, which Charlotte had long since chosen to support? They were all mad, weren't they? All tarred with the same brush?

Driving back from Bridge House one night shortly afterwards, Mark and Charlotte saw a glow in the sky and realised with a sickening sense of horror that it came from Priors.

Bert and Izzie were already running down the track towards the house together with workers from the other three cottages close by. It was a barn that was burning, not the house itself, and the blaze was under control before the fire brigade arrived on the scene. No very great damage was done, though Mark was grieved that he had lost the winter feed for his beasts and that the barn itself would cost close on a hundred pounds to repair. The aftertaste of the incident was bitter.

"How can they hate us so much?" Mark asked, looking baffled. "I'm the same man as I always was. Neither of us has changed, and nothing we have done has hurt anyone."

"It makes them feel better," Roger said cynically. "It takes their minds off their own grubby, sordid little sins."

"But to fire a barn! Why, in heaven's name? Any amount of damage could have been done."

"Mark, you know very well why." Charlotte's head was resting on her hand. She would not look at him. "And you know what must be done. I must go away."

"No!" Mark slapped his clenched fist into the palm of his hand. "Damn it, no! I won't give in to them whoever they are. There must be some sort of redress. Maybe the police will find out who's responsible."

But the police got nowhere and it was hard to ignore the suspicion that they were not over-exerting themselves.

As if affected by the atmosphere, Catherine grew worse. With only Izzie in the house, it was almost impossible to keep a close watch on her all the time and it became increasingly obvious that someone, somewhere, was supplying her with liquor. It was strange that one so lethargic, who had apparently taken no interest in life for years, could prove so devious and energetic in procuring the drink for which she now craved.

When she was drunk her eyes glittered and her temper was ungovernable. One winter's evening when Izzie was lighting the lamps in the hall, she heard a strange hissing noise behind her and turned to find Catherine with wild hair and eyes, a kitchen knife raised in her hand. Fortunately for us all she remained calm and talked gently to Catherine until Charlotte, who was upstairs, came down and took in the situation with one horrified glance and was able to come up behind Catherine to disarm her.

It was a situation which could not continue, and once more Mark took her to London, to the nursing home in Wimbledon where she had always been looked after so well and where her relations would be able to visit her.

Now that Catherine was removed from her care, Charlotte felt she had no alternative but to go away and planned a visit to other relatives in Somerset. She did not say so, but I felt that this was to be a kind of trial—to see if she could, in fact, live without Mark or he without her. Christmas was only days away, however. Peter was due home, so rather against her better judgment she agreed to stay until after the festivities were over—not that the adults had any heart for them.

Ellie was loving Oxford. Already she had become involved in the debating society—the Somerville Parliament, based strictly on Westminster lines—and although I gathered that she had not yet summoned enough self-confidence to speak herself, she attended every one of the debates and was becoming politically aware.

She was full of indignation concerning a meeting that she had attended at which Keir Hardie had addressed—or attempted to address—his patrician audience. The undergraduates had refused to give him a hearing and had behaved disgracefully, pelting him with tomatoes and eggs.

"*Men!*" Ellie said in disgust. "Do they call that democracy? It's so absolutely typical of them—just exactly the same reaction they have to any talk of women's suffrage. They're terrified of the working classes, just as they're terrified of women. So come on, boys—don't bother to listen! Just jeer and mock and throw things."

"There's a letter in the *Chronicle* that would interest you," Roger said, lifting his eyes from the paper one breakfast time. "A Colonel Fanshawe gives it as his opinion that the vote is too strong a wine for women—that they will lose their femininity and modest self-restraint, and that in their own interests the vote should be withheld from them."

"I'd like to boil him in oil," Ellie muttered darkly.

"Come, come, my dear. Where is your modesty and restraint?"

"Lost somewhere between here and Holloway Gaol."

I looked at her in consternation.

"Ellie, you wouldn't—"

"Not if I can help it, Mother. I hate violence as much as I hate bigotry."

This, at least, was a relief. I had imagined that perhaps the charismatic presence of Christabel Pankhurst, who had also spoken in Oxford during that eventful first term, would have its effect on Ellie; but apart from thinking that she was an effective and sincere speaker, she seemed to have avoided falling completely under the spell of this woman who was adored to the point of idolatry by so many.

We did not greet 1911 with a great deal of enthusiasm.

The children scattered once more to their various places of

education and Charlotte made definite plans to go away. I was with her one January day at teatime, toasting muffins by the fire. The curtains were drawn against the chilly, relentless rain that had brought a premature darkness to the afternoon. We were in the small sitting room as the hall was much too draughty on a day like this and were talking over arrangements for her departure when we heard the telephone ringing in the distance.

"Izzie will answer it," Charlotte said. "She's terrified of it, but at least she's schooled herself to pick the thing up and speak into it."

There was a tap on the door and Izzie looked into the room. "Excuse me, Mrs Mannering, I think you'd better come," she said, her manner agitated. "There's a telephone call from London for Mr Leyton, but I can't make head or tail of it, the line's that bad."

"London?"

That surely could mean only one thing. Catherine. Charlotte went swiftly from the room and I rose from my knees by the fire to follow her. Through the open door I could hear the raised pitch of Charlotte's voice, though could not distinguish the words, and full of disquiet I went out into the hall.

"But surely," she was saying, "you must have *some* idea? No, Mr Leyton isn't here. I'll send for him at once. Have you tried her relatives in London? You have their address, I'm sure. Well, if she's not there, the police *must* be notified! The reputation of your nursing home is of minor importance, Matron—it's Mrs Leyton I'm thinking of. Yes, I'll get him to ring the moment I can find him."

She hung up the receiver and turned round to look at me. "She's gone," she said. "Vanished. No one knows how or when or why."

"Surely that's impossible! I thought the whole idea was that she was constantly supervised."

"She was supposed to be. Nevertheless, she's gone."

"Do they think she's making for home?"

"She had no money and only indoor clothing. And the weather is as bad in London as it is here. Jenny, she'll freeze, she'll be soaked to the skin! Izzie, can you please try to find

262

Mr Leyton? I'll go and look in the stables if you'll find someone to go further afield. I've simply no idea where he might be."

Izzie ran into the kitchen and Charlotte was shrugging into a raincoat when Mark strode in having been caught in the yard by Izzie even before she had needed to leave the house. He returned the call to the nursing home at once, fidgeting and pacing round the hall in his mud-soaked boots until it came through, cutting off the bell after one short, shrilling ring.

"Matron, is that you?" he barked. "Am I through to Whitelands Court? This is a terrible line! Matron, this is Mark Leyton here. What is all this about my wife?"

He listened closely, his face dark with anger. After a few peremptory remarks he slammed the receiver down.

"My God, the incompetence of it! How much do I pay them, just to look after her—just to see that she's safe and well? I don't expect them to cure her. I don't ask for miracles. Just simple, kindly effective care. Charlotte, I'll have to go up there."

"Yes, of course. I'll put some things together for you." She ran up the stairs leaving me in the hall with Mark. He looked at his watch.

"There's a train at ten minutes past seven from Witney, isn't there? I must wash and change but I should be able to catch it."

"Roger can take you in the car," I said. "He's in Collingford today, I know."

"Thanks. That would be a great help."

He stood for a moment, his face bleak. It was as if he were trying to summon sufficient energy to galvanise himself into action.

"Mark, I'm so very sorry," I said. "Surely she can't have gone far—not on a night like this."

"No." He took a breath and pulled himself together. "You'll ring Roger for me?"

"Yes, of course. You go and get ready."

He walked slowly and heavily up the stairs as if every step were an effort and I watched him go, seeing in my mind's eye the young man he had once been, leaping up the staircase two at a time, full of liveliness and vigour.

I reached for the telephone and asked for the Ring of Bells. There was a suppressed air of excitement about Mrs Harmsworth's voice as she answered me.

"I hope there's nothing wrong, Mrs Leyton," she lied, her voice greedy for sensation.

"I think not," I replied glacially, and quite uselessly. She quite certainly knew as much as we did about the affair and so, shortly, would everyone else in Collingford. How, I wondered, would they twist matters to make it appear Charlotte's fault? For I felt quite sure that somehow they would find the ingenuity to do so.

"Can you bring the car to Priors at once?" I asked Roger.

"What's the trouble?"

"I'll tell you when you get here. Just hurry."

He did so and was soon on the way to the station with Mark. I insisted on Charlotte coming back with me to Bridge House, she looked so forlorn and abandoned as they drove away.

"Was there ever such a time as this?" she asked, as later the three of us were at dinner. "One wonders if it can possibly get any worse."

"On the basis that it can't," Roger said, "the builders are starting work incorporating the cottage into the Ring of Bells. Popular opinion is so much against me that there seems no point in putting it off. They might as well say all they have to say and get it over."

"Is business bad?" Charlotte asked. She and Mark had been so weighed down by their own problems that we had refrained from talking too much of ours. Roger and I now exchanged a rueful glance.

"Worse than it's ever been since the day we opened, but no doubt we'll survive," he said. "Anyway, it all pales into insignificance beside this latest caper of Catherine's."

"She surely must be found quickly," I said. "A woman like that—just in a dress, with slippers on, no proper outdoor clothes. Someone will notice her and see that there is something wrong."

"I have a terrible feeling of—of crisis." Charlotte looked gaunt with worry. "As if whatever happens, this will bring things to a head."

"You need a holiday," said Roger. "Both you and Mark are absolutely worn out. You should go somewhere miles away from Collingford where the sun is shining and you can forget all the beastliness of the past few months."

"And who'd look after the farm?"

"I would," Roger said. "I wasn't a bad farmer in my time, you know—I'd probably be one still if it weren't for the influence of this woman here. There I was, perfectly happy in the midst of all my sheep and cows, until she snared me and dragged me behind the bar of the Ring of Bells."

"A travesty of the truth if ever I heard one!"

How terribly bright we were being, I thought. Whistling in the dark, nothing more, both making a desperate attempt to be cheerful. I was hardly surprised that it did nothing to lift Charlotte's depression.

"If anything happens to her," Charlotte continued, "my position in Collingford would be completely untenable. Instead of merely being suspected of being a witch, the case would be proved beyond doubt."

We both spoke soothingly and assured her she was wrong; but she looked unconvinced by our words and so, if the truth were to be known, was I.

We telephoned for news the following morning, but found that although Catherine was still missing, the picture had changed a little. It had been discovered that one of the domestic staff had confessed to pawning a brooch for her in return for a proportion of the money received.

Mark was furiously angry at this disclosure and talked of legal proceedings against the nursing home; they, in their turn, had instantly dismissed the maid and were moving heaven and earth to find Catherine without publicity in order to preserve their good name.

"I'm totally amazed that she could have done something that needed so much organisation," Charlotte said when we were discussing this latest turn of events. "Still less to have stirred herself to run away."

"It's the same sort of cunning that she used to get hold of the liquor," I said. "You never did find out how she did that, did you?"

"No. Nor who supplied it." Charlotte sighed wearily.

"She wasn't sensible enough to take a coat with her, though."

"Did Mark say what the police are actually doing?"

"Combing Wimbledon Common, apparently."

"With money she could have gone further afield—up west, anywhere. Your relations live in Putney, don't they?"

"Yes, but Mark says she isn't with them. They haven't heard a word from her."

I thought back to my early days in Fulham, now long distant. Surely I was right in thinking that Putney was not so far from Wimbledon Common. Catherine might have been able to see the main road from her room—I was sure that Mark had mentioned that the house stood close to the road. Suppose she had seen buses passing with 'Putney' written on the front? Might it not have put the idea of going to her relations into her mind? I suggested as much to Charlotte.

"I suppose it's a possibility," she admitted. "But the motor bus from Wimbledon passes nowhere near their house."

"She may not have known that. If she just saw the destination—"

"Should we suggest it? Wouldn't they have thought of it? I don't like to keep bothering Mark."

"Perhaps it would be wrong not to explore the smallest possibility."

"I'll ring again," Charlotte said, suddenly making up her mind.

The call came through after a wait that seemed endless and even then it was impossible to speak with Mark as he was out on the common with the police. Charlotte asked to speak to the matron.

"Tell Mr Leyton to try Putney," she said. "It was a sudden thought. Mrs Leyton might perhaps have caught a motor bus to try to find her aunt and uncle. It's possibly a wild-goose chase, but I thought it best to make the suggestion."

Having made the call there seemed little we could usefully do, yet it was equally impossible to settle to anything else. There were things that needed my attention at the Ring of Bells, but I did not like to leave Charlotte. We drank endless cups of tea and fruitlessly discussed the subject from all angles.

During the afternoon we received a call to say that an

omnibus driver had been found who remembered picking up a woman on the road that led past Wimbledon Common in the late afternoon of the day before. He remembered her particularly as it was drizzling and she had no coat, and as far as he could recollect, she got off the bus at Putney Bridge. Enquiries had been made in the area to no avail and the police were preparing to drag the river.

Charlotte shuddered when I reported this to her.

"It must have been quite dark by the time the omnibus arrived at Putney Bridge," I said.

"Yes—dark and wet." She wrapped her arms around herself, as if for warmth. "You would think someone would have tried to help her, wouldn't you? That someone would have realised that she wasn't responsible for her actions, out in the wet like that with no coat?"

"That's London for you," I said. "Nobody cares."

"I suppose you're right. How did you think Mark sounded?"

"The line was terrible, as always. He just sounded miserable, and rather impersonal. One is always so conscious of the wretched Mrs Harmsworth at the exchange."

"She ought to be reported," Charlotte said, but without heat or conviction. Of course it was wrong for the operator to listen in, but we recognised the fact that there were few who could ignore a scandal of these proportions.

"I wish I were with him," she added.

"Of course you do. The waiting is terrible."

"If there's no news tomorrow, I'm going up, Jenny. After all, the Godfreys are my relations too. I can always stay with them."

The next day brought no news and true to her word, she caught the London train. I returned to work and absorbed myself in the flood of small matters that needed my attention. It was just as well that we both had plenty to occupy our thoughts, since we had to wait until the following evening before the telephone rang.

Roger reached it before I did. His wooden expression and monosyllabic replies told me nothing and I was in a fever of suspense until he had replaced the receiver.

"Catherine is dead," he said baldly. "Drowned."

267

My hand flew to my mouth. "How? What happened?"

"Mark said little. He obviously didn't want to talk about it over the telephone, but it seems that she fell into the river somewhere along from Putney Bridge. He said he would tell us all when they get back."

"When are they coming?"

"Not yet. A few days, Mark said—I suppose there are arrangements to make; there will have to be an inquest before the funeral."

"How awful. Oh Roger, how *awful*!" I whispered, as the horror of Catherine's end struck me. I had never liked her, and it would be hypocritical to pretend otherwise, but I would not have wished this for her—terror and loneliness and cold and confusion, and finally the icy Thames sucking at her, pulling her down into its murky, polluted depths.

"I wonder what they'll do, Charlotte and Mark?" he said. "If they have any sense they'll get married."

"Not right away!"

"Why not? Collingford would be horrified, but whatever they do Collingford is bound to be horrified. They might as well make the whole thing legal and let the gossips get on with it—it's exactly the same principle as going on with the extension at the Ring. They'll talk themselves out. Eventually some other scandal will come along to take the place of our affairs."

"Perhaps you're right," I said doubtfully.

But he was not right and my uncertainty was justified.

No doubt following the same thought processes as Roger, Mark persuaded Charlotte to stay in London with him until after the inquest and funeral were over; he then purchased a special licence and on a snowy day in January 1911 they were married in a civil ceremony with two strangers from the street as witnesses.

After the brief ceremony they telephoned to tell us of it and asked if Roger was agreeable to keeping an eye on Priors for a week so that they could at last have a break.

"A week!" Roger said. "What use is that? Take a month, old chap. Get right away. Give the dust time to settle."

But Mark was adamant. He had made no plans for being away, he said. A long holiday would need preparations. As it was he'd only taken enough clothes for a couple of nights and had been forced to buy more. And he'd promised to take the bull over to Syke's farm next week, and there were the wages to pay, cheques to sign.

"Poor Charlotte," Roger said after he had hung up. "I have the feeling that Collingford will provide a somewhat bleak honeymoon for her."

They arrived and Roger met them at the station, taking them straight to Priors at their own request. The invaluable Izzie had cleaned the house and lit fires and prepared a meal, and their spirits must have risen to think that they were at last husband and wife, able to live openly together. All the slanders and venomous words would seem only half as hurtful now and surely even the worst of the gossip-mongers would tire of them eventually and find a new target.

They were tired that night and slept soundly, though Mark said that at one time he was aware of the dogs barking and sleepily thought that there must be a fox about. They were thus ill-prepared for the sight which met their eyes when Charlotte drew back the curtains the following morning. On the side of the barn which was in full view of their bedroom window, in red letters three feet high, was scrawled one word: MURDERERS.

"Now do you believe you should have gone away?" Roger asked Mark when later the four of us were together.

"What difference does it make? If that's what they think of us, a month's absence won't make them change their minds."

"They need time to forget and so do you."

"No." Mark's mouth was set in a grim line. "I shall never be able to forget this. I've lived in this place all my life. I've loved every stone, every blade of grass. I thought these people were my friends."

"Most of them are. How many would be involved in a hideous thing like that? Two—perhaps three louts, no more. Give them time, Mark."

I was quite sure he was right. Collingford would forget, given time.

A few days later I was in the kitchen at the Ring of Bells checking the stores, the open cupboard door hiding me from view. The hatch between the kitchen and the tap-room was open and the sound of voices which had been rumbling on for some time without me being more than half aware of it suddenly formed itself into recognisable words. I heard a name and paused to listen, realising that the sages in the tap-room were talking of Priors.

"Stands to reason that Mrs Mannering ill-wished 'un, didn't 'er? First to last she were guilty, I'd stake me life on it."

"Ar—you're right, Nobby. And I'll tell you 'ow I know. It were 'er that telled Mr Mark where to look for 'un. 'Ow do you account for that, then? Shouldn't be surprised if 'twasn't 'er 'ad an 'and in poor old Mrs Oliver's death, neither. 'Tis all in the family, after all."

"It's wickedness like we've never seen! Coming 'ere with 'er votes for women nonsense—burning churches and driving good people crazy! Bitches like that should be locked up."

Trembling with rage, I carefully set down the huge jar of salt that I had in my hands and was about to put my head through the hatch to give them my opinion when I heard my own name mentioned.

"Don't know as you can blame Mrs Mannering for every-thing. I mind when Mrs Roger were a girl, afore she married Mr Roger." I recognised the voice as that of Goosey Parslow, now incredibly gnarled and ancient. "There was talk then about the old girl—old Sarah, as used to run the inn. Died very sudden, she did. There was some then as said it was unnatural. Some as said Mrs Roger might 've given 'er a shove. I mind being told as they 'ad the father and mother of a row."

"Hold your tongue!" I blazed at them, suddenly coming to life and appearing in front of the hatch. A circle of gentle, vacant country faces turned towards me, mouths hanging open.

"You'll all be locked up for slander if you say things like that. You know nothing, do you hear? Nothing!"

I tried to say more but could feel angry tears rushing to my eyes so left them speedily, making my way to the wash house at the end of the kitchen. By great good fortune there was nobody about but me. It was sheer fury that made me cry. I was angry with myself and mopped at my eyes, thinking of all the things that I ought to have said.

When I had regained control, I walked back to the hatch and looked through. The tap-room was empty. Amaze your friends, I thought. How to clear a bar in one easy movement. Go bankrupt overnight.

I grasped the wooden base of the hatch and leaned my head against the wall, suddenly overcome with fear and misery. It was frightening to think that the events of the past were still so close beneath the surface. I knew now how Mark felt when he had commented so bitterly on his disillusionment with those he had always regarded as friends. It was the same with me.

How many times had I joked with Goosey Parslow? How many times had he smiled at me and told me I was bonny and asked me why I couldn't always serve his beer? How many times had he stopped to have a word with the children, and talked of Roger's batting average and boasted to me of the size of his marrows and runner beans?

Yet how pleasurably he had savoured the gossip about Charlotte—and how ready he had been to bring up the old talk about my grandmother's death. Thank God, I thought, that Bella had left Collingford. What capital she would make of this!

"Are you all right, Mrs Leyton?" Alfred asked, coming into the kitchen to start preparations for the evening meal.

I straightened up and took a breath.

"Just a little tired, Alfred," I said.

It took Bert and one of the other labourers a week to remove every bit of red paint from the side of the barn, but it was done at last.

The very next night, Mark and Charlotte were woken by the dogs barking furiously. Mark grabbed the shotgun he had taken to keeping by his bed, pulled on a dressing gown and, stopping only to cram his feet into the boots that stood in the kitchen, rushed out into the yard.

The dogs were going mad. Normally they slept inside and had done so until the night the barn was defaced; now they were justifying Mark's decision to leave them outside by giving the alarm. Shadowy figures were racing away across the field and shouting at the top of his voice Mark gave chase, only to lose them at the road. Lights had come on in the cottages and the men emerged to join him, but although they scattered in all directions, the intruders had got clean away. It remained to be seen what damage they had done back at the farm.

"Look around, men," he told his labourers, and with torches in their hands, they did so.

It happened to be Mark himself who found what they had done. His chestnut hunter, Rob Roy—the apple of his eye, the companion of years—lay dying, a gunshot wound in his head.

He was grey-faced when he came to tell me about the events of the night before and still had to fight for control when he came to the moment when he had actually found Rob Roy.

I was alone at Bridge House. Roger was president of the Licensed Victuallers' Association that year and had gone to Oxford for their annual dinner the night before, staying over at the Angler's Rest. I put my arms about Mark as I would have comforted Ben or Philip.

"That's not all," he said after a moment. "They left this, nailed to the door. I haven't shown it to Charlotte."

He handed me a square of paper, jaggedly torn where he had ripped it from the door.

"Next the red-haired bitch," it said.

"Mark, you must give this to the police! It's horrible."

"Yes." His voice was dull, totally without life. "They'll have the bullet, of course; the one that—that—" he faltered and turned away. "Jenny, I've come to a decision. Last night, in the stable."

"What decision, Mark? I don't think you're in any state—"

"There's only one decision I *can* make. Rather ironic, really, that I should tell you before anyone."

"Before Charlotte?"

"Charlotte is too upset to think rationally—besides, she hasn't seen the threat to her. I, on the other hand, suddenly feel very clear-headed. I know that this is the right thing to do."

"Mark, what are you talking about?"

He faced me again and put his hands on my shoulders.

"At last Charlotte and I have a chance to be happy. We're

together, legally, with nothing and no one between us after—how long? All of ten years. There's no need now for secrecy and subterfuge. The only thing that's between us and happiness is a few acres and a heap of Cotswold stone. Priors."

I stared at him, my lip caught between my teeth.

"It's not worth it, Jenny. I'm not going to let it spoil the rest of our lives. God knows how many years we have left—there have been too many wasted already. There are other places, other farms."

"But Priors—"

"I love it. You more than anyone know how I love it."

"Then how can you let them drive you away?"

"Because I can't afford to wait and see what else happens before this village is satisfied that I've paid the price."

"It's not the village as a whole—only a few senseless hooligans!"

"It only needs one. No, Jenny. No. It simply isn't worth it. Remember when Roger said he was leaving Priors to me? Well, I'm handing it back again. He can pay me what it's worth and I'll be off to pastures new."

"You should stay and fight, Mark."

He put his head on one side and looked at me, a small, mocking smile on his lips.

"Are you trying to tell me you don't want it, Jenny?"

Dumbly I continued to stare at him. There was no need for me to answer. He knew my feelings; he had always known my feelings.

A sob tore at his throat as wordlessly we clung together.

17

If ever we needed evidence that goodwill was an essential part of our business it was presented to us over that dreadful winter.

It's hard to say what makes one inn more popular than another. 'Atmosphere' is something difficult to qualify. It depends not only on the service offered by the licensee but also on each person who crosses the threshold. When even Goosey Parslow, Nobby Clark and Dutchy Holland removed their custom we were left with an empty tap-room and no atmosphere at all where once all was warmth and friendliness.

It was a depressing sight and it upset Roger more than anything that had happened in recent years.

"You know they'll come back eventually," I said.

"I suppose so. It's just that I've suddenly become aware of how fragile it all is."

I did my best to cheer him, but he remained low in spirits until the day when the news broke that Mrs Oliver's intruder had been tracked down and arrested.

It seemed that her son had returned, knowing that it was her habit to keep her savings in the upholstery of her armchair. His intention had been to break in, take the money and leave without disturbing her, but things had not gone according to plan. Noah Dandridge told us that the wretched man had not found the money in the chair as he had expected, and had been surprised by his mother while rummaging through her drawers. He hadn't meant to kill her, he assured the police. He hadn't laid a finger on her. She had apparently not recognised him and, as Richard Fenwick had surmised, had died of fright.

"Well, thank God that's cleared up," Roger said. "It certainly took the police long enough to find him. The whole incident must have lost us hundreds of pounds."

"We should have lost it anyway," I said. "Our stock has been at a low ebb for more than one reason this winter."

"It's no time to lay out money on a house that's far too big for us. Do we really need Priors, Jenny? What would we do with all that acreage?"

He was sitting at his desk with his back to me as he spoke, but as if conscious of the horrified nature of my silence, he turned to look at me. I was staring at him, completely stunned, and he laughed as he saw my expression.

"You really want it that much?"

"You know how I love it! Oh, I know the roof leaks and there's damp rot in the kitchen and you don't want to farm the land, but we can lease a few acres to George Goodson and just keep enough to grow our own fresh produce. Think what an advantage that would be, Roger! And think how we should hate to see strangers living there."

He lifted his hands in mock surrender.

"All right, all right—I give in! We'll have an independent survey to have it valued and if the sum isn't too horrendous you shall have Priors."

So in the end it was agreed. Mark and Charlotte managed to find a farm in Somerset that appealed to them, close to a place called Huish Episcopi. It was called Paternoster Farm and the house dated from pre-Reformation days. It was beautiful, Charlotte said, set in countryside softer and more lush than that which surrounded Priors. To both of us it seemed a good omen that once again the house had in the past been owned by monks.

Charlotte was the best friend I had ever made and I missed her sorely; but no words could express my emotions as we took possession of Priors and I was able to look at it and to know that at last it was mine, and I could make of it what I wished. Lucy blossomed into an able adviser on its decoration, far better than I at visualising which colours combined well together, and we had many shopping expeditions in Oxford to this end.

By Christmas 1911 we had finished, and Priors glowed like a jewel. Gone were the dark, fusty furnishings, replaced with light colours and flowered chintzes. The best of the furniture was repolished, the rest discarded, and in the kitchen was installed the very latest gas stove. Did I want to ruin him? Roger asked. But in spite of the question he was as delighted as the rest of us at the result and was determined to hold an enormous Christmas party as a housewarming.

Not unnaturally, Mark and Charlotte felt that they were unable to return to Collingford just yet, but the Gough grandparents came from Cheltenham and duly marvelled at the changes we had wrought.

There was some doubt before the invitations went out as to whether or not we should invite the Bollingers. They had never made any gesture of friendliness towards us, nor did we particularly want them to. However, it would be the natural thing for us to invite them in their capacity as squire and first lady. Certainly, in days gone by, it would have been unthinkable to have such a function without inviting the old lord.

Roger was in favour of asking them. I was less sure, but finally agreed to do so simply because I was fairly certain that they would be away for Christmas and therefore would refuse. I was proved wrong. They accepted with thanks, and I was left to wonder about their attitude to me. Did they accept the apparently generally held belief that I had ingratiated myself with their uncle only for what I could get out of it? I was uncomfortably aware that the events of that night when we had dined at Watersmeet could easily have given rise to this view.

Still, all was gracious amiability on the night of the party, and the shadows of the past months seemed to be receding at last.

We had chosen Christmas Eve because Roger felt that by so doing we would forestall other parties and catch our guests before they had become sated with revelry. Perhaps it was for this reason that all our friends seemed to be in the highest of spirits as they drew up to our front door, most of them still in horse-drawn carriages.

The house looked beautiful, Alfred and I had prepared a magnificent buffet supper, and we had arranged for an orchestra to come from Oxford. My dress was lace over satin in a shade of blue that matched the necklace of sapphires that Roger had given me for our previous wedding anniversary—our twenty-second. He was easily the most distinguished man present. The touch of grey at the temples only enhanced the distinction, and he always looked well in white tie and tails. We started the dancing together, circling decorously in a waltz, smiling at each other with happiness.

"Oh, Roger—don't our girls look lovely?" I said with justifiable pride.

Ellie was wearing a dress of rose-coloured lace which suited her far better than the pale pinks and blues and whites that most of her contemporaries were wearing. I had wondered if the gown were not too sophisticated for her, but recognised now that her choice had been perfectly right. It was so typical of her to know unerringly what she wanted and to persist quietly but firmly until she had achieved her aim. She looked both chic and distinctive.

But it was undeniably Lucy who was the belle of the ball. Her dress was a froth of white tulle with little pink roses scattered here and there and a pink satin sash—sweet and girlish and as delicious as a dish of meringue glacé. The young bloods of the neighbourhood clustered around her, laughing at her every word, masterfully sweeping her on to the dance floor when their number on her programme had been reached.

Lord and Lady Bollinger seemed to be enjoying themselves. There were a sufficient number of the hunting set amongst our guests for them to feel at home, and Lady Bollinger became positively animated when leaping about the floor with Roger in a military two-step.

To me she was pleasantness itself, complimenting me on the house, on the food, on the orchestra and my daughters. She even complimented me on my dress, though spoiled it somewhat by adding that she had always liked blue and had indeed possessed herself a dress of the same shade last year when it was fashionable. A slip of the tongue, I felt sure; or did I? I could not help remembering her totally false solicitude for the old lord and her crocodile tears at his funeral. She was not a woman with whom I could feel at ease.

As they took their leave, both she and her husband said that another meeting must soon be arranged. We must visit them at Watersmeet, they said.

"I think she finds country life dull," Roger said as we made our way back to our guests, for the Bollingers had been the first to leave.

"Lady Bollinger thinks that daddy is *devastating*!" Lucy giggled. "I overheard her saying so to Mrs Irwin."

"Does she, indeed!" I was feeling a little flat the following day, now that all that was left of the party were empty glasses in odd corners of the house, burst balloons and the remains of french chalk to be cleaned from the hall floor. I was glad that we were to go to John and Angela for Christmas dinner.

"It really was the most splen*dif*erous party," she went on dreamily. "I had the best time of my whole life."

"Did you enjoy it, Ellie?" I asked.

"Oh yes, it was great fun," she said, but in rather a lukewarm way as if not wanting to hurt my feelings.

"You seemed to have a great many partners!"

"Oh yes," she said again, and sighed. "I just wish that some of the young men around here could talk of something other than hunting, shooting and fishing, though. I must say I grow very weary of agreeing that unmarked barbed wire is a sin and that Lord Branstead should be hung, drawn and quartered for poisoning foxes to preserve his pheasants. One of these days I shall tell them what I really think about fox-hunting."

"But Ellie," Ben said, with an entirely false air of sweet reasonableness, "don't you know that the fox *enjoys* it."

Ben was fifteen and a half now, tall and lanky, and would be quite good-looking once his spots disappeared, which we all assured him would occur in due course. Meantime he was inclined to gaze at himself despairingly in any mirror that he passed, looking embarrassed and off-hand if actually surprised in the act. Academically he was doing well—so well, in fact, that he was a year ahead of his contemporaries and was being pressed by his housemaster to stay another year in the sixth form so that he could be assured of a scholarship to Oxford.

Ellie was still blissfully happy at Somerville. She had actually spoken in a debate to which the Somerville Parliament had been challenged by the Arnold Society of Balliol College—"That this house is resolved that in matters of franchise no distinction should be made between men and women," and she reported delightedly that the supporters of equality had carried the motion by eighty-six votes to twenty-six.

She and Roger were inclined to argue about politics. Roger, as a life-long Liberal, had always regarded himself as sympathetic to reform. Indeed, there were many in the district who regarded him as a traitor to his class—though what could one expect of a feller who gave up the land and went into trade, what?

But Ellie went further. Glib phrases fell from her lips: 'capitalist tyrants', 'toiling masses', 'solidarity of the workers'. I could almost see Roger wince at their banality but Ellie was totally sincere. She burned to improve the lot of the underdog. Roger sometimes grew impatient with her but on the whole felt that the desire for change was a healthy one. She would undoubtedly mellow with the years, he said comfortably.

Which were, I thought, passing all too quickly.

When at the end of July Lucy left the high school for good, her report said: "Lucy is an agreeable and popular girl, and with self-discipline she will no doubt settle down to a fruitful and rewarding domestic life."

Neither Roger nor I was in any doubt that this was tantamount to saying that as far as the high school was concerned, she had been wasting her time and theirs for the past six years. In September she went to Mrs Brimacombe's college in Cheltenham, ostensibly to learn the rudiments of office work plus a smattering of culture—though I doubted whether Mrs Brimacombe would succeed where the Oxford High School for Girls had failed.

She was to board at the college, but naturally would spend a large amount of her free time with her grandparents whose house was in the next street. Granny was full of excited plans. She and Goffy knew some charming people in Cheltenham, she said. She would make it her business to see that Lucy would meet the most eligible and desirable young men.

"She's supposed to be working, Granny," I pointed out.

"Not all the time, surely? It's important for her to meet the right kind of people, Jenny. I mean to see that she does."

Philip, now almost eleven, was at something of a loose end that summer. He missed Peter badly and in fact went down to Somerset to spend a couple of weeks at Paternoster Farm. Amos had less leisure time than of yore for he spent a great deal of time with Bert, working on the small-holding which was all we had retained of the original acreage of Priors.

For want of anything better to do, Philip began hanging around the kitchen of the Ring of Bells. It had always been a favourite port of call since Alfred was generous with left-over pieces of pie or cake, but now Philip took a more practical interest and began peering over Alfred's shoulder, asking questions and generally getting in his way.

More to keep him occupied than anything else, Alfred set him small tasks. He learned the correct way to chop parsley and blanche almonds and whip up white of egg. One day I discovered him shrouded in one of Alfred's aprons, its hem reaching to the floor, tears pouring down his cheeks as he sliced onions. I begged Alfred to send him packing if he should become a nuisance, but was assured that this was far from the case and that he was beginning to be quite useful.

"We'll make a chef out of him yet," Alfred said.

As I had predicted, our old customers drifted back. Mrs Earnshawe at the Waggon and Horses did something to irritate them and the tap-room grew busy again, once more filled with noise and smoke, tall stories and laughter. I felt it had been a timely reminder of our vulnerability.

Lucy's year at Cheltenham finished on the last day of July when she was due to return home, her education completed. Roger was going to meet her at the station, but on the morning she was supposed to come we received instead a telephone call telling him that it would not be necessary.

"A friend is bringing me," she said. "It's all right, Mummy—don't fuss! Granny knows him and thinks he's most frightfully sweet."

I passed the telephone over to Roger who spluttered helplessly when he heard this message.

"It's all *right*, Daddy! Honestly! He's a simply marvellous driver, *very* responsible and sensible. And Granny knows his mother very well—they play bridge together every Thursday—and he went to Winchester and is a *perfect* gentleman. So you see, there's not the slightest need to worry."

Roger did worry, nevertheless. He regarded any young man who cast his eyes upon Lucy with the deepest suspicion, which made for a distinctly unquiet life since practically everyone in trousers appeared to be overcome by her.

Lucy and her escort arrived during the afternoon. A smart, maroon-coloured Lagonda drove up to the front door with a spurt of gravel, Lucy waving gaily from the passenger seat. He turned out to be a dark-haired young man by the name of Nicholas Marchant, recently graduated from Cambridge. He had handsome brown eyes and a luxuriant moustache, agreeable manners and a strong determination to spend as long as possible in Lucy's company.

Naturally I asked him inside for tea. Roger was polite, if a little distant, until the subject of cars was broached, whereupon his natural curiosity got the better of him and the Lagonda was discussed in minute detail. Lucy lifted her eyebrows at me in comic resignation. There was something a little different about her, I thought. She was growing up.

Just as Nicholas Marchant had been taking his final Tripos at Cambridge and had come down with an honours degree, Ellie, too, had been taking her finals at Oxford. The results showed that she had done very well, but while Nicholas—with his third-class honours—was entitled to put BA after his name, Ellie had to be content with a mere certificate and a pious hope that some time in the future, justice would be done. She seemed in a wistful sort of a mood, no doubt sad that the Oxford interlude had come to an end. She had no clear idea of what she wanted to do next, except that she did not want to teach—the destiny of most of her contemporaries.

That summer we went down to Somerset to stay with Mark and Charlotte and were pleased to find them busy and contented. Their house was charming and Mark looked less drawn than I had seen him for many a long year.

"Are you looking after Priors for me?" he asked me once when we happened to be alone.

I smiled at him. How strange it was that it was Mark who shared this strange, almost mystic feeling about Priors with me and not Roger, who shared everything else.

"You can depend on it," I said. "I wish you would come and stay. Would it be too painful?"

He took a few moments to answer.

"One day," he said. "We'll come one day."

Ellie stayed behind when we returned to Collingford. She

had always got on well with Charlotte and in many ways I knew she found it easier to discuss important issues with her than she did with me. Charlotte was an objective adviser. I trusted her judgment, knew that she would be helpful to Ellie, and readily agreed that Ellie should prolong her visit.

Lucy, on the other hand, could hardly wait to get back. She had received several fat letters while we were staying at Paternoster Farm which I knew were from Nicholas Marchant. We had a carriage to ourselves on our way home by train and were able to converse freely. I teased her gently about her admirer and she laughed happily.

"He is rather a darling," she said.

Roger gripped his newspaper and glared at her over the top of it.

"I don't know that I trust that young man," he said.

"Daddy! What an awful thing to say."

"Well—what does he do, eh? He seems an idle sort of a fellow."

"That's not at all true! He's just looking around at the moment, trying to find the right opening."

Roger snorted. With some amusement I remembered my grandmother's verdict on him. A rackety sort of a fellow, she had said. Not the sort to settle down.

"I used to know someone rather like your Nicholas," I remarked innocently to Lucy. "He went to America, even, and tried working in a Wall Street bank, but he didn't like it at all. So then he tried farming—"

"You've made your point," Roger said, smiling in spite of himself.

"Mummy, you like Nicholas, don't you?" Lucy asked me when we arrived home. She had come into the bedroom and was perched on the end of my bed watching me as I unpacked.

"I don't really know him very well, do I?" I asked cautiously, feeling my way. "He seems very agreeable. The point is, do you?"

I sat back on my heels and looked up at her. Suddenly for all her newly acquired poise she looked very vulnerable.

"Oh yes" she breathed. "I like him very much."

"Better than all the others?"

"Much better. Much, much better. I love him, Mummy."

"Oh Lucy! You've known him for such a short time."

And what, I asked myself, does that have to do with it? What short memories adults have sometimes.

"Does he love you?" I asked.

She nodded at me, smiling. "He wants to marry me. And don't say that I'm too young, because you were eighteen when you married daddy, weren't you?"

"I was older in some ways. I hadn't led such a sheltered life."

"Oh, Mummy," she came and knelt down on the floor beside me and put her arms around me. "I know that I love him. People think that because I'm quite pretty and not clever like Ellie that I'm flighty and silly, but I'm not—not at all. I just want to marry Nick and have lots of babies and be faithful to him, till death us do part, just like you and daddy."

I fought back a few sentimental and pleasurable tears.

"If he really wants to marry you," I said, turning briskly to my unpacking again. "He'd be well advised to get himself some gainful employment. I don't suggest mentioning it to your father until he has established himself in some sort of job with decent prospects. Unless, of course, he comes from a very wealthy family. Has he an independent income?"

"Unfortunately not. He's the younger son of a younger son, and doesn't have what you might call great expectations. But I don't care! We'd be happy in a cottage."

"Hmm!" I felt a little doubtful on that score. Lucy's taste ran to simple but expensive clothes and even as she spoke Izzie was unpacking for her. Nicholas, I had noticed, enjoyed fast cars and good brandy. "Even so," I said, "a job would be a good idea."

"Oh, he knows!" Lucy said. "He is trying, honestly."

He tried to some purpose and the following month managed to secure a position with some promise of advancement in the University Press in Oxford.

"You see," crowed Lucy in delight. "He really is awfully clever. He's *very* literary!"

Ben had attained his scholarship at Christ Church and was

reading Greats, working hard for Responsions, his first major hurdle.

"What do you think of Nick?" I asked him privately, having considerable regard for his opinion.

"I like him," he said, which soothed my doubts. "I think," he added, which brought them to life again. "Oh, he's a nice chap, mother, and he's obviously mad about Lucy. He'll probably do her very well."

"Do I detect a note of reservation?"

"Well, he's not exactly my cup of tea, but then I'm not proposing to marry him, am I? I have the feeling that he regards me as a dangerous Bolshevik."

"And are you?"

"Hardly! But I probably appear that way to Nick. I would say he was ultra-conservative, wouldn't you?"

"With a big C or a little one?"

"Both, I would guess."

"But still, you like him?"

"I think he's basically good and kind. A sound man. And really whether I like him or not hardly enters into it, does it?"

"I respect your views about people."

"Thank you kindly, ma'am." He pulled a forelock and grinned at me and I thought how like his father he had become.

Nick was not the only one who had found a job. Ellie, armed with introductions from Charlotte, had presented herself at the London headquarters of the NUWSS and was working on a weekly magazine put out by them. She earned a pittance which had to be augmented by a contribution from Roger to allow her to live in a respectable girls' hostel—somewhat, I think, to her disappointment. She had been rather looking forward to starving in a garret, suffering for the cause, but Roger was adamant. Either she lived in the hostel or she did not live in London at all. Gracefully she gave in.

Roger's mother was horrified. Young ladies did not live in London, in or out of hostels; still less did they become members of the Fabian Society and spend all their time working for lost causes such as women's suffrage. How, she asked us, did Ellie expect to find a husband that way?

"I don't think she's looking for one just yet," I replied. "She's very busy and very happy. That's sufficient for the moment."

"Well, I'm glad Lucy seems to have more sense. She couldn't do better than Nicholas Marchant. His mother is a dear friend of mine and the family is very well connected."

Roger was not as happy as everyone else—but then he would probably not have approved of any young man produced by Lucy, with the possible exception of the Prince of Wales who was currently up at Oxford too. And now that Nick had found suitable employment, there seemed few objections that he could possibly make. He was a thoroughly decent, well-mannered young man, and he was head over heels in love with Lucy.

The engagement was announced that Christmas and by way of celebration we arranged a large and formal dinner party for New Year's Eve.

The dining room at Priors looked just as I had imagined it could, in all the splendour of lace napery and crystal glasses. The silver gleamed in the light of the candelabra, and hot-house roses and carnations graced the centre of the long table. The Marchants could be as full of consequence as they fancied, but by all that was holy, I would show them that the Leytons had nothing to be ashamed of either.

Colonel Marchant, ex-Indian Army, was tall and thin, with a hawk-like nose and stern mouth. It was a mouth made for barking orders; a mouth that seemed to find it difficult to smile, and I thought with sympathy of the junior officers who had served under him. Mrs Marchant was plump and affable and seemed cowed by her husband. This did not surprise me. I had to work very hard not to be cowed myself.

Around the long table sat the Leytons—all six of us, with the addition of John and Angela and their two elder daughters, Jessica and Hester. Mrs Marchant sat on Roger's right hand, the colonel on mine. On my left was Dr Gough—dear Goffy, now a much-loved friend—and next to Roger sat his mother, white haired and bespectacled but as vehement and vigorous as ever. And in the middle of everyone sat Lucy and Nick with no eyes for any but each other.

Conversation was never laggardly when two or three of the Leyton clan were gathered together, and on this occasion it rollicked along very happily in spite of Colonel Marchant's grim presence. I felt he was making a great effort to be affable, and he succeeded reasonably well until Goffy was unfortunately inspired to ask Ellie about her work with the NUWSS.

"You—you are a *suffragist*?" the colonel asked, as if he could hardly believe the evidence of his own ears.

It needed little imagination on my part to see my delightfully civilised dinner party collapsing about my ears. Ellie was already drawing breath to reply to him as I shot a despairing glance towards Roger, who gallantly responded by launching at once into a vivid but totally irrelevant account of an exhibition we had visited in Oxford. The moment was saved.

We moved to the hall long before the stroke of midnight, and champagne was served in good time for everyone to drink to the coming year. We had already drunk to the newly engaged couple, to the Marchant family, to the Leyton family. But now it was time for another toast. As the grandfather clock chimed the twelve strokes of midnight, we all raised our glasses.

"To 1914," Roger said. "Happy New Year, everyone!"

"Happy New Year," we all chorused gaily, embracing each other with joyful innocence. "Happy New Year! Happy New Year!"

It was going to be wonderful. How could it be otherwise? Lucy and Nick would be married, Ben would do well at Oxford, Ellie would follow her star and change the world, and Philip—why, Philip would follow in his father's footsteps.

And I? I had Roger and I had Priors. I was the luckiest woman in the whole world.

If I had to acknowledge a small cloud on my horizon it was only that Roger was being drawn inexorably into the Bollingers' circle, not because he found either of them congenial, but simply because Lord Bollinger frequently invited him over for an evening's gaming, and this seemed something that he found impossible to resist.

could do. Europe is a powder-keg at the moment. It
eeds one spark."

was being just a little tiresome, I thought. It was all
nd good being aware of world events, but this was a
ing, not a wake.

en thank heaven for the English Channel," I said,
tartly.

few miles of water won't save us."

en, not now." Ellie had come up behind us and was
ing at his sleeve. "Not today."

No," I said, feeling suddenly cold. "Let him finish."

f Germany attacks France or Belgium, we'll be drawn in
There'll be no alternative."

stopped and faced him, there on the path with the scent
lowers all about us and the comforting bulk of Priors
ming behind.

"What are you trying to tell me, Ben?" I asked.

"That there's going to be a war. A war with Germany."

It was very still in the garden. From somewhere near at
nd one of the dogs barked, answered by another across
e valley. And from inside the house came the sound of
ughter.

18

ow was it possible for a cataclysm of this magnitude to
al up on us so imperceptibly? So easy, afterwards, to say
we should have seen it coming. We didn't want to see,
n't want our pleasant, ordered lives to be disturbed. Even
ve had seen the signs and read them correctly, there was
one of us who would have known what to expect.

en went back to Oxford early from the summer holiday.
had been withdrawn and thoughtful for the entire month
August. I suppose we should have been prepared, but

"It's perfectly harmless, Jenny," he said, when I raised objections. "I promised you that I'd never play for high stakes again, and I haven't. By the by, they've invited us to join their party for the Gold Cup. Lydia was saying how long it is since she's seen you."

I smiled to myself somewhat cynically. So it was Lydia, now? That was a new development. I did not fool myself that any of the invitations we received were because of her wish to see me; it was Roger whose company she desired—and that, I felt sure, only because she was bored to tears in Collingford.

I said nothing to him of my conviction. There was nothing whatever in his manner to make me think that he regarded her with anything more than a lukewarm friendliness. I stifled my objections to the gambling, too, for the excitement seemed to be something that he needed.

The wedding date was fixed for the last week in July. Excellent, wrote Mark—right between haymaking and harvest! He and Charlotte would certainly be coming. It put the final seal on a joyful occasion and I threw myself into the preparations with the greatest enthusiasm.

Ellie was to be bridesmaid, together with her four cousins, which necessitated a great deal of correspondence to ensure that all were in agreement over their dresses. The reception was, of course, to be held at Priors. To me it seemed made for occasions such as this. That year it was a perfect summer. As one sunny day followed another, we asked ourselves if it could possibly last until the end of July. It was a matter of enormous consequence that the sun should shine.

"Oh, getting married is *such* fun!" Lucy said, opening presents and scattering paper to the four winds for the patient Izzie to clear up. "It's like having a birthday every day. That makes four toast racks and six biscuit barrels."

"No home should be without four toast racks and six biscuit barrels," Roger said, laughing at her. "Not to mention several dozen Chinese vases."

"The very worst thing is that elephant's foot umbrella stand that Nick's uncle and aunt gave us," Lucy said, shuddering. "I've never seen such a monstrosity. Mummy, you will come to my dress fitting, won't you? And be sure to back me up when I tell Miss Ponting that the skirt isn't tight enough, because I want it really tight, tight, tight! A hobble skirt to beat all hobble skirts."

The day when it finally dawned was perfect. I thought it just possible that I might cry at my daughter's wedding, but I didn't, because she was so gloriously happy and had to take such ridiculously tiny steps in her hobble skirt to beat all hobble skirts; and my dearest Charlotte and Mark were there and all our menfolk looked wonderful in morning dress. Ellie was beautiful in her own distinctive way in her bridesmaid's dress of palest gold, and I was happy about my own dress and hat which had cost me more than anything I had ever bought before in my life.

There was champagne in plenty back at Priors—and the fact that Mark was there and didn't seem to mind that the house belonged to Roger and me now made everything perfect. He approved all the changes and admired the new colour scheme—then waxed enthusiastic about renovations he had carried out at Paternoster Farm, which made me feel that he had truly made the transition from Oxfordshire to Somerset and had no regrets.

"Dear Mark," I said, and reached up to kiss his cheek. It was strange to think that we had been enemies, once, a million years ago.

There were speeches—a witty one from Goffy, a halting one from Nick's pale and sweating best man, and finally a short but rather touching one from Nick himself. Then it was time for Lucy to go upstairs and change for they were to catch the train to London, where they were to spend the night before going on to Paris the following day.

She threw her bouquet as she came down the stairs, but Ellie did not even try to catch it. It landed in Jessica's arms. Jessica was John's fourteen-year-old daughter, and everyone laughed and cheered and she looked delighted with herself, and suddenly I felt a pang because it seemed such a short time ago that Lucy was fourteen and her wedding day impossibly distant.

We escorted them to the train, and I know as I stood by Roger's side on the platform that he was thinking of our wedding, just as I was. Did Lucy wonder what marriage

288

would entail, I asked myself? Was she apprehensive? At least I had made sure ignorant as I had been—yet how, in w explain love?

There were still guests at Priors when relations—Marchants and Leytons—tha And there had been no time yet for a long with Charlotte.

I longed suddenly for quiet. I looked out saw that it was bathed in the lambent light The shadows were already lengthening, peace and a stillness there that seemed to cal

I stepped outside and stood for a second b of the fragrant summer air, noticing how the h stones of Priors were turning to grey as the lig turned my head a little and saw that Ellie sitting side by side on a wooden bench beneath bush and I stepped down from the stone terrac towards them, the scent of the white blosso towards me. They were engrossed in conversati

"Wasn't it all lovely?" I called to them as I ap They turned to look at me, not smiling, and fo I hesitated, stopped in my tracks, before cont walk.

"Is there something wrong?" I asked. Neither of them spoke.

"Well, come on, one of you! What's the trage Still they said nothing. Then Ben got up and around my shoulder, turning me back toward and together we walked between the clumps of

"We were talking of Europe, Mother," he sa "Of Europe? You mean the assassination? been some archduke killed, I remembered. It that Lucy had gone for the last fitting for her that the fourth toast rack had arrived. The eve penetrated my consciousness. People were a themselves assassinated in these Balkan states, It was what one expected of foreigners.

"What of it?" I asked. "It doesn't really it?"

289

"It's perfectly harmless, Jenny," he said, when I raised objections. "I promised you that I'd never play for high stakes again, and I haven't. By the by, they've invited us to join their party for the Gold Cup. Lydia was saying how long it is since she's seen you."

I smiled to myself somewhat cynically. So it was Lydia, now? That was a new development. I did not fool myself that any of the invitations we received were because of her wish to see me; it was Roger whose company she desired— and that, I felt sure, only because she was bored to tears in Collingford.

I said nothing to him of my conviction. There was nothing whatever in his manner to make me think that he regarded her with anything more than a lukewarm friendliness. I stifled my objections to the gambling, too, for the excitement seemed to be something that he needed.

The wedding date was fixed for the last week in July. Excellent, wrote Mark—right between haymaking and harvest! He and Charlotte would certainly be coming. It put the final seal on a joyful occasion and I threw myself into the preparations with the greatest enthusiasm.

Ellie was to be bridesmaid, together with her four cousins, which necessitated a great deal of correspondence to ensure that all were in agreement over their dresses. The reception was, of course, to be held at Priors. To me it seemed made for occasions such as this. That year it was a perfect summer. As one sunny day followed another, we asked ourselves if it could possibly last until the end of July. It was a matter of enormous consequence that the sun should shine.

"Oh, getting married is *such* fun!" Lucy said, opening presents and scattering paper to the four winds for the patient Izzie to clear up. "It's like having a birthday every day. That makes four toast racks and six biscuit barrels."

"No home should be without four toast racks and six biscuit barrels," Roger said, laughing at her. "Not to mention several dozen Chinese vases."

"The very worst thing is that elephant's foot umbrella stand that Nick's uncle and aunt gave us," Lucy said, shuddering. "I've never seen such a monstrosity. Mummy, you will come to my dress fitting, won't you? And be sure to back me up when I tell Miss Ponting that the skirt isn't tight enough, because I want it really tight, tight, tight! A hobble skirt to beat all hobble skirts."

The day when it finally dawned was perfect. I thought it just possible that I might cry at my daughter's wedding, but I didn't, because she was so gloriously happy and had to take such ridiculously tiny steps in her hobble skirt to beat all hobble skirts; and my dearest Charlotte and Mark were there and all our menfolk looked wonderful in morning dress. Ellie was beautiful in her own distinctive way in her bridesmaid's dress of palest gold, and I was happy about my own dress and hat which had cost me more than anything I had ever bought before in my life.

There was champagne in plenty back at Priors—and the fact that Mark was there and didn't seem to mind that the house belonged to Roger and me now made everything perfect. He approved all the changes and admired the new colour scheme—then waxed enthusiastic about renovations he had carried out at Paternoster Farm, which made me feel that he had truly made the transition from Oxfordshire to Somerset and had no regrets.

"Dear Mark," I said, and reached up to kiss his cheek. It was strange to think that we had been enemies, once, a million years ago.

There were speeches—a witty one from Goffy, a halting one from Nick's pale and sweating best man, and finally a short but rather touching one from Nick himself. Then it was time for Lucy to go upstairs and change for they were to catch the train to London, where they were to spend the night before going on to Paris the following day.

She threw her bouquet as she came down the stairs, but Ellie did not even try to catch it. It landed in Jessica's arms. Jessica was John's fourteen-year-old daughter, and everyone laughed and cheered and she looked delighted with herself, and suddenly I felt a pang because it seemed such a short time ago that Lucy was fourteen and her wedding day impossibly distant.

We escorted them to the train, and I know as I stood by Roger's side on the platform that he was thinking of our wedding, just as I was. Did Lucy wonder what marriage would entail, I asked myself? Was she just the smallest bit apprehensive? At least I had made sure that she was not as ignorant as I had been—yet how, in words, can one really explain love?

There were still guests at Priors when we returned, still relations—Marchants and Leytons—that I had to talk to. And there had been no time yet for a long heart-to-heart talk with Charlotte.

I longed suddenly for quiet. I looked out at the garden and saw that it was bathed in the lambent light of early evening. The shadows were already lengthening, and there was a peace and a stillness there that seemed to call me.

I stepped outside and stood for a second breathing deeply of the fragrant summer air, noticing how the honey-coloured stones of Priors were turning to grey as the light grew less. I turned my head a little and saw that Ellie and Ben were sitting side by side on a wooden bench beneath a philadelphus bush and I stepped down from the stone terrace and walked towards them, the scent of the white blossoms wafting towards me. They were engrossed in conversation.

"Wasn't it all lovely?" I called to them as I approached.

They turned to look at me, not smiling, and for a moment I hesitated, stopped in my tracks, before continuing my walk.

"Is there something wrong?" I asked.

Neither of them spoke.

"Well, come on, one of you! What's the tragedy?"

Still they said nothing. Then Ben got up and put his arm around my shoulder, turning me back towards the house, and together we walked between the clumps of flowers.

"We were talking of Europe, Mother," he said.

"Of Europe? You mean the assassination?" There had been some archduke killed, I remembered. It was the day that Lucy had gone for the last fitting for her dress; the day that the fourth toast rack had arrived. The event had hardly penetrated my consciousness. People were always getting themselves assassinated in these Balkan states, weren't they? It was what one expected of foreigners.

"What of it?" I asked. "It doesn't really affect us, does it?"

"It could do. Europe is a powder-keg at the moment. It only needs one spark."

He was being just a little tiresome, I thought. It was all well and good being aware of world events, but this was a wedding, not a wake.

"Then thank heaven for the English Channel," I said, rather tartly.

"A few miles of water won't save us."

"Ben, not now." Ellie had come up behind us and was tugging at his sleeve. "Not today."

"No," I said, feeling suddenly cold. "Let him finish."

"If Germany attacks France or Belgium, we'll be drawn in too. There'll be no alternative."

I stopped and faced him, there on the path with the scent of flowers all about us and the comforting bulk of Priors looming behind.

"What are you trying to tell me, Ben?" I asked.

"That there's going to be a war. A war with Germany."

It was very still in the garden. From somewhere near at hand one of the dogs barked, answered by another across the valley. And from inside the house came the sound of laughter.

18

How was it possible for a cataclysm of this magnitude to steal up on us so imperceptibly? So easy, afterwards, to say that we should have seen it coming. We didn't want to see, didn't want our pleasant, ordered lives to be disturbed. Even if we had seen the signs and read them correctly, there was not one of us who would have known what to expect.

Ben went back to Oxford early from the summer holiday. He had been withdrawn and thoughtful for the entire month of August. I suppose we should have been prepared, but the news that he had joined the 1/4th Battalion of the Oxfordshire and Buckinghamshire Light Infantry came as a shattering blow. Even Roger—usually on the side of adventurous youth—felt that he had been far too precipitate.

"You could at least have finished at university," he said. "Going back after a break will make everything far harder."

"But, Father, I don't finish for another three years! Greats is a four-year course, remember? How could I wait that long?"

"But why go at all?" I demanded. "You're not a soldier. You even hate swatting flies or stepping on a spider! And what about the OTC at school? You did nothing but complain about how much you hated it."

"I know all that," he said. "But the issues are clear, Mother. Germany has been rearming for years. It's quite ridiculous for people to say that it will be over by Christmas. Germany is arrogant and overbearing and I, for one, don't intend to stand by and let it happen. After all, I did get my certificate A in the OTC."

Izzie was furious and banged saucepans about in the kitchen.

"Certificate A, certificate A—what do that signify? I don't care if he's got certificate XYZ! You shouldn't let him do it, Mrs Leyton, dear."

But it was too late to stop him and I had to confess that the sight of him in his subaltern's uniform made me very proud. He was to go away immediately for training—but only to Essex, which didn't sound too frightening. I cherished the hope that in spite of his gloomy forebodings the war would be over in a few months, or at least well before his training was completed.

Ellie had gone back to London immediately after Lucy's wedding and had become involved with the organisation that provided tea for the soldiers at main-line stations. The first hospital trains from Mons came through after only a few weeks. She wrote moving accounts of the humour and bravery of the men; the boy with the bandage across one eye who said that he was happy as long as he could still see a girl as pretty as she; and the grey-faced man with bloodless lips who smiled and said in a hoarse, north-country whisper: "Ee, that were a short war, that were an' all."

Faced with stories like these our own problems seemed insignificant, yet nevertheless they had to be dealt with. Suddenly, almost overnight, there was enormous pressure on our bed space. So many people were on the move throughout the country. Army camps were set up in rural places which had never seen a soldier and stately homes were turned into hospitals. There were strangers everywhere. All this meant that our hotels were in demand, and while we were at first able to cope with the influx, things grew more and more difficult as many of our trained staff left. We were forced to bring in anyone who was able and willing to wield a broom or make a bed.

"The halt, the lame and the blind," Roger murmured ruefully to me on one occasion, watching poor old Gimpy Gower hobbling across the dining room with a tray of glasses, spilling ale at every step.

By the end of March 1915, spilling beer over the customers was the least of our worries, for Ben was overseas with his battalion in Ploegsteert Wood—Plug Street, as the Tommies called it. He wrote amusing letters making light of the dangers and discomforts, telling us only of his friends and the jokes that were made and the wonderful times when they marched back from the line to Pont de Nieppe and were able to soak their exhausted bodies in huge vats of water at the old brewery.

It was left to the *Oxford Chronicle* to tell us of the gas attack at Ypres and of the fact that the 1/4th Battalion had been issued with respirators. The growing lists of casualties told their own story. It was as well that Alfred had left the Ring of Bells to join the Army as a cook (oh, most fortunate of soldiers!) and that I had therefore to resume my old duties in the kitchen, for I would surely have gone mad with nothing to do but worry about Ben.

As it was, food was beginning to get short and it took all my ingenuity to ensure that we still offered adequate meals, even though luxuries disappeared. Posters urged everyone to make economies and those who continued to quaff their champagne and demand cigars and caviare and smoked salmon were said to be in league with the Kaiser. Roger turned nurseryman and worked in the few acres we had retained at Priors, as proud as anyone in the village of his fresh vegetables.

Watersmeet was turned into a hospital and the patients in their bright blue uniforms often walked into the village, many on crutches or with sticks. I spoke to one of them who had recently returned from Flanders.

"It's sheer 'ell in the trenches," he told me, not knowing that I had a son there. "We was 'alf-buried in mud—all me mates was wiped out. I was the only one what come out alive. I never thought I would, straight—I lay there all night, stuck fast, with me mates 'eavin' and 'ollerin' all round me, till one by one they went quiet and didn't 'oller no more."

His words were to come to me night after night as I lay sleepless, worrying about Ben. I found that I was so tired that usually I fell asleep the moment my head touched the pillow, but by three o'clock I was awake and worrying and nothing could induce peaceful sleep again—not the Lord's Prayer, nor the twenty-third psalm, nor trying to think of new ways of serving turnips, swedes and parsnips, nor wondering what my grandchild was to be like. For Lucy was to have a baby in November.

What a world for the poor child to be born into, I thought. Nick was still at home and would continue to resist the enlistment posters and his father's accusations that he was dragging his feet until after Lucy was safely delivered of her baby, but he suffered dreadfully under the barbs he received from passers-by. A group of shop-girls walking four abreast down Broad Street had turned round to look at him in his civilian suit and had sung pointedly: "We don't want to lose you, but we think you ought to go!" and yet another woman had walked up to him and presented him with a white feather.

Poor Nick! His gesture in staying with Lucy was the bravest thing he could have done for he was the most conformist, conservative patriot it would be possible to find. His father wrote pointed letters that hurt him deeply, but every slur and innuendo was forgotten when a dear little daughter was born—pink and white and perfect, just like her mother.

Nothing now could prevent Nick from 'slipping across to help' as the posters phrased it—just as if it was the work of a moment and that he would be free to slip back again as soon as the fancy took him. He joined his father's old regiment, the Worcesters, and basked in the old war-horse's approval, which perhaps was some consolation when he, too, after a short training, was sent to the mud and misery of Flanders.

"Surely it's time Ben came home for some leave?" I said to Roger one day towards the end of 1915.

"Mmm?" He turned round and looked at me guiltily. I had caught him unawares, staring at himself in the mirror—not for the first time. He reminded me of Ben when he was fifteen and worried to death about his spots.

"I was saying that I thought it was time Ben came home. It's been well over a year."

"So it has," he said absently.

Lucy and her baby, who was christened Elizabeth but always known as Beth, came home to live at Priors after Nick went away. Their little house in Oxford was rented to a senior physician at the Radcliffe Infirmary and I thought sadly of her excitement when she and Nicholas had furnished it together.

It was a wrench for her to leave it, but it made sense for her to come home and I was hopeful that Roger would find her presence cheering. He had grown silent of late—almost morose, which was strangely unlike him, however worried.

The following day I once more caught him peering at himself in the glass, stroking his greying moustache and frowning.

"Tell me honestly," he said. "Do I look fifty?"

"Yes," I said brutally—and quite untruthfully since all the gardening he had been doing had made him lean and tanned with not a spare ounce of flesh on him. "Darling, you're surely not thinking of trying to enlist?"

"I feel so useless," he said miserably. "Even Bollinger has gone."

"Only to some dreary desk at the War Office! Besides, he's younger than you are."

"He doesn't look it!"

He went off in a huff and I looked at his departing backview with exasperation.

Hugh Bainbridge went, leaving a very elderly man in his place as agent at Watersmeet, and Lydia Bollinger seemed to think this good enough reason to send for Roger at any hour of the day or night to deal with all manner of domestic problems. He reported that she wore an especially tailored nurse's uniform and floated about dispensing gracious words to the wounded men, but little else. There was a tough little Scottish sister and a handful of overworked nurses who actually did the work; however, she had given up her home so I felt it ill behoved me to feel quite so resentful of the way she continued to take up Roger's time.

At first, he was reasonably good natured about it and dealt capably with her problems concerning tenants and tied cottages, overflowing streams and broken fences; but as time went on and our own staff problems grew more pressing, he became a little restive.

"You are an idiot," I told him. "You should turn round and tell her."

"Easier said than done. It's very hard to lay down the law to her when she's sitting there looking soulful, like some latter-day Florence Nightingale."

"You're far too kind," I said.

I was quite certain that there was nothing more to it than that, although I would be less than honest if I did not admit that I resented the time he spent at Watersmeet.

He had put in a hard day in the garden and was relaxing by the fire with a glass of whisky in his hand after a hot bath when the telephone rang one evening.

It was Lydia Bollinger.

"There's an emergency," she told me. "I hate to bother Roger, but I'd be so grateful if he could come—truly, nothing but the gravest necessity would make me call him out."

I pulled a face at Roger who was listening to me from the other side of the room.

"He's very tired," I said.

"My dear, aren't we *all*? I mean, it is wartime, isn't it? One does have to make just that little extra effort. Sometimes

I feel that the strain is all too much for me—all these poor, sick, gallant men!"

"You'd better speak to him yourself," I said, resignedly.

It ended as I knew it would. He would be up just as soon as he had finished his dinner, he said. I was a little tight-lipped about it, and grew more and more so as the evening lengthened and he failed to return from Watersmeet.

"Still up?" he said in surprise when he finally came home and found me downstairs by the fire, stabbing my needle in and out of one of his work shirts I was mending. I put it down and glared at him.

"And just what emergency kept you up until this time?" I asked.

I thought that he faltered a little on the threshold.

"You're not angry, are you? Lydia was going through a sort of *crise de nerfs*. The whole thing is getting on top of her."

"Just so long as it's not you who's getting on top of her!"

For a split-second he looked at me in stunned amazement, then blew out his cheeks in an explosion of laughter.

"Well! Jenny Leyton, you shock me to the core, you really do! What very coarse company you must have been keeping. What your poor, dear grandmother would say I simply can't imagine."

"My poor dear grandmother would probably take a rolling pin to you—and to the lady at Watersmeet. Surely it's bad enough that I have to lend you to her during the day as a substitute husband without having you take over at night as well."

He came over and sat beside me, still laughing as he rubbed his cheek against my hair.

"Oh Jenny, if you only knew how you wronged me!"

"I'll eat my hat if I'm wronging Lydia, though. Admit it, Roger, she's had designs on you for years."

"Do you mind?"

I sat up straight and pushed him away from me.

"Of course I mind, you fiendish man! Stop laughing this instant. How do you think I've felt, sitting here hour after hour wondering just what's happening up at Watersmeet?"

He looked at me thoughtfully, through narrowed lids.

"It's a fair cop," he said. "I'll come quietly—confess everything—throw myself on your mercy. It will do you the world of good to hear all. It'll show you that other women appreciate my finer points and my unique talents."

"Ha!"

He rose to his feet and stood on the hearthrug looking down at me, his thumbs stuck into the armholes of his waistcoat.

"When I arrived at Watersmeet," he said, "Lydia was having, as I told you, a *crise de nerfs*—or what in the nursery would have been called a tantrum. She and the Scots sister had all but come to blows over whether a handyman could be spared from essential work in the kitchen to repair Lydia's plumbing, the lavatory having seized up for some reason and flooded the bathroom. Having pacified the sister, commiserated with the handyman, plied Lydia with brandy, I then had to get down to finding the blockage and clearing up the mess. So far from spending the hours in dalliance, my sweet and suspicious love, I was for the most part locked in battle with a pipe wrench and a leaky cistern."

It was my turn to laugh.

"Serve you right," I said. "You shouldn't be so *willing*!"

"Lydia has had enough. She's through with the whole charade—Gerald needs her more than the poor, brave boys at Watersmeet, she says."

"Well, thank God for that."

There was still a smile on his face, but one of extreme self-satisfaction.

"I must say it does the old ego a lot of good to think that jealousy reared its head to such an extent after all these years. Suddenly I don't feel such an incredibly ancient has-been after all."

"Tell me honestly," I said. "There was something, wasn't there?"

He came and sat beside me once again and reached out to stroke my cheek gently with his fingers.

"On her part, perhaps," he said at last. "Through sheer ennui, I'm certain. In her London milieu she would have thought me a country bumpkin. But you don't need me to give you assurances, do you, Jenny? There'll never be anyone else for me—never, ever. Believe it."

"I do," I said, and reached up to kiss him.

He continued to fret about what he chose to call his uselessness, though we were supplying vegetables not only to our own hotels but to two hospitals in Oxford.

"It's nothing that an older man couldn't do," he said. "Or a younger one, come to that. Amos put in a wonderful day's work today. He's a fine, strong boy."

"So I believe. And *he's* talking about trying to volunteer too."

"But he's hardly fourteen."

"That's no more ridiculous than a man of your age talking of passing himself off as a thirty year old!"

He glared at me but said no more.

A few days later, Roger returned from a visit to Oxford and without a word got down to work, more morose than before. Even though he had no middle-aged spread, I could only assume that he had been unable to convince the recruitment board that he was of a suitable age to enlist.

Both the NUWSS and the WSPU had suspended the fight for women's suffrage for the duration of the war and Ellie found herself out of a permanent job. For some months she worked on the tea-stalls but it did not satisfy her, and during 1915 we had received a letter telling us that she had been accepted as a probationer nurse at a hospital in Paddington.

"I don't like it," Roger said testily. "I can't bear to think of her dealing with all the frightful things a nurse has to do."

"Nonsense!" his mother said briskly. She was staying with us on a brief holiday taken for the purpose of seeing her great-grandchild. Goffy's nursing home had been turned into an Army hospital and he was busier than ever. She was only sorry, she said, that she herself was too old to train as a nurse. It was the only job worth doing.

By the spring of 1916 Ellie had completed her training and had volunteered to go to France. Ben was still in and out of the trenches at Hebuterne, retiring to rest billets in Courcelles for short spells, but always returning to the line.

"He *must* be due for leave now," we said to each other as 1916 went on its way. He wrote of it in the early summer and he and Ellie even planned a visit home together, but on the 1st July the Somme offensive started and all leave was cancelled.

The casualty lists were terrifying. I almost dreaded going to church every Sunday for nearly always we would hear of a Collingford boy either dead or wounded. I think the bravest man I ever knew was Reverend Chalmers, who stood up and preached a simple and moving sermon on the day after he had heard his only son had been killed on the Somme.

One day I happened to be standing at the door of the Ring of Bells and as I glanced idly towards the main road I saw the telegraph boy turn the corner and come bicycling towards me.

I felt as if all the blood had drained from my body, as if heart and lungs and all the organs inside of me had been wrenched out and replaced by a single, heavy block of ice. Dumbly I watched as he approached, whistling; and closed my eyes in thanksgiving as he passed me by and went round the corner to one of the cottages that faced the green to the side of the Ring of Bells. Thank God, I thought; oh, thank God! Then went inside and buried my head in my arms and cried, there in the privacy of my office, because the war had reduced me to this; that I could be glad that it was some other mother's son who had died and not Ben.

That summer Lucy donned breeches and worked on the land. We still kept three horses which were in constant use as the delivery van used by the Ring of Bells had been requisitioned by the Army, and Lucy took on the job of looking after them. Her delicate skin grew weatherbeaten and her hands were like sandpaper, though she dedicatedly rubbed them with lanolin every night. The few cows we had also became her concern—a hard enough job in the summer, but cruelly hard in the winter when the windows were icy even on the inside and her boots crunched over frozen puddles in the yard on the way to the cowshed.

Izzie looked after the baby. Izzie looked after everything and everybody except Amos, who looked after her. Bert had rejoined the Navy at the outbreak of war and Izzie accepted his departure with resignation. She watched Amos constantly, fear in her eyes. She knew that he, too, was desperate to be gone.

Amos was a tall, strapping lad, in appearance far older than Philip although they were much of an age. Philip was still a coltish schoolboy, moving pins on a map and anxious that the war should not end before he was old enough to join the Royal Flying Corps. He and Peter planned to do so at the earliest possible moment and Philip was envious because the time was almost ripe for Peter. He would be seventeen at Christmas.

Meantime, Philip spent his holidays helping out at the Ring of Bells. It was no longer a case of finding him something to do merely to amuse him. When he put in an appearance in the kitchen it was like having an extra pair of hands, and I was sorely tempted to give in to his earnest request that he should be allowed to leave school and help full-time.

"They won't take you in the Flying Corps if you're half-educated," Roger said.

To me, this seemed an excellent reason for curtailing his education forthwith, but I knew that I was being illogical. Of course he had to stay at school. The war would not go on for ever and it was essential that he should be prepared for the world that must eventually come after it was all over, however remote and insubstantial that world might seem now.

In December 1916 it could hardly have seemed more distant. The struggle at Verdun had been going on since February; there had been many more Zeppelin raids; Kitchener had been drowned when his ship had been mined; Britain had lost confidence even in her sea power since the Battle of Jutland. And Ben had been in Belgium and France for the past eighteen months, almost constantly in battle, his chances of survival diminishing with each succeeding day.

Then suddenly we heard that he would be home for Christmas. Home for Christmas! The words echoed round Priors and everyone's heart grew lighter—until the telegram came for Izzie. Bert's ship had gone down in the North Sea, lost with all hands.

If Izzie shed any tears, she did not let me see them. She

went about her work with a kind of grim fury, her black-circled eyes looking even more desperately at Amos.

There was again talk of Ellie coming home with Ben, but it was only a possibility and we heard no positive confirmation of it. It would have been wonderful to have them all at home, but in another way, I told myself, perhaps it was better like this—first Ben and then Ellie. That way we could spread our pleasures. There would still be something to look forward to once Ben had gone back to the front.

But oh, it was impossible to think of him going back when here he was at last, striding down the station platform towards us. Was he always so tall, I asked myself? Or did he look taller because he was thinner? His face was pale and he had lost the last vestige of boyish roundness from his cheeks. He looked gaunt and deathly tired.

John Leyton, angry because he had volunteered for the Army and was still languishing behind an office desk in Whitehall, was also home on leave and he and Angela and their family came over for Christmas Day.

Our party was determinedly jolly. Ben smiled and joked and teased his cousins and played charades, and said nothing at all about the life he had left beyond the channel. Even when directly questioned, he was evasive.

'Not frightfully pleasant,' was his verdict on trench warfare, and 'perfectly splendid' described the spirit of the ordinary fighting man.

"How do you get on with the French?" Angela asked him.

"Oh, quite splendidly," was his reply.

Did he talk more to Lucy, I wondered? Perhaps—but then again, perhaps not, for what could he say of comfort to a girl whose husband was at the front! It was a shame that Ellie was not at home for he had always been able to talk to her—and still could, it seemed, for we learned that he had managed to snatch a 'perfectly splendid' day with her before coming home.

It all went so quickly. He walked a lot and went ferreting and played with Beth and helped Lucy with the horses. And sometimes he just sat and looked into space.

"I've never known ten days fly so fast," Lucy said on his

301

last night, looking at him with something like desperation in her eyes.

"Yes, it has gone awfully quickly," he agreed, smiling politely. I almost expected him to say 'Thank you for having me', like a well-brought up little boy.

"As long as you've enjoyed yourself—" Roger said.

"Oh yes, thanks. It's been perfectly splendid."

"Do you think he *has* enjoyed it?" I asked Roger when, much later, we had retired to our bedroom.

"Of course."

"Don't you find him a little difficult?" I asked. "Remote. As if we are strangers he has to be very polite to."

"We are strangers," Roger said after a moment. "He must feel that this is quite unreal. The life out there is what is real to him."

"But we love him so!"

"He knows that. Perhaps it's simply that he daren't let himself get too involved with us. The change when he gets back would be too shattering."

I found it impossible to sleep. I heard the grandfather clock in the hall strike midnight and half-past midnight and one o'clock, and still I could not sleep.

I would make myself a warm drink, I decided, and slipped carefully out of bed so that I would not wake Roger. I put on my dressing gown and slippers and crept softly from the room.

The top corridor was illuminated by a full moon that flooded through the tall windows at the top of the stairs. There was no need to switch on the light for me to see my way, and as I passed Ben's door I could see quite clearly that there was a line of light beneath it.

So he could not sleep either.

I hesitated for a moment, then tapped on the door and looked into the room.

"I was going to get myself some cocoa," I said. "Would you like some?"

"Mmm?" He was sitting fully dressed in an armchair with his back to the door and he turned at my words, a look of polite enquiry on his face.

"I wondered if you would like some cocoa," I repeated.

"Thanks—but I think I'll stick to this." He lifted a bottle that was on a small table by his side. I recognised it as Roger's best brandy. "Would you like some? There is another glass."

I hesitated, not really wanting brandy; but there was something in the atmosphere that made me feel that if I walked out of the door I would be walking away for ever from the chance to talk to Ben.

"Perhaps I will," I said, coming inside and pulling up another chair. "But for heaven's sake make up the fire, Ben. It's freezing in here."

"Is it?" he said, looking surprised. He got to his feet and put coal on the fire, attacking it with the poker until it burst into life, then poured some brandy into the second glass and handed it to me.

"I haven't had much to drink," he said defensively.

"I can tell you haven't," I agreed. And indeed, he seemed perfectly composed and completely sober.

"But somehow," he went on as if I had said nothing, "I feel I could drink the whole bottle without it having any effect. I wish it would. I wish it would . . ."

His voice trailed away into silence.

"Ben," I began. "Ben."

I leaned forward gripping my glass tightly, not knowing how to phrase what I wanted so much to say, conscious only of the seconds dripping inexorably away like the grains of sand through an hour glass.

"We must seem so remote here—remote from the life you lead in France, I mean. If we do, it's not entirely our fault. You haven't told us anything!"

He was silent for a moment, swirling the brandy around in the glass, his face drawn into lines that belonged to a much older man.

"I wanted to talk about it," he said at last. "Before I came, I kept thinking—I must try to make them understand what it's like. But somehow, seeing you all here, just the same as ever, not touched by it, the words won't come. I don't know how to begin."

"There was a sergeant," I said. "One of the patients at Watersmeet. He talked to me one day about the mud and the blood and the awfulness of it all, and my imagination did the rest. I never stop thinking of you, Ben. And it's not true to say that we are untouched."

"You can't *begin* to imagine it!" His voice was angry, but immediately he glanced at me penitently. "I'm sorry, Mother. I know I'm edgy. I'd give anything in the world to say thank you, gentlemen—I've had enough! I will now resume my academic career, if it's all the same with you. But of course, that's impossible, and even if it were not, I don't suppose I would do it. I still believe Germany must be stopped."

"Ben, you won't do anything terribly brave and foolish, will you?"

He laughed at that.

"Only by accident. I'm not a very good soldier, you know. Oh, I manage to endure the hardships as well as any—maybe life at a British public school is the best preparation for the trenches that you can get! But when it comes to killing people . . ."

His voice trailed away into silence again and I remembered that it was always Ben who was sorry for the fox when the Meet set out in full cry.

"It must be indescribably dreadful," I said.

"Yes," he agreed woodenly. "Yes, it is, rather."

That impenetrable glass barrier was down again.

"How did you think Ellie was when you saw her?" I asked. "Really, I mean. And," I added, "if you say 'perfectly splendid', I don't think I shall be answerable for the consequences!"

"Ellie?" He looked up with a smile as if grateful that I had steered the conversation away from him. "She's all right. Thin and pale and overworked, like every nurse, but in tearing spirits. A little exaltée, I should say."

"Exaltée?"

He paused and grew serious again as if considering his words carefully.

"She's in love, Mother," he said at last. "Madly in love. Madly," he repeated, as if surprised at himself for using the word but standing by it just the same.

"Who with?" I asked. "Have you met him?"

"Yes, I have. I had dinner with both of them. He's a

captain in the Lincolnshires who was wounded. She nursed him."

"What's he like?"

"Oh—a perfectly splendid—"

"Ben!"

"Sorry. He's thirtyish, perhaps a little older. Brownish hair, grey eyes. Very intelligent in a quiet sort of a way. He's quick-witted. Amusing. Well-read. Mad about Ellie."

"He sounds quite perfect!"

"There's just one small flaw. He's due to go back into the front line at any moment. Nothing perfect about that."

"Oh, the poor darling," I whispered, agonising for Ellie. "There wouldn't be any half measures about the way she fell in love, would there? I wish she could have come home for Christmas."

"Yes, indeed," Ben agreed, in his polite voice. "Mother—I'm not too sure I should have told you."

"I'm glad you did."

"I didn't want to go back without—I mean, if anything happened to him and if anything happened to me, then you might not have understood quite how seriously she was involved." He had dropped the remote manner. He was suffering for Ellie too, but for a moment I had abandoned the thought of my daughter and was concentrating only on what he had said of himself. His voice had been so matter-of-fact as he mentioned the possibility of something happening to him that the full impact had not hit me for a split-second after he had finished speaking. I swallowed hard and tried to ignore it. It was, after all, a thought that had lived with me for the better part of two years and putting it into words made it neither more nor less possible.

"But she's happy just now?"

"Luminous," he said and grinned at me, sharing the knowledge of just how luminous Ellie could be.

"What's his name?"

"Lawrence Durward."

"And he's quite recovered now? He's back in the trenches?"

"Not yet. He's having some leave in Paris before going back."

There was a silence that lengthened between us. Hurriedly he turned and put some more coal on the fire.

"Ellie's with him, isn't she?" It wasn't really a question. I knew, suddenly, why she had been unable at the last moment to come home on leave.

Ben expelled his breath slowly and leaned back in his chair.

"I rather gave the game away there, didn't I? Yes, Ellie is with him. Do you blame her? It wasn't something she did lightly."

"No. No, I don't suppose it was."

I thought of my sensitive, courageous Ellie, in love and facing squarely the fact that this might be all she would ever have of her Lawrence. "I don't blame her," I said. "How could I?"

"I don't think you'd better mention it to dad," Ben said.

"He'd be across the channel with a horse whip, wouldn't he?"

"Which neither of them deserves. Lawrence isn't a depraved seducer, I promise you. He really loves Ellie."

"As well he might," I said, tears suddenly springing to my eyes as I thought of her. Oh God—why did I never suspect that there were so many tears to be shed?

"Lucy has really turned up trumps, hasn't she?" Ben said. "I never suspected her capable of such hard work. I'm so glad to have had the chance to see Beth."

I nodded and smiled. There he goes again, I thought—implying that this might be the only chance given him. I suddenly felt exhausted, any reserve of strength I might have was wholly depleted, and I saw from the clock on the mantelpiece that it was after half past two.

"We must both get some sleep," I said. "You have a long journey tomorrow and I have to work." Yet I got to my feet slowly, reluctant to leave him. "Ben, I'm so glad we talked."

He rose too, and stood facing me, fidgeting nervously with the empty glass in the hand.

"Will you sleep now?" he asked.

I nodded and reached up to kiss him.

"Good night, darling. God bless you, always."

I went to the door and he followed me awkwardly as if there was still some last thing left unsaid.

"Mother," he said as I was about to leave. "Thank you."

Good heavens, I thought. He really is thanking me for having him!

"I don't mean just for this leave," he added quickly, seeing my expression. "I mean for everything. Nobody could have had a happier childhood than I did. It's all been perfectly—" he broke off and laughed a little in his nervousness, shrugging his shoulders.

"Splendid," I finished for him. "I'm glad, darling, because it's been perfectly splendid having you. And will be again, please God."

I left the room quickly before he saw me start to cry again, and I even managed to smile as his train drew out of the station the following day. At least, I thought, he is safe for another day or two. It will take that long for him to get back to the line. I don't have to worry yet.

And it didn't mean anything special when he spoke of the possibility of not coming back. How could it? He couldn't know. Everything was just speculation.

But one thing had been made clear by Ben's leave. Whatever the outcome of this war—however many men returned, however vivid the imagination of those at home, there would always be an unbridgeable gulf between the men who had experienced the battle at first hand and the ones who had stayed behind.

19

Nobody thought beyond the end of the war.

Lucy, so recently a high-spirited, carefree schoolgirl, grew pale and quiet, uncharacteristically preferring solitude to the company of friends as if only when alone could she concentrate on keeping Nick alive. I recognised the feeling. Strangely, it seemed as if by worrying about them and bearing them constantly in our thoughts we were contributing something positive towards our menfolk's well-being.

Peter had joined the Flying Corps and was receiving his initial training in Gloucestershire, not too far away from us, so he came for occasional visits. We had not seen him for several years and to me it seemed that he had changed out of all recognition. He had always been full of self-confidence. Now that he was in the coveted uniform, he positively overflowed with bounce and swagger. His conversation was larded with flying jargon and Philip hung on his every word.

"Flying's not a bit as I imagined," Peter told us. "I always thought there would be a sort of soaring sensation, as if you were a giant eagle with enormous wings. But it's not like that at all. It's more as if the earth is dropping away from you."

I shuddered.

"I don't know how you can!"

"Have you been solo yet?" Philip asked.

"Lord, yes! It's a lonely sort of sensation, but absolutely ripping when you get used to it. The instructor says I'm a natural."

"Lucky swine," Philip said, with feeling.

I forbore to mention, and tried not even to think, that the life of the average pilot these days could be measured in days rather than weeks. They were sending half-trained boys up, I had been told, so great was the loss of life in those fragile planes that flew over the enemy lines.

"What's the news from your father?" I asked Peter.

"He's madly busy trying to keep the farm ticking over with hardly any men left to help him. He tried to join up, but they wouldn't have him. They said growing food was just as valuable."

"Quite right, too," I agreed.

"That's all very well," Lucy said dismally. "But one doesn't feel part of anything."

"Poor old sis," Philip said.

I looked at Lucy. She had just come in from outside and was rubbing her chilled hands before a meagre fire. She was dressed in a strange assortment of clothes against the cold, layer upon layer, and no one could have guessed that underneath them all there was an exceptionally shapely young girl of twenty-three.

She must feel as if she is in a state of suspended animation, I thought. As a young married woman in peacetime she would be busy with friends and home and family. As a single woman in wartime she could at least have benefited from the sense of purpose and comradeship others experienced. For Lucy there was no feeling of oneness with her generation. Just dreary routine, hard slog, worry and loneliness and, at the end of the day, a fretful baby to cope with, for Beth was teething and had been sleeping badly.

"I have an idea," I said suddenly. "Lucy, let's take French leave! Peter and Philip can look after the livestock for once and Izzie will be only too pleased to have Beth. We'll go to Oxford for the day and buy ourselves some new clothes."

She brightened a little at the thought and I, too, found the prospect of a carefree day appealing. It still seemed strange to see Oxford full of khaki uniforms instead of the flying black gowns of prewar days. But a weak sun was shining and Oxford could never change in essence. As always we enjoyed its timeless beauty and for a few brief moments we were frivolous, forgetful of the cares that had weighed us down for so long.

I could not tempt Lucy into buying much. She still had all her trousseau in mint condition, she said, and to acquire anything else would be positively unpatriotic. She did buy a hat, though, and I splashed out on a pretty green coat and skirt which revealed more ankle than anything else I had ever owned.

Over lunch at the Mitre, Lucy suggested that we should go to the cinema.

"I saw a poster in the town," she said. "It's this man Chaplin. Do let's go, Mother! He's supposed to be awfully good."

"Do you think we should?" I asked doubtfully. I should have preferred to go with Roger, were I to go at all. There was a feeling of daring about going to such a place; but Lucy looked brighter than she had been for months and on reflection there seemed little harm in the idea.

The film was *Shanghaied*, and we enjoyed it enormously.

It was not our first taste of moving pictures as for some years there had been a tent at the Hiring Fair which exhibited short films, but we had never seen anything half as entertaining as this. Charlie Chaplin was superb as the man dragged aboard ship and it did my heart good to hear Lucy laughing beside me as he went through the motions of waiting at table in a heaving sea. It came to an end amid a final burst of arpeggios from the pianist.

Escapist entertainment it was called in the paper. Aptly too, for we had escaped into another world for one brief moment where the war did not exist. From then on Lucy and I occasionally escaped to Witney where there was a cinema called the People's Palace. We saw Theda Bara and Pearl White and Lillian Gish. We laughed at the Keystone Cops and yearned over Douglas Fairbanks. It was all fantasy, of course, and we recognised it as such. But it helped a little.

The increased submarine warfare caused losses to the Americans as well as to the Allies and in April they finally decided that our struggle was also theirs. It gave us an enormous boost to feel that new and vigorous forces were joining us. Ellie wrote that the American troops looked like a race of supermen beside our worn-out Tommies.

"It can't be long now," we said. "Surely not long."

And still Ben was safe, and Nick too—though according to Lucy, Colonel Marchant prayed nightly for him to win the Victoria Cross. She went to stay with her in-laws in Cheltenham from time to time and always came back full of pent-up anger and frustration.

"I don't think he would care if it were to be granted posthumously," she said bitterly. "He pretends to care about Nick, but it's his own honour and glory that's important. I spend all my time there biting my tongue."

"They're all heroes," I said. "Every last one, medals or no."

The news that Ben had been awarded the Military Cross, however, did fill me with pride, though my first reaction was outrage.

"I *told* him to be careful," I said. "Oh, he is naughty! He never listens to a word I say."

310

In the same engagement Nick was mentioned in dispatches. His father regarded this as a very second-rate award, almost a disgrace, and Lucy swore that it was only her presence that prevented him turning Nick's picture to the wall. Mrs Marchant for once defied her husband and said that he was a son to be proud of, a fine brave boy, so there!

I had mentioned casually in a letter to Ellie that Ben had told me of Lawrence Durward and how much I hoped that he would be kept safe. She replied that she was glad we knew about him. She had been meaning to mention him herself but had been hoping to see us, face to face, to explain how she felt about him. It was difficult, she said, to convey in black and white quite how she felt without sounding like a lovesick sixteen-year-old! But love him she did, and after the war they would be married. So far, she said, he was safe; and thereafter she only mentioned him casually, either to say that she had just had a lovely letter from him or that it seemed ages since she had heard.

I was delighted when Ben wrote that his battalion was withdrawing for seventeen days during July for intensive training, though less delighted when it dawned upon me that the training must surely mean that some big push was in the offing.

"At least Peter is still in England," I said to Roger. "And Nick's been given leave. Isn't that wonderful?"

His grim expression melted into a smile.

"Lucy is so excited, I think we'll have to tie her down before next week or she'll fly higher than Peter. She's going to London to meet Nick, I take it?"

"Yes. They plan to stay there for two nights, come back here to pick up Beth and then go off to Cheltenham to stay with the Marchants."

It was impossible not to feel more cheerful, with Lucy singing about the house again. Lloyd George's Coalition Government was in power; Winston Churchill was at the War Office; the Americans were pouring over in force; the sun was shining. And Ben was behind the lines, in training. I could forget to worry, just for a few weeks.

Lucy left for London looking her old, delightful self, the layers of woolies discarded, but the week's leave was so short—even to me it seemed no time before they were back from Cheltenham. To them it must seem as if it had all happened in the winking of an eye. Nick was to stay one night at Priors before returning to London en route for France. All through dinner Lucy was feverishly bright, her eyes fixed upon him, and as soon as it was decently possible they left us to spend their last night together.

I lay beside Roger staring into the darkness, rigid with misery.

"What's wrong, darling?" he asked, drawing me to him.

"Oh, Roger," I sobbed into his chest. "Oh, I can't bear it! Lucy and Nick, counting every minute—and Ellie, knowing that the man she loves is in danger, and Ben, loathing every second of it. Do you remember how he cried about the dancing bear? He hated to think of the poor thing suffering! I can't bear it for them, Roger—I just can't bear it for them!"

He said nothing for a while, just held me close and stroked my hair.

"Of course you can't," he said, his voice little but a sigh. "We none of us can bear things for other people, even our children. They have to bear their own burdens ultimately, just as we have to bear the burden of loving them. It's what makes them, after all. The bad things along with the good— they all mould their characters."

"But to sit back and let them suffer!"

"I'm not saying we can be indifferent. Heaven knows, I'd give my life in an instant if it would solve anything. All I'm saying, Jenny, is that we have to accept life as it is, not fight and worry at it like you do, every minute of the day. They'll do their own agonising, just as they'll do their own loving and rejoicing. You can't experience their pain, any more than you can experience the love that Nick and Lucy are probably sharing at this very moment. You'll wear yourself out, trying to channel every one of their emotions through yourself."

I expelled my breath slowly, forcing myself to relax.

"You're right, of course. I'll try to be calm."

Before the end of that week, Peter came to tell us that he was leaving for France. He had a week's embarkation leave which he was going to spend in Somerset, so for us this was his farewell visit.

312

He had been almost like one of our own children before Mark and Charlotte left Priors and even now, though mildly amused and irritated by his bumptious self-satisfaction, I regarded him with great affection. He was so very young and so very proud of being a member of the Flying Corps. But Izzie was, perhaps, more affected than any of us since for many years she had looked after him with as much devotion as she had given to Amos.

"I've brought you this, Master Peter," she said, folding up a Balaclava helmet she had knitted and tucking it into his kit bag. "It'll be cold up there. Don't forget to wear it, mind—I know what you're like about clothes, never a scrap of sense when it comes to dressing up warm. Now, be a good boy for Izzie and don't do anything silly."

"You're an angel, Izzie dearest, and I'll wear it always," Peter said, with a concealed wink in Philip's direction. "And I'll be thinking of you every time I put it on."

He bent to kiss her cheek and she accepted the kiss woodenly, her mouth clamped into a straight line.

"Dear old girl," he said, when she had gone. "I'm surprised she didn't turn round and tell me what a foolish occupation flying is."

"If God had meant you to fly," Philip said, in a fair approximation of Izzie's voice, "He would have given you wings."

"Your turn next, old boy," Peter said, bending to adjust the angle of his cap in front of the mirror that hung on the wall.

"It'll be all over long before Philip is old enough," I said sharply.

Philip pulled a face at Peter.

"She's probably right, you know—I'm still only sixteen. I've another year at school before I can even think of volunteering."

"Too bad, old son." Peter grinned at himself in the mirror, well pleased with the dashing appearance that confronted him. "Well, I'd better be off, or I'll miss the train."

At the end of July the third Battle of Ypres began. This, then, was the offensive for which Ben and his battalion had been in training throughout the month.

Roger had already gone over to the Red Lion and I was about to leave for the Ring of Bells one morning in August when I glanced from the front window of Priors and saw the telegraph boy cycling down the track. It was a sight I had often rehearsed in my mind. I had wondered how I would react. Now I knew; I simply stood and watched him, all feeling suspended. I could not move or think.

I saw Lucy come round from the yard to intercept the boy and watched her disappear from my view as she made for the door tearing at the envelope. Still I could not move.

"Mother." I heard her voice behind me sounding strangled and strange and with an enormous effort I turned my head.

She came to me and put her arms around me.

"Mother, it's Ben."

I took the telegram from her and stared at it, trying to get the words into focus.

"Regret to inform you . . . Captain Roger Benjamin Leyton . . . Missing believed killed."

"Missing," I said, seizing on the word. "Only missing. There's still hope."

"Of course there's hope," Lucy agreed. "The confusion must be terrible over there."

Ellie said the same thing in a letter. There were times when I knew that he was still alive. Equally, times when I felt quite certain that he had been killed. All through late summer and the lovely, golden autumn days I alternated between hope and despair.

Amos ran away and joined the Navy at about this time. He was only sixteen, but could easily have passed for seventeen and a half, he was so tall and strong.

"He can't join without your permission, Izzie," I said, when she came to me stony faced to say that he had gone. "You could get him back."

"He's was set on it," she said resignedly. "Ever since Bert was lost, he's been set on it. I've turned round and told him, time and time again—" but her words were lost as quite literally she turned round to hide her tears from me.

It was on a wet night at the end of October that Roger, Lucy and I, having eaten, were sitting in the smaller drawing room. Izzie had moved back into Priors since Amos left, partly for reasons of economy and partly because she was lonely, and I could hear sounds from the dining room where she was clearing up after our meal. Lucy was writing a letter to Nick, Roger was shaking his head over the paper, and I was knitting mechanically, my thoughts miles away.

Suddenly I heard the crash of china and a yelp of surprise from Izzie. I wondered briefly what particular item had come to grief and what had happened to startle her, but I was so sunk in my own gloomy thoughts that I paid little attention. The loss of the china, whatever it was, did not distress me as it might have done even a year ago. What did china matter? What, even, did houses matter, compared with the lives of one's family? In times like these, one's priorities had a way of sorting themselves out without the slightest doubt or hesitation.

The door between our sitting room and the hall opened and we all looked up to see a slight figure, plainly dressed in a damp, all-enveloping navy blue overcoat with an ugly hat pulled low. We sat transfixed for a split second.

"Ellie!" I cried, leaping up from my chair.

The three of us began to talk at once, pulling her in towards the fire, hugging her, unbuttoning her coat. It was a full minute before it dawned on me that she herself had not said a word.

"Darling child, you should have phoned from the station," Roger said. "Why on earth didn't you let us know?"

She didn't answer him, but just looked at us all, her face a small, white triangle beneath the cloud of dark hair that was revealed when she had pulled off the extinguishing hat. She looked at me, her huge eyes blank with misery, then seemed to launch herself at me, sobbing as though her heart would break.

"Is it Lawrence?" I asked.

She nodded, gulping back her sobs.

"I kept writing to him. I didn't know. They didn't tell me because I wasn't his next of kin—they told his parents, of course, but not me. Then all his letters came back."

Roger picked her up and carried her to his armchair where he cradled her on his knee as if she had been a baby. Lucy knelt beside them both, silent tears slipping down her cheeks.

I went outside to find some hot food and drink for Ellie, leaning for a moment against the door behind me, my eyes closed. Was there to be no end to it?

I was aware of Izzie talking to me.

"I'm that sorry, m'm, I was startled, seeing her there, not expecting anyone, like. She looked like a ghost! It would be one of the best plates that got broke, wouldn't it? Always the same! There aren't many left now."

"It doesn't matter, Izzie. Don't worry about it. Is there any of the soup left?"

"I've already put it on to heat, and I'm just going to get the bed made up. She'll need plenty of hot bottles by the look of her: Peaky, isn't she—the blessed lamb! Lucky the fire's laid in her room—I'll only need to touch a match to it."

Oh blessed, invaluable Izzie! If only it were possible to soothe the hurts left by the war with hot bottles and fires and soft beds.

"Do you have to go back?" I asked Ellie at the end of her leave, already extended by a week at Richard Fenwick's insistence after he had examined her and pronounced her totally exhausted.

"I have to, Mother. I just have to."

"Well," I said. "I expect you know your own business best."

"It's not that I want to go."

"I understand."

"I wish you could have known Lawrence!"

"Ben liked him a lot. I'm sure we should have done so, too."

"I wanted to bring him here, so much. I talked about you all often. He liked Ben, too."

"Ellie—what about Ben? Am I a fool to keep hoping?"

She shrugged helplessly.

"How can one *not* hope?"

The telegraph boy made another journey to Priors just before Christmas, but this time I was spared the sight of his approach. I knew what news he had brought when I went into the kitchen to find Izzie crying into her apron.

Amos.

"Oh Izzie, Izzie!" I held her and we wept together.

"It's no more than I expected," she said grimly when at last she could speak. "It's a judgment on me."

"What on earth can you mean?" I asked.

"For my sin. For giving birth to him in the first place."

"You can't believe that! Izzie, I will not have you saying such a thing—it's sheer nonsense! As if God would exact that kind of retribution!"

"I don't believe in a God of love," she said. "Not any more."

"Reverend Chalmers does, and he's lost a son too," I said. "Talk to him, Izzie. Perhaps we should both talk to him," I added as an afterthought. It was all too easy, these days, to believe that God must have abdicated responsibility for us all.

There was not much time in my crowded day, but I took to going across the green to St Peters—sometimes to pray, sometimes just to sit and absorb the prayers of the generations that had gone before. All over the country, people were turning to the church. I wondered if God minded that when things were going well, we were inclined to forget Him, yet always turned to Him as a last resort.

I was walking back across the green towards the Ring of Bells one afternoon as the early dusk was already beginning to fall when I saw a figure coming towards me. I did not immediately recognise the woman, but as she drew nearer my heart began to beat faster. There was something horribly familiar about her—nightmarishly familiar. Perhaps I was hallucinating? Surely, it couldn't possibly be—

" 'Afternoon," she said, stopping in front of me.

"Bella!" I said faintly.

I stared at her in disbelief. It was—how many years? Seventeen?—yes, seventeen years since she had left Collingford, and they were years that had wrought changes in her.

She was still loudly dressed but looked far more prosperous than when I had seen her last. Her fat had somehow solidified giving her the appearance of being upholstered, and her jaw-line had folded into dewlaps. Beneath her eyes were little pads of fat and her mouth had in some way become smaller, pushed into second place by the expanding flesh.

"Yeah," she said, smiling. "Surprise, eh?"

I could find nothing to say. I was vaguely conscious of two women from the neighbouring cottages who passed and greeted me. A pony-trap went along the lane on our left at a spanking pace and there were children calling. I stood, stonily silent, and looked at Bella.

"Ain't yer going ter say nothin', then?" she asked.

"You're—you're looking well," I managed to say at last.

"Best thing I ever did, leaving Collingford," she said.

"Yet you've come back!"

She laughed and came closer to me, standing over me just as she had in the old days, and I edged away a little. Even as I did so I knew that I was being illogical and foolish. There was no reason now to dread what she might reveal—too many years had passed for her to harm me. The feeling of revulsion was a hangover from my youth, nothing more. Surely I was too old—had gone through too much—for her to affect me.

"You'll never guess," she said.

"Guess what?"

"What I'm doing 'ere. I'm in the money meself, see. Remember Wally? 'Course you do! Our Vera's Wally. Well, 'im and me, we teamed up when I left 'ere. 'E left Vera—well, silly cow, she asked for it, no one can say different—and I ran across 'im up in Liverpool. Luckiest thing that ever 'appened. I'd just about run through the money you give me."

"That was very fortunate," I said, making as if to continue towards the Ring of Bells. Her voice ran on, jangling at my nerve ends, not changed in the slightest.

"We started a café for the sailors—all sorts you get, up in Liverpool, it don't do to be fussy. Lascars, Chinamen, Negroes, we got 'em all. When the war come we 'ad to make it bigger—there was the demand, see. Wally's a fly one, 'e is. We turned it into a doss-house. Never enough places to sleep there ain't, in Liverpool."

"So you made plenty of money?"

" 'Sright, dearie. And I made bloody sure I took my cut and locked it away nice and tight where Wally couldn't get 'is mitts on it, 'cos I knew bleedin' well 'e would, given 'alf

318

a chance. And I was right, too. 'E grabbed 'is share and 'opped it with a black whore from Cardiff! I'd be in a right two-and-eight if I 'adn't made provision."

"You were always able to look after yourself."

"No one else would, dearie." She grinned at me and I noticed another difference. She now had a set of gleaming white porcelain teeth.

By this time we had reached the inn and I stood in the doorway and faced her.

"You still haven't told me why you've come back to Collingford."

"You won't 'arf be surprised! I've taken over the Waggon and 'Orses. 'Ow about that, then?"

"You mean you're the landlady?"

" 'Sright. I saw it advertised in the paper, so I bid for it and got it. The brewery owns it, o' course—it's not me own place. Still, it's a start, ain't it? Laughed me 'ead off when I found I was coming back to Collingford after all these years. And in the same business as you, wot's more!"

She put out a hand and gave me a push on the shoulder.

"Old friends is best friends, I always say."

"Yes. Well." I stood and looked at her, not knowing quite what to say. I hated to think that she was back in the village, but really—what possible harm could she do me now?

"I'm prepared to put the past behind us," I said. "The war seems to have made everything else unimportant."

"That's right, dearie. Let bygones be bygones, and I'll do the same."

She extended her hand to me and although I still shrank from touching her, I managed to take it with a show of warmth.

"I wish you luck," I said.

"Thanks, dearie." She retained her hold of my hand and I looked at her, knowing that she still had something to say. "You need luck in our business, don't you? 'Eard about all that nastiness when your sister-in-law died. Didn't do you no good, did it?"

I looked into her eyes and saw that she had not changed. They still glittered with malice, pushed by the cushions of

319

flesh into two pinpoints of spite. A trickle of apprehension coursed down my spine.

I went inside and made my way to the kitchen where I sat with my feet on the fender, my two hands clasped round a cup as if for comfort. I felt cold. Since the word had come about Ben, I thought that nothing else could touch me, but still I felt depressed at Bella's return.

There's nothing she can do, I said to myself, full of sound common sense and logic. Our paths won't really cross. Yet I felt sure that she still nursed her childhood jealousy of me and would find a way to hurt us if possible, and of course, at some time it would be possible. The whole affair of Mark and Catherine and Charlotte had proved to us how vulnerable we were. Something unpredictable could happen at any time.

When once again I saw the familiar red bicycle of the telegraph boy bumping down the track towards Priors, my overriding thought was that I must reach him before Lucy. There was still no news of Ben. Nick was the only one left.

We knew he was in great danger. His division had been moved to the Italian front where a fierce battle was being waged against the Austrians. He had survived so much on the Western Front, it seemed almost impossible that his luck would hold out for ever, and I could tell that the strain on Lucy was growing steadily less bearable. If it were bad news, I had to know first; I could not bear it, to think of her seeing the words in cold print.

But though I ran quickly to the front door and out through the porch she had seen the boy from the yard and had beaten me. She was already tearing open the yellow envelope with shaking fingers and I stopped short, my hand pressed to my mouth.

The face she turned to me was one of joy.

"Mother, it's Ben—it's Ben! He's a prisoner. He's safe!"

The boy sat on his bicycle scuffing the ground with the toe of his boot, watching us and grinning, no doubt pleased for once to be the bearer of good news. I rushed inside to look for my purse, anxious to give him a tip, calling to Izzie, calling to anyone who was there to listen that Ben was safe, bursting with frustration that Roger was in Oxford for the day and could not be contacted.

We did not delude ourselves that being a prisoner of war was likely to be a pleasant experience; but he was alive, and life was all. And once again the telegram had not brought bad news of Nick. His charmed life went on.

"It can't go on much longer," we said to each other. "More and more Americans are pouring over. How *can* Germany hold out against them?" But apparently they could, and did.

Eventually, in April on a beautiful spring morning, we had a brief letter in Ben's own handwriting, months old and saying little. Anything could have happened since the day it was posted, but it cheered us immeasurably.

Izzie was knitting him a warm Balaclava helmet. They were her speciality and she knitted them one after the other with a grim, relentless fervour. When she met acquaintances in the High Street, she would ask after their relatives at the Front, closely followed by a second question: "Would he like a Balaclava helmet?" She had even been known to send one to Davey English who was in Egypt.

"I've heard about them desert nights," she said, her lips pursed knowingly, when Roger teased her about it.

Ben, I felt certain, would welcome one. Wherever he was, I was sure that it would be cold and comfortless—but surely, surely, we would not have to endure another winter of war?

Izzie's face grew craggy and her eyes seemed to retreat into her head. It was almost as if she wanted to repel sympathy as she went about her work, cleaning and polishing and ironing harder than ever, and in her moments of relaxation she would sit in the wooden wheel-back chair by the kitchen range and the steel knitting needles would fly.

I came into the kitchen one afternoon about tea time just as she threw down the knitting in a limp, khaki pile on the floor.

"Drat!" she said. "I've gone and made a mistake *again*! I should have decreased four rows back. Fifty-three of them things I've knitted and never a mistake; now I can't seem to get it right no matter how I try. Dratted things! I never want to see a bit of khaki wool again as long as I live—no, nor navy blue wool, either."

She rested her elbow on the arm of the chair and covered her face with her hands. Little Beth was with me and she stood transfixed, her thumb in her mouth, looking at Izzie in consternation.

"Granny," she said. "Izzie has the hiccups."

"Go and find mummy, darling," I said, giving her a little push in the direction of the back door. "See how the baby chicks are getting on."

Obligingly she went out into the yard and I crossed the room to Izzie.

She was not the kind of woman to take kindly to embraces, but this time she clung to me. "You've been brave for too long," I said. "You're having a holiday, Izzie. You're going right away from here to some lovely place where people are going to wait on you for a change."

"Whatever next!" Sheer indignation made her stop crying at once. "I'll have a holiday when the Kaiser is beaten and not before."

"I won't take no for an answer," I said. "You give it some thought. We'll arrange the hotel."

It took her some days to come round to the idea, but eventually she said rather diffidently that she had always wanted to go to Bognor.

"It must be lovely there," she said. "It's where the King goes, and *he* must know what's what."

And so it was decided.

It was while Izzie was away that Lucy heard that Nick was wounded—not in action but in a climbing accident in the Italian mountains, where his battalion had gone for training for the engagement that was coming with the Austrians on the Asiago Plateau. He had fallen and broken his pelvis.

"They're sending him home," she said, her face glowing. "Isn't that the most wonderful news in the world?"

A strange world, I thought, where one could consider a broken pelvis wonderful—but of course she was right. With any luck, his war would be over.

Nick, apparently, didn't view it in quite the same light. He was furious at what he considered the ignominious character of his accident.

"Aren't men strange?" Lucy remarked one day, looking up with a frown from a letter she had just received. "He's really ashamed of having fallen, though from what I can gather it was no fault of his—he was lunging to save one of his men who slipped from a rock. He says that being wounded in action is one thing—that's an honourable way to go, he says—but this is quite another. He feels he has let his battalion down. He says he's writing to his father to—to *apologise*! Can you imagine that?"

"No," I admitted. "But then I find it hard to imagine any of Colonel Marchant's thought processes."

"Oh well," Lucy said philosophically, tucking the letter back in the envelope. "The important thing is that he's coming home. I expect he'll see things more in proportion when he gets here—after all, no one can say he hasn't done his bit. Wouldn't it be marvellous if we could get him to Watersmeet?"

In the event he was sent to a hospital in Gloucester, and in July Lucy and Beth went to stay with the Marchants in Cheltenham so that she was near enough to visit him frequently, her joy at seeing Nick considerably tempered by the thought of an unspecified period spent beneath the roof of her parents-in-law.

The house seemed strangely quiet and empty when she and Beth had gone. It seemed to be brooding but at peace, as if it knew that all the children were out there somewhere but would return, bruised and scarred and needing its solace.

As summer progressed, the Americans counter-attacked in strength and suddenly Germany did not seem so invincible. The end of the war became a real possibility, no longer something as unattainable as the pot at the end of the rainbow.

And women had the vote at last—or at least those of us over thirty did. Charlotte wrote to me, a letter that mixed joy with cynicism.

'So at last we have it," she wrote. "And it took a war! I still think that with less militancy we might possibly have achieved it earlier—though who can tell? One can only be grateful to those who strived, I suppose, though in my view the more drastic the tactics, the less likely were the politicians to give in to them. It would have seemed as if they were succumbing to blackmail, however much they might have agreed with the cause in their hearts. But what a price to pay, Jenny! Will anything ever be the same again?"

I stood looking over the wall on the top road with Priors dreaming in the sun below me. It was autumn with the leaves turning to gold and the hedgerows full of red berries and trailing old man's beard. From here I could not see those farm cottages that Mark had built at the time of Izzie and Bert's wedding. They lay round the bend of the lane. The land beyond Priors was leased to another farmer and the sheep that grazed on the hillside were not Leyton sheep. But the scene before me was the same as when I had gazed at it with lifted heart that winter so long ago when I was a girl of seventeen.

Miraculously we had all come through.

We had heard from Ben only days before, saying that he was well. Charlotte's letter had told me that Peter was in the highest of spirits and so far had come through unscathed. Nick was already in England.

What did Izzie think? I asked myself. How would I feel in her position, having lost both husband and son?

I closed my eyes and leaned against the wall in an excess of physical pain. Quite literally, it didn't bear thinking of. How unfair life could be, and how fortunate I was, with my children safe and my husband beside me and Priors to live in.

Priors!

I opened my eyes and looked at it once more, warm and golden in the sunlight, every window and gable and chimney-stack dear and familiar to me.

"They'll soon be coming back to you," I said silently to the house across the valley.

Book III

1923–1939

20

"The shades of long-dead monks must be running for cover tonight," Roger said to me as we stood to one side of the hall listening to the revellers jigging madly to the explosive, insistent rhythms of the jazz age.

"Let them," I said.

To me it wasn't only Philip's twenty-first birthday we were celebrating some months after the event but a new, carefree era when we could enjoy life without looking over our shoulders, fearful for the safety of those we loved.

It was not that I was totally unaware of the world outside our four walls. I knew that Lloyd George's promise of a land fit for heroes to live in was proving a poet's empty dream. I knew that there were industrial troubles; unemployment and hunger and misery. And if I had not been aware of such things from my own observation, Ellie would undoubtedly have brought them to my notice.

But there was a gaiety too and a release from tension, and a childish exuberance that didn't seem to me so very sinful. I loved to feel that the house was full of colour and laughter again. I envied the girls their corsetless figures and the ease with which they mingled with the young men. It must be wonderful, I thought, to be young in 1923, for there was nothing ahead now but peace and eventual prosperity.

"What do girls do with their bosoms these days?" Roger asked me under his breath, his eyes gleaming with amusement.

I giggled. "Heaven alone knows! The power of fashion over the human frame is quite phenomenal, isn't it?"

"Come on, you two—join in," called a young, scarlet-clad blonde, turning to smile at us over her bare shoulder as she bobbed past us in Peter's arms. "This is a ripping tune!"

"I'm waiting for a nice quiet waltz," Roger replied, smiling in return—but the girl was gone, lost in the throng of similarly bobbing heads.

The orchestra was at one end of the hall on a raised platform, and we had opened the doors to the dining room so that the dancers could spill over from one room to the next. The buffet supper was laid in the smaller sitting room and the bar was in Roger's study. It had taken a full week for Alfred, Izzie and me to prepare it all and it was good to stand on the side-lines now and see the whole thing falling into place.

I surveyed the scene, the professional in me never far from the surface. It seemed to be going well. Waiters were circling with trays of cocktails and fruit punch. There were animated groups on each side of us, for Philip had many friends, and of course the Leyton clan had gathered, or most of it. I was sorry that Mark and Charlotte had not been able to come, as it was the first really large party we had held since Lucy's wedding, far off in those carefree, innocent days before the war, but I appreciated the difficulties a farmer experienced when leaving his farm at any time.

John and Angela, not looking much changed, were there with their two younger daughters, Christina and Virginia, who were now sixteen and eighteen. Jessica and Hester were both married—Jessica to a South African farmer she had met whilst doing war work in London and Hester to a naval officer.

Peter had pitched up rather late the night before. One never really knew whether Peter was going to be present at functions or not. He came and went without warning and it was impossible to pin him down about times and dates.

He had emerged from the Flying Corps with, it seemed, an ability to fly and little else, unless one counted an outsized helping of charm. For some months after he left the corps he did nothing very much but fly back and forth to the south of France with a group of rather raffish friends. He was saved the immediate necessity of finding gainful employment by the fact that he had inherited a certain amount of money from his mother. He bought a small, light plane and devoted himself with great industry to enjoying life to the full and getting through his inheritance with all speed.

I knew Mark was worried. He had refrained from playing the heavy father immediately after the war, feeling that it was time Peter enjoyed some of his youth released from the constant fear of death, but for some time now we had all felt that he should begin behaving more responsibly. Mark had taken him to task—with the result that Peter had now gone into business with an ex-Flying Corps friend and between them they were running a Flying Circus, travelling from town to town giving stunt shows—wing-walking, death-defying spins, and so on. We could only assume that he *liked* death staring him in the face!

There was no doubt whatsoever that he liked the company of pretty girls. There were times when I wished that just one of them would give him his comeuppance; so far he seemed to bowl them over like ninepins.

"Would you believe that Lucy is a sober matron and mother of three?" Roger asked me, breaking in on my thoughts. He was looking across to where she sat on the edge of a table, swinging one foot in an emerald green satin shoe and holding court among a group of bright young things.

"It's good to see her enjoying herself," I said, smiling. Indeed, it seemed some time since I had seen that particular expression on her face. First there had been the war and then the dreary anti-climax of Nick's long-awaited return to civilian life.

Not that she had complained to me. It was all too obvious, however, that Nick had returned a different person from the handsome, uncomplicated young man who had left home in 1915. Incredibly it all seemed to stem from the fact that he had been wounded, not in action, but in an accident that could have happened at any time and in any place.

The rest of his battalion had been completely wiped out on the Asiago Plateau. Why the fact that at the time he was safe in hospital in England should seem like a betrayal was something that the feminine mind was unable to grasp; but I had a shrewd suspicion that his father's attitude had added considerably to his feelings of guilt.

Where was he now? I looked round the room and saw his backview over by the door. He was looking down at Ellie, not saying anything, I guessed, though I could not see his face. I could see Ellie, though, and she was talking enough for two.

Please Ellie, I said, trying to transmit thought waves across the room. Please—not the League of Nations, or the deplorable policies of Stanley Baldwin, or the growing number of unemployed; not tonight, and not to Nick, for he was inclined to take her socialist views as a personal affront and I did so want everything to go smoothly. But even as I looked at them I saw Nick throw back his head and laugh and I was relieved at the thought that just for one night even Ellie must have filed away the problems of the world into a drawer marked 'pending'. It really seemed as if she might be indulging in frivolous conversation.

Ellie had come down from London the night before in her newly acquired Austin Seven. She was thirty now. (Could Roger and I possibly have a daughter of *thirty*?) Being small and slight she looked younger and I knew from experience that on a political platform she presented an incongruous picture, with her neat figure and fashionable hats. Yet she had a brisk way with hecklers and was a powerful and impassioned speaker, totally committed and sincere.

I admired Ellie. I could see my younger self in her. There was a time when I would have thrown myself into her cause with an equal fervour and it was, perhaps, to be deplored that middle age had blurred the issues in my mind so that I no longer saw clearly who and what was to blame for the ills of the world. I thought of my righteous anger when Jed and Annie had been forced to leave Collingford and how I had fulminated against the system. I could still see its inherent injustice, but there was more than one side to it. The rights and wrongs no longer seemed so clear cut.

I admired her, but I worried about her too. If only, I frequently said to Roger, she could find a *nice* man! She had friends in plenty—all very left-wing and inclined towards long hair and dandruff and marital problems and minds above simple things like marriage and raising a family. She worked much too hard. She travelled all over the country lecturing on behalf of the Labour Party and the League of

Nations. At the same time she held down a job in the Home Office; she was too thin and she smoked too much.

I asked her once: "Aren't there any *eligible* men in that group of friends you go about with?"

She had laughed at me. "Don't worry about me, Mother. Believe me, I'm happy. I'm not consciously mourning for Lawrence still, even though I'll never forget him. It's just that I've never met another man I can imagine seeing across the breakfast table from now until the day I die—and with so many millions of my generation dead in Flanders, I consider myself lucky to have work to do that satisfies me."

And with that we had to be content.

It was the war that was to blame, I told myself. Not only because of the lost generation that Ellie mentioned, but also because it had made people reluctant to settle down. There was a restlessness abroad that there never had been in the pre-1914 world. Even Ben was still a bachelor.

My heart gave a small lurch as I thought of Ben and surreptitiously I scanned the room for him. He couldn't be serious about that girl he had brought with him, surely? It wasn't, I assured myself hastily, that I was a snob—oh no, it wasn't that at all. Simply that of all people . . .

There she was. Zoë. She was leaning against Ben and screaming with laughter and he was looking down at her as if she were all the art treasures of the Louvre rolled into one.

She was a matron at the school in Somerset where he taught English and he had sprung it on us over the telephone that he wanted to bring a girl to the party, if it was all the same with us. Of course, we said expansively. She'll be more than welcome.

"Oh Roger, I do hope she's nice," I said. I had been wanting him to meet the right girl for a long time. It would settle him down. Ever since the war he had seemed a little on edge, though recently I had thought him more serene, which seemed to justify his choice of teaching as a profession.

Ellie had been furious.

I smiled a little as I thought back to the time when, on a summer's afternoon soon after Ben's return from the prison camp, his future had been under discussion. I had been sitting in a deck-chair supposedly sewing but not very

331

wholeheartedly. Ellie was sitting on the ground hugging her knees while Ben lay at full length on the grass, his arms folded behind his head.

"Ben can't make up his mind whether to go back to Oxford," Ellie said despairingly.

"You're wrong," Ben said, opening one eye. "I'm going back. The thought depresses me, but I'm going back. The only thing is that I'm going to see if I can change Schools. I've decided to read English instead of Greats."

"That's good," I said, innocently beaming at him, at the same time that Ellie leant forward towards him, her face a mask of fury.

"Oh Ben, honestly! How could you?"

"What's wrong with reading English?" I asked.

Ben didn't wait for Ellie to tell me.

"It's generally regarded as a soft option," he said, smiling. "But I don't care. I just want to get the whole thing over as soon as possible."

"Ben, you'll enjoy it!" I said.

"Will I?" He closed his eyes again. "I don't think so, Mother. I'll feel like a visitor from another age—a revenant. Anyway, that's what I've decided to do."

"And then what?" Ellie asked in the tone of voice that seemed to expect him to announce his intention of becoming a rag-picker.

"And then I'm going to teach."

"Teach!" She sounded amazed and scornful, almost as if she would have preferred the rag-picking. "Honestly, Ben—you can't coast through life just doing the easiest thing that comes to hand."

"Now just hang on!" He sat up, no longer smiling. "You change the world your way, Ellie, and I'll do it mine. You can put your faith in politicians if you like; I prefer to put mine in the next generation. I actually *want* to teach—don't you understand? It seems a sane, worthwhile sort of job to me."

"It's the refuge of the destitute," Ellie said. "Those that can, do. Those that can't, teach."

"If that's true—which I don't believe—then it's deplorable!"

332

"Ben you've got a brain—a first-class brain. Can't you see you'll be wasted as a glorified wet-nurse, arranging sports days and placating parents? You had ideas and convictions once. You're articulate, you can express yourself. You can sway people."

"Oh, rats!" Ben said, but tolerantly and with amusement, lying down and closing his eyes again. "I have no faith in my ability to change the world, but if I can open the eyes and expand the minds of just a handful of boys I shall feel I haven't lived in vain."

He had not been moved from this point of view and had been teaching at a boys' school in Somerset for the past year.

And now Zoë! Her laugh split the air again. There was noise everywhere, but her peals of merriment had a peculiarly piercing quality that grated on the ear.

"What can he see in her?" I asked Roger.

He lifted an eyebrow at me. "Don't you know?"

Well, of course I knew. She had a creamy complexion with the texture of a magnolia petal and enormous brown eyes such as poets might immortalise in verse. Her hair was lustrous and her nose piquantly tip-tilted. It did not take much understanding to see that her superficial attractions were overwhelming.

I did not—I *would* not—criticise her voice with its overtones of whiny gentility superimposed on a London accent; nor the fact that she applied rouge to her lips in public; nor the fact that she said 'Please-to-meet-chew' when introduced, and, ignoring me, simpered at Roger, fluttering her enormous eyelashes like a vamp in a Hollywood movie. None of those things would have counted—or so I told myself—had she seemed kind and generous, intelligent and loving. But I saw no evidence of any such attributes.

She and Ben had arrived from Somerset the night before the party and I watched her over dinner. From my vantage point at the foot of the table it seemed to me that she played him like a fish, smiling at him one moment with the tip of her tongue coquettishly between her teeth, and the next turning a smooth shoulder towards him as she flirted with Peter.

"Lovely to get away from all those little boys," she said

to him, smirking at him from under her lashes. "Lovely to meet some big boys for a change."

"However did they entice an exotic creature like you down to the wilds of Somerset?" Peter asked. "That's my home ground too, you know—so I know just how wild it can be!"

"It's lovely down there, isn't it? A bit quiet of course, but ever so nice reelly. I've always loved the country."

"Do you come from Somerset, Miss Patterson?" Roger asked her.

"Ooh no, not me! I'm a town girl reelly—from Harrow—but me and my sister, we used to ride round the lanes when we were children."

"Oh, you ride, do you?" asked Roger. "Well, I daresay we can find you a mount—"

"I think Zoë meant bicycles, Father," Ben said gently.

"Give me wheels any day," Philip said, leaping in to cover her embarrassment. "I'll have to take you for a spin in my new car, Miss Patterson. I touched forty-five on the Cheltenham road this morning."

"Philip, you must be careful," I said, shocked to the core. "We didn't give you a car so that you could kill yourself and be a danger to others."

"Don't worry, mother—I'll settle for one or the other," he said. "You'll risk a drive with me, won't you, Miss Patterson?"

"That was your birthday present, was it? A new car? Aren't you a lucky boy, then?" She leant forward and touched his arm. " 'Course I'll come with you. And call me Zoë, won't you?"

"Can I call you Zoë, too?" Peter leaned close to her, giving her the sort of look that stripped every particle of clothing from her body. "Never mind his car. I've got a plane, you know. I'll fly you up, up—halfway to paradise."

She giggled.

"Oh, you are a one! Listen to him, Ben. Isn't he a naughty boy?"

Yes, I thought—yes I think he is rather a naughty boy. I looked across the room at him now, to where he sat with his head close to the glossy blonde tresses of the girl he had been dancing with, whispering in her ear. She somehow managed to look both outraged and delighted at the same time. Whatever he's saying, don't believe it, I wanted to tell her.

"It's a waltz," Roger said to me suddenly, breaking into my thoughts. "Come on, let's show these young things the way to do it."

"Do you know who taught me to waltz?" I asked him as we drifted together.

"Yes. John, on the village green. You've told me before."

I pulled a face at him.

"Sorry! That's old age for you. I'm as bad as Goosey Parslow."

But I didn't feel old. In spirit I felt very much the same as the girls who were jigging in their skimpy dresses to the ragtime tunes and it was only when I came face to face with myself in the mirror that hung on the long wall that I realised that a considerable gulf separated us.

It was not something that bothered me unduly.

Ben's happiness was. He danced time after time with Zoë, holding her close. She had decided to give him all her attention, it appeared, and he was in his seventh heaven, entirely oblivious to the charms of the many other girls who had been invited.

"Ben, please be a good boy and do your duty with little Doris Westerby," I said at one point, cornering him in our improvised bar between dances. "She's been sitting out for ages and looks so miserable."

"Blast little Doris Westerby! Sorry mother—you're quite right and I'm being an awful bore. But honestly—isn't Zoë a peach? Isn't she the most wonderful girl you ever saw?"

Fortunately for my immortal soul he had gone, bearing two glasses aloft, and I was saved the necessity of perjuring myself.

"I'll dance with her," a voice said in my ear, calm and reassuring.

Thank God for Philip.

I turned and smiled gratefully at him.

"Don't worry," he said. I knew he was speaking of Zoë.

"I can't think of a single reason why I shouldn't," I said.

"It won't last. Old Ben has too much sense—"

"Sometimes I wonder! You know what your father says—there's no fool like an academic fool."

Philip laughed and went away to do his duty by Doris Westerby.

There was a naivety about Ben—an innocence, almost, that made him an easy prey for someone like Zoë, I felt.

Philip was far more practical, rather like Roger. He had the same singleness of purpose, too. He had known right from the days when he helped Alfred in the kitchen of the Ring of Bells that his future would be tied up with the hotels. He wanted no other. He had been disappointed that the war had not outlasted his schooldays and that he had not been able to join the Flying Corps like Peter, but now he soberly acknowledged that he had been fortunate.

He had left school in 1919 and had spent a year at the Angler's Rest, working under Marie Jepson. Edward Jepson had been badly gassed during the war and was invalided out of the Army, never again able to do more than light gardening. They were both glad to have Philip at the hotel, able and willing to turn his hand to almost any job, and the training was invaluable to him. At the end of that year he went to the Ecole Hotelière in Lausanne, where he had just finished his course—hence, his long overdue twenty-first birthday party—and now he was destined for a spell in the Savoy in London.

My mind was at rest about Philip, more than any of the other three. He was happy and fulfilled in the work he was doing. He enjoyed life in an uncomplicated sort of way. He was a person to rely on.

The dancing continued until two o'clock and it was almost three before the last car had gone from the front of the house. I collapsed against Philip's shoulder as we waved away the last load of singing revellers, totally exhausted and yet at the same time wound up and disinclined for sleep.

"That was *some* party," Philip said, his arm around my shoulders. "Who's for some more bubbly? Come on, everybody—don't let's stop yet."

"You can do what you like," Roger said. "You're twenty-one, after all. But I'm considerably older and feel at least a hundred, so I'm off. Are you coming, Jenny?"

"I'll be up in a minute," I said.

I collected up some of the best glasses that had been left in various places around the hall, shrugged at the utter hopelessness of attempting to clear up the place at that time of night and went through to the kitchen where Philip had led the way, Ben, Zoë, Lucy, Nick, Peter and Ellie trailing behind him.

"Oh, don't bother to clear up tonight, Mother," Ellie said, seeing the glasses in my hand.

"I'm not," I said. "It's hopeless."

"I've never seen such a sordid sight." Philip was leaning over to pour yet more champagne.

"No," I said to Philip, "No, I won't have any more, thank you. I'm off to bed now."

"So are we," Nick said. "Lucy, don't have any more champagne."

"Oh, Nick, I don't want to go yet! You go, if you're tired. I'm enjoying myself." Her voice was light and full of laughter.

"Lucy—I said don't have any more, didn't you hear? Put that glass down! You've had quite enough to drink."

"I haven't! Oh Nick, don't be so stuffy. We haven't been to a party for ages and I've had a lovely time."

"Come on, old boy—don't be a spoil sport," Philip said. "Where's the harm? We can sleep in tomorrow."

"I want to go to bed!" Nick's voice was tight with fury.

"Is that an invitation? Charmed, I'm sure," Zoë giggled.

"It's an order," Nick said, glaring at Lucy.

Still she did not move but continued to sip her champagne, looking challengingly at Nick over the rim of her glass.

"Yes, *Sir*. Certainly, *Sir*."

"Oh, look," said Ben, always the peacemaker. "Nick's probably right. It is pretty late and we've had enough to drink."

"Yes, come on Lucy, there's an angel," I said, trying to sound off-hand. "I shall never unhook this dress by myself and I expect your father is asleep and snoring by this time."

"Ellie can do that," Lucy said. "I'll just stay on for a while. Peter, give me a cigarette, will you?"

"Of course." Peter produced his cigarette case and handed

it to her. "I didn't know you smoked," he commented, as he lit her cigarette for her.

"I don't as a rule. I just feel like breaking rules tonight."

"Lucy—" Nick began.

"I'm staying, Nick. In fact," she said, puffing inexpertly, "I was thinking. I'll probably stay at Priors for a few days— or weeks, or months."

"Don't be absurd," Nick said. "You don't know what you're saying."

"On the contrary, I suddenly feel remarkably clear-headed."

"Look," I said. "It *is* awfully late."

"Yes," Ellie said, suddenly decisive, stubbing out her own cigarette. "Come on, Lucy."

Philip, standing at the door, switched the light on and off and on and off.

"Time, gentlemen, please," he said, in an authoritative barman's voice.

Somehow, between us, we herded Lucy out of the room. Nick, grim-faced, bade everyone good night and followed her quickly, cutting off her retreat. It was a sour end to a lovely evening. No doubt, I told myself, everyone would have calmed down in the morning and Lucy would happily return home with Nick. If only he were not quite so serious, I thought as I lay sleepless in bed.

Why, oh why, was insomnia made doubly annoying by the insensitive snores of one's nearest and dearest? The grandfather clock struck four and then half past. This was ridiculous! I'd been up since crack of dawn and I'd had a busy day. I was tired out—and yet I could not sleep. The champagne had made me thirsty. I thought longingly of a cup of tea and wondered if I could summon the energy to go down to the kitchen and make myself a pot. The prospect of the tea was alluring; the actual effort necessary to get out of bed and make the journey to the kitchen far less so.

But eventually, with sleep apparently receding further away with every moment that passed, I went downstairs. My mind was far too active, that was the trouble. Nick and Lucy—Ben and Zoë; my thoughts went round and round. Oh God, I thought, *surely* not Ben and Zoë! It wasn't a case of my thinking no girl good enough for my precious son. I desperately wanted him to get married and was certain that he needed the stability that marriage could bring. But a *good* marriage! I knew with absolute certainty that he would be bored to tears with her in six months, at a generous estimate. She had a brain the size of a pea.

Down in the kitchen I made my tea and sat at the table to drink it. The clock over the mantelpiece coughed and whirred as it had done for as long as I could remember. There were other noises. Mice? I didn't think so, though Tibbles, the kitchen cat that was asleep on the chair by the range, got to her feet and stretched luxuriously before giving me an incurious glance and collapsing once more into a limp heap of ginger fur.

Not mice, no. But something. Someone was creeping down, just as I had. I turned towards the kitchen door and saw Lucy there with her hand on the latch, surprised into stillness by the sight of me.

"Couldn't you sleep either?" she asked.

I shook my head. "No. Too much champagne—it always makes me thirsty. Would you like some tea?"

"Mm. Please."

She pushed across a cup which she unhooked from the dresser and I filled it for her, passing it over to her as she sat down opposite me. For a moment she sipped in silence.

"Sorry about the scene," she said at last, not meeting my eye.

"Does that sort of thing happen often?"

She considered the question.

"No, not really. But it could. These days, I seem to have to hold myself in all the time, trying not to lash out—trying not to resent being tied down." She stared moodily at the table, her chin supported on her clenched fists.

"I can't help wondering, Mother. Is this all there is?"

"Lucy—you have three lovely children."

"Oh, I know that. When Nick first came home and the twins were born, I was as happy as anyone could be. I thought life was going to be wonderful. I was busy. Nick was proud of his sons and glad to be home. Everything was just grand."

"And now it's not?"

"No. Ever since Nico and Jamie went to kindergarten I've been bored to tears. Nick seems to want me to be the sort of wife who's content to live entirely in his shadow. He doesn't seem to appreciate the fact that for over four years I had to make decisions for myself, force myself to be self-sufficient. I can't make myself accept the sort of life his mother has always led."

"Darling, you're exaggerating! Nick is nothing like his father."

"Well he is, up to a point. He hates anything that isn't entirely conventional and *comme il faut*. Appearances are everything."

"What particularly are you talking about?"

"Do you remember Prudence Wintringham? She was a friend of mine at school—you must remember her, she was called Prudence Fellowes then. Well, her husband was killed during the war and she's been desperately hard up ever since; she was left with two little children. She's just opened up a dress shop in Oxford—very expensive, very chic—and she wanted me to go in with her."

"And Nick wouldn't allow it?"

"Nick nearly had apoplexy. You know, I thought that all I ever wanted was to have a home and husband and babies; now I find myself envying Ellie her freedom."

I crashed my cup back on its saucer and glared at her angrily.

"Don't you ever *dare* say such a thing to me again, Lucy! Do you think there's a day in your sister's life when she doesn't think about the man she loved—the man she might have married? Ellie's got grit and determination and she's getting on with making a good life for herself, knowing that the chances are she'll always be alone."

"I know, I know. I'm sorry, I didn't mean that, exactly."

"I should hope not."

"If I'm dissatisfied, it's partly your fault, you know—yours and dad's. You set a pretty high standard of marriage for anyone to follow. I can't tell you how I've envied you when I've heard you laughing together; you seem such good friends, as well as husband and wife."

340

Were we so unique? I wondered. Mark had remarked on the very same thing.

"We weren't always quite such good friends," I said, remembering. "And now I come to think of it, the reason we weren't happy was much the same as the reason you give."

"When weren't you happy?" Lucy asked. "I don't remember."

"Well, you wouldn't would you? You were very small— and anyway, parents aren't supposed to go through crises and have emotions."

"What did you do about it?"

I was silent for a moment, reliving that horrible time again. I shouldn't be hard on Lucy, I thought. It still hurt me to think of it, even after so long.

"I went back to work," I said.

"Well, there you are." She leaned across the table towards me to give emphasis to her words. "We're much the same, you and I. We need something else, not just home and children. I wish I were different, I do really."

"Is there any chance of persuading Nick?"

"None. Believe me, I've tried."

"He loves you, Lucy."

She reached for the pot and poured herself another cup of tea.

"I know," she said. "And really, I love him. I just wish—" she broke off and sighed heavily.

"Is something else worrying him? He seems very solemn and subdued these days."

"It's just the weight of his responsibilities, I think. That and the ridiculous business of the accident at the end of the war—he's never got over feeling guilty for not dying with the rest of his men; and of course, his father hasn't helped. If ever the subject of Nick's war service comes up when we're with them he always seems to make Nick feel ashamed of himself."

"And I suppose your wanting something beyond marriage and the home makes him feel even less of a man."

Lucy pondered the question.

"I hadn't looked at it like that," she said. "But that's

ridiculous, Mother. Daddy isn't less of a man because you've worked in the hotels all these years."

"Everyone's different. And people change, Lucy. Because Nick feels this way now, it doesn't necessarily mean that he'll feel the same way for ever. I think your best course of action is to concentrate on bolstering him up a bit."

"But I'm not a saint, Mother. I'm an ordinary sort of person and I'm unhappy *now*. It makes me wonder—" she stopped abruptly and looked up at me through her lashes, just as she did when she was a little girl and was about to say something particularly shocking.

"Wonder what?" I prompted.

"How important is fidelity? I mean—there's a man at the tennis club. He's an architect, the one that designed Daisy Taggart's new house. He's madly attractive, Mother, and he's made it pretty obvious that he's attracted to me. Sometimes—sometimes I feel so *old*! I don't seem to have had any time for being silly and frivolous. One moment I was a schoolgirl and the next I was married and now I'm staid and middle aged. When Arthur Courtney talks to me it makes me feel like kicking up my heels and doing something quite mad."

"Don't," I said quickly. "Please don't, Lucy. Infidelity is a terrible, destructive thing and it won't solve anything. Look." I reached across the table and grasped her hand. "Look darling, during the war you showed you had more courage than anyone ever dreamed. We all admired you— up at crack of dawn, summer and winter, working twice as hard as anyone could have expected. You proved you had self-discipline then, and that's what you're going to need now. I know it's easy for me to talk. I had a husband who was only too pleased for me to go back to work and our problem resolved itself. But the more confident Nick is, the more likely he is to relax his Victorian paterfamilias attitude. Don't you think so?"

"Perhaps." She sounded drearily unconvinced, and I was hardly surprised.

"Hold on to the love you had," I urged. "Marriage isn't a happy-ever-after, fairy-tale sort of thing! Everyone has good times and bad times—"

"But to live like this for ever more!"

"Lucy, it won't *be* for ever more! Nothing is for ever more! That's what I'm trying to say. People change. Circumstances change."

She sighed. "Oh well," she said, inconclusively. "You needn't worry that I shall do anything silly. There are the children to consider, after all. But it's not easy, Mother."

"Things seldom are," I said.

"I pray to God that Ben doesn't marry that silly little strumpet he's brought with him."

"Lucy!" Much as I agreed with her in private, I hardly thought her language was seemly.

"Well, honestly! I'm absolutely astounded that he's taken in by someone quite so obvious."

"I'm equally astounded that she finds him attractive," I said. "I would have thought he was much too serious and bookish for her. Peter would be more her type."

"She was getting on pretty well with him tonight—maybe she'll transfer her affections." Lucy was thoughtful for a moment as if wondering whether to speak, then suddenly made up her mind.

"She said something strange to me," she said. "About Peter. She said that he had told her that by rights this house should have been his."

I stared at her in bewilderment.

"He said that? Peter?"

"So Zoë maintains. A crying shame, she said it was—her very words. Done out of his birthright, she says."

"By whom, pray? We bought it, fair and square. Your Uncle Mark set the price and we paid without quibbling."

"Mother, she's a troublemaker—honestly, I wouldn't pay any attention. I shouldn't have mentioned it, but I thought you ought to know the kind of person she is."

"I think I know the kind of person she is," I said.

But the thought of what Lucy had told me nagged at me long after we had said good night and gone to our respective bedrooms.

I knew the sort of person that Zoë was. She was shallow and brainless and not nearly good enough for Ben. But what sort of person was Peter? Did he honestly think Priors should be his, or was that simply a remark made by Zoë with the purpose of stirring up trouble, as Lucy had suggested?

I found, on reflection, that I had no idea what sort of person Peter was. Not any more. Not an idea in the world.

21

"After Alfred comes back," I was wont to say to Roger during the war, "I'm never setting foot in the Ring of Bells again."

A ridiculous statement, and one which I had no wish to be taken seriously, for I would have found it impossible to stay away altogether. The place was part of me now, and I felt as much at home there as in my own kitchen. Each of the bedrooms had its own atmosphere and I loved every inch of it, sloping ceilings, creaking boards and all.

I cooked no longer. There was no need now to scrimp and save and devise recipes that combined two parsnips and a beetroot to make a tempting dish, but there was still plenty of work for me. There was the linen cupboard, the furnishings, the stores; all received my attention and I often visited the other hotels, too, to authorise repairs or replacements to the fabric and equipment.

I enjoyed this. It did not mean an early start or regular hours and by the end of 1923 I, too, had a car of my own, though cravenly I never learned to drive it. We employed a young man called Sidney, an ex-Gunner with the Royal Artillery, to act as chauffeur and to drive me between the hotels. It was also his job to meet guests at the station with the hotel car, although Dick had made the transition to the internal combustion engine quite easily and still looked after the vehicles and drove for us.

Quite often Roger and I were able to travel around

together which we both enjoyed; but at other times he was closeted in his office with account books and income tax returns. More and more frequently these days I found, among the papers on his desk, half-finished plans and drawings.

We had made money out of the war. It was something about which we felt guilty, though in all honesty I could not justify the guilt. There had been a need and we had supplied it; we had not profiteered or ever patronised the black market. We had worked hard and given value for money, yet I knew that Roger felt on a par with those who had made fortunes from supplying the Army with shoddy goods. He donated mightily to the War Memorial which now stood close to the church on the green, the names of the dead inscribed upon it and—more constructively, to my way of thinking—contributed to the extensions to the cottage hospital which were being undertaken also as a memorial to the men of Collingford who had fallen. He gave of his time, too, being now a member of the Parish Council.

I knew that there was still a lurking feeling of guilt, though—that is until his plans for the new hotel became crystallised and he became so excited about the project that the past was forgotten.

Philip was in London and working odd hours at the Savoy, so that he was not often able to come home. However, on the weekends that he managed it, the conferences between him and his father were endless and there was a marked increase in the plan-drawing activities. Many sheets of paper ended as screwed-up balls in the waste-paper basket or were impatiently ripped and thrown into the fire; but others survived and were mulled over, and gradually it seemed that through all this maze of plan and counter-plan a dream was emerging. It was to be the perfect hotel; a building that would blend with the Oxfordshire countryside, built with the traditional stone and incorporating features such as the gables and chimney-stacks that made old farmhouses like Priors such a delight to the eye, yet would be luxurious and modern inside.

Philip, who for a twenty-two-year-old already had a wealth of experience behind him, had no doubts at all what he wanted and constantly brought home pictures of new equipment and brochures of kitchens that looked to me more like operating theatres.

I became aware of how very amateurish we still were. Of course we had learned a lot since the time we had first taken over the Ring of Bells, but Philip's ideas, learned first in Switzerland and now at the Savoy, made our somewhat bumbling, rule-of-thumb methods look out of date. Even the kitchen at the Rose Revived, which was the newest of them all, seemed antiquated in comparison with the illustrations in the catering magazines he produced for us to see. In this new hotel of ours there were to be acres of stainless steel. Many of the bedrooms would have their own bathrooms. There would be central heating and a ballroom and comfortable lounges.

"Tennis courts," Philip said one breakfast time to Roger, without preamble.

"Grass?"

"Hard. Golf Course?"

"Nine-hole. Enormous attraction."

"Well, perhaps."

I became used to this kind of verbal shorthand as ideas flew between them like tennis balls at Wimbledon.

"Where is this palace going to be built?" I asked.

"I don't know exactly," Roger admitted, "but I'm looking at some land near Woodstock. We want somewhere within easy reach of Oxford, yet quiet. Somewhere in the country but near a main road."

"Woodstock would be a good idea," I agreed. "It's becoming more and more popular with tourists. I even saw a party of Americans there the other day. How small the world is getting."

"Americans, eh? That's something new," Roger said.

It was, indeed—but new things were happening all the time in 1923. Ellie was on top of the world when the socialists took office for the first time in December of that year. True, it was a minority Government and only kept in power by the somewhat tentative support of the Liberals, but it affirmed the status of the socialists as the second major party and was by way of being a personal triumph for Ellie, as she had campaigned vigorously for a successful Labour candidate in an East London constituency.

We had no Labour candidate in our constituency, which perhaps was just as well as it contributed to the cause of peace within the family. Roger and I were therefore able to vote Liberal, as always, without the necessity of having to defend our choice to Ellie. But as usual, the Conservatives were returned, as they were in most rural areas.

Excitement ran high in Collingford, despite the predictability of the outcome. There were political meetings on the green with a great deal of heckling on both sides, but on the whole people were inclined to be reticent about which candidate would receive their vote.

It was during the election campaign that I met Clare Matheson. I had seen her at church and knew her to be the new teacher at the school (now enlarged and divided into Boys, Girls and Mixed Infants), but although we smiled and said good morning when we met we had never actually come across each other socially.

We had both volunteered to help fold election material on behalf of the Liberal candidate—at least, Clare was to fold and I was to place in envelopes—and by the time we had worked our way through the pile of paper in front of us there was a bond between us that was none the less real because of our difference in ages.

She had a quick, dry wit that immediately struck an answering chord in me, and the sort of face that even in repose looked as if it was on the point of breaking into a smile. Her eyes were a warm, peaty brown and shone with intelligence and life.

I don't remember at what point in the conversation I learned that she had been engaged to a soldier who had died at Mons. She did not labour the point or ask for sympathy. Her tears had obviously all been shed long ago, and like Ellie she was facing the future with courage and gaiety.

She would be exactly right for Ben, I thought.

But Ben was bringing Zoë home again for Christmas, which was something I was not looking forward to, and he had even hinted in his letters that he might possibly have 'something to tell us'.

"They can't be going to announce their engagement, can they?" I asked Roger anxiously.

"Ben wouldn't be such a fool," said Roger.

I wasn't so sure.

"Is Peter coming this year?" Roger went on, after a moment's thought.

"I don't think so. But then, you know what he's like—he's just as likely to drop in at the last moment as not. Why do you ask?"

"I merely thought we might be able to press ten shillings into his hand and bribe him to seduce the delectable Zoë," Roger said. "Though come to think of it, he'd probably do it for five."

"Roger, really!"

"Ben ought to have his eyes opened. I've always said it—there's no fool like—"

"An academic fool. I know. But even if Ben does err on the innocent side, I'm glad he's not like Peter, aren't you? I have a theory about Peter. Two theories."

"Which are?"

"One—that he doesn't really like women at all, which is what I used to think about Mark. Oh, he loves to flirt and he loves their company and for all I know he may be the world's greatest lover, but he doesn't *like* them. Once the flirtatious badinage is over he doesn't have a word to say to them; have you noticed?"

"Hm. You may be right. What's your other theory?"

"That he's too much like Catherine for his own good."

"Like Catherine? Oh, come now, Jenny!"

"No, I mean it. He's amusing and cheerful while he's the centre of attention, but take that away and he grows almost sullen."

"I thought you were fond of him!"

"I am. I always have been—you know that. It's just that I've been seeing him in a different light just lately."

"Well, I'm sure he'd oblige us where Zoë is concerned. Still, if he's not coming, we'll have to think of something else."

I was, in fact, too busy to think of anything except purely practical things like the annual collection of toys for the children in the workhouse and all the usual Christmas preparations that had to be made for the family party that was to take place. Goffy, now sadly alone since Roger's mother had died in the influenza epidemic, was coming to stay for a week and Lucy and Nick and the three children were arriving on Christmas Eve. Ellie would be coming then too, but Philip had telephoned to say that he would be working and would not be arriving until Boxing Day. Ben and Zoë were due to arrive as soon as their school broke up, which was a week or so before Christmas.

On the day they were due, I was placing the latest batch of Christmas cards on the mantelpiece when I heard the unmistakable sounds of Ben's arrival, as heralded by a volley of bangs and backfiring his car finally spluttered to a halt. I braced myself to go outside and welcome Zoë.

To my astonishment, he was alone.

"Where is she?" I asked him, after we had hugged in greeting.

"She's not coming," he said briefly.

"Oh?" I looked at him enquiringly, but he added no more, merely hurrying inside to the warmth of the fire.

"It's good to be home," he said, holding out his hands to the blaze.

"Did she change her mind?" I asked.

He pulled a face at me over his shoulder.

"It's all over, Mother—for which I know you'll be heartily thankful."

"Ben, I'm sure I gave you no reason—"

"I know perfectly well that you didn't like her. You're about as transparent as a piece of plate-glass."

"Well, I'm sorry," I said. "I tried. Surely that's not why—"

"Why it's all over? No, I don't think so. If there'd really been anything—anything substantial between us, I expect it would have withstood the icy draught from my esteemed parents."

"Oh, darling," I said miserably. "I'm sorry if we let you down."

"You didn't," he said. "It had nothing whatever to do with you. We had an almighty bust-up, and you know how

I hate rows. Funny thing," he added thoughtfully, as if the point had only just struck him. "Zoë seemed to glory in it. She really came alive when she was shouting at me, defending herself."

"Defending herself?" I raised my eyebrows at him. "Against what?"

He shrugged.

"Oh, it was all too silly and petty and squalid—the sort of storm that blows up in isolated communities that are a bit turned in on themselves. She'd left undone various things that she ought to have done and when all was discovered she contrived to fix the blame on one of the boys. It just happened to be the one who was least able to stand up for himself. I told her what I thought about it, she accused me of being a prig, and it all progressed from there."

I felt suddenly light-hearted as if a weight had rolled from me.

"You must be dying for tea," I said. "We'll toast some crumpets, and Izzie's made you some gingerbread, just for old time's sake."

We sat companionably in front of the fire, Ben squatting by the hearth with the crumpets on the end of a long fork, and I watched the glow reflected on his face. Thank heaven that awful gaunt look has gone, I thought, remembering what he was like when he had returned home in 1919.

"Do you mind terribly about Zoë?" I asked him.

He sighed, then shook his head.

"No, not really. She's so wonderful to look at that I invested her with a character to match. The girl I thought I was in love with only existed in my imagination—which was hardly fair to the real Zoë Patterson. Don't worry, Mother—I'm perfectly all right."

"And you're really happy in that school of yours?"

"Yes." He smiled to himself, his eyes on the crumpet that was just turning brown. "So yah-boo, sucks to Ellie!" He turned round to grin at me, suddenly looking much younger and not at all cast down by the loss of Zoë.

"Ben," I said, just remembering. "You'll be on your own after dinner tonight, I'm afraid—unless you care to come with me to the concert at the school. Your father is out at some dinner or other."

"You're going to a school concert?" He looked at me in astonishment. "Why on earth? You're a masochist, Mother. Surely you sat through enough of those when you actually had children performing. Why bother with this one?"

I told him about my friendship with Clare but forebore to dwell on her charm and intelligence. I had learned over the years that any fulsomeness on my part would only lead to complete rejection on the part of my children. Clare's charms would have to speak for themselves when the time came.

"Well, I'm glad you've found a friend," Ben said, in what I regarded as an avuncular and somewhat patronising manner. "But if you don't mind, I'll stay at home and play some new gramophone records I've brought with me. I've been up to my ears in school concerts for the past week and couldn't stand any more."

Anxious as I was for him to meet Clare, I was content to postpone the occasion until a later date as I felt sure that Clare would have no opportunity for socialising that evening. I was proved right. I hardly had a chance to speak to her, though I did invite her to Priors for our family party, which was that year to be held on Boxing Day so that Philip could be with us.

On Christmas Eve Roger arrived with Goffy, having met him from the station, and a little later Ellie came, bringing with her the news that it was freezing hard and looked like snow. Lucy and Nick and the children arrived soon after tea and with each new arrival the pile of gaily wrapped presents grew under the tree, and we laughed and were glad to be together again.

For once in their lifetime the children went to bed without protest, anxious for morning to come, but not before we had invited the staff, both indoor and out, into the hall, where Beth could distribute our presents to them and we could all take a Christmas drink together.

The stockings were carefully fixed to the ends of the children's beds.

"You don't have to worry," Beth assured Nico and Jamie. "I wrote to Father Christmas to tell him we would be staying at Priors. He'll know where to find us." And she turned her little, contained face to me and gave me a conspiratorial look. It was up to us older people to keep the legend alive, her look told me. I hugged her and she giggled delightedly, suddenly not the least bit old but just as excited at the prospect of a filled stocking as Nico and Jamie.

Once they were tucked up we left them with Izzie, who was entertaining on her own account in the kitchen, and we all went to the Ring of Bells for dinner.

Several small tables had been put together to accommodate our large party and for me it was a special pleasure to see the place humming with life and full of warmth. Like Priors, it seemed made for special occasions. It seemed to respond to bustle and excitement and I looked down the table to exchange a long and smiling look with Roger. There were people in that dining room who had been coming every Christmas for years. There were others who had come for the first time. It would not be our fault if they did not come again—the meal, as always, was superb.

We had reached the coffee stage when in came the carol singers. I remembered, as I remembered every year, the young girl who had been so entranced by them that very first Christmas at the Ring of Bells. The inn had changed, but not the glowing Christmas spirit that made our customers reach into their pockets to fill the collecting boxes.

"Do you think Lucy and Nick seem any happier?" I asked Roger that night, just before we went to sleep.

I heard him sigh in the darkness beside me.

"I suppose the fact that she's older might account for the fact that she seems so subdued. On the other hand . . ." His voice trailed away. He's just as worried as I am, I thought.

"On the other hand, what?" I asked.

"There's an awful—deadness about them. They're so polite to each other."

I knew exactly what he meant. We had been the same, all those years ago, and I still hated to think of it.

"I wish I knew what the answer was," I said. "I wish Nick wasn't so pompous and that he'd let her do something outside the house. I wish they could have some *fun* together."

"I wish you'd go to sleep," Roger answered. "Stop worrying, darling. Tomorrow's Christmas."

Next morning we went to church and walked back over

grass stiff with frost to presents and turkey and plum pudding.

"I'll never take prosperity for granted again," Ellie said to me. "Not after campaigning in the East End. The conditions that people live under are unbelievable to people like us, Mother—there's such poverty and misery! Life's a treadmill, a vicious circle of unemployment and hardship and under-nourishment. Yet with it all people are so brave, so kind and humorous. It's the system that's got to change—and it *is* changing, Mother. We're in. The party is actually in! It's the beginning of a new age."

"It would be nice to think so," I said. "We shall await great things. At least the women's cause is won."

"*What*?" Ellie stopped dead in her tracks and looked at me as if she hardly knew whether to laugh or cry. "Mother, honestly! If you believe that, you'll believe anything."

"I expect you're right, dear," I said absently, my mind occupied with foolish domestic issues, such as wondering if Izzie would remember to put more brandy in the brandy butter as instructed. There had been a few light-hearted complaints last year. And would Goffy have already read the book I bought him?

He appeared to be delighted with it. The brandy butter—and everything else—was perfect, and the rest of the day passed pleasantly, with Ellie forgetting deeper issues to play games with the children in common with the rest of us.

I was amused to overhear part of a conversation between Ben and Philip, who arrived in time for lunch the following day.

"Mother's asked the school-ma'am this evening, I hear," Ben said. "Now, there's a treat for you!"

"Not that little dried-up biddy with the teeth?"

I watched with cynical amusement their momentary shock when Clare arrived. She was dressed in cream-coloured lace which set off her chestnut colouring to perfection and never would the expression 'dried-up' spring to anyone's mind.

The evening started quietly enough, but true to custom we warmed up to charades, which had become a tradition over the years. We were not in the least sophisticated. We laughed year after year at the same jokes.

Clare and Philip danced, after the dressing-up clothes had been put away, to music played by Lucy; a quiet, thoughtful Lucy, who watched them over the top of the piano, an unreadable expression in her eyes.

And Ben? I could not tell what Ben was thinking, either—but he danced with Clare too, and after it was all over, it was Ben who took her home.

All in all, I thought, as I curled up beside Roger, it had been a highly satisfactory day.

22

The distance between Oxfordshire and Somerset seemed to shorten that winter and it was surprising how often Ben found himself able to come home for the weekend. But I still could not tell how he felt about Clare.

"She's one of the chaps," he once said to me, which seemed to me an unlikely basis for romance.

But one day in April when Ben had just come home for the Easter holidays and there were lambs in the fields and a watery sun shining on hedges filled with catkins and pussy-willow, I happened to look out of the window and saw them in the meadow beyond the front garden laughing helplessly together—and I laughed too, because it was good to see and, in view of Lucy's testimony, the power of a shared joke was something I would never underestimate.

I still worried about Lucy. We saw her frequently, often dining with them in Oxford and occasionally going to the theatre, sometimes just with the two of them and sometimes with John and Angela in the party too.

The six of us were together after an evening of Gilbert and Sullivan, having gone back to John's house for a late meal, and it was Angela who unwittingly set the cat amongst the pigeons.

"I was in Prudence Wintringham's little shop the other day," she said casually and quite without guile. "She seems to be making an awfully good thing of it."

"Yes, I believe she is," Lucy agreed stiffly.

"She told me she's thinking of expanding," Angela went on, oblivious of undercurrents.

"I know. She wants me to go in with her."

"Does she? That would be rather fun, wouldn't it?"

"It's out of the question," Nick said, smiling paternally at Lucy. "Lucy has quite enough to do at home."

"But I haven't, Nick. That's the point."

"Darling, please don't bring this whole thing up again." He raised his shoulders and looked around at the rest of us. "My adored wife has many good qualities." He reached out and patted her hand. "She's a good cook; I've never yet found myself without a clean shirt or a neatly pressed suit. But what gives her the idea that she could sell dresses, I have no idea!"

"I'm interested in fashion," Lucy said stonily, removing her hand from his reach, but stealthily.

"Darling, I'm interested in music, but it doesn't mean I think I can conduct a symphony orchestra!"

"It's not quite the same thing, is it?" I asked, stepping in, as always, where angels would fear to tread.

"There is no *need* for her to work," Nick said, staring fixedly at me.

I looked down at my lap, a small flame of anger springing to life as I realised that he was laying the blame for Lucy's restlessness at my door.

"Lucy, I'm banking on you to help me with the Red Lion," I said, lifting my head and looking directly back at him. "She has such good taste," I went on, "and we have to refurnish the sitting room. I remember how invaluable her advice was when we were furnishing Priors—do you remember, Roger? She was quite wonderful, wasn't she?"

"She was always artistic," Roger agreed.

"I'd love to help," Lucy said.

"Well, that's settled then." I smiled sweetly at Nick. "I'm sure we can make sure that she's back in good time to see that you don't miss your perfect dinner."

He had little option but to agree and Lucy began to travel with me more and more to the hotels, impressing me with her flair for colour and her assurance in seeing exactly what the finished picture would be like—whereas I, so often, had to wait until the chairs were covered or the curtains hung before realising that something quite different might have been an improvement.

Roger had found the perfect site for the new hotel close to Woodstock and suitable plans had been drawn up by a firm of architects in Oxford.

I experienced the strangest feeling as I stood on the site watching the builders marking out the foundations. It was such a huge undertaking—exciting, but daunting too. Where would we ever find the people to fill such a large building? To me it seemed a hair-raising gamble, but Roger had been right too often in the past for me to give voice to my doubts.

The project absorbed Roger utterly and Philip came down from London as often as he could to look at the growing walls lovingly and to issue a continuous stream of suggestions. I feel sure that between the two of them they must have driven the architect and builders mad; but because of—or perhaps in spite of—their involvement, throughout the summer of 1924 the new hotel rose steadily, golden stone on golden stone.

We did not see much of Ellie during the first half of the year. She had given up her Civil Service job and was now working full-time at Labour Party headquarters, still spending many of her evenings lecturing at halls all over London on the subject of socialism.

Towards the end of March she paid us a flying weekend visit and in the car beside her was a small, swarthy young man with dark eyes and a thin, serious mouth. I greeted him in some surprise as I had not expected her to bring a friend.

"This is Robert Stephens, Mother. Annie's son," she said.

"Annie's son! Of course, you're Robbie—I can see it now. How lovely to see you again! It's years since I heard from your mother—"

"She died during the war, I'm afraid."

"Oh, no! Oh, poor Annie. She stopped writing to me years ago, but I often thought of her. What happened to her?"

"It was pneumonia, plus overwork and undernourishment."

"Oh, poor Annie," I said again. "I wish I'd known. And your father, and the rest of the family?"

"All well and living in Manchester still."

"I'm glad to hear that. Come inside do—I'm so glad Ellie brought you. How on earth did you ever meet? And why didn't you give us some warning, Ellie?"

"I only met him last night; this was a spur of the moment decision, wasn't it, Robert? He was one of the organisers of a meeting in Maida Vale where I spoke, and it was only after a very nasty cup of coffee afterwards that we discovered we both originated in Collingford and that his mother used to work at the Ring of Bells."

"Is your father still interested in politics?" I asked.

"It's his whole life. He's worked for the Trades Union movement as long as I can remember."

"And you're following in his footsteps."

"I do what I can."

"You look like him," I said. And indeed, now that I came to study Robert, I could see that the likeness to his father was quite uncanny. Although his features were different, the shape of his face was the same and the way his hair grew. More than that, there was a likeness of expression; a quiet watchfulness which seemed all too ready to manifest itself in a sneer.

As far as I could tell, he thought and spoke in clichés, and as I sat and listened to him holding forth over the dinner table, I grew a little less delighted that Ellie had brought him home. Yet there was gallantry there too, I thought. He sat in the shiny blue suit in which he had arrived, his cuffs frayed, yet he held his head high and looked Roger straight in the eye as he spoke of the toiling masses oppressed by capitalist lackeys awaiting the glorious revolution—the phrases churned out with a relentless inevitability, one after the other.

"The fellow's an awful bore," Roger said to me afterwards in private. "Ellie can't be interested in him, surely?"

"Only as a fellow-worker, I think. She thought I'd be interested to meet him again. You know, the more he talks, the more he reminds me of Jed."

"Jed never said very much!"

"No, but what he did say was always tinged with the same sort of barely-controlled anger—don't you remember?"

"I remember the man was a bloody fool," Roger said.

Ellie and Robert walked up to Berry Cross to see the cottage where the Stephens family had spent their early years, and they called into the Ring of Bells for a drink on the way back. Somehow the weekend passed, but it was with a slight throbbing behind the temples that we waved goodbye to them as they drove back to London.

"It is perfectly possible," I said to Roger, "to have a little too much of politics and the underprivileged masses. I propose to put some Beethoven on the gramophone, put my feet up, and relax with Elinor Glyn."

"You're depraved, woman," Roger said. "Come the glorious revolution, your head will be the first to roll."

"Oh, go and eat cake," I told him.

Ellie phoned a couple of times during the next few weeks, but although I asked about Robert she was uncommunicative about him and I sensed she had no wish to talk of him. Thankfully, I dropped the subject, only too pleased that we were not likely to be called upon to undergo another visitation.

It was in June that Ellie appeared again, this time alone and with no warning whatsoever. I had been over at the Rose Revived and returned home to find that in my absence she had arrived and had gone straight to bed.

"She doesn't look at all well, Mrs Leyton. I'm that worried about her," Izzie said. "Like a ghost, she was. She had some tea, but wouldn't take anything to eat."

I went upstairs to Ellie's room. She did indeed look ghastly. Her face was a greenish white and there were dark shadows round her sunken eyes.

"Ellie, darling," I said, looking at her in shocked concern. "What on earth's the matter? You're ill! I'm going to send for Richard."

"No—no, please mother, don't do that! I'm all right, honestly. I'm tired, that's all. I've been overdoing it."

I sat down on the bed and looked at her.

She looked exhausted, pinched and small-faced, just like the time she had come back from France knowing that Lawrence was dead.

"Is there anything I can get you?" I asked. "Have you a headache?"

She shook her head.

"Just let me sleep," she said.

She closed her eyes, and after studying her for a few moments feeling sick with worry, I tiptoed out of the room and back to the kitchen.

"It's that rackety life she leads," Izzie said, crashing pans around in the sink to signal her disapproval. "Honestly, Mrs Leyton, you should turn round and tell her—"

"I think she's a little too old for that," I said. "But I'm sure you're right, Izzie. She works hard all day, then rushes across London to do her lecturing, then sits up half the night talking with her friends."

"And she smokes too much," Izzie said.

"I'm afraid she does."

"And never a square meal, unless I'm very much mistaken."

"I'm sure you're not! But what can one do with a daughter who is thirty-one? She's her own mistress now, Izzie."

"That's as may be," Izzie muttered darkly.

The following day I was relieved to see that Ellie's colour was a little better, but she was still subdued and merely picked at the food I brought her on her breakfast tray.

"Ellie, there's something wrong, isn't there?" I asked her tentatively.

"I said I was tired!" Her tone was sharp, but she looked contrite the moment she had spoken. "I'm sorry, Mother," she said penitently. "But really, I need to rest, that's all. Please don't fuss."

"What's Ellie doing in the garden, alone and palely loitering?" Roger asked later in the day, standing at the tall window.

"I don't know," I said. "But come away, do—she'll hate it if she feels we're watching her every move."

"I don't like the look of her," he said.

I could only agree with him, but if Ellie chose not to confide in us, there was little we could do.

During the course of the evening, long after she had retired to bed after a silent supper, I went upstairs to fetch some mending from my room. I hesitated for a second outside her door, but she had indicated so clearly that she wanted no interference that I passed on, resisting the temptation to go in to her. It was only seconds later that I passed her room again on my return journey, and this time I stopped, more torn than ever; for now I could hear that she was crying.

She was not a person to whom tears came easily. She had cried when she had returned from France, after Lawrence had been killed, but since then I had never known her give way to emotion. She was normally so poised and contained; I knew she would hate to be caught with her guard down. Yet it was quite beyond me to pass by her room again. Rightly or wrongly, I would have to go in.

She was in bed, curled into a ball, sobs tearing her apart. I ran to her and held her and for a few moments she clung to me as if she were a little girl again and I the all-powerful mother-figure who could make everything right.

"Ellie, darling, what is it?" I asked at last as gradually her sobs lessened. "What's happened to you?"

She shook her head dumbly.

"I'm just—just at the end of my tether," she said at last.

I held the back of my hand to her forehead.

"You have a temperature, I'm sure. Ellie you're not well—I don't care what you say, I'm going to send for Richard."

"*No!* You're not to, Mother—I won't have it."

"Darling, why not? You're quite obviously ill."

"Once and for all, you are *not* to send for Richard!"

I stood looking down at her, puzzled and concerned. Richard was an old friend; she had always seemed fond of him and found him easy to talk to. There was no reason on earth why she should not consult him now, when quite obviously there was something badly amiss with her; I had never known her so distraught, so pale.

Suddenly, as I looked at her, I thought of a reason. At first it seemed such an enormity that my mind refused to accept it, and I pushed the thought away; but the more I thought about it, the more it seemed that little else would explain her despair or her reluctance to see Richard.

"Ellie," I said. "Ellie, darling—are you pregnant?"

She had been looking away from me, but at this she turned to stare at me, her eyes blank with astonishment, before she began to cry again, silently this time, the tears forcing themselves between her closed lids.

Silently she shook her head, and for a few moments I stood there helplessly, chiding myself. What a question to ask her, I thought. Ellie, of all people—sensitive, fastidious Ellie.

"Would you have minded?" she asked suddenly.

"Minded?" I shrugged and laughed briefly. "Well, it's not exactly the sort of thing one wants for a daughter, is it? But we wouldn't condemn, if that's what you mean. We wouldn't have told you never to darken our doors again!"

She sighed, a long shuddering sigh.

"I was pregnant, Mother. But I got rid of it."

There was a moment of utter silence; a moment when I felt as if all the breath had been knocked from me. I opened my mouth and tried to speak, but no words would come. The silence lengthened between us.

"Mother, before you sit in judgment, just consider what a baby would have meant to me," she said, in a high, rapid voice. "What would I have done with it, in heaven's name? How could I have coped? There's a chance—just a small chance—that I might be adopted as a parliamentary candidate at the next election! Just imagine having to turn that down because I was tied with a baby I didn't want. And look at it from the baby's point of view. Who wants to be a bastard?"

"Don't pretend you were thinking of the baby!"

"Well, not entirely, of course."

"You had an abortion!"

"I said so, didn't I? I didn't mean to tell you—I wish I hadn't!"

"Oh, Ellie!" I turned my back on her and walked towards the window.

"Mother, I didn't have any choice." Her voice was quieter now, less defensive.

"You could have had the baby. You could have married the man."

"No! That was out of the question."

361

"Why?" I turned to face her and looked at her stonily. "Was he married already?"

"No. I—I just didn't love him, Mother. It was a mistake, the whole thing—a horrible, ghastly mistake that would have been compounded a hundred times over if we'd married."

"Did he offer marriage?"

"It didn't arise. I didn't tell him about the baby."

Nothing in my experience had prepared me for this. Women became pregnant; that happened all the time. Out of wedlock it was something to be deplored, but it was understandable. But this—this! To me, it was evil, unthinkable, ugly. It was murder, nothing less.

"You're—you're all right?" I managed to say at last. "I mean, it can be dangerous."

"Oh yes," Ellie said. "You don't have to worry about me. It was all very sterile, and very, very expensive."

"Don't pretend to be hard, Ellie," I said. "You're not hard. If you were, you wouldn't be crying."

She lay back on the pillows again, her eyes closed, her face hardly differing in colour from the linen that supported her head.

"Oh, God," she said bitterly. "How we work and agitate for women's equality, and how futile it is, really, when it comes down to this: that men can have their brief moment of fun and walk away, whereas we have to pay, mentally and physically maybe, for the rest of our lives. Why *should* we, Mother? You've always been a believer in equality and freedom for women; tell me, where's the justice in being forced to go through an unwanted pregnancy? Why should our bodies enslave us this way?"

I shook my head helplessly, then went to sit down on her bed, putting my arms around her, loving her so much.

"I don't know, Ellie," I said. "I'm not clever. I can't answer things like that. I just think—hasn't the baby rights, too?"

"That's such a Victorian point of view!"

"Perhaps. If it is, can you blame me? I was a Victorian for a good number of years. I can't help thinking that for all your fearless, modern point of view, you're not exactly happy about it yourself, are you?"

"I had no choice."

"Then why are you so sad? What makes you cry as you cried tonight?"

She had no words to answer me, but instead gave a kind of gasp and began to cry again in rending, gulping sobs.

"My life is a mess," she said, her words muffled. "A hopeless, hopeless mess."

I held her close, wanting more than anything in the world to draw her sorrow into me and knowing that it was impossible. She did not ask me not to tell Roger, and indeed, I was so upset that it would have been impossible for me to keep my feelings a secret from him. He was struck as dumb as I had been, but his outrage, when he could finally give voice to it, centred more on the man involved.

"I wish I could get my hands on him!" he raged. "My God—a decent girl like Ellie—"

"Roger, she isn't sixteen! One can hardly accuse him of taking advantage of an innocent young girl."

"I've always hated her living in London, right from the beginning," he said. "It's no life for a woman. And all these Bolsheviks she's mixed up with—"

Upset though I was, I ventured a protest at that, but he ploughed on, raging up and down the room.

"Is this what emancipation means? Is this the new, liberated woman? If so, then the sooner we return to the old ways the better."

"The old ways are gone," I said. "There'll be no return to them." His anger made me plead Ellie's cause. "Freedom means that we have choices now—choices that were out of the question a few years ago."

"And choice implies responsibility!"

"Ellie's not irresponsible. Mistaken, perhaps—but surely not more irresponsible than men who have fathered unwanted children for centuries without a thought to the consequences."

"Jenny—you're not condoning this, are you?"

Miserably I rested my head against the wing of the armchair, staring at nothing.

"No," I said. "I keep thinking of the baby. I feel lost and confused. In theory I can see Ellie's point: why should women be the ones to bear the consequences? If I believe in the equality of women—which I do—then surely I should believe that too. I suppose I'm too much a product of the Victorian age after all, because the thought of it makes me sick."

"To hell with thoughts and theories! I'm not letting her go back."

"Roger, we both know that Ellie is far beyond the stage of asking our permission for what she does."

"We'll see about that!"

He was full of sound and fury, but when he came face to face with Ellie the next day he took her in his arms and I was not surprised, minutes later, to see him walking and talking with her calmly in the garden.

Over the next few days she regained her composure, though was still pale and quiet. She yielded to our pleas to stay at home for a complete rest for a week or so, and although at first she raised objections, saying she had appointments to keep and lectures to deliver, a few telephone calls relieved her of these immediate commitments and she surrendered herself to unashamed idleness. She was aided and abetted by a succession of warm and langorous days that made it a pleasure to lie in the garden. Sometimes she read; more often she slept.

"The less one does, the less one wants to do," she said to me one day when we were strolling through the garden together. "I ought to go back." But she said it without conviction. It was as if her London life had become unreal; lost somewhere in the smoke from the belching chimneys.

"Do you feel better?" I asked.

"Much." She smiled at me. "It all seems like a nightmare now."

"Stay a little longer," I begged. "London will be impossibly hot just now."

"I know. Even the thought oppresses me."

"Then leave it a while."

"You shouldn't tempt me! I have work to do."

"Surely Parliament goes into recess in summer?"

"Not for a while yet; and even when it does, there's plenty of work at headquarters."

"Even so, don't rush away." I put my hand through the crook of her arm. "We love having you."

"I can't imagine why. I'm nothing but a headache to you."

"Nonsense!"

We reached a seat and sat down by the white philadelphus bush—the same seat, I remembered suddenly, where I had discovered Ben and Ellie after Lucy's wedding.

"What a glorious evening," I said, as I sat down. "Why can't it always be like this?"

"Nothing is ever like this always," Ellie said. "Every Eden has a serpent in it somewhere, just waiting to strike."

And all I wanted was for my children to be happy, I thought; realising even as I formed the words how nonsensical the idea was—as if happiness was a simple thing, a small thing to ask for. But it's not a small thing, I thought. It's an enormous thing to expect.

"Oh, Ellie," I said. "I wish I could help you."

"Have you forgiven me?"

"You're more unforgiving of yourself than I could ever be."

"Perhaps. I've thought about it all so much, Mother, and I still can't see what other course I could have taken."

"You don't think the father had a right to know?"

"No!" She was silent for a moment, idly twisting the head of a daisy in her fingers. "Aren't you curious about who the father was?"

"Yes," I said after a moment. "Yes, I suppose I am."

"I want to tell you because I think it will help you to understand why marriage was out of the question. It was Robert Stephens."

I turned to look at her, remembering with amazement the swarthy little man in the shiny suit, with his angry eyes and stream of clichés.

"Annie's son!" I said.

"Jed's son. A strange character, Mother. A fanatic. Bitter and hating and black with despair. I could never have married him."

"But Ellie—why on earth—"

"Did I let him make love to me in the first place? I told

you, it was a mad, impulsive sort of thing. I suppose we were both a little drunk—on words, I mean, not wine, though we'd consumed a fair amount of that, too. We'd been to a meeting in somebody's house and he saw me home. Suddenly the loneliness seemed to overpower me and it seemed preferable to allow him into my bed rather than sleep alone. There's a sort of magnetism about him, you know. I admit it wasn't very obvious when he stayed here, but believe me, he can exert a powerful charm when he wants to."

"Jed was like that," I said. "And I don't think Annie ever refused him, either."

"And look what happened to her! No Mother—it was a regrettable and bitter experience, and I would never allow myself to go through it again; but I can see no other ending to it."

She said no more about leaving for London, seeming content to bask in the sun or walk over the hills or along by the river, our old spaniel at her heels. Sometimes she would walk to the Ring of Bells to meet Roger or go with him to the green on a Saturday to watch the cricket match. It must have seemed a strangely peaceful contrast to the frenetic pace of her life in London and Izzie and I noted with satisfaction that her appetite had improved and she seemed altogether more relaxed.

One day she mentioned that Kim, the spaniel, had picked up a thorn in his foot while she had been watching the cricket on the green, but that fortunately the new vet was a cricketer and had been on hand to extract it.

"I haven't met him yet," I said. "Is he nice?"

"A useful bat," Roger said. Ellie and I exchanged amused glances.

"What more can anyone say?" I murmured.

"He seems agreeable," Ellie said, only marginally more informative. "He has a pleasantly craggy sort of face."

It was only two or three days later that I returned from a day at the Red Lion to find the owner of the pleasantly craggy face taking tea with her on the lawn at Priors underneath the copper beech tree. He was introduced as Geoffrey Maskell, and gave a lame and halting explanation for his presence; he was calling to check on Kim's paw, he told me.

A likely story, I thought. No veterinary surgeon—overworked and underpaid as they were—had ever gone out of his way to pay an unsolicited call on a dog whose injury was not only superficial but long since forgotten; but I was not inclined to query his motives. It was sufficient for me that Ellie appeared to be happy in his company. She was conversing with much of her old sparkle and Geoffrey was regarding her with an amused and delighted disbelief, as if he had always hoped to meet someone like her but had never thought such a fate possible. Before he left he had invited her to go with him next day to a remote farm where he had to carry out tests on a herd of cows, and she had accepted.

Later the following day we received a telephone call to say that Ellie would not be home to dinner; she would be dining with Geoffrey at the Rose Revived.

"I hope she's not going to be hurt again," Roger said as we sat together over our meal. "What did you think of him?"

"He struck me as being very nice," I said. "Not the sort of person who would want to hurt anybody. There's a kind of quiet strength about him."

Stability, I thought. That's what Ellie needs, and that's what Geoffrey Maskell has.

He took to dropping in for tea when he could spare the time and occasionally they went to Oxford to the theatre or a concert. "He's very easy to be with," Ellie said. "Undemanding. I like him enormously. But don't go getting ideas, Mother—we're friends, that's all. Just friends."

And I was pleased because I felt that friendship could never be overrated. Friends could well become lovers; whereas without friendship a relationship to someone such as Ellie would be dead from the start.

Roger and I had been out to dinner with the Fenwicks one evening and it was late when we returned, but late as it was we passed Geoffrey's battered car turning out of the Priors track just as we approached it.

The summer evenings were long and darkness had not long fallen. The house was unlit except for one small lamp burning in the hall and I switched on the main light as I went in, revealing Ellie curled up in the window seat leaning against the mullioned panes and blinking at us like a cat.

"Goodness me, I didn't realise anyone was here," I said. "Why are you sitting in the dark?"

She uncoiled herself and stretched.

"I was thinking," she said. "And the effort has quite exhausted me. I think I'll go up to bed."

She said good night and left us and I knew as surely as if she had told me that Geoffrey had asked her to marry him. I found myself quite unable to guess her reply.

I liked Geoffrey. I would love nothing better than to have Ellie living close by, raising a family, living a normal life. But could I really imagine her as a country wife? She had hardly mentioned politics since she had been at Priors and had told me that she never discussed them with Geoffrey; yet to her politics had always been the breath of life and I could not picture her away from the hub of things.

She was quiet and thoughtful for several days and we saw nothing of Geoffrey, but one evening towards the end of July I saw them from afar sauntering down the track hand in hand, stopping every now and again to talk and to kiss, and I knew then what her answer had been.

"Think how useful it will be to have a vet in the family," Ellie said, after they had reached the house and we had drunk to their happiness.

"Just so long as he resists the temptation to put his mother-in-law down." I smiled across at Geoffrey and he smiled back from his place by Ellie's side.

"I hope you're pleased," he said to me when for a brief moment we found ourselves alone.

"Ellie needs someone like you," I assured him. "We couldn't be more delighted."

"I can't really believe it." He gave a short, breathless laugh. "I can't think what she sees in me."

"Don't underestimate yourself. You've made Ellie happy—you have only to look at her. I think she's a fortunate woman."

"I'm the lucky one," he said, his eyes never leaving her.

The following morning there was a letter from London in the post for Ellie. She came down to breakfast in the highest spirits, kissed the top of Roger's head in passing and pulled

Kim's ear as she went to the sideboard to help herself to eggs and bacon.

"Did you ever see anything like this weather?" she asked. "Isn't it heavenly? Day after day one thinks it must surely end and day after day the sun keeps shining." She rattled on happily as she studied the envelope by her plate and opened it with her knife before tackling her breakfast. I thought how young she looked—young and vivid and beautiful. Oh please God, I thought, let her be happy. She's suffered so much.

She was reading her letter and her words died. She put the paper down with a hand that trembled and in a single, abrupt movement got up and went to the window, thrusting her hands deep in the pockets of her skirt and hunching her shoulders as she stared out into the garden.

"What is it?" Roger asked. "It's not bad news, is it?"

He turned in his chair to look at her anxiously and she moved to face us with a quick, nervous shake of the head as if she were flicking the hair from her eyes.

"No," she said. "Not bad news, exactly. The timing of it leaves something to be desired, however." Her voice was high and tight with strain.

"Ellie?"

She turned to me, seeming to swallow with difficulty.

"It's something I've always wanted—something I've longed for as long as I can remember."

Her face was as white as if it had been carved out of bone.

"The government's going to the country at the end of this session—and they want me to stand. Do you hear that? They want me to stand."

She stood for a moment with her lip caught between her teeth and wide-eyed we stared back at her, bereft of words. Then she picked up her letter and ran from the room.

23

The election at which Ellie stood as a candidate was lost by the socialists, but she had reduced her opponent's majority and was not unduly cast down by the result. If she ever had any private regrets about Geoffrey, she did not confide them to me. He, poor fellow, seemed to avoid us, for which I could hardly blame him. I saw him sometimes driving his battered little car about the countryside, giving the impression of a confirmed and rather lonely bachelorhood.

It was disappointing, too, that I was left at the end of Ben's summer holiday not knowing whether his relationship with Clare had progressed or not.

"That wretched war has a lot to answer for," I said to Roger crossly one day. "It seems to have made Ben far too cautious."

Roger laughed at me.

"That's a strange complaint, coming from a mother. I thought a parent's role in life was to bemoan the rashness of youth."

"Ben's forgotten the meaning of the word. He seems terrified of committing himself one way or the other. You know, Roger, I think there's a lot to be said for arranged marriages."

"Oh yes? And where do you imagine that would have left us? You would be behind the counter of a butcher's shop in Witney and I should have been matched up with the horsy Miss Dodwell of Standlake. What you really mean is that there's a lot to be said for marriages arranged by *you*!"

I laughed ruefully.

"Yes, I suppose that just about sums it up. Still, it does rile me to see a couple like Ben and Clare, so ideally suited that everyone in the world can see it except themselves, circling around each other in this inconclusive sort of way. One minute it seems that Ben is advancing while Clare is retreating, then Ben takes fright and it looks as if Clare is the one that's keen. They remind me of starlings on a lawn—one flies off as the other swoops down."

"There's nothing you can do about it, my love. They'll take their time and make their own decisions."

I agreed that they would. But I still had the desire to shake them at intervals.

It was Christmas again before we could turn round, which meant that they had known each other for a whole year. With a grim sense of purpose I fastened several bunches of mistletoe in strategic places, but as far as I could see it was only Peter, who had come to spend Christmas with us that year, who reaped the benefit. He was meeting Clare for the first time and was exerting himself to charm her. Ben seemed to stand off a little and to watch him sourly, doing nothing whatever to establish any claim to Clare on his own part. My desire to shake him grew stronger than ever.

Goffy went to his brother in Nottingham that year, but John and Angela and Mark and Charlotte came to us, which made everything perfect. It was many years since the three brothers had been together—not since their mother's funeral, which had hardly been the happiest occasion. Both Roger and John were now grandfathers and Mark's hair was snowy white, but they were as happy as schoolboys to see each other again.

And I was overjoyed to see Charlotte. We were able, it seemed, to pick up a conversation just where we had left it years before. With Charlotte I always knew that there was no need to explain myself or my thoughts. In nine cases out of ten, she was there before me. As we exchanged our news and observations, I knew for certain that I would never find another friend like her. Friendship such as ours, I felt, had to be forged in youth and strengthened by shared joys and sorrows.

With the house full of people the opportunities for quiet conversation with Roger had been limited for some days, but while we were both preparing for the ball, he contrived to deliver something of a bombshell.

"Peter buttonholed me this morning before the Meet," he said.

"Oh, yes?" I was more interested in fixing my earrings than in anything Peter might have to say and was paying scant attention.

"He wants to come into the business."

"*What*? Why, Roger? What's happened to this flying show thing?" He had all of my attention now.

"It's a joint enterprise, as you know—he's dependent on this friend of his whom I gather is a rather wild character. Peter's plane is still serviceable, I'm told, but the other one needs more money than they're prepared to pay for it to be given a certificate of air worthiness. The other chap wants to pull out."

"What did you say?"

"Merely that I'd think about it. I'd like to help the boy, of course."

"Darling, do be careful!"

"The gypsy's warning! Careful of what?"

"I don't know. I don't know what to make of Peter these days."

"There's no reason why he shouldn't be a perfectly competent manager if he's willing to train and to work hard."

"If," I said sceptically.

"He has a way with people. That's important in a business like ours. And Miss Perkins is leaving in the spring."

"He couldn't possibly take her place! She types and answers the telephone and makes out bills and shows people to their rooms—all the tedious little jobs that are so necessary but don't make any show at all. That's not Peter's style."

"No—but even so, there might be a place for him." He was silent for a moment as he wrestled with his tie.

"Here—let me." I went over to him and reached up to straighten the white bow. "Mm—I always think you look so distinguished in tails. There, that's better."

"Don't say anything to Mark, will you?"

"Not if you don't want me to. Why, though?"

"Peter wants to get himself sorted out before worrying him."

We left the conversation there, but I found the possibility of Peter's permanent presence disturbing. We were a big party at the Ring of Bells and he was at some distance from me. I looked down the table towards him and wondered just how he would fit in.

He was obviously in the highest of spirits that night, and Peter in high spirits was a formidable force. He had his mother's looks and wilfulness, but there was also something of his grandmother about him; a strength of personality that inspired both attraction and annoyance. However one felt about him, no one would ever ignore him.

There was a great deal of shimmery material about that year, with oriental embroidery and beads and bright, flaming colours. There were floating panels and jewel-encrusted bandeaux and gilded turbans sprouting feathers. There were more bobbed heads than ever before, only Charlotte and I among our party still wearing our hair long. Some of the younger bloods among the men were wearing double-breasted dinner jackets instead of the more usual tails.

"Looks a bit caddish, doesn't it?" Mark remarked to me. "I don't think it will catch on."

"I said the same about the horseless carriage," I said.

"Not to mention the aeroplane! What do you think of that, Jenny? A son of the soil like me siring a son who earns his living looping the loop."

But perhaps not for very much longer, I thought.

"I wish he'd give it up," Mark went on. "I worry so about him. Sometimes it seems as if the war isn't over at all."

I looked down at my plate and wondered whether to speak, but decided against it. I had given Roger my promise, after all. But from then on I began to feel a little differently about taking Peter into the business; perhaps it was something we should do, for Mark's sake.

"At least he's not getting shot at," I said, trying to be comforting. I looked once more down to the end of the table where Clare was sitting with Ben on her left and Peter on her right. "Though I have the sort of feeling that he might just get shot at tonight."

Mark followed the direction of my eyes. Peter was monopolising Clare, his head close to hers. He was laughing, demonstrating with his hand the approach of a plane. He turned his head to include the others sitting near him, to carry them along with him as he told his story. Lucy, Nick and Clare exploded into mirth.

Ben alone sat glum, biting the inside of his cheek and drawing patterns on the table cloth with his fork. Later he seemed to make an effort and rallied himself sufficiently to dance with Lucy and Ellie. He danced with Clare, too, but they circled the floor with stony faces, looking over each other's shoulders and saying nothing.

My heart sank a little and the occasion lost something of its glitter, so that when Mark yawned and said that he was far too old to hunt *and* sit up late and, please, could he go home? I was quite ready to agree that the younger members of the family should be left to continue the evening without us.

"Do you mind?" I asked Roger.

"Good Lord, no! I've had more than enough late nights recently. We're getting old, Jenny."

"Speak for yourself," I responded tartly; but thought later, as I waited for sleep, that this was a night when I felt very old indeed.

I still grieved over Ellie's failed romance, particularly as she had not been elected to Parliament as she had hoped.

"I never really expected it the first time," she said. "There'll be another chance. The party is quite pleased with me."

That's as may be, I thought to myself. What comfort is that going to be in her old age?

My face must have expressed my feelings.

"I can't help being this way," she went on. "After all, you influenced me, you and Aunt Charlotte. She supplied the theory of women's emancipation and you the practice. Knowing you two, how could I ever subscribe to the view that women were in any way inferior to men? And really, all my other political beliefs grew from that major premise."

I was only partially mollified, my worries far from allayed. It still seemed to me that a copy of Hansard would make a cold bedfellow in the years to come.

Then there was Lucy.

She seemed more resigned to her life with Nick; but what

fun was there in being resigned, I asked myself? If only she could exercise her brain and her undoubted artistic talents in some way, she would be a great deal happier.

As for Ben—well, I could cheerfully throttle him! He deserved to lose Clare, to Peter or to anyone. He seemed to be turning into a dry-as-dust academic before my very eyes; or was that only in comparison with Peter's urbane charm? Was that the way Clare saw him, now that she saw him alongside his cousin?

I drifted off to sleep eventually, but was woken later by the arrival of cars. I heard doors bang and the sound of voices, followed by deafening 'shushing' noises as one half of the company appeared to be urging the other half not to wake the entire household. The young have returned, I thought; but not, if I knew my family, to sleep. There would be hot drinks in the kitchen and conversation lasting half the night.

I wonder who took Clare home, I thought sleepily? I hoped it was Ben—but was then jerked fully awake by the sound of her voice outside our window. The least the girl could do, I thought testily, was to keep her voice down. What could she be thinking of, making such a racket? It dawned on me that everyone was being uncharacteristically noisy. They were not usually guilty of thoughtless behaviour of this kind and I frowned into the darkness trying to make out the cause of all the fuss—for fuss there undoubtedly was. I could hear Lucy's voice suddenly raised.

"Ben," she shouted. "Don't be an idiot!"

There was the sound of scuffling on the gravel, the dull crash of something breaking and a stifled feminine scream.

"Stop being fools, the pair of you!" That was Nick, crisp and military and authoritative. It appeared that the pair of fools took not the slightest notice and the scuffles continued. Fully awake now, I shook Roger and leapt from the bed.

"What the blazes is going on out there?" he asked sleepily.

"Roger, they're fighting. Wake up, for heaven's sake."

I ran to the window and pulled the curtains open, peering out into the garden where, clearly illuminated by the light spilling out from the open front door, I could see Ben and Peter locked in combat.

Lucy was capering around them making ineffectual grabs at their clothing, pleading with them to stop. Clare was standing to one side, wringing her hands. Philip appeared to be holding Nick back from interfering, at the same time trying to herd both Ellie and Clare into the house.

"Silly young idiots," Roger said, joining me at the window.

Ben landed a swift upper cut to Peter's chin which sent him staggering backwards. He recovered his balance and came charging back towards Ben, his overcoat flying open to reveal his gleaming shirt front and his tie, now definitely askew. The pair closed together and I opened the window, leaning out into the cold night air to call down to them, my words quite inaudible against the grunts and muffled swearing that was going on below.

"Roger, can't you do something?" I said helplessly, turning to my husband who was watching with every appearance of enjoyment.

He ignored me.

"That's it, Ben," he was saying softly. "Now's your chance—a quick right—"

"Roger, stop it! They'll kill each other."

"Nonsense," he said. "There's been bad blood between them the whole of this holiday; maybe this will get rid of it once and for all."

"They'll disturb everyone."

"The guest bedrooms are at the back. Oh my stars, look at this!"

I had not noticed that Ellie had left the scene until I saw her return, armed with a white enamel bucket. Just as if she were quelling a dog fight, she threw the contents of the bucket over Ben and Peter, drenching them from head to feet with what I imagined was ice-cold water.

Gasping, his hair plastered to his head, Ben turned towards her looking murderous, but before he could utter a word of protest she had neatly covered his head with the bucket, which immobilised him more effectively than one might have thought possible only seconds before.

Peter stood for a moment as if thunderstruck, but then he looked at Ben fighting his way out of the bucket and his mood changed. He began to laugh. Ben, winning his battle, stood with the bucket in one hand glaring at him with impotent fury until all at once he was laughing too—great, whooping paroxysms of mirth which rose to match Peter's laughter until they were both staggering and holding on to each other, all antagonism apparently forgotten.

"Men!" I said, shaking my head in total bewilderment.

"What did I say?" Roger asked, looking smug.

"But they must come in—I must go down—they'll be soaking wet and freezing cold."

"Leave them," Roger said. "For heaven's sake, come back to bed. If they haven't enough sense to get out of cold wet clothes at their time of life, then they deserve everything that comes to them." He chuckled. "How do you like that Ellie, though? That was as neat a trick as I've seen in a month of Sundays. She keeps a cool head in a crisis, doesn't she?"

"No cooler than those two boys are at this moment, I imagine," I said, curling up beside him again.

Not surprisingly we were all late waking the following morning, and my slumbers that followed the brawl outside the window were undisturbed by the sound of cars or anything else.

"I don't know what these are doing here, I'm sure," Izzie said in surprise, having found two suits of tails drying in front of the kitchen range.

"It's a long story," I said.

I had eaten breakfast and was in my bedroom a little later when Ellie put her head round the door.

"I imagine you were not entirely unaware of the fracas last night," she said.

"You imagine right! What was it all about? Clare?"

"Yes. I think you'll have two very contrite young men apologising to you this morning—but neither of them is a fraction as contrite as Clare. By the way, she slept in my room last night. Do you have anything she could borrow to wear this morning? All my clothes would be much too small."

"I expect I can find something," I said. "What was the trouble, exactly?"

"I rather think that Clare felt that if she paid a little attention to Peter, it might bring Ben to the boil—and my goodness, it certainly did, didn't it? Did you ever imagine that sweet-natured, peace-loving Ben could actually *attack* anyone? Clare was quite overcome when she saw what she had unleashed."

"Did it have the desired effect?"

Ellie shrugged. "Time alone will tell. I shouldn't be at all surprised, though. She was fussing around him like a mother hen last night, getting him hot bottles and hot drinks, while Peter was left to fend for himself. I can't find it in my heart to blame Ben, you know. Peter is an awful tom cat!"

"They were very naughty," I said severely, "all of them, including Clare. Ellie, that was an *awful* thing to do, drenching them like that—and on such a cold night, too!"

"It was effective though, wasn't it?"

And she grinned at me, unrepentant, as I handed her some clothes for Clare.

The boys did apologise and Roger and I graciously forgave them, on the understanding that such childish behaviour would never happen again. Clare, too, came to me privately and said how sorry she was to have been the cause of the quarrel.

"It was a terrible way to behave," she said. "I'm thoroughly ashamed of myself. I was never the slightest bit interested in Peter, really—just that I was desperate to know, once and for all, how Ben felt about me."

"And do you know now?" I asked.

She looked at me and smiled, a slow, irradiating smile that lit up her face.

"I believe I do," she said.

I was delighted, when I next had the chance to talk to Roger, to report that everything between Ben and Clare seemed to be going well.

"That's good," he said, sounding abstracted.

"Is something wrong, Roger?"

"Not really. I've just had another talk with Peter."

"And what have you decided?"

We were on our own in the small sitting room. He thoughtfully knocked out his pipe before replying.

"I can't really think of a suitable niche," he said at last. "And I said as much to Peter. I was a bit taken aback by his reaction. He more or less implied that I owed it to him—or at least, owed it to Mark."

I digested this remark with astonishment.

"Then he does feel that we've done him out of his inheritance," I said. "Zoë said as much—you remember, I told you what Lucy said."

"I must confess that he irritated me," Roger went on. "I suppose he was too young to understand all the facts of the case—that Mark was anxious to leave Collingford at the time, and that we bought the place at its market value."

"I hope you spelled it out for him."

"Oh, I did—I did. But somehow I don't think I convinced him."

"Then what did you decide?"

He shot me a wary glance under lowered brows as he concentrated on lighting his pipe again.

"I said I'd give him a chance. He's in financial trouble up to his neck, it appears."

"But he had all Catherine's money!"

"Nothing lasts for ever. The way he's been spending it these last five years, I'd be surprised if there was any left at all."

"But what is he to *do*, Roger? You said yourself there wasn't really a place for him."

"I suppose we can make one. When Violet Perkins goes we can get a young girl just to do the typing and make bookings. Peter can start immediately learning the more complicated bookkeeping from Violet and I can show him the ropes concerning the liquor sales. There's really no other way to learn a job like ours but by actually doing it."

"There's no reason why you should feel obligated—"

"I know. But he is my brother's son, and I ought to give him a chance."

Mark was worried about Peter's flying, I reminded myself. He and Charlotte would be overjoyed to think he had a job where he could keep both feet on the ground.

"Oh, well." I picked up some sewing, prepared to accept the situation. "Let's hope you can lick him into some sort of shape. You'll have to read the riot act to him about female guests! The last thing we want is to have irate husbands and fathers complaining that he's seduced their wives and daughters."

"What? Oh, even Peter will have more sense than that, surely!"

I did not feel so sure. I did not feel sure of anything, except that I had a soft-hearted husband who was an easy mark for any hard-luck story that was presented to him.

24

Ben and Clare were married during the Easter holidays on a showery April day in 1925, with Beth dressed in gold and apple green as Clare's one bridesmaid, and Nico and Jamie as two wayward page-boys.

Part of Roger's present to them was a honeymoon in Florence and Venice, and I was glad that they were out of England when the news came that dear Goffy, who had been present at the wedding and had enjoyed every convivial moment of it, had been instantaneously killed in a car crash on his way back to Cheltenham. It was the very first time that he had ever come to us by road. He had always maintained that he enjoyed the train journey, which was an easy one; but this time he had thought to favour his arthritic knee by hiring a car and driver, door to door, and it was this decision which led to his death.

We all grieved for him. He had become part of our family and sometimes it was hard to remember that he was not Roger's real father, so shadowy had become the memory of Mr Leyton.

It was Roger's sixtieth birthday that year, but far from slowing down he seemed to have gained new life from the dream that was beginning to take shape on the land near

Woodstock—the new hotel that he and Philip had planned between them.

It had once belonged to the church, this land—and that to me seemed a good omen, since Priors, the Ring of Bells and Paternoster Farm had all been church property at one time. After a great deal of family discussion, it had been decided to call it Chantry Court, which we thought sounded both regal and ecclesiastical.

All through the summer of 1925 it seemed almost the sole topic of Roger's and Philip's conversation, and if I failed to join in with total enthusiasm, it was merely because it dawned on me that both had gaily assumed that while Philip would be responsible for all its equipment, I would take on the job of planning its decoration and furnishing.

The thought filled me with horror and I gave voice to my misgivings.

"What nonsense, darling," Roger said. "You've always managed such things beautifully."

"But this is bigger." I said desperately. "Philip wants it to be quite different from anything I've done before."

This I knew to be a fact. I had intercepted a speaking glance between him and Lucy one day when the three of us had been contemplating the empty shell and I had remarked, with innocent enthusiasm, how well a heavy gilt mirror that had once hung in the Red Lion would look in the hall. It was obvious to me that in their opinion, both the mirror and my Victorian ideas should be consigned to the scrap heap.

"It's got to be modern, Mother. Light and rather bare," Lucy said.

"Then why don't you take charge?" There was a distinct note of huffiness in my voice.

"I only wish I could." She gave a sigh as she walked away.

Peter had taken up his duties at the Ring of Bells and had all the maids eating out of his hand in no time. Alfred, however, was less bedazzled. I was concerned that there seemed to be an atmosphere of unrest in the kitchen where once all was harmony.

My fears about the female guests proved fully justified. I went there unannounced one morning to check on an old invoice from Elliston and Cavell. I was buying new curtains for the Rose Revived and was interested to see what we had paid the previous year for similar material and accordingly went straight to the filing cabinet in the office.

There could have been only a few seconds' warning of my approach and I found a very flustered young girl straightening her hair at one side of the tiny room while Peter, desperately nonchalant, shuffled papers at the other. I stood and surveyed the room coldly.

"Er—good morning, Aunt Jenny. Have you met Miss King?" Peter's voice was striving for normality.

The girl ducked her head, looking embarrassed.

"Spiffing morning, isn't it? Peter—Mr Leyton—was just telling me about all the lovely country around here."

"Indeed?" I suddenly had a picture of myself standing there, looking every bit as forbidding as my grandmother ever had. The girl shifted from one foot to the other, shot a desperate look at Peter, and edged to the door.

"I was just off, actually. Thank you for your help, Mr Leyton."

"My pleasure, Miss King." Peter looked wickedly amused.

I waited until she had left the area well behind.

"Peter," I said sternly. "This simply will not do."

"Come off it, Aunt Jenny!" It was a joke to him, nothing more. "Daphne King has been chasing me from the moment she crossed the threshold."

"With no encouragement from you, naturally."

"Well—I'd hardly say that. Who am I to refuse gifts so readily offered?"

"You are, supposedly, the manager of a respectable hotel. That girl, I presume, is the daughter of Mr and Mrs Howard King of Bristol who happen to be valued clients. They've been coming here for years. I've heard them speak of a daughter, but they've never brought her before. I don't imagine she's long out of school."

"Girls like Daphne were born old."

"Her age makes things worse, but it doesn't materially affect the issue which is that a manager of a hotel does not take advantage of his position where the female guests are concerned. It simply can't be tolerated."

He turned his eyes to heaven and raised his shoulders.

"No, Aunt Jenny."

"I mean it, Peter. We can't risk the reputation of the hotel."

"Of course not, Aunt Jenny. I'll be the soul of propriety, never fear."

I found the invoice I was looking for and left the hotel, far from satisfied. I did not mention the incident to Roger, feeling that he had enough to worry him at that moment, but I was sorry I had not done so when two or three weeks later another guest complained to Roger that he considered Peter's attentions to his daughter offensive and over-familiar.

"Did you tackle Peter about it?" I asked him.

"Naturally—but I'm inclined to accept his protestations of innocence. If you ask me, I think it could be a case of wishful thinking. The poor girl was undoubtedly behind the door when looks were given out."

"I wonder," I said, and proceeded to tell him about Miss King.

"Not the Howard Kings' daughter? The people from Bristol? My God—when was this?"

I thought back.

"Two or three weeks ago. Somewhere about then. I gave him a fairly stern warning and hoped that would be sufficient."

Roger had business at the Ring of Bells that afternoon, which happened to be Peter's afternoon off, and came back to Priors in the evening looking thoughtful.

"You're quite certain that the Kings stayed at the Ring?" he asked me. "I couldn't talk to Peter because he wasn't there, but I looked in the visitors' book and couldn't find any record of their visit at all—no registration, no bill."

"I saw the girl myself!"

"I made other enquiries. According to Alfred, there were forty breakfasts served last Saturday, yet only sixteen double and three single rooms occupied, going by the records."

We exchanged a long, troubled look.

"Duplicate bills?" I suggested.

"Surely it's not possible! Peter wouldn't do a thing like that—though takings are down a bit for the time of year."

The implications were too unpleasant to contemplate but

once the suspicion had presented itself it was impossible to dismiss it.

"I'll talk to him," Roger said. "I'll get him to come here so that we can have some privacy."

Summoned to Priors, Peter came that evening with a bad grace. I left them alone the moment he arrived, but heard his voice as I went upstairs.

"I say, damn it all, it is my day off, Uncle Roger. Can't this wait till morning?"

"It won't take long."

I shut myself in my sewing room and heard no more, and when at last I went downstairs I found Peter on the point of leaving. He smiled at me, handsome and charming and apparently unabashed.

"Aunt Jenny! No star of stage or screen could descend those stairs more gracefully than you."

I looked back at him, unamused. A little-boyish expression of guilt came over his face.

"You're not going to be frightfully pleased with me, Aunt Jenny."

"No?"

"Fact is, I've been a cad. I can only admit it, regret it, apologise for it and throw myself on your mercy."

I had reached the bottom of the stairs by this time and his eyes, shining with sincerity, looked into mine.

"You've always been marvellous to me, you and Uncle Roger. This has been my second home."

"Yes." I was disinclined to help him and felt angry that in spite of myself I was experiencing the usual mixture of annoyance and affection that Peter always produced in me.

"We'll talk more about this in the morning, Peter," Roger said, coming towards us.

"Meantime, no hard feelings?" Peter stretched out a hand and after a second's hesitation, Roger took it.

"He's been systematically siphoning off the takings for the past three months," Roger explained wearily after Peter had gone.

"That's unspeakable! And you say there are no hard feelings?"

"It was a loan, he assures me. He meant to pay it back."

"But *why*? Has he really run through all Catherine's money?"

"It would appear so. He has enormous debts, he tells me." Roger sighed and sat down in his favourite armchair looking tired and worn. He leaned his head against the back of it.

"I can't help feeling guilty," he said.

"*You* feel guilty? That's a good one!"

"He explained that he'd always rather admired the fact that I've lived rather more recklessly than Mark—he's impressed by the way we've expanded, my business sense and so on. He said he caught the gambling bug from me."

"So you've been a bad influence on your innocent nephew."

"Evidently. I took Peter to his first Ascot Gold Cup, remember? He was only about thirteen at the time. It was the year I backed a twenty to one outsider that romped home, and he's never forgotten it. He's been following my example ever since—got in over his head—didn't know which way to turn—"

"And it's all your fault! When will you realise that Peter always blames everyone but himself for his own shortcomings? He'll never grow up until he learns responsibility, and you're not helping him by making excuses for him. If I remember rightly, you took Philip to the same race meeting and as far as I know he is neither in debt, nor has he robbed anyone."

"It was all going to be paid back—Peter assured me of that."

"So you're giving him another chance?"

"I told him I'd think it over—but yes, I suppose so. He did seem contrite."

I shook my head slowly as I looked at him. I was full of misgivings.

"I don't trust him, Roger. He's such a smooth, slick talker. He'll say anything to get himself out of a tight spot— witness all that soft soap about Priors being his second home and how wonderful we have been to him. It's not what he's said before, you know. Why, even to you he implied that we'd somehow done him out of his birthright and that we owe him a living."

"I know, I know." Roger sighed. "But you can't gainsay the fact that I've been a rotten example. What is it that makes a man gamble, Jenny? It's a sort of itch. I love it—I always have, and I've always felt guilty about it."

"Except when you won £2,500 and cleared off all our debts!"

"What an enormous sum that seemed to us at the time—and what a difference it made! But you're wrong. I felt guilty about that, too. In the circumstances, I don't think I can do other than give the boy another chance—wipe the slate clean and hope that he'll be appreciative enough to stay on the straight and narrow from now on."

I said nothing but my misgivings remained.

Meantime the new hotel progressed apace and the subject of its decoration continued to worry me. I brought it up in conversation a few evenings later when we were dining in Oxford with Nick and Lucy, and I expressed my opinion that Lucy, with her artistic gifts, would do a far better job than I.

"But she has no experience," Nick said, smiling at her fondly.

"She has flair," I said. "I've always been grateful for her help when we've been redecorating the other hotels. She's far better than I am when it comes to choosing colours."

"Well, I don't suppose she'll mind popping in from time to time." Nick transferred his benevolent smile to me. "Of course, she's quite busy, aren't you, darling? We have a hectic social life, you know. There's the golf club and bridge every Friday, and of course the boys are getting to be a handful."

I looked at Lucy, but she said nothing.

He's worn her down, I thought. By sheer, implacable kindness, he's worn her down.

In the car going home I mentioned this thought to Roger.

"Lucy seems to have lost all her spirit," I said.

Roger gave me a quick glance of surprise.

"I thought she seemed happier these days."

"Perhaps. They say long-term prisoners become resigned to living behind bars."

"Oh come now, Jenny—don't exaggerate!"

386

I sighed and said no more, for I felt sure that somewhere inside her those earlier dreams of fulfilment must still be lurking. And I sighed again when I thought of the formidable task of furnishing the new hotel to Philip's satisfaction.

At last I could put the task off no longer and a date was set when I should meet with Philip and an architect to try to formulate plans for the basic decoration. I told myself I was being foolish to allow myself to be thrown into such a panic. I'd done it before, I thought. Surely I could do it again?

I went to the extent of going into Oxford to browse around furniture stores in the hope of being struck by inspiration, but instead grew progressively less happy with the task before me, and returned home tired and dispirited.

When I awoke in the night feeling nauseous with a griping pain in my stomach I knew immediately where to apportion the blame. I had abstractedly eaten lunch in Oxford at an inferior little café close to the furniture emporium, feeling too weighed down with care to walk across town to the Randolph Hotel, and was now paying the price. I was ill so seldom that Roger was terrified; indeed, I was not at all sure myself that my last hour had not come.

"We'll call Richard first thing in the morning," he said, as I staggered for the tenth time to the bathroom and back. "Can't I get you something, darling? Brandy, perhaps?"

I shook my head weakly as another wave of nausea hit me.

"I'm supposed to go to the hotel to meet the architect tomorrow," I said at one stage between spasms.

"You're not to worry about that. We can postpone it for a day or two."

I groaned. I had been hoping to seize this opportunity not to go ahead with the hotel decoration.

"Oh Roger, I feel terrible! This'll teach me to eat fish in strange restaurants."

Richard confirmed that I seemed to be suffering from a classic case of food poisoning.

"But not really serious," he said briskly. "You'll be right as rain in a day or so."

Again my hopes were dashed but nevertheless I decided to make the most of my illness and stay in bed longer than necessary, so that they would have to look elsewhere for an adviser—if I had my way, to Lucy.

"I do feel a *little* better," I said to Roger the following day in a weak voice. "But not able to get up, darling. And as for going to the hotel—truly, I can't see myself doing that for at least a week."

"Then we'll have to wait."

"I don't think you ought to. There's so much to be done."

"Well, I suppose Philip can make the preliminary arrangements."

"He has enough to do as it is. Darling, let's ask Lucy to take it on. It would be such a load off my mind."

"Nick would never allow it, surely?"

"You ask him, Roger. He might agree if you tell him she would be getting us out of a hole."

"*Could* she do it, Jenny?"

"Oh yes!" I said enthusiastically, remembering only at the last moment that I was so feeble and moderating my voice accordingly. Roger looked at me with a worried frown and I felt horribly guilty—but still determined.

I have no doubt that he sounded equally worried when he spoke to Nick, telephoning him at his office, and rather reluctantly Nick agreed that Lucy should take on the burden, in view of the fact that my old and ailing frame was in no fit state to bear it. Philip was delighted.

"Not that you wouldn't have done it beautifully, Mother," he hastened to assure me. "But working with old Lucy will be fun. She's got some good ideas."

"I know," I said. "She won't let you down."

For what proved to be the hardest ten days of my life I stayed in bed. For the first few days I was happy enough to lie and read, but I soon became restless and thoroughly tired of a diet of steamed fish, egg custards and milk jelly.

Lucy dropped in full of talk about materials and colours and for the first time in years I thought that she looked like the girl we used to know; lively and vivacious and full of plans. I was happy just to watch her enthusing and was smiling a small, self-congratulatory smile when she stopped in mid-spate, looking at me accusingly.

"Mother, you're not listening!"

"Oh darling, I am! You were talking about wallpaper."

"That was at least three sentences ago. Mother, there's nothing seriously wrong, is there?"

"No, of course not. I'm strong as an ox," I said. "But I'm not getting any younger, Lucy, and I did really have a bad bout of sickness. It's an enormous relief to be able to hand all this over to you."

"I rather think Nick expects me to drop everything the moment you're better."

"Do you want to?"

"Oh, *no*! I'm having more fun than I ever had in my whole life. I take the children to school before I leave, and of course Molly keeps the house immaculate, as always. This is much better than filling my days with tennis and bridge and good works."

"Then stand up to Nick!"

"Mother!" Lucy pretended to look shocked. "That sounds strange coming from someone who has always urged me to be dutiful."

"You can be a good wife without being a doormat."

"I'll remember that."

"And you're happy about the way things are going at Chantry Court?"

"Yes—the tilers have just about finished with the bathrooms and some of the kitchen equipment came today. Philip's over the moon about it."

"That's nice." I lay back on my pillows, grateful to be able to enthuse from afar.

A sudden thought struck Lucy as she was on her way to the door.

"Oh—I'll tell you a strange thing, Mother. You know that frowsty old Blewett woman who keeps the Waggon and Horses? I've seen her several times up at the hotel."

"Doing what?" I felt the old twinge of anxiety, the merest stirring of misgiving.

"Well, nothing much—simply looking. It's odd because, after all, it's a fair distance from Collingford. I mean, she can't just be passing by, she must make an effort to get into that funny little cart of hers and drive up there. Strange, isn't it?"

389

"Very," I agreed. "Has she spoken to you?"

"Oh no. She just drives past very slowly, or sits and stares. Philip says she was there for a full twenty minutes yesterday afternoon. It's a bit unnerving, in a way. She's such a sinister old girl, she gives me the creeps."

I forced a laugh.

"I expect it's the same instinct that makes people stand and watch men digging holes in the road. Or perhaps she's hoping for a few tips on how to improve the Waggon and Horses."

"That wouldn't be difficult!"

"Just ignore her. She can't do any harm."

"No, I don't imagine she can. It's just odd, that's all."

Lucy dismissed the subject from her mind, but it was not quite so easily dismissed from mine.

Why on earth, I wondered, was Bella still interested in our doings? It must be a kind of impotent jealousy that made her go and stare at Chantry Court. She begrudged it to me—the girl who, like her, had been brought up in that squalid house in Ackerly Street.

Poor Bella, I thought, rather surprised at the sudden feeling of pity I had for her. She had terrorised me when I was young and unsure of myself. I found her repulsive to look at and unlikeable as a character and even now I distrusted her motives. But in spite of all that, I could look across the chasm of the years and feel compassion for that unlovely, unloved child who had waited, cold and neglected, outside the public house on the corner. What chance had she had? In Ellie's world, the paradise that she dreamed of, all such inequalities would be swept away, and a good thing too.

But in Chantry Court rested all our dreams and all our resources, and it was small comfort to me that Bella must know it as well as I.

25

The troubles of the miners dominated the headlines that spring of 1926. Ellie came home for the odd, rushed weekend and was vocal and impassioned about their wrongs. I could only agree with her, as most of the country agreed, that their lot was insupportable; that *something* must be done for them. There was talk, even, of revolution. But when it came to the point the average, tolerant, easy-going Englishman proved himself disinclined for such extreme measures, and the General Strike degenerated into a bit of a lark, with students driving buses and clerical workers shovelling the coal to keep the trains running.

Blacklegs, Ellie called them. Traitors to their class. For the first time ever a hint of rancour crept into her arguments with Roger. He had not personally voted for Stanley Baldwin but was impressed with the effect that his policies appeared to be having on the country. There was more prosperity in Britain than at any time since the war, he said. Slums were being cleared and houses built. Unemployment had dropped. To all these things he drew Ellie's attention, and by all she remained unimpressed. So they went on, neither one of them conceding ground. It was a debate that could never be resolved.

Thankfully, I attended to my own concerns and left Lucy alone with Chantry Court. My own concerns were worrying enough, in all conscience.

I called in to see Alfred in the kitchen of the Ring of Bells one day and found him undergoing what verged upon a nervous breakdown. The maids were silent, going about their business with frightened glances towards the chef, who was crashing implements about with tight-lipped fury.

I had innocently dropped in for a chat. I had known Alfred for a good number of years—had, in fact, trained him—and I respected his skill and dedication. Given his head, he was a chef in a million. Peter, it appeared, was not giving him his head.

"I'm *so* glad to see you, Mrs Leyton," Alfred said to me. "In fact, if you hadn't dropped in, I was going to ask to see you—wasn't I, girls? I said to them 'Mrs Leyton's got to hear of this' I said. I mean, it's not right, it isn't, really. Not after all these years. It's as if I'm not trusted."

"Alfred, *please*!" I pressed him down into a chair and he took off his chef's hat and mopped his forehead. "Now, tell me what the trouble is."

"I don't really like to speak of it," he said, but dismissed the girls to the wash house and proceeded to do so. "It's Mr Peter. I'm sorry, Mrs Leyton, but I have to say it. It's him or me."

"Oh, Alfred—I can't believe whatever is wrong can't be resolved! What's happened?"

"It's the interference, Mrs Leyton. And the incompetence. *He's* supposed to do the ordering! I tell him if I'm running short of anything, just like I used to tell Miss Perkins, but it's two weeks now since I had any garlic, and it won't do, it won't do at all. I'm *hamstrung*, Mrs Leyton, that's what I am. Now, take almonds. That's something we've always bought from Reids. Now, suddenly I'm not allowed to send round for them—I have to wait until Mr Peter goes into Oxford with a big order for Robinson and Whites."

"Robinson and Whites? We don't normally deal with them, do we?"

"We do now, Mrs Leyton. And nasty, cut-price stuff it is, too."

"But why? I don't understand."

"Well, of course, it's not up to me to make accusations— but it just happens that Mr Peter was at school with young Mr Robinson, and if you ask *me* there's some sort of hanky-panky going on."

"Haven't you mentioned this to Mr Leyton?"

"We don't see him here these days. He's all taken up with the new hotel."

That was true. I would have to remind Roger not to forget our old inns in his enthusiasm for the new.

"I'll look into the whole matter," I promised. "And

Alfred—you know how valuable you are to us. We appreciate everything you do, and always have done, so please try to bear with us until everything is straightened out."

"It's just not the atmosphere I'm used to any more," Alfred said, refusing to be mollified. "And it's not only the stores, Mrs Leyton. I'm not one to gossip, as you well know—"

"But?" I said, knowing that there was always a 'but' after a statement such as that.

"Well!" Alfred looked uncomfortable. "I don't like trouble, Mrs Leyton. It upsets me. I'm not used to it."

"What sort of trouble?"

He leaned closer to me and darted a swift look over his shoulder as if to check that the maids were still out of the room. "Women, Mrs Leyton. *That* sort of trouble."

I stared at him.

"I think you'd better tell me," I said at last.

"There was a Mr Foster and his wife staying here last week. Quite an elderly gentleman he is—very wealthy, I'd say—drove a Rolls-Royce, or at least his chauffeur did. His wife was much younger."

My heart sank. I hardly needed to know the rest of the story.

Alfred cast another glance over his shoulder and lowered his voice still further. "There was a to-do in the middle of the night. Not that I heard it, of course—I was asleep, but the next morning they were paid up and gone, before breakfast. No one told *me*, naturally. I was left with two breakfast trays prepared and no one in Number Three to eat them. I was just told after that Mrs Foster had been found in Mr Peter's room and that Mr Foster whipped her away there and then."

I was bereft of anything to say.

"Perhaps I shouldn't have spoken," Alfred faltered, looking unsure of himself.

"No—no, you were quite right to tell me. We should know these things. But Alfred, please don't speak of it to anyone else, will you?"

Effusively he assured me that his lips were sealed.

I went through to the office where Roger, present at the

Ring of Bells for once, was looking remote and abstracted behind his glasses, adding up columns of figures. Peter was nowhere to be seen. I closed the door behind me.

"Roger."

"Mm?" He went on adding up.

"Bad news."

He looked up at me, and I told him everything that Alfred had said. Roger took his glasses off and stared at me miserably.

"Oh, God," he groaned. "What a fool the boy is! I was congratulating him only minutes ago for doing so much better. In fact I even mentioned to him the possibility of his taking over the Angler's Rest. Mrs Jepson wants to give up at last. I thought with Peter showing signs of pulling his socks up, that we could engage a cook and put him over there to manage the place. Still, that's out of the question if there's a word of truth in all of this."

"I can't believe he'd attempt to chisel us over the food," I said. "Not after the last time. But this thing with Mrs Foster has the ring of truth about it."

Roger sighed.

"I'll have to talk to him, of course. He has the right to put his case, after all."

At dinner that night I heard the outcome.

Mrs Foster had, according to Peter, literally forced herself into his room. No—he had not given her the slightest encouragement! The woman was unbalanced—hysterical, there was nothing he could do. Mr Foster would not listen to any explanations. It had all been the most devastating experience! And as for Robinson and Whites—why of *course* he would go back to the old system, if that's what everyone wanted. He was just trying to help an old chum.

"I hope you made it clear to him that Alfred was far more valuable to us than he," I said grimly.

"I left him in no doubt whatsoever," Roger assured me. "I don't think there'll be any trouble from now on."

I found myself unable to share his optimism, but it did seem that, for the time being, the Ring of Bells settled down once again into its accustomed calm.

Chantry Court was, on the other hand, as full of activity

as an ants' nest, or so Lucy reported to me. I forbore to go and look at it until the curtains had been hung and some of the furniture delivered.

When I finally made the journey I was in for a shock.

Eagerly I went through the big front doors to see what she and Philip had made of it, for I knew that they had conferred on most aspects. I was prepared to overflow with maternal pride and congratulations and had no difficulty in doing so at the sight of the entrance hall with its leather-faced reception desk, deep leather chairs and glass tables.

"It's not quite finished," Lucy said hastily. "There's going to be a table in that alcove with a large picture over it—we're having that specially commissioned, painted by an artist I came across in Oxford."

"It's lovely," I said enthusiastically. "Very warm and welcoming. Doesn't it look enormous? The carpet seems to go on for ever."

"Come and see the lounge," Lucy said, leading me towards a shallow flight of three steps which led out of the hall.

I went up them already formulating fulsome phrases of delight; but was rendered speechless by the sight of the room that Lucy had created. There were none of the rococo trappings that I knew I would have chosen. No gilt cherubs or ornate carvings; just space and a bare, honey-coloured coolness that was almost austere.

"I didn't want it cluttered," Lucy was saying.

"Well, it's certainly not that," I said faintly.

The carpet was a pale, misty blue and the huge french windows were curtained in an even lighter shade of the same colour. The walls were plain and the big-square cut chairs and settees were the colour of new Cotswold stone. There was a great deal of white—the walls, the tables, the cushions, the row of pillars on each side of the dance floor at the far end of the room. How impractical, I thought.

"You don't like it, do you?" Lucy's voice was anxious.

"It's—it's unusual," I said hesitantly. "It looks like a film set by Cecil B. de Mille."

"It's wonderful," Philip said. "Look at the ceiling, Mother."

I directed my gaze upwards and saw that on the white ceiling were painted delicate flowers in the soft blue and gold of the other furnishings.

"That's very pretty," I said, with no reservation at all.

"Try to imagine it with lots of flowers about the place," Lucy said. "I'm putting a classic sort of pillar here between the door and the window with a huge Grecian urn that we'll keep full of flowers, and there's going to be a table by that wall over there with another bowl. And the mirrors haven't arrived yet."

"It's very nice, darling," I said.

"But you're not sure," said Lucy, in a small voice.

"It's so very different!"

"That's what we wanted," Philip said, his voice full of enthusiasm. "It's different and completely modern— absolutely 1926—yet it's not in the least brash and it's very luxurious. Just sit down in this chair, Mother, and feel it. Isn't that the most superlative comfort? And look at the room. Take your time. Don't you think it's restful?"

I did as instructed and looked about me.

"Yes," I said, and was silent. "Yes, it's certainly restful. I *do* like it, Lucy." Now that the initial shock had worn off, I was surprised at the appeal the room had for me.

"Has your father seen it yet?"

"Not since we hung the curtains."

"He gave me no idea what to expect."

"I know what you were expecting," Philip said, laughing at me. "Chintz and cherubs, and the odd aspidistra."

"And antimacassars," added Lucy.

"There's no need to make me feel as if I've come out of the ark! Come on, show me what other surprises you have in store for me."

They took me on a tour of inspection and I duly marvelled at the gleaming kitchens and the bathrooms and the soft, pastel-coloured bedrooms. The dining room was oddly medieval, with chairs made of leather on natural oak and a huge wrought iron chandelier.

"I said you had flair," I told Lucy. "Come on, I want one more look at that lounge."

I stood in the centre of the room and studied it slowly,

letting my gaze travel from the blue draped doors at one end to the pillar-encircled dance floor at the other.

"Will there be pictures?" I asked.

"Yes, two, one on each side of the window. Impressionist, sort of blurry blues and greens."

"Ashtrays?"

"Solid chunks of clear glass. Too heavy to take away as souvenirs."

"Ha!" I doubted whether anything could be that. "Is the lighting sufficient?"

"I think so." Philip touched a switch and I saw that as well as the wall lights there were also concealed lights behind the swathed pelmets.

I nodded.

"You've done well, both of you," I said. "And all I can say, Philip, is—thank heaven Lucy did it and not me, because I should never have dreamed up anything like this. I should have disappointed you sorely."

Lucy had wandered over to the window and was looking out idly, watching the army of gardeners who were clearing the builders' rubble.

"She's there again," she said. "Peering over the hedge. Beastly old crone—what does she want, for heaven's sake? She looks as if she'd like to put a curse on us."

I joined her at the window, knowing immediately that she was talking about Bella.

"She's never liked me," I said lamely. It was all too complex, too difficult to explain, too long ago. "There's nothing she can do to hurt us."

I tried to sound confident but could I really be certain? The success of this new hotel meant everything to Roger. I felt a small and superstitious pang as I realised how vulnerable we were.

True to Roger's custom we were planning to celebrate the opening with a lavish party to which anyone of note in the district had been invited. Even Lord and Lady Bollinger, in Collingford on one of their periodic visits to the family seat, were to honour us with their presence.

It was about a week before this event that I went to the Ring of Bells for a routine check of the bedroom furnishings.

Before going upstairs I stopped in the kitchen for a brief word with Alfred, who seemed considerably happier than on my last visit, learned that Peter had gone to Oxford to pick up some urgent supplies, and passed through the hall on my way to the bedrooms.

A fashionably dressed young lady, rather thin and gaunt, was standing by the reception desk, looking lost. Miss Parker, who was supposed to deal with arriving guests, was nowhere to be seen, so I approached the young lady myself, asking if I could help her.

"I need a room," she said, her manner agitated.

I went behind the desk and reached for the book which recorded reservations.

"I made no booking," she said hastily. "I merely called in, hoping you would have a vacancy."

"How long would you wish to stay?" I asked.

"Well—" she looked harassed and undecided. "Really, my plans aren't very definite. Just a night or two. I imagine—though on the other hand—"

"We have a single room for tonight and tomorrow," I said. "But after that I'm afraid we are fully booked. Of course, there's always the chance of a cancellation."

"I'll take it," she said. "Er—is Mr Leyton about? I rather wanted to see him."

I raised my eyes and looked at her, full in the face. She was in her late twenties or early thirties, I supposed, blonde and pretty, but with a strained look about her eyes, which were puffy, as if she had shed recent tears.

"Mr Peter Leyton?" I asked.

She nodded.

"He's in Oxford for the morning. Perhaps if you would just register?"

I passed her the book and she signed her name, just as Miss Parker put in an appearance from somewhere at the back of the building. I reached for the key of Number Seven.

"Oh, Miss Parker," I said. "Would you be good enough to show—" my gaze fell to the visitor's book to read the name, and my voice faltered—"Mrs Foster to Number Seven. If you leave your bag, Mrs Foster, I'll have it sent up directly."

She thanked me and followed Miss Parker up the stairs, while I stood and thoughtfully regarded her retreating back-view.

Mrs Clementine Foster, the book said. It could, perhaps, be a different Mrs Foster—but no, she had asked for Peter.

What was I to do? Intercept Peter on his return to the hotel and read the riot act yet again, I supposed. Or should I have a word with the lady herself? No, on the whole I thought not. It was something I should have to rely on Peter to deal with in as tactful a way as possible—and surely, after Roger's last confrontation with him, he would realise the importance of behaving with restraint. Just as long as Mr Foster didn't turn up, I thought, before we had time to persuade his wife to leave.

Mrs Foster stayed in her room all morning, while I busied myself about the hotel until Peter returned. I called him into the office and told him what had happened.

"Well, my God, Aunt Jenny, I never asked her to come, I promise you," he said.

"You must persuade her to go," I said. "We don't want her husband roaring up here demanding pistols for two, or anything of the sort."

"I should say not!"

"With Chantry Court opening next week, the last thing we want is adverse publicity or unpleasantness of any kind."

"I'm with you, Aunt Jenny, every step of the way. Don't give it another thought. I'm sure I can make her see reason. It's not as if I've given her any encouragement—"

"Of *course* not, Peter," I said, with heavy irony. "There never was a man pursued by predatory females quite so determinedly as you are. Just explain to this particular predatory female that your job depends on her departing from the Ring of Bells with no fuss and no trouble."

The light died from his eyes.

"My *job* depends on it?"

"That's what I said, Peter."

"But with all respect, Aunt Jenny, I hardly think it's up to you—"

"Your uncle will not disagree with me, I can assure you."

"Now look here—that's damned unfair!"

"Peter, you've had warning after warning. You've been told time and time again that everything depends on goodwill in this business—if we lose that, we lose everything."

He glared at me with his mouth set mulishly.

"I've said I'll get rid of the woman."

"Just as long as you understand the position." I picked up my gloves and my handbag. "I'm relying on you, Peter. Don't let me down."

I left him to think the situation over and returned home to Priors for a solitary lunch, Roger having gone over to Chantry Court. I was worried by Mrs Foster's arrival, particularly as she seemed so upset, and wished that I could have talked it over with Roger.

I told him about it that evening, but his mind was miles away at Chantry Court. There had been a last minute hitch about the supply of glasses. The suppliers, for some reason, had been unable to deliver the whole of the number ordered, which would mean that we should be short for the party. It was not a major problem. We could send plenty up from the Ring of Bells and the Angler's Rest, but it was annoying.

The problem of Peter and Mrs Foster was shelved for the time being, but I did not forget it and the following morning I called in yet again to the Ring of Bells. Peter was quite clearly angry that I had seen fit to check up on him.

"I've talked to her," he said, "but what do you expect me to do, Aunt Jenny? She's booked for two nights. I can hardly throw her out into the street. Believe me, I'd be glad if she left right now—I never want to see her again."

"Where is she now?"

"Heaven knows. She went out somewhere—where, I didn't enquire."

"And she's definitely leaving tomorrow?"

"She'll have no alternative. After Friday, we haven't an inch of space."

There I had to leave it. As Peter said, one could hardly throw the woman out bodily, but I offered a small prayer that without any further ado she would indeed be off the premises by the time I returned.

After speaking to Peter that morning I continued to Oxford by train, for I had a pressing engagement with my new dressmaker—an excellent woman discovered by Lucy. She was whipping up a glorious confection for the Grand Opening, scheduled for the Saturday evening of that week.

I needed shoes, too. I told myself I had been foolish to leave everything until the last moment like this, but somehow there was never enough time—which brought me to another decision. I stared out at the passing countryside from the train window and pondered deeply. Should I, at last, have my hair bobbed? I was the last woman in Oxfordshire not to have had it done already, Lucy assured me, and there was added pressure in that the fashionable cloche hats fitted extremely badly over long hair. It would be a good opportunity, perhaps—but Roger disliked the idea and I was not altogether convinced myself that a new style would suit me.

It was with these sort of problems that I occupied myself on the journey to Oxford. The question of Mrs Foster receded to the very back of my mind, and I was hopeful, as the train brought me back home again late on Friday morning, that the whole affair would have resolved itself.

Sidney was at the station to meet me and I knew at once that he had something to tell me. However, he avoided my questions until he had handed me and my small overnight case into the back of the car and had gone round to the front to swing the starter-handle. Then he took his place behind the wheel and turned to face me, one elbow on the back of the seat.

"I'm afraid I've got bad news, Mrs Leyton," he said.

There was a twist of dread in my stomach.

"Not Roger? Not Mr Leyton? He's all right, isn't he?"

"It's a young woman at the hotel." I could see his Adam's apple jerking as he swallowed convulsively, and he reached into his pocket for a handkerchief to mop his brow. "I'm sorry, Mrs Leyton—it was a terrible shock. Alfred called me to go up with him, see, and we was the ones found her first. It was a sight I'll never forget, worse than during the war, being a young woman like that. I've never seen so much blood."

I felt as if my own blood was slowly draining away leaving me cold with fear. For a moment I stared at him, unable to speak.

"She's dead?" I asked at last.

He gulped again and nodded, then with a convulsive movement turned to put the car in gear and drove towards the Ring of Bells.

26

She had haemorrhaged after an abortion.

Roger was, of course, already at the hotel and was able to give me this information as Richard Fenwick had been quickly on the scene and had been able to sum up the situation immediately, though of course there would have to be a post-mortem. There was a hushed air of shock about the place and other guests were uneasy, sensing that something dramatic had occurred, even though the full details were not made public.

Roger was in the office, trying to contact Mr Foster who was said to be in Edinburgh on business.

"Where's Peter?" I asked him.

"God knows!" He slammed the telephone receiver back into its rest. "Foster's office is going to call me when they find out exactly where he is. As for Peter, I told him to get out of my sight."

"But what happened?"

Roger ran a shaking hand through his hair.

"Jenny—d'you think you could rustle up some coffee? I haven't had time for anything so far, what with the doctor and the police."

I went swiftly to the kitchen where a white-faced Alfred sat motionless by the range surrounded by silent, scurrying maids.

"I knew he'd bring trouble," he said when he saw me.

"Alfred, I don't think we should discuss it—"

"I saw him, you know. Yesterday afternoon. Taking Mrs Foster somewhere in his car."

"Alfred, could you please send some coffee into the office?"

I returned to Roger.

"I shall go mad if someone doesn't give me some *facts*!" I said.

"I've talked to Peter. At first he was all injured innocence—he knew nothing, hardly knew the woman, had no idea what was in her mind." I nodded, knowing exactly how it would have been. "But Alfred saw him taking her somewhere yesterday afternoon and eventually he admitted that he'd given her a lift into Oxford and dropped her in the High. It was his afternoon off and he went on to have a picnic on the river with Binkie Robinson and a few friends."

"So he didn't bring her back?"

"No. He went on to some other party and returned after midnight."

"And he didn't know she was going to have an abortion?"

"So he says. But I don't believe it."

"Nor do I!"

The door of the office opened, and expecting a maid with the coffee I turned to receive it, but it was Peter himself who came into the room, closing the door behind him. I looked at him coldly, without speaking. My feelings for him were no longer in the least ambivalent.

"She was carrying your child," I said. "That's why she came to find you."

He shrugged.

"How could I, or you, or anyone know for certain it was mine?"

I ignored him and ploughed on.

"You must have known she intended to have an abortion. I don't believe for one moment that under the circumstances she would not have told you where she was going or what she proposed to do. I believe you took her wherever she had to go and there you left her—to go on a picnic with Binkie Robinson! I hope it didn't spoil your afternoon too much, remembering what she was going through on your account. Did you spare her a thought from time to time, while your

403

friends were playing their ukuleles and making futile jokes? Was there another girl there you had marked out as your next victim, trailing her hand delicately through the water, fluttering her eyelashes at you, while Mrs Foster was suffering pain and shame and danger and utter, utter degradation because of the way you used her? And the very *worst* thing," I said, hardly pausing for breath, "was that you left her to face it alone. You weren't even there afterwards to be any sort of comfort to her."

"She didn't want me to wait." His face was bone white and had somehow thinned. "I arranged a taxi to bring her back—"

"Such consideration!"

"She said she'd be better alone—"

"It's a pity she didn't think that earlier. But surely even you must realise the dangers of going to a back-street abortionist? You mean you didn't even check on her condition when you came back home?"

"It was late. I thought she'd be asleep."

"You disgust me," I said.

There was silence in the little room, during which one of the kitchen maids edged in with the tray of coffee. She appeared to be holding her breath as she set the tray down and she flicked a quick, scared look around at us all before scuttling out again. Peter turned to follow her.

"Wait," Roger said, rapping out the order with such authority that he obeyed automatically. "The police will be asking questions, you know. It'll be better for everyone if you tell them the truth. Did you furnish her with the name of this—this butcher she went to see? She was a stranger here; she must have found it from someone locally."

Peter stood with his back to the door, his face thrust forward aggressively.

"It was her idea. The whole thing was her idea. When I found out that she'd arranged it all on her own, I simply fell in with it."

"But how did she know where to go?" I asked.

Peter shuffled uncomfortably.

"I suppose indirectly it was through me. I did just mention that I knew of only one person in Collingford who might possibly know of someone who—who would do the necessary. I didn't know for sure, of course. It was just gossip."

"Who was that?"

I was curious. I could not, for the moment, think of anyone in that sleepy, somewhat puritanical little town who would have access to an abortionist. It seemed something that would be quite alien to any of its inhabitants. Then suddenly I thought of one person who had not been brought up in the simplicity of the Oxfordshire countryside—whose mother had had friends who 'helped girls in trouble', who had been exposed from her earliest days to gin-shops and back streets and squalor, and my heart missed a beat.

"Who?" I asked again as Peter stood silent.

"That Blewett woman," he said at last. "The landlady at the Waggon and Horses."

I might have known, I thought. I might have known.

"You'll have to tell the police," Roger said.

"No!"

They both turned to look at me.

"But Jenny, he'll have to," Roger said reasonably.

I was silent, biting my lips. He was right, of course; but what timing!

"What about the opening?" I asked.

Roger sighed and shook his head, his face grey with worry.

"I've thought of cancelling it, but how can we at this stage? We've got half the county coming to Chantry Court in just over twenty-four hours—it can't be stopped now."

I looked at Peter.

"The dream of your uncle's life," I said. "I hope you're pleased with yourself."

The telephone rang. Mr Foster had been contacted, and Roger began to break the news to him. Peter left the room, and I was left to agonise over events. I thought back to the day, so recent, when I had seen Mrs Foster in the hotel and had noted that she seemed troubled. Would it have helped if I had been more sympathetic—had enquired the reason for her agitation? Impossible not to blame myself a little for thinking primarily of the good name of the hotel.

Now Bella had a stick to beat us with, bigger than she had ever dreamed—and she was unlikely to refrain from using it if she became involved with the police through Peter's evidence. Only a few miles away stood that beautiful new hotel, repository of all Roger's hopes and labours and the end product of months and months of work on the part of Lucy and Philip, the venue only the next night of the biggest party we had ever given! What were we to do?

Go through with it, Roger insisted. Hold our heads up high and show the world that we had nothing to reproach ourselves with. It was a tragedy, certainly, and he was desperately sorry both for Mrs Foster and her unfortunate husband, but nothing now could bring her back to life and we had everything to lose by assuming too great a share of the guilt. Besides which, it was too late to cancel, that was the fact of the matter. Visitors from farther afield had already arrived at Chantry Court and it would be almost impossible to stop the momentum now.

So we went through with it, and if our smiles were forced, it was not obvious to the majority of our guests. The story had so far been played down. That a young woman had died while staying at the Ring of Bells on Thursday night was common knowledge among the locals, but no details had as yet been published abroad.

I stood with Nick at Chantry Court before the great influx started and we surveyed the scene in front of us.

"I did say she wasn't very experienced," he said. He sounded apologetic, as if he felt responsible for the fact that Lucy had surprised everyone with this extraordinary room; yet he was on the defensive, too, ready to do battle for her if necessary.

"I like it," I said.

The look he turned on me was one of astonishment, but before he could say anything, Lady Bollinger was upon us.

"My dear, what *stunning* decor," she gushed, talking in the exaggerated, swoopy voice that seemed all the fashion. "I hear your daughter is responsible for it."

"May I present her husband, Lydia? This is Mr Nicholas Marchant. Nicholas, Lady Bollinger."

She flashed him a smile.

"You must be *frightfully* proud. I'm quite *desperate* to speak to her. Where is she hiding herself? Oh, I believe I see her! Do excuse me, won't you?"

"Well!" Nick said expressively, looking none too pleased at the encounter.

"You see? Some people like it."

"Seems a rum sort of room to me. Half-furnished, I'd say." He looked around it again as if there must be some aspect of it that he had missed.

"Lucy wanted it to look uncluttered," I said in a matter-of-fact voice, just as if I hadn't myself been winded by the first sight of it. "I think it looks absolutely charming now that it's finished, with flowers and people to give it warmth. Excuse me, Nick—I must go and mingle."

I left him to greet our guests who were now pouring in in great numbers. I talked to the Goodsons and then moved on to Sloane Bryson, our local Member of Parliament, who was conversing with John and Angela. I was receiving their congratulations when we were joined by Philip.

"Ain't it grand?" he said, smiling broadly.

I dismissed any lingering doubts about this reception being in bad taste, coming as it did so soon after Mrs Foster's death. It had been right not to take this moment of triumph away from Philip and Lucy.

"It's lovely," Angela assured him.

"How long before it makes a profit?" John asked.

"Well, not this year or next, I daresay; but never fear, Uncle John, we'll be raking in the shekels before long."

He turned to acknowledge the congratulations of one of Oxford's more notable hostesses.

"Thank you, I'm so glad you like it. This room? That's all my sister's doing—Mrs Marchant. Yes, indeed, most unusual."

I left him to join Roger who was doing his duty by circulating among the guests. He turned and greeted me with a smile.

"It's a triumph, darling. I'm glad we didn't cancel."

"People seem to approve, don't they?"

"A dream come true."

"Tarnished a little by Peter, nevertheless."

"Forget Peter—yes, and forget Mrs Foster, too, poor woman. You've earned a memorable night, Roger."

"So have Lucy and Philip. I'm glad they're part of it."

"Lucy must be desperately sorry her part is ended," I said.

Peter had kept very much out of sight at the Ring of Bells all that day, but he, too, was present at Chantry Court, all charm and swagger again. In spite of my best efforts to avoid him, I came face to face with him halfway through the evening.

"Corker of a party, Aunt Jenny," he said to me, glass in hand.

"So glad you're enjoying it," I said distantly.

"Ouch! It's still a bit chilly around here."

"You're surprised?"

He *is* surprised, I thought in amazement. He really thinks that even now he can bounce back with a smile and that all will be forgiven.

"I have news that will please you," he said. "I've written to the friend I ran the flying show with. He's in Australia operating an outfit somewhere in the bush—just a couple of planes—and he's been wanting me to join him for some time. Last night I decided I'd go."

"How soon?" I asked.

His smile died.

"As soon as possible. May I get you another drink? Sure? Then you don't mind if I—"

"Please do."

I watched him make his way across the room towards a waiter with a tray of glasses. He had collected a girl on either hand before he was halfway.

Lucy was still talking to Lydia Bollinger or, more accurately, listening to her. I could tell from Lucy's expression that she was delighted by the tone of the conversation, though I thought I detected a look of uncertainty when she glanced over her shoulder towards Nick at one point.

I drifted over to Ben and Clare.

"Well?" I said.

"Wonderful. Pity Uncle Mark and Aunt Charlotte couldn't come."

"That would have made everything perfect. Still, I know what Mark would have said: 'You're taking a big risk, old man!'"

Ben laughed, but I thought there was a worried look in his eyes.

"He would have been right. Dad must really have stuck his neck out to do all this. I hope he gets a good return on his investment."

"Surely you can trust his business acumen by this time."

"He's backed losers before now."

"Only on the race course!"

"Ben, stop being so gloomy," Clare said. "It's all lovely, and Lucy has done wonders. What imagination she has! Here she is—Lucy, you're so clever! Come here at once and be congratulated."

"Thank you—glad you like it. You'll never guess what!" She paused and grinned at me, hugging her secret.

"Do tell," I urged her.

"Lady B. is so impressed with the decor that she wants me to do Watersmeet."

"*Do* Watersmeet?"

"Redecorate it, Mother. All of it! She said that she wouldn't dream of talking business at a party, then proceeded to talk of nothing else. Anyway, the upshot of it all is that I'm to go over there and see just exactly what is to be done and give her an estimate of what it would cost."

"Good heavens," I said faintly, this aspect not having occurred to me. "You mean she intends to pay? You're quite sure, Lucy? She's inclined to think that all we peasantry should rally round for the good of our souls. You ask your father about that."

I did not mind in the least that on the rare occasions they were at Watersmeet now, Lydia Bollinger had retreated somewhat from the brief spurt of friendliness with which she had favoured us previously. But I felt a little irked still when I remembered how she had made use of Roger during the war.

"She said quite definitely that she had been looking into the prospect of employing someone from London but that I had the very style she was looking for and that she would rather I did it than anyone. It seems they intend to spend more time at Watersmeet in the future. Isn't it wonderful? It hasn't been touched for ages, of course. It's still full of the Victoriana that the old lord introduced."

My mind went back to the strange night that he had produced his son's picture from the old roll-top desk and had told me that my mother was also his child.

"Some of the furniture was far older than that."

"Lady B. says most of it is hideous and should be thrown out, but naturally I won't let her scrap anything valuable. That's the beauty of this cool, uncluttered style—it makes the most of the odd, lovely piece of furniture. I simply can't wait to get started."

She was alight with enthusiasm, but sobered a little as she glanced towards her husband who was standing at a little distance from us.

"Of course," she added, "I don't know what Nick will say."

"Let's hope you can talk him round."

"I expect he'll be delighted," Clare said. I smiled, but did not agree.

It was some time later that they came to say their farewells before leaving to go back to Oxford and for some reason I gained the impression that Lucy was being propelled away from the scene, like a prisoner under escort. Yet Nick was as affable as ever as he said good night and his hand rested only lightly on her arm. I was probably imagining things, I told myself; seeing what I expected to see.

Ellie went back to Priors with Ben and Clare. Philip had taken up his new quarters at Chantry Court, and so Roger and I returned home on our own.

Roger was quiet as we drove away.

"It went well, in spite of everything, don't you think?" I said.

"Yes, I think so."

We neither of us spoke again for some time. I watched the hedgerows slipping past as we drove along the lanes towards Collingford, the headlights illuminating bushes and stone walls and five-barred gates and the odd, flashing scut of a rabbit.

Now that it was all over and I could relax a little, the nervy, apprehensive feeling was back—the feeling that we were on the edge of a precipice. Had Peter mentioned Bella's name to the police, I wondered? If so, I did not need to ask what her reaction would be.

"Roger," I said tentatively, after a long silence. "It's not too ambitious, is it?"

He gave a short laugh.

"It's a little late in the day to have doubts."

"I suppose so. Just how much have you gambled?"

Even as I asked him, I appreciated the strangeness of the fact that I had not questioned him before. I had always been content to deal with the small practical problems as they arose, never bothering myself unduly with the wider financial implications of his wheeling and dealing.

He did not answer for a moment, then he took one hand from the wheel and reached for mine.

"Everything," he said. "I've put everything on Chantry Court. Mortgaged the lot."

My heart seemed to plummet downwards.

"Even the Ring of Bells?"

"Everything. It was that or go public and I disliked the thought of that. You must trust me, Jenny, just as you always have. We can't fail, I promise you."

I was silent. What drove him, I wondered? Into his sixties, yet still staking everything that we had painstakingly built up over the years for the sake of a dream—a beautiful dream, I could only agree, but still an extravagant building which would surely be difficult to fill in spite of the nine-hole golf course and the tennis courts and every other attraction.

"Please stop," I said suddenly, when we had turned left at the crossroads in Collingford High Street and were driving past the green. He did as I asked.

I opened the door of the car and stepped out, drawing my silk stole round my shoulders as the evening had grown cool, and I walked a little way across the green, skirting the churchyard in which lay old Sarah and Joe, together with Aunt Millie and our first baby son, and so many other good friends that we had known during our many years in Collingford.

Roger joined me as I stood beneath the chestnut trees and looked across the expanse of grass to where the Ring of Bells crouched like a sleeping cat, long and low and blessedly familiar, not planned, not designed. Full of strange nooks and crannies and awkward corners; of imperfections and in-built inconveniences.

"It's a wretched place to keep clean," I said.

"The kitchen has been inadequate for years."

"Those top bedrooms have always been freezing cold, no matter how we try to warm them."

"And the dining room isn't big enough any more. Tell you what, Jenny—we'll tear it down, brick by brick."

I whipped my head round to look at him, my mouth open with shock, and he reached out to put his hands on my shoulders and give me a small shake.

"Jenny, that was a joke! You were supposed to laugh."

I looked at him for a moment without speaking, far from mirth.

"I couldn't bear it," I said at last, my voice a whisper. "It's part of me, Roger—my youth, my marriage, my very flesh and blood. I've backed you in everything, every step of the way. But don't lose me the Ring of Bells. The very thought makes me feel . . ." my voice trailed away as I turned to look at the inn again.

"It'll never come to that."

He sounds old, I thought; old and unsure of himself. I took his arm, throwing off my mood of doubt.

"Come on," I said. "This entire week has been too much for both of us. Let's go home and have a nice cup of tea."

Ben and Clare were at Priors before us and with them I chatted determinedly about Lucy's desire to 'do' Watersmeet, steering the conversation firmly away from the future of Chantry Court.

"What could Nick possibly object to?" Clare asked.

"A wife's place is in the home," I said solemnly. "He's never approved of me, you know."

"I'll talk to Nick," Roger said. "I've always got on with him perfectly well. I'm sure he'll give in, once he realises how much it means to Lucy."

"I hope you're right. Just be tactful," I warned him.

His opportunity came only a few evenings later when we went to stay with them after a visit to an afternoon organ recital in Oxford. The subject arose over dinner.

"It seems a harmless sort of occupation," Roger said genially, echoing my thoughts on the subject.

Nick sat in silence stirring his coffee, his mouth tight with disapproval.

"I can't see why it should be regarded as any different from doing watercolours or embroidery," I said. "After all, it's a form of art."

"Art?" Nick looked at me with anger only thinly disguised with a show of mild amusement. "I'm afraid I can't agree."

"It's because I'm going to be paid for my efforts that Nick disapproves," Lucy said. "To paint futile little pictures and donate them to the parish bazaar is one thing, but actually to go into business turning people's houses into places of beauty is quite another."

I could tell from the quiet desperation in her voice that this was no new argument but a continuation of a long-standing disagreement.

Nick drew in his breath slowly and patiently.

"You know my views," he said. "A married man supports his wife. I'm sorry if that seems old-fashioned, but to me it represents the values I fought for. I will *not* have my wife hawking herself round the market place—"

"I'm not exactly contemplating going on the streets, Nick!"

"Lucy, really! That's quite enough!"

"No, dammit, it's not. And I'll swear just as much as I like, so take that look off your face! Nick, this is something that's really important to me. Oh, I know you can support me, that's not the point. This is something I enjoy—something I'm really good at. The only reason you don't want me to do it is because your manly pride would be damaged." Her voice had risen and her mouth was trembling, her eyes bright with tears.

"Lucy," I said, pacifically, "maybe Nick would rather not discuss it in our presence."

"Nick *never* wants to discuss it. Well, he's got to! I'm bored, Nick—bored, bored, bored. Can't you understand that? You go off to work every day, full of importance, while I'm supposed to stay at home and fill my days with bridge and tennis and Primrose League coffee parties. The children don't need me any more—"

"Utter rubbish!" Nick had flushed bright red and was glaring at her furiously.

"They're at school all day. I must do something or go mad."

"There are plenty of things you can do. What do other wives do?"

"I don't *care* what other wives do! If they're happy arranging the flowers for church or gossiping over bridge teas, then that's wonderful for them. I'm happy for them. But it isn't wonderful for *me*!"

"And you imagine it would be wonderful for me, I suppose, admitting to my friends that my wife has taken paid employment—"

"*Oh!*" Trembling with fury, Lucy rose from the table. "You haven't listened to a word I've said, have you?" She made as if to say more, then shook her head helplessly and ran from the room, her tears spilling over.

She left an awkward silence behind her. I half rose from my seat, then sat down again.

"Isn't it perhaps something you could think over a little more?" I suggested diffidently. "After all, it's a perfectly ladylike occupation."

"This is a matter on which I have to make my own decision." Nick's voice was icy.

"Very well." I rose from the table. "I'd better go to Lucy, I think. I wouldn't like her to do anything silly in her desperation." As I reached the door of the dining room I looked back at him over my shoulder. "Such as leaving you," I added.

I did not wait to see the result of this parting shot, but went up to Lucy's room where she was lying face down on her bed, sobbing bitterly. I sat down beside her, patting her shoulder, and tried to comfort her with meaningless words.

"Don't worry, darling. It'll all work out—don't upset yourself so. I'm sure he'll come round."

"You don't understand," she said when finally she was in sufficient control of herself to speak. "It's not just the fact that I want to do this particular job at Watersmeet. It's more that Nick doesn't seem to be making any attempt to appreciate how much it means to me. Saving his manly dignity is the only thing that matters."

"I don't really believe that. It's important to him, I know, but he does love you, Lucy."

"As a sort of extension of himself, perhaps. I'm not supposed to want any life outside his orbit."

"Poor Nick," I said.

"Poor *Nick*?" She blinked at me in amazement.

"He married a sweet, tractable, rather empty-headed little girl who wanted nothing but a home and babies and he came back from war to find her gone for ever. You've matured into someone quite different."

"I grew up, I suppose. I had to!"

"I know."

"And I come from a long line of independent women."

"I know that, too!"

I rose from her bed and moved around the room, picking up a stocking that had fallen to the floor, straightening the brushes and the jars on her dressing table. Lucy watched me, saying nothing for a few moments.

"You never speak of your mother," she said at last. "What was she like?"

I went back and sat at the foot of her bed once again.

"Obstinate," I said. "Strong-willed and full of pride. Mistaken in many ways, but admirable too. I have much to thank her for."

"And your grandmother? She was formidable, I gather. How can Nick really expect me to be a meek sort of woman? Look at Ellie!"

"There must be an answer to this. Perhaps if you could explain to him . . ."

"Oh, I've explained until I'm blue in the face! He simply won't listen. He has it firmly fixed in his mind that nice, well-brought up wives of gentlemen do not indulge in gainful employment."

"Couldn't you simply do it as a friend? Advise Lady Bollinger for nothing, I mean, simply for the fun and satisfaction you would get from it?"

"No! She'll take far more notice of me if I go in as a paid consultant. Besides—who knows where it might lead? Chantry Court led to Watersmeet; Watersmeet could lead somewhere else. I might start a regular business."

"Oh come, Lucy! If Nick won't allow this—"

"Mother, since when did you talk about husbands not *allowing* their wives to do this or that? We're not in the Victorian era now, you know."

"I don't want you to wreck your marriage, that's all."

"I have the feeling that my marriage is already wrecked," Lucy said bitterly.

I moved up beside her and put my arm round her.

"I don't think that's true," I said.

"I can't go on like this."

We talked for some time longer until her calm was almost restored, and I persuaded her to undress and go to bed. It occurred to me to wonder what was happening downstairs. Roger had kept very quiet at the dinner table, merely sitting and listening and smoking his cigar reflectively. Unless I missed my guess, however, he would have had something to offer once he and Nick were left on their own.

Personally I felt exhausted. I said good night to Lucy, went along to my own room and went to bed, thankfully escaping into the pages of *The Green Hat* by Michael Arlen and the far more complicated problems suffered by his unfortunate heroine.

Eventually I dozed with the reading lamp still switched on and my glasses on my nose, waking with a jerk as the book fell off the bed and on to the floor. I looked at the clock by the bedside. Two o'clock, and still no sign of Roger! What on earth could be going on downstairs? At least all seemed quiet. I had heard no raised voices or angry door-slamming.

As I listened, I did discern a thump, followed by a muffled voice uttering what might well be a curse. I leapt from my bed and, wrapping my dressing gown around me, went to the door, memories of Ben's fight with Peter all too vivid in my mind. They wouldn't be so infantile, surely—but then again, hadn't Roger cheered Ben on? I seemed to have lost a great deal of faith even in the most peaceable of men.

Somewhat fearfully I opened the door and peered out.

The top portion of the staircase was in full view and as I watched I saw Roger and Nick lurch into my range of vision, slowly and with difficulty. It would have been hard to say which one of them was supporting the other.

Roger, who was slightly in the lead, looked up and saw me framed in the doorway of the bedroom.

"Hello, darling," he said with great joviality. "Thought you'd've been asleep hours ago."

"I was," I said, icily.

"Hey, stow the noise, old man," Nick said in a penetrating whisper, giving him a friendly shove in the back. "You'll wake the children."

The blow, however friendly, caught Roger by surprise and he collapsed on to the stairs, and since Nick was hard on his heels he too fell headlong. They lay in a welter of arms and legs, giggling helplessly.

By this time Lucy, too, had appeared at her door, and we exchanged looks composed of amazement, amusement and exasperation in almost equal parts, before heading towards the stairs to help our incapacitated husbands into an upright position.

"Roger, you've been drinking!" I said severely. "This isn't like you."

"Dashed good brandy you keep, old boy," he said, turning to put a paternal arm round Nick's shoulders. "Man can't be all bad when he keeps such dashed good brandy."

Nick leaned against the wall and laughed helplessly.

"The last two," he said, hardly able to speak. "The last two—" he doubled over, wiping tears of laughter from his eyes.

Roger blinked at him owlishly.

"What about the last two, old boy?"

"Cooking brandy," Nick said. "We finished the Napoleon. You—you didn't even know the difference."

Roger looked at him in shocked silence and I could see their new-found friendship crumbling before my very eyes. He removed his arm from Nick's shoulders.

"I say, rather bad form, wasn't it, old chap? Giving a fellow cooking brandy? After all, I'm a conno—conno—"

"Sewer?" I supplied, angry with him yet quite unable to keep from laughing too.

Roger's outraged expression broke into a smile and he, too, leaned against the wall sobbing with laughter.

"For heaven's sake, come to your senses!" I pulled at his arm and still hiccuping with mirth, he allowed himself to be led off towards our bedroom.

"Well," I said next morning, when he finally opened his eyes. "That was a fine performance last night."

He groaned and closed his eyes again.

"Jenny, I feel terrible," he said.

"Not without reason. Here—I've brought you some tea."

"What time is it?" He struggled to a sitting position, wincing with agony.

"Ten o'clock and high time we were on our way. Lucy is taking the children to church and we have to get back to Priors. The Fenwicks are coming to Sunday lunch—remember?"

"Oh, Lord!"

He groaned again, but accepted the tea and sipped at it with an expression of distaste.

"Remind me never to do that again!"

"What *were* you doing all that time, besides drinking?"

"Mm?" He raised a puzzled eyebrow at me as if he had forgotten the dramatic events that had led up to Lucy's sudden departure from the dinner table. "Oh, we were just talking. Everything's settled."

"What do you mean, everything's settled?"

"Well, Lucy's to do this job. Nick agreed to it."

"I don't believe it!"

I sank down on the bed in amazement, and Roger winced again.

"Darling, do be careful! Any sudden movement—"

"How did you persuade him?"

"Just tact," he said. "We covered a lot of ground; talked about life and women and marriage. I gave him the benefit of my experience."

"Oh, you did, did you?" I raised my eyebrows at him.

"I did. My not inconsiderable experience."

"And he actually listened? And took note?"

"Of course. I think I managed to persuade him that in spite of the fact that my wife has always worked in the business, I'm no less of a man."

I began to laugh.

"Because you can hold your liquor? My dear, if you could see yourself!"

"He's all right, is Nick. He agreed to give it a try, at least." He frowned at me. "Darling, do you mind removing yourself from the bed? You're making it shake."

"Only if you promise to get up now. We really must make a start soon, Roger."

I took his empty cup and went downstairs to where Lucy and the children were breakfasting together.

"No Nick?" I asked.

"No Nick. Believe it or not, he's feeling a little under the weather this morning."

"Has he mustered enough strength to speak yet?" I asked.

"He has! Whatever daddy said seems to have done the trick. He says that if my happiness really depends on doing this decorating business, then I ought to give it a try."

"I'd love to have been a fly on the wall, wouldn't you? Your father said they discussed life and women and marriage. I might have learned a bit myself."

"I'm so grateful! I was determined to go ahead and do it anyway, but it's wonderful to think that it has Nick's blessing, even if grudging. I'll just have to prove to him that I can be a better wife when I'm happily employed than when I'm not."

"I'm sure you will, too. I couldn't be more pleased for you, darling. And Lucy—I'm glad you put all thoughts of that man—what was his name? Conway? Courtney? out of your head. An affair is never the answer."

She got up from the table.

"Coffee, Mother? No?" She poured herself a cup and brought it back to the table, concentrating very hard on stirring it.

I regarded her with sudden suspicion.

"Lucy?" I said, tentatively.

She smiled at me, a small and secret smile.

"You're right, Mother. It isn't the answer. Come on—I

419

must clear this lot away before we leave for church, but I can leave it in the sink. Molly has gone to mass, but she'll be back to deal with it."

I rose to help her remove the crockery from the table and said no more.

The journey back to Priors was accomplished mainly in silence. Roger was subdued and complained bitterly that they didn't make aspirin as effective as they used to; but I was occupied with happier thoughts. It was, I felt, a new beginning for Lucy.

27

A week had passed since Mrs Foster's tragic death, and still Bella had kept away from me.

I was not sure what form I expected her revenge to take. I did not even know if the police had taken any notice of the fact that Peter had suggested her name to Mrs Foster as one who might know of an abortionist. Cravenly I kept away from the Ring of Bells, occupying myself with Ben and Clare who had stayed a few days and then with my trip to Oxford with Roger at the end of the week.

Mr Foster had come to Collingford and had arranged for the transport of his wife's body from the cottage hospital where it had been taken for the post-mortem back to Birmingham for burial, but I had not seen him. Roger said that he was a quiet-spoken, kindly man, apparently knocked almost speechless by the tragedy that had befallen him.

There had been a short, non-commital paragraph in the local paper, published before the result of the autopsy had been made known. Roger was worried that there would be a bad reaction to the report that would appear now that the reason for her death had been made public and I did not add to his worries by telling him of mine. He still had no idea of my past connection with Bella.

Why hadn't I told him? I was hard put to it to remember my reasons, my past fear of her seeming childish now; but the reasons had seemed valid at the time. There was the time when she had asked for money before our wedding, when the last thing in the world that I wanted was that the Leytons should have any further reason to disapprove of me. Then I had weakly given in over the reference because I thought she threatened the children—and Roger had come home excited about buying Bridge House and I could not bring myself to tell him of the threat she posed to our business. And then, the third time, he had been ill and I had been tired to death, anxious only to be rid of her.

Since her return to Collingford towards the end of the war, she had kept her distance from me and the thought of her only brushed the edge of my consciousness—that is, until Lucy had drawn my attention to her unnatural curiosity about Chantry Court.

However I might have mellowed towards her, I felt quite sure that she still harboured resentment against me—for I lived in a beautiful house, and Roger and I owned businesses that made her inn look like the dirty, down-at-heel tavern it was. We had a standing in the community which she could never aspire to. Roger was on the Parish Council and people deferred to him. Tradesmen were anxious to please me and old men in the village touched their forelocks when I passed by. I had no doubt whatsoever that such treatment infuriated her and I was only surprised that she had not seen fit to broadcast details of my background well before this time.

What was she waiting for? What else but this—the chance to finish us, once and for all.

There was a much longer report in the local paper the following week in which the true reason for Mrs Foster's death was clearly stated. Although Roger was determined that Peter should not go on working for us, he was in no hurry for him to go. He felt that he should carry on normally for at least a month or two, giving the appearance of a man with a clear conscience; but Peter had other ideas and decamped without warning at the end of the week with the contents of the petty cash box.

It was, of course, the worst possible move. The talk and speculation swelled in volume. Peter had actually killed Mrs Foster; I had gone into Oxford that day and had organised the whole thing; Alfred had refused to call in a doctor in the middle of the night because of the scandal it would cause; Roger had arranged for the abortion to take place at the hotel, but had ensured that I would be in Oxford, out of the way. Each rumour was more far-fetched than the last, but as we might have expected, they began to have their usual effect; custom fell away.

It was over two weeks after the tragedy when Izzie showed Bella into the small sitting room at Priors, disapproval written clearly all over her bony features.

"I was expecting you," I said, standing up to greet Bella. "Izzie, would you bring tea, please?"

She looked as unsavoury as ever. Her black coat had food stains down the front and the ruffles at her throat were edged with grime. And the smell—that same old smell!

"Do sit down," I said.

She sat, clasping a cheap, cracked handbag before her on her fat knees, and shifted from one buttock to the other, settling into the chair.

" 'Ow's business?" she asked me, grinning

"Not so bad," I said. "And yours?"

"Likely to get a lot better, I'd say. Wait till it all comes out—all about that poncy nephew of yours and the lady what died. It's early days yet, but the talk's beginning. You made a bad mistake putting the police on to me."

"That was nothing whatever to do with me; but you deserved it. It was you who told the poor woman where to find an abortionist, wasn't it?"

"Lies," she said flatly, "all lies. I never said nothing, and no one can say different. Where's yer witnesses, dearie? There ain't none."

We were silent as Izzie brought in the tray with the tea things and I busied myself pouring the tea.

"Is it money you're wanting this time?" I asked pleasantly. "Milk and sugar? There, I hope that's to your taste."

Bella took the cup in her hand and glared at me.

"Don't try to pretend it don't mean nothing to you," she said.

I stirred my tea, not looking at her.

"I wouldn't dream of it. Of course I am concerned. In our business public opinion is all-important."

"Lady Bloody Muck!" Her voice was wondering—almost, I thought, admiring. "You 'aven't changed a bit, 'ave you? Still use 'alf a dozen fancy words when one would do."

"I'm sorry, Bella," I said. "It's the way I'm made."

"Don't make me laugh! You always spoke to me like I was dirt."

"I didn't mean to—not when we were children. Can't you see that I was frightened of you?"

"Teacher's pet, you was. Mother's pet. Never a word to throw to me."

I shook my head wonderingly. It was all so long ago, so unbelievably distant, yet she spoke with such venom.

"I thought about you when I was away from Collingford all those years," she said, leaning towards me. "I'd see that snooty look what come over your face whenever you seen me. 'I'll get that bitch one day', I'd think, never believing the chance would really come my way. Then I seen the advert about the Waggon and 'Orses—the name 'Collingford' fairly jumped at me out of the paper—and I thought 'Right, Bella my girl—now's your bleedin' chance. You go back and sooner or later Lady-bloody-Lah-di-Dah will fall right into your lap.' And I was right. You copped the lot, you did. 'Andsome 'usband, pots o' money—it's not fair, it never 'as been fair. And then you set the narks on me!"

"The woman died, Bella. Because of you, not me."

"No witnesses. Nothing proved. When I've told the papers what I know about you, your business will be finished."

"I shouldn't bank on it," I said wearily. "We've weathered other things over the years—"

"But you've never 'ad a grand place like that Chantry Court before, 'ave you? A pretty penny that must have cost. I'd laugh if it closed before it ever opened."

"Would you, indeed?" I asked. "And will you laugh when

you are in court facing a charge of criminal libel? Because if all those lies are put into a newspaper, that's what would happen, I promise you. My husband would see to it."

"Well," she said after a moment. "Forget the papers. It's the people round 'ere that really matter, after all. I'll enjoy telling all your regulars what are now coming to *my* pub all about when we was kids together."

"More hot water, Mrs Leyton?"

Izzie had come into the room without my noticing her, and I jumped. It occurred to me that she had been lurking somewhere very close by.

"No, thank you," I said. "Miss Blewett is just leaving."

"And not before time." Izzie fixed Bella with a baleful look. "I'll show you out."

"Don't trouble."

Bella got to her feet and swaggered to the door, but stopped just before she reached it and slowly looked round the room, her gaze taking in the pictures, the covers, the rugs and ornaments.

"Lady Bloody Muck!" she said softly.

"Get out of here, you foul-mouthed creature," Izzie said, turning upon her and literally shooing her from the room. She returned to look at me with concern.

"Ooh, that nasty besom," she said. "What has she been saying to you, Mrs Leyton, dear? You look really ill."

"Oh, Izzie, it's such a long, long story." I felt too weary to begin, but after a moment I did so and I told her everything, right back to my schooldays and even earlier, to the time when Bella would wait round dark corners to terrorise me, and Izzie listened without interrupting, though she clicked her tongue disapprovingly upon occasions and snorted with disapproval when I told her about the money I had given Bella.

"Mrs Leyton, dear, that was very unwise. Whatever possessed you?"

I sighed.

"Honestly, I can hardly remember. For years she frightened me, and always she seemed to choose just the right moment—and there was the chance that something could be proved against me. Things are different now."

424

"That they are," Izzie said, and began to clear away the cups with a determined air as if she had come to a decision. "That woman needs a good talking to. You should turn round and tell her—"

"Izzie, it's no good. It's best to leave it."

"Hm! If you don't fancy the job, I'll do it myself."

"My dear Izzie," I said, "I doubt if even you turning round and telling her would have much effect—"

"Now, don't you mock me, Mrs Leyton, dear, because I'm getting an idea, and I think it's a good one. I did tell you, didn't I, that young Gladys is courting the young policeman?"

"I could hardly fail to know; with his bicycle propped up outside the back door every afternoon."

"I'm very lenient with Gladys," Izzie admitted, as one confessing to a fault. "But Jim Trubshawe is a decent fellow and I'd like to see her settled with him."

"So what do you intend to do?"

"With your permission I'll talk to Jim about it. He's got a good head on his shoulders and he'll know what to do—what's more, it suits him to keep in with me."

"So you're not above a bit of blackmail yourself, then!"

"Mrs Leyton!" She drew back and looked at me in outrage, then laughed. "Oh, you always were one for a tease. I'm glad to see you looking a bit more cheerful."

"There's something reassuringly sane about you, Izzie."

"Don't you worry any more. Jim and me will sort it out between us."

I had a momentary feeling of alarm.

"Izzie—just ask Jim's advice and see if he can warn the wretched woman that she'll be guilty of slander if she spreads lies about me. Don't get involved—do you promise?" I had ample evidence over the years that Izzie's turning-round-and-telling-'em activities sometimes got out of hand.

"Don't you give it another thought," she said.

"Izzie, you're a dear. What would I do without you?" I asked her. She went bright red and made a hurried, embarrassed exit.

I was surprised at how calm I felt. Perhaps, I thought, it was the calmness of despair, or perhaps advancing age had taught me that it was sheer foolishness to run around like a chicken with its head chopped off.

This time I would definitely tell Roger everything. He should be the one to confront Bella—to tell her exactly what was in store for her if she damaged our business by spreading slander. He and Jim Trubshawe together, perhaps. I went to the bookcase and took out an encyclopaedia, turning the pages until I came to the part that dealt with legal matters. I found a whole page on defamation. Excellent, I thought, as I read. She would not have a leg to stand on.

I closed the book with a satisfied bang and returned it to its place on the shelf. Roger had gone over to the Red Lion and there was little I could do until he returned home. My thoughts wandered to Chantry Court and a few doubts raised their heads again. Could Bella harm us? We had such a lot to lose.

Damn Peter to hell, I thought, with uncharacteristic profanity. It was all his fault. If he never returned from Australia, it would be too soon for me.

I sat for a while thinking of him, and of Mark, wondering what, if anything, he had told his father. I didn't for one moment suppose that he had given anything like a true account of his departure from the Ring of Bells—but on the whole I thought we should let it stand.

It was more than time that I wrote to Charlotte, however. I went upstairs where I had left my pen, and from my bedroom window I happened to glance out towards the track which led upwards to the lane. Making their way up it were two figures—Izzie dressed in her best black with her hat set very straight upon her head, and Constable Trubshawe, pushing his bicycle. I looked at my watch. It was just after opening time and I had no doubt at all about their destination. There was an eagerness for the fray in the straight line of Izzie's back.

I had to stop them! It was not that I did not appreciate Izzie's partisan attitude; I loved her for it, but felt certain that she was hopelessly wrong to tackle Bella in this way. She was not the sort of person to back down after a lecture on right and wrong delivered by such as Izzie. A quiet visit from Jim Trubshawe might possibly have been effective, but a harangue from Izzie could tip the scales the other way.

I hurried downstairs. It was a warm evening and I needed no coat, and hastily I put on a hat—any hat, the first one that came to hand—and I ran out of the house after them. They were already out of sight on their way to the village. Swiftly I went up the track and out on to the top lane, past the church and the Ring of Bells. By this time they had turned into the High Street, going up the hill in the direction of the Waggon and Horses. I was becoming breathless, but hurried even faster.

I knew by the time that I reached the corner that I would never catch them in time and for a second I hesitated. Being such a fine evening there were many people about. Some were sitting at the open doorways of their cottages and I felt they were staring after me as I made up my mind and went on towards the Waggon and Horses. Izzie must be mad, I thought. A *quiet* word with Bella was what I had in mind. At this hour the bar would be full—surely it was sheer lunacy to attempt to talk to her there.

But that, it appeared, was their intention. I continued up the street, my steps slowing as I approached it. Now I was here, what could I do? From the street I could hear Jim shouting for order. What could be going on inside? I had only my imagination to supply the answer, for there was only one tiny window giving on to the street and this was obscured by the backs of the men sitting against it.

There was an alley at the side which I guessed would lead to the back. I went along it and into the yard which was a jumble of crates and boxes and empty bottles. Here there was a larger window into the bar, wide open to catch the summer breeze. I sidled over to it and pressed myself to the wall at the side where I could hear all that was going on.

Jim had succeeded in claiming everyone's attention and was addressing himself to Bella.

". . . acquaint you with the law," he was saying, his voice with its Oxfordshire burr taking on a portentous cadence. "Defamation is committed by a person who attacks the reputation of another by the publishing of a false and defamatory statement concerning him—or her, mark you—to a third party. If the defamatory statement—Miss Blewett, I must ask you to hear me out—is written, it's libel. If it's spoken, it's slander. And you can be sued for damages if by such defamatory attacks you disparage a person in the way of his—or her—business, or if you imply that such a person has committed a crime punishable by imprisonment—"

This was obviously a great deal too slow for Izzie.

"And that's what you're threatening to do, you nasty creature," she said, her voice coming clearly to me through the open window. "And me and Jim, we've come here to say that if you have anything to accuse Mrs Leyton of, lovely lady that she is, then you'd better speak up now, in front of witnesses—people, I may say, who're supposed to be her *friends*. Yes, I can see you, Mr Parslow, no use cowering behind Mr Holland there, not to mention George Fisher and Nobby Clark—yes, I see you."

Oh no, Izzie, I thought, leaning against the wall with my eyes closed. Leave it—leave it for heaven's sake! We had known that our customers would defect. Nevertheless I edged round a little to peer into the room and was astounded at the number of regulars I could see in the small section that was visible to me. Goosey Parslow, now incredibly old and wrinkled, was making chewing motions with his toothless mouth as if bereft of words, and Dutchy Holland, the friend of his bosom, bent forward to look at Izzie, leaning heavily on his stick.

I could hear a noise from the portion of the bar that was out of sight. From the sound of it, Bella was coming forward to do battle with Izzie.

"You got a bleedin' nerve coming in 'ere," she began.

"That will do, Miss Blewett, no violence if you don't mind," Jim said.

"You let '*er* say what she likes!"

"I've got right on my side," Izzie said self-righteously. "And we're still waiting to hear what it is you've got to say about Mrs Leyton. Because all that about libel and slander and defamatory statements, that wouldn't apply to you, would it? 'Cos you've got witnesses, I understand, and proof. And when the Leytons take you to court and sue you for every penny you've got, you'll be able to laugh at them, won't you?"

"Er—Mrs Noakes," Jim Trubshawe said. "Perhaps you'd better leave it to me."

Yes, Izzie, I begged silently. Leave it to Jim. She ignored us both.

"Come on then—out with all the accusations! Why so quiet all of a sudden, Miss Blewett? Now's the time to tell us, if there's anything at all to tell—right here, with twenty people to hear you. Why should you worry about being sued? You got no worries—you know it all, so tell the rest of us."

"Gawd, I'll smash your face—" There was the sound of a chair or some other heavy object crashing over and I winced. The room erupted into uproar, though whose side most of the men were taking I could not make out. The most piercing cry was from Goosey Parslow.

"Bloody women," he cried. "We don't come here to 'ave bloody women a-'ollering at us. We can get that at home."

"Quiet," yelled Jim Trubshawe. An uneasy peace, broken by subdued mutterings, fell over the room. "That's better," he went on, in a lower voice. "I just want to make sure you understand the position, Miss Blewett. Slander is a serious matter and will be dealt with as such."

"I know what I know," Bella said. I edged round to the other side of the window so that I could see her end of the room. She looked grotesque and strangely helpless, purple in the face and fists clenched by her sides.

"Speak now or for ever hold your peace," Izzie said, taunting her.

"What's all this about?" someone asked from the body of the room. "I don't know what's going on."

"Miss Blewett does," Izzie said walking round her as if to study her from a different angle. "Miss Blewett knows well. She's been using her nasty, poisonous, slanderous tongue to hurt innocent folk and Jim and me are going to see she don't do it no more. Anything you got to say, you say right now, do you hear? Cat got your tongue?"

"Gawd," Bella said, shaking her head so that her dewlaps wobbled. "Gawd, I'll get you for this."

"Careful now—we've got the law here. You can't threaten in front of the law, not to mention all these witnesses." Izzie

429

looked around the room as if assessing the strength of the support she could count on. Clearly she thought little of it.

"I wouldn't like to put my trust in you lot," she went on. "I suppose it's your business if you give up taking your drink in a nice cosy place like the Ring of Bells to come to this filthy hole. Look at it—look up there, at the cobwebs. Did you ever see anything like it? What would you say if your wives kept your home like that? Look at those corners! Catch anything, you could, drinking in a place like this. Do you think those tankards are ever given a decent wash? Yes, it's your business if you catch typhoid—*or worse!*" The drama with which she invested her last words would have made me laugh out loud in any other circumstances. Now I could only silently beg her to stop—to leave while she appeared to be winning. But she was far from finished; hardly, yet, in top gear.

"Rats there are, running about out there," she said, flinging out a hand towards the window where I cowered. "And what started the Great Plague of London? I'll tell you—rats! But it's your business, of course. I don't know how you could, though; I tell you honestly, you fair beat me, all of you. Every night at the Ring of Bells, day in and day out, all smiles to Mr and Mrs Leyton. Then comes the first hint of trouble and do you rally round? No, you do *not* rally round. How could you? I ask—how could you?"

The men were watching her now as if mesmerised. Even Jim Trubshawe had pushed his helmet to the back of his head and was looking at her with a kind of rueful amusement, his arms folded.

"You and you," she said, pointing to Freddie Summers and Ollie Winslow. "Friends of Mr Roger, I thought you were. Mates together, you were, playing cricket when you were young 'uns—stood you many a pint, he has. No one like Mr Roger, you used to say. No side about him, treats everyone the same, always good for a laugh. Laugh? There never was such a one as Mr Roger. You remember him at the parish concerts, Goosey Parslow. Laughed so hard one night you fell over backwards! I suppose you know he bought the new operating theatre at the cottage hospital? Saved your life, didn't it, when you got appendicitis a few years back?

"And as for you, Dutchy Holland, have you forgotten the way Mrs Leyton went night after night to sit with your missus when your Leslie was lost at sea? Too busy getting drunk and drowning your sorrows, you were, but Mrs Leyton cared. There's many a poor soul in this village can vouch for that, for all she never drove about with her soup and her good advice like the Lady of the Manor. Do good by stealth, the Good Book says, and that's what Mrs Leyton's done all her life. Ask how many sets of baby clothes she's made; find out the number of people she's sent a good hot meal to, when they've been in need."

Oh, God, it'll be the Christmas collection of toys next, I thought, listening to this tirade in astonishment—and heaven alone knows that wasn't me, that was the rest of Collingford. All I did was donate space at the Ring of Bells and arrange the dinner.

"*And* what about the toys for the workhouse," came Izzie's voice, as if on cue. "Not to mention the dinner for the inmates, year after year. But what do you lot do when misfortune strikes them? Do you help? Do you support them with friendship when they need it most?"

She paused for breath, and Bella seized the opportunity to come forward and grab her by the shoulder looking at least twice as tall and twice as wide.

"Out," she said. "Out of my pub, you. I've stood enough."

Izzie brushed her hand contemptuously aside.

"I've finished," she said. "I'm going." She seemed to take a firmer grasp of the bag she carried on her arm and she squared her shoulders. "I always believe," she said, "in talking straight." And with her head held high she made for the door.

She had barely reached it when she stopped.

"I don't believe it," she said. "No—not even in this hole, I don't believe it!" Delving into the shadows behind the open door she emerged holding a dead rat by the extreme end of its tail, very fastidiously and with an expression of outraged repugnance on her face. Without a word she threw it at Bella and swept out.

The rat fell to the floor with a dull thud, landing on its

431

back with its pathetic little paws curled in the air, and for a second there was complete silence as the assembled company contemplated it. Then Ollie Winslow cleared his throat noisily, emptied the dregs of his tankard and banged it down on the table in front of him.

"Well," he said. "You lot can do what you like, but I'm off to the Ring."

He got up and began to walk out alone, but before he reached the door, Fred Summers had called to him, swallowing hastily.

"Wait a bit, Ollie, hold on there," he said. "I'll come with you."

They left together, leaving silence behind them. Jim Trubshawe had produced a notebook and was writing busily.

" 'Ere," Bella said. "What d'yer think you're doin'?"

"Just making notes, ma'am," Jim said, in a detached and official voice. "Item: one rat, found in bar. Large amount of dirt present. Unwashed spittoons."

"She was right, Dutchie," I heard Goosey Parslow say, over a mounting barrage of protest from Bella. "What she says about Mr Roger and his lady. Quite right, she was. I'm a-going back."

"Well, dang it, Goosey," Dutchie said. "I didn't want to come 'ere in the first place, did I? 'Twasn't my idea."

"Damn sure it weren't mine," Goosey argued. "I said to you, where be we going tonight, then, and you said to me, damn if I don't feel like a change, you said . . ." Still arguing, they left the Waggon and Horses together.

I watched full of amazement as several others drank up and left, and then I, too, slipped away.

Was it the rat or the rhetoric, I wondered? Which one had worked the magic?

It didn't really matter. There was a blessed feeling of peace in my heart as if an evil spirit had at last been laid. I had seen Bella for what she was; a bully, full of sound and fury, but with little stomach for a fight. I even felt rather sorry for her.

Oh, God bless Izzie! She had really turned round and told them as she had never told them before—and although one rat was very like another and I obviously could not be sure, why did I have the feeling that the rat lying on the floor of

432

the Waggon and Horses was a Priors' rat, the sort that could be found in the barn any day of the week?

I laughed to myself as I sped homeward—but stopped short when I reached the Ring of Bells and instead of going past it on my way to Priors, I turned aside and went into it.

The sound of a cricket bat smiting a ball came to me and a delighted shout of 'Howzat!' The team was out on the green, practising as usual, and soon would be in for their pints.

Inside all was cool darkness and polished wood and the comfortable smell of old kegs. I smiled and nodded a greeting to those that I knew. There was a couple from Cheltenham who came every year, and an elderly Commander RN, Retd. and his imposing wife who were also regular visitors.

I greeted one of the maids as she was flitting past to the dining room. She looked at me warily as if afraid that my unexpected appearance might herald yet another drama. It would be a long time before our staff could forget Mrs Foster.

I made my way to the kitchen, said good evening to an astonished Alfred, and looked through the hatch to the tap-room where sat Goosey Parslow and Dutchie Holland, Ollie Winslow and Freddie Summers, Nobby Clark and several others, all looking as if the very idea of defecting to the Waggon and Horses had never so much as entered their heads.

"Good evening, gentlemen," I said to them, leaning through from one side to the other.

They all responded in their various ways, though I detected a common embarrassed disinclination to look my way.

"I *am* delighted to see you all," I went on. "I don't often come in at night nowadays—not like the old days, eh, Goosey? What a long time it is that you've all been coming here! It struck me tonight that it's good to have friends like you. We appreciate it, my husband and I." There were a few uncomfortable stirrings and clearings of the throat. "I'd like to show my appreciation. How about a pint all round, on the house?"

They looked at me then, embarrassment giving way to beams of approval and rapid acceptance of the offer.

"Thanks, missus," Goosey said. "Oh, you're a bonny maid, I always did say so. Didn't I, Dutchie?"

I waved their thanks aside, called the pot-boy to give the order, and left them to enjoy it.

28

The redecoration of Watersmeet marked a turning-point in Lucy's life. Lady Bollinger was delighted with it, and through her Lucy gained introductions to a number of her friends, all anxious, it seemed, to cast off the last remnants of Victoriana and embrace the bare, cubist style that Lucy favoured.

It would not be true to say that Nick withdrew all his objections overnight. He still refused to be put out in any way by her work. Her visits to craftsmen and wholesalers had sometimes to be curtailed in order to fit in with his arrangements, and he invariably insisted on a formal, four-course dinner, for which they changed, being ceremonially waited on by Molly.

But somehow Lucy seemed to be charged with energy, bearing out the theory I have always adhered to: the more one has to do, the more one *can* do. It is only when there are long, pointless, empty hours to fill that everything in life seems too much trouble.

It was some two years later that Lucy began to consider opening business premises in Oxford where she could keep selected materials on hand.

"There's a shop empty in Little Clarendon Street," she said. "I hear the lease is for sale. It would be absolutely perfect for me."

"What does Nick say?" I asked cautiously.

She laughed.

"I think we'd better unleash daddy and another bottle of

brandy on him. He's not too happy about it, but I intend to talk him round. After all, I'm almost financially independent these days."

"For heaven's sake don't flaunt that aspect, Lucy. That might be enough to sink the whole thing."

"I'm not flaunting it—but it's still true, Mother. I'm sure I could raise a bank loan for the property on my own account."

"We could lend her the money, couldn't we?" I asked Roger later.

"If Lucy really needs money, I expect we can find some," he replied. But he looked gloomy as he spoke and I knew that his financial situation was giving him cause for concern. After the initial splash when everything seemed set fair, Chantry Court had settled down to unremarkable business and it was seldom more than three-quarters full—a state of affairs which both Philip and Roger robustly declared to be nothing more than they expected.

Poor Philip! He worked so hard and put so much enthusiasm into the hotel, I felt it must be dispiriting for him to see the rooms so empty, yet he refused to be downhearted. I sighed now as I thought about him.

"Something wrong?" Roger asked me.

"No. Well, only Philip. I just wish—"

"He would settle down and find himself a *nice* girl," Roger finished for me.

"Yes, I do."

He was twenty-seven now and growing more like his father every day, though he had also acquired a highly-polished, man-of-the-world veneer which owed not a little to Noel Coward, currently both delighting and shocking London with his gems of wit. Even his voice seemed to have become off-hand and brittle, just like the master.

There were times when I felt he mocked everything I held sacred: the church, home, family affection. Yet at the very next moment he would demonstrate with a word or action that this was not really the case and that underneath the cool cynicism he was the same loving, warm creature he had always been. He would be all right, I felt sure. Ben had been in no hurry to settle down either, but when he had done so, he had made the right choice. Philip would be the same.

I turned my attention once more to Lucy.

"Will you talk to her about the shop?" I asked Roger. "They're dropping the children off here tomorrow when they go to Cheltenham for the weekend."

He agreed to do so, and I smiled when I heard him in conversation with the pair of them the following day. He would have made an excellent diplomat, I thought. By the time they left, he had somehow contrived to convince Nick that such an excellent idea must have originated with him and that only with his help in negotiating the lease of the shop in Little Clarendon Street could the venture get off the ground. Nick even managed, as they got into the car, to throw in some artistic ideas for good measure.

"Not too much in the window," he was saying. "Just some draped material and a Grecian vase."

By the end of 1928 the shop was a reality, and Lucy's business seemed to be developing very satisfactorily.

It was a memorable year in other ways, too. It was the year when the vote was given to all women over the age of twenty-one, putting a stop to the ridiculous anomaly by which a labourer of twenty-one could vote whereas a woman graduate was forced to wait until she had reached thirty.

We broke with tradition that year and went down to Somerset for Christmas to stay with Mark and Charlotte, for Clare was expecting a baby and did not feel able to make the long journey to Oxfordshire.

Clare positively glowed with health and happiness and I was delighted, too, by the look of Ben. He had put on some badly-needed weight and there was a serenity about him that was something new. Gone for ever was the tension. I had not known him so relaxed since he was a boy and blessed Clare in my heart for working this miracle. He was thrilled at the prospect of a baby.

"If it's a girl," he said, "we're going to call her Genevieve."

"Oh, you're not! The poor thing!"

"I think it's a lovely name," Clare said.

"My grandmother said it sounded hoity-toity, and I don't think she was far wrong." I smiled as I remembered the day

I had first entered the Ring of Bells. "Still, I appreciate the honour," I said. "And no doubt the poor child will live it down."

But the child was not called upon to do so, since he turned out to be a boy and was christened Roger Benjamin at St Peter's Church, Collingford, dressed in the same christening gown that his father had worn before him.

Nick and Philip had been asked to stand as godfathers, and Ellie was to be godmother. I knew that she was delighted to have been asked, but from the moment she walked into Priors I was aware that some deeper excitement had her in its grip. We were not long in discovering the cause.

"It seems that Baldwin is likely to go the country in May," she said. "And I've been asked to stand for Broxton. Isn't it wonderful? I'm so thrilled I can hardly believe it."

"But surely Broxton is solidly Conservative, isn't it?" Roger asked.

I had only the vaguest notion of its whereabouts. It lay somewhere to the south of London. I seemed to remember I had heard that it had once been a rural country town, until the tentacles of suburbia had reached out and encircled it, so that now it was almost part of London.

"There are some vast new factories there and several council estates," Ellie said. "It's regarded as a marginal."

"Who's the present Member of Parliament?"

"Sir Horace Vigar."

"Never heard of him."

"Nobody has! That's the whole point! He's a silly old buffer who's sat for donkey's years doing absolutely nothing except watch his majority dwindle with every passing election."

"What about the Liberal candidate?"

"There's been some almighty row in the local party, the man who stood for them last time is standing as an Independent, so the vote's split right down the middle. The time is absolutely ripe for someone with a bit of go in them!"

"It's wonderful news," I said, hugging her. "I'm so pleased, darling. Roger, isn't it wonderful?"

"Tremendous," he said.

There was a note of forced enthusiasm in Roger's voice

and I glared at him. This was no time to let his own political convictions prevent him from rejoicing with Ellie. He took the hint graciously, and hugged her in his turn.

"I'm proud of you, my dear. The party must think highly of you."

"I hope so! Well, yes, I think they must do."

"You know we wish you well—but promise not to try to convert me, won't you? You'd be wasting your time."

"I promise!" She clung to him for a second. "You're not a bad old codger," she said. "If all the old lot were like you, the world wouldn't be in such a terrible state. Now, don't say a word to the others, will you? I don't want to steal the baby's thunder. This is his weekend—his and Clare's and Ben's."

It was yet another of the family parties that had become traditional at Priors and Roger Benjamin covered himself with glory by smiling angelically at the vicar and promptly going to sleep for the rest of the service.

Ellie went back to London to be caught up immediately in preparations for the forthcoming election. She took a flat in Broxton and we saw nothing more of her, which did not surprise us one bit. It was entirely characteristic of her that she would devote every waking moment to getting to know her constituency.

"I hope she's looking after herself," I said worriedly to Roger one day.

"She's wn up, Jenny."

"I know that. But she doesn't eat when she gets absorbed in what she's doing! She'll make herself ill."

"Jenny, for heaven's sake . . .!"

I lapsed into an unhappy silence, but was not comforted.

"I'm going to see her," I announced suddenly. "At least I can make sure she has a square meal."

Roger laughed at me.

"Go if you must," he said. "I expect you're dying to be part of the fun, if the truth were known."

"I suppose that's part of it," I admitted.

Accordingly, I packed a small case and caught the train to London the following day. Broxton was only a short ride on the Underground, and I emerged from the station into a street where the first thing that caught my eye was a life-sized picture of Ellie on a hoarding bearing the legend, 'Eleanor Leyton Cares'. It would have looked more impressive had not a moustache been drawn upon her upper lip by an unknown hand; but even so, I felt a mounting excitement to think that in only a few days the residents of this town would be casting their votes in an election where a daughter of mine was a candidate.

Whatever her politics, it was an achievement, say what you will. I had a daughter to be proud of.

I had no idea where I might find the headquarters of the Labour Party in Broxton, but a little way up the street I could see a policeman and I made my way towards him thinking, rightly, that he could direct me there.

"It's not far," he said. "Straight on for a couple of hundred yards, then left into Gladstone Street. You can't miss it."

I thanked him and he sketched a salute.

"Whoa—hold on, ma'am," he said as I started off in the direction he had indicated. "Here comes the other lot."

I saw a large Rolls-Royce draw to a halt beside the green, followed by several other smaller cars which looked like a flotilla of little vessels surging round a battleship. All were decked with posters and blue ribbons. Out of one of the small cars jumped hordes of supporters who quickly erected a platform. When this was ready—and not one moment before—out of the Rolls emerged a tall and impressive figure in black coat and striped trousers, an enormous blue rosette in his button-hole.

"That's Sir Horace Vigar," the policeman said. "Makes you laugh, don't it?"

I was not quite sure what aspect of Sir Horace was supposed to encourage mirth. To me he looked intimidating.

There were pictures of him about the town, as well as those of Ellie; but no one would draw a moustache on his beaming countenance for the simple reason that he already possessed one of the most magnificent growths I had ever seen, large and blond and curling. A broad pink forehead rose above bushy eyebrows. I crossed the street and mingled with the shop-girls and office workers who were beginning to gather round the platform. I edged as near to him as I could, intensely curious to see the strength of Ellie's major opponent.

His speech began predictably enough, so much so that I felt I could have written the whole thing for him. As an exercise in the use of high-sounding words that said absolutely nothing, it could hardly have been equalled.

Things livened up a little when the heckling started.

"What about unemployment? Are you going to give us jobs?" shouted a young, thin-faced man in a collarless shirt and cloth cap.

"It's the most important issue facing us!"

"Then what are you going to do about it?"

"Expansion is the answer—expansion that can never take place under a socialist government."

"It don't take place under the old gang, neither," yelled the man.

"You're wrong, Sir! There are over one hundred thousand less men unemployed at this moment than there were at the last election, when we were left with the mess made by the Labour Government."

The figure seemed to silence the heckler effectively and Sir Horace took the opportunity to spread his arms wide and beam paternally at his audience.

"My friends," he said. "For so, I feel, I may call you, since I have represented you for so many years. Your fears are my fears—your aims, my aims. You've seen the posters, haven't you? 'Eleanor Leyton Cares'." He invested the words with a wealth of sarcasm. "Oh yes, my friends. Eleanor Leyton cares, all right. She cares for one thing—" and here he leaned forward, emphasising his words with blows from his clenched fist upon the rail of his platform. "She cares for the propagation of her own extreme political views, dictated not by what Broxton needs; not even dictated by Westminster; but by Moscow!"

He stood back, his face expressing outraged patriotism. But he had by no means finished, and leaned towards them again.

"Is this, I ask you, what we fought shoulder to shoulder in the trenches for? So that we can hand this glorious, noble country over to a group of cranks whose loyalties lie not here but elsewhere—"

"How *dare* you!" I shouted, my voice cleaving a path through the red film of rage that seemed to have formed in my brain. "Eleanor Leyton is no less a patriot than you! She may not have fought in the trenches but she nursed in Army hospitals in France throughout the war. You won't find her talking of it, though, because she believes it's the future that matters, not the past."

"Well, well," Sir Horace beamed down at me. "So Miss Leyton has one supporter. She's a plucky little lady—I don't grudge her that."

"The lady's right," shouted a bald-headed man standing close to me. "The past is behind us—and what have you done with it? Nothing!"

"And what did the Labour Party do with power when they had the chance? They created such chaos, my friends, that we're still clearing it up. It's a job for someone of experience, my friends; a man's job! It was our government that gave you ladies the vote. I plead with you to use it to support the candidate who has a proven record of success, not a young woman attempting to cut her political teeth on you, the people of Broxton."

"She's a lot prettier than you," one wit called out.

"I can't argue with you there," Sir Horace agreed, wagging a finger and looking rogueish. "But handsome is as handsome does—"

"Name one thing that you have ever done," I demanded loudly.

He chose to ignore me. The meeting was coming to an end, the crowd breaking up and drifting back to their places of work. Sir Horace stepped down from his platform to walk among those still gathered there, clapping men on the back, bending to pat children upon the cheek, clasping hands and smiling, smiling.

The bald-headed man who had been standing near turned to speak to me.

"I wouldn't trust that man as far as I could throw him," he said. "He couldn't have given you an answer, not if he'd thought about it all night."

441

"Eleanor Leyton *does* care," I said.

"I know."

"And she doesn't take her orders from Moscow!"

"Lady, you don't have to tell me. I work for her!"

"You do?" I smiled at him and held out my hand. "Well, I'm glad to meet you. I'm her mother, and I'm just about to go to headquarters to find her."

"I'll take you there," he said. "If we're quick we'll just catch her before she starts on her afternoon tour."

When I reached the headquarters in a seedy, semi-detached Victorian house quite close to town, Ellie's greeting was warm but harassed. She should have been speaking in some remote Oddfellows Hall ten minutes ago, her frantic aides informed her, and as a consequence I found myself presented with the key of her flat and was told to go and make myself at home.

Home! Was anywhere less like it than these three dusty rooms over a newsagent's shop? A greasy pan stood on the stove and dirty crockery filled the sink. Unwashed laundry was piled so high that I marvelled Ellie had anything left to wear. I removed my coat and hat, rolled up my sleeves and got to work. They'll never get me knocking on doors or making speeches, I thought, but in this area at least I could be useful. I could play Martha to Ellie's Mary.

It took all of a week before I became so deeply involved with Ellie's cause and so at one with her body of enthusiastic helpers that I, too, was campaigning with the best of them, realising suddenly that I'd never had so much fun in all my life. There was a closeness between us all, a camaraderie that manifested itself in late-night and often hilarious sessions in Ellie's flat, where we picked over the bones of the day and planned the next.

I telephoned Roger frequently and was relieved that he was accepting my prolonged absence with resignation tinged with lightly veiled amusement. He had expected nothing else, he told me.

"But I miss you," he said. "I'll be glad when you're home."

I missed him, too. On polling day itself we were nervously drinking coffee in the kitchen of campaign headquarters when a helper arrived to tell me that someone was asking for me—'a tall, white-haired toff', the man said. I rushed out, my heart full of hope which was fully justified when I saw Roger standing in the front office, regarding with a quizzically lifted brow the bare floor and trestle tables, the pamphlets and pictures of Ellie. We embraced as if I had been away a year.

Ellie clung to him, tense fingers digging into his shoulders. His arrival caused a welcome diversion in a day which seemed endless. Later we went to dine at the White Hart. Ellie's face seemed to have grown smaller and had taken on a greenish pallor. Infuriatingly she tapped on the table with her fingernail, on and on, until I snapped at her to stop, apologising immediately as she turned anguished eyes on me.

"We might as well get over to the Town Hall and have our nervous breakdowns in company," Roger said.

The votes were still being counted. Someone told us that it would be a close thing. Another proffered the information that Sir Horace had said he was confident of winning. Ellie said nothing and even Roger fell silent, his attempts to maintain normal conversation falling on unreceptive ears. Then, suddenly, the returning officer was among us and we were all being ushered out on to the balcony of the Town Hall where down below us was a crowd so large I could not see the extent of it.

I reached for Roger's hand and gripped it tightly. My throat was constricted and a lead weight seemed to have lodged itself in my stomach. Ellie stood as if carved from stone.

"Sir Horace Vigar, 20,560 votes," announced the man who held her future in his hands. There was a brief spatter of applause, quickly stilled as he went on. "Mr George Carson, 5,409 votes. Mr Edward Thomas, 3,282 votes. Miss Eleanor Leyton, 22,375 votes. I therefore declare—"

He went on speaking, but his words were lost in an upsurge of cheering from Ellie's supporters below, a spontaneous burst of joy as they seized each other, dancing and whooping with delight. Ellie turned to us, her eyes shining.

"You did it, you did it!" We hugged her with tears of joy

and pride in our eyes, and smiled mistily at each other as she went forward to speak to the crowd.

I did not register her words. I was looking at her slight figure, still girlish; her face alight with idealism and dedication.

"She did it," I whispered again to Roger. "Oh, isn't it wonderful?"

And of course he agreed, though the following day when it became apparent that the Labour Party had romped home, he was somewhat less euphoric.

"Ramsay MacDonald will make a mess of it again," he said. "Mark my words, Jenny."

Such views could not be stated at Ellie's headquarters, not on that day of all days, but over the following months it became only too obvious that the victory of the Labour Party was not to usher in a new age of prosperity.

29

After all the excitement, Ellie was only in Parliament for two years.

By the autumn of 1931, the number of men out of work had risen to such an extent and so great were the financial troubles of the country, that once again Ramsay MacDonald went to the country, this time to ask for a 'doctor's mandate' with which to cure them. This meant a Coalition Government—a concept to which Ellie was totally opposed. Roger and I inclined to the other view. We saw a National Government as the only solution to Britain's difficulties, but we had long since stopped arguing with her about our differences. I merely felt sorry that all the hard work and excitement at Broxton had apparently been in vain.

"I'll get back before long," she said. I felt sure that she was right.

Times were hard everywhere. Roger brooded over his account books and his face became lined and worried—a look which seemed to age him overnight. We were forced to cut back on the staff at Chantry Court since the place was never full, and the turnover at our country inns fell dramatically. Alfred tore his hair and indulged in hysterics when I urged economies upon him, but he soon came to realise that more expensive items on the menu were never ordered. It reminded me of wartime, the way we had to trim our sails and cut corners. The men still came for their drink in the evenings, but it was more likely to be a half-pint than a pint.

Even though it was never full to capacity, Chantry Court still attracted the rich, who somehow seemed to survive the slump without altering their way of life in the slightest. The golf course still rang with cries of 'Fore' from well-heeled business men in plus-fours and their tweedy wives; and in the evenings the subtle lighting fell on gleaming hair and jewels and bare shoulders. There were times when I sat apart and listened to the high, well-bred voices and wondered if they even knew, let alone cared, what seventy-five per cent of the population was going through. I doubted it very much.

At a time when many inns went to the wall, the Waggon and Horses closed altogether and Bella left Collingford—where she went I neither knew nor cared. I was far too worried about our own situation.

"There's only one thing for it," Roger said to me one morning. I felt a pang at his haggard expression. "We'll have to sell the Angler's Rest. I hate to let it go. It's the only place that's making any money at the moment, but for that reason alone it will be the easiest to sell. At least our loan repayments will be reduced."

"But we'll have less income to make our repayments *from*! What does Philip say?"

Roger smiled and lifted his shoulders.

"Philip has the optimism of youth. He says hang on—but frankly, Jenny, I don't think I can stand the pace any more."

"Trust Philip," I urged. "He's like you were, Roger, thirty years ago. Remember how horrified I was when you bought the place, how you swept me along with your enthusiasm and confidence. It worked out, just as you said it would."

"But everything was on the up-swing then, Jenny. Now we're in a slump."

"It can't last," I said desperately.

Chantry Court, I thought murderously. That's what has brought us to this. I was beginning to hate the very thought of it.

Roger said no more about selling the Angler's Rest just then but I knew that the subject was one he constantly turned over in his mind, in spite of Philip's urgings to keep it. For myself I could not believe that we were so close to parting with even the smallest of our beloved inns after so many years. We had experienced ups and downs before and had somehow weathered everything. Surely Roger's luck would not desert him now?

Salvation came from a totally unexpected quarter. A letter with an American stamp arrived for Roger one morning, the return address being that of his cousin with whom he had worked so briefly in New York many years before. Rather like Roger, Charles Leyton was a survivor. The family bank had foundered, but he had bobbed to the surface again in an entirely new area of activity—the travel business. Leyton's Luxury Tours, it seemed, was thinking of entering the British market. Could we cope, Charles enquired, with parties of wealthy American tourists?

"I thought America was suffering from the slump more than we are," I said.

"Like everywhere else, I expect the rich get richer." There was a vibrant note of hope in Roger's voice that had been missing for many a long day. "Charles goes on to say that they want to soak up the atmosphere of the Oxfordshire countryside and any culture we may care to throw in."

"Culture?" I reached forward and seized his hand eagerly. "We're surrounded with it. There's Oxford and Blenheim Palace and even Stratford-on-Avon not so very far away."

"I'll drive them there myself, if need be," Roger said. "Declaiming Shakespeare every inch of the way. Darling, this could make the difference between life and—total extinction, do you realise that?"

"Then God Bless America," I said softly.

It naturally took time to organise, and Leyton's Luxury Tours did not begin crossing the Atlantic in our direction until the following year, but by the summer of 1934 we were in business again and our hopes were buoyant. We renewed beds and other furnishings, and the curtains that I had been afraid to have washed, knowing that they would immediately fall into tatters.

Local trade began to pick up, too. In the next two years we found it necessary to establish a small office in Collingford High Street (a converted cottage with 'Leyton Hotels' on a brass plate by the door) where a young man called Michael Blanchard, a friend of Philip's from his Savoy Hotel days, took over the paperwork which seemed inseparable from running the administrative side of the five hotels.

What golden years they were, those that followed. We were freed from the threat of losing our hotels. We were able to relax and enjoy the company of our children and grandchildren; every year the beauty of the countryside seemed to give us more pleasure—sometimes, I felt, because we were seeing it afresh through the eyes of our American visitors. We visited the theatre in Oxford and took several leisurely trips through Europe. Roger would never admit that he had retired from active work, but with Philip and Michael and our excellent managers he felt able to take longer and longer holidays, which amounted to the same thing.

We listened to the wireless and read our papers, untroubled by disquieting echoes that were beginning to make themselves heard from Germany. Had anyone asked us our opinion of Adolf Hitler, we should probably have said that he seemed to be pulling his country out of the doldrums, so blindly contented were we. If I had any worries at all at that time they were centred on Philip who seemed to have two passions: Chantry Court and the pursuit of pleasure. Sometimes I felt that the pursuit became an end in itself. To me he did not seem particularly happy as he whirled from one social affair to the next, Michael Blanchard giving the impression of hanging rather breathlessly on to his coat-tails.

"How I wish he'd settle down," I said to Roger one day. "He's getting a bad reputation. I overheard a girl describing him to another as one of the 'kiss and ride away brigade' the other day. And it's nothing to laugh at," I added sharply, as Roger seemed amused. "He'll be an elderly roué before he can turn round at this rate."

"Nonsense—he works hard and plays hard, that's all," Roger said comfortably.

I had hopes that at last he had met the right girl when he brought a vivacious, dark-haired young woman called Kitty to the house twice in the space of a week, but when she came no more to Priors and I enquired what had happened to her, he laughed.

"It occurred to me that she didn't so much speak as *quack*," he said. "And quite frankly, Mother, I prefer my ducks à l'orange."

"Philip! She was a thoroughly nice girl."

"What a dreadfully damning thing to say! Kitty would be mortified."

"Philip, you're insufferable," I said, angry at his man-of-the-world pose. "It would do you all the good in the world to get married."

"Doesn't that put marriage on a par with cod-liver oil?" he asked, with an amused lift of his eyebrow.

In July 1934 Lucy and Nick had been married for a staggering twenty years. Where had the time gone? I remembered the pretty little bride who had insisted on the hobble skirt to beat all hobble skirts, and the slim, handsome officer who had gone to war in 1915. Thankfully they had achieved harmony now. Perhaps age would have brought it anyway; but I still held that the fact Lucy was busy with work in which she had achieved artistic fulfilment had a great deal to do with it. She had grown into a serene, mature woman and, almost in spite of himself, Nick had become interested in her business. He had long since forgotten his objections regarding his wife's earnings. The two boys were at Winchester and Beth was studying art in Florence. They had been able to move to a delightful house on the outskirts of Oxford where they entertained an interesting circle of friends. I no longer worried about Lucy.

In the spring of 1935 we were much engaged with the King and Queen's Silver Jubilee—not the minor affair that was taking place in London, but the far more important junketings that went on in Collingford, as in every other town and village throughout Britain. Great fun it was, too, and good for business.

Only weeks later there was another General Election at which Ellie was once more swept back to Parliament as the member for Broxton, so that although Stanley Baldwin and his Conservative majority dominated the National Government, she formed part of a vocal opposition party.

She was forty-three now, but still as slim and vital as ever, her dark hair only lightly touched by grey. She had changed in other ways, however. A softer, more tolerant approach to life was clearly discernible; not tolerance towards poverty or greed or inefficiency, but a less aggressive way with those who disagreed with her. She liked nothing better than to come to Priors for a weekend when she would relax in the garden, wear old clothes and walk in the fields, enjoying the company of her nephews and nieces.

She would even go out with Geoffrey Maskell sometimes—to a play or to dinner. They were friends now and I was glad to be able to welcome him again to Priors.

Ben and Clare and their three sons, Roger, Christopher and Alan, came frequently. Ben was now a housemaster at his school and lived in part of a gracious old Georgian house which seemed to me, on the few visits I paid there, to swarm with boys from attic to cellar and to pulsate gently with the noise they generated. Clare complained that she felt hopelessly outnumbered amongst such a monstrous regiment of men and vowed that she would not give up until she had produced the daughter she wanted so much. By the summer of 1935 she was once again pregnant. This time, she said, it *had* to be a Genevieve.

Philip was still a bachelor. He had a flat at Chantry Court where he lived an independent existence most of the time, but his room at Priors was always ready for him and often he came home when he felt the need to escape altogether from the demands of the hotel. Things were going well there, justifying his and Roger's earlier optimism.

As for Roger and I—well, both of us suffered a little from twinges of rheumatism and our eyesight was not what it

449

had been. Roger's hair was completely white, though still abundant, and mine was an undignified sort of pepper-and-salt colour which I disliked intensely. We were both well into our sixties, but both—thank heaven—fit and active and still vitally interested in the business.

I was walking back from the Ring of Bells one day in autumn. It had been a good harvest and now the yellow-hammers and starlings were busy amidst the stubble. The hedges were feathery with traveller's joy and ripe with blackberries and elderberries which drooped heavily from their overhanging branches which earlier had been a mass of white blossom. The chestnuts were tinged with gold, and up in the spinney to my left were flashes of flame and russet where maple trees and sycamores shouted their presence.

I rounded the bend and my footsteps faltered. There was a girl looking over the wall towards Priors, her elbows resting on the grey stones. She was young and slim and dark-haired, and she was completely absorbed in the scene before her. She turned to look my way as I approached and I saw that she was smiling, whether in greeting or with pleasure at the sight of the house I could not tell.

"Good morning," I said, as I drew level with her.

"Hi, there!"

So she was American. A member of Leyton's Luxury Tours, I supposed. Her jacket and skirt, though plain, were superbly cut and expensively fashionable. She had a high cheek-boned gamin face under dark, crisp curls cut short in a boyish style, and there was a shining, well-groomed look about her which I had come to realise was typically American.

"Excuse me," she said as I passed her, sounding a little diffident. "Could you tell me—who lives in that house down there?"

"Indeed I could." I stepped up on the bank beside her as I had done so many times before and I, too, leaned my elbows on the wall and gazed at Priors. "It belongs to me—to my family. I am Mrs Roger Leyton."

"Oh!" She laughed in some confusion. "Please forgive my curiosity. It's just that I think that's the most beautiful house I've ever seen. My name is Laura Maybury, and I'm on holiday from the States."

"That much I gathered." I looked at her curiously. There was something about her that teased at my mind. Perhaps I had seen her before. "Your second visit?" I asked.

"Oh no, I've never been before. That's what's so strange! The moment I saw that house, I felt—I felt—" vaguely she gesticulated. "I don't know, it sounds crazy. But I felt that somehow I'd seen it before."

I turned to study her even more closely.

"That *is* extraordinary," I said. "It had the same effect on me when I saw it for the first time. I was quite a bit younger than you are now—just seventeen—and very new to Collingford; yet I had this strange feeling of home-coming."

"That's exactly it!"

"Would you like to see it from the inside? Do walk home with me and have some coffee."

"May I really? I would love that."

She adjusted her long-legged stride to mine and fell into step beside me as we went along the lane together.

"Are you staying at the Ring of Bells?" I asked her.

"The hotel back there in the village? Oh no, I'm visiting relatives. They live in a very grand house, but to me it isn't half as attractive as yours."

I stopped in my tracks, and she stopped too.

"Watersmeet?" I asked.

"That's right. I guess you know the Bollingers? In a place as small as this, everyone must know everyone else."

"Especially the Bollingers! Let me work this out. You must be descended from the last Lord Bollinger's daughter."

"She was my grandmother. The present Lord Bollinger was her cousin. She died about five years ago."

"Of course!" We resumed our walk towards Priors. "I remember old Lord Bollinger telling me that his daughter had married a Yankee and that he had a number of American granddaughters."

"My mother was one of five. Did you know him well?"

I hesitated.

"A great deal better than I know the present lord," I said

451

after a moment. "He was a wonderful man—warm and humorous and kind. I was very fond of him."

Her lips twitched.

"He sounds a whole lot different from the present Lord Bollinger."

"I would agree with you there."

Our eyes met and we laughed, a little guiltily.

"You're like him," I said. "The old lord, I mean. There's something about your smile and your eyes . . ." My voice trailed away as I remembered his saying much the same thing to me on the night he had shown me his son's photograph. "And another thing—Priors, the house you were admiring, used to belong to the Bollinger family before they built Watersmeet. Perhaps deep in your subconscious there's something that recognises it."

It was her turn to stop.

"It really belonged to our family, that lovely place? And they sold it to build that—that mausoleum? They must have been crazy!"

"I've always thought so."

"I wonder if it's possible—I mean, your theory that in some strange way I have a memory of it? That's really rather fanciful, isn't it?"

I rejected the sudden impulse that made me want to tell her of my own connection with her family. What was to be gained after so many years?

"Tell me, are your mother and father with you on this trip?"

"No." Her tone was flat and dismissive. So she did not want to talk about her parents. Well, she would not be the first young lady to want to prove her independence. She looked the strong-willed, spirited sort, I thought, and I could easily imagine that parental control would be irksome to her.

"Are you staying long?"

"Just a week. I really came over to Europe on business but I couldn't leave without taking time out to look up my family. I'm an assistant to the fashion editor of *Chic*—you can imagine how thrilled I was when they sent me on an assignment to Paris!"

"My goodness, yes." I looked at her with respect. *Chic* was a magazine that had come my way only by courtesy of our American guests at the hotel and I had been vastly impressed by the glossiness of its pages and the quality of its pictures and reporting. Was there a clue here about her relationship with her parents? Perhaps they disapproved of their daughter having a career.

We had arrived at Priors by this time, and I ushered her inside. The autumn sun filtering through the mullioned windows turned the beech leaves which I had put into a copper urn to brightest gold, and chrysanthemums and michaelmas daisies glowed from a bowl which stood on the stone mantelpiece. Laura looked around her with appreciation.

"It's simply lovely," she said. "It surely is the most beautiful house in the world. It has such perfect proportions—those windows, the staircase!"

I smiled at her.

"I'm so glad you like it. Please sit down while I go and organise some coffee."

"Thank you. You're being very kind."

No, I thought. Not kind. Just strangely drawn to this tantalisingly familiar stranger. She turned to me as I rejoined her in the hall.

"You know, I'm not a particularly superstitious person, but I can't help feeling that the house welcomes me. Maybe it welcomes everyone! It's a benevolent sort of house, I guess—warm and rooted in history."

"Do tell me more about your work," I said, sitting down in a chair close to hers. "It sounds fascinating."

"It is—yet even so I came to Collingford partly to give myself time to consider a break from *Chic*. Since being over here I looked up my godfather who's the editor of *Here and Now*."

"I take it regularly!"

"It's good, isn't it? The thought of working on it never entered my head—I simply wanted to see Paul Maddox again. He left America years ago, but I always remembered him like a kind of favourite uncle. My father and he were big college buddies, but they've drifted apart since Paul came to England."

"But he offered you a job?"

"Isn't it amazing? All unbeknown to me he's been keeping tabs on my work, just like a perfect godfather, and it seems he really approves of me!"

"Yet you have doubts?"

She accepted the coffee I offered her and stirred it thoughtfully.

"I feel a certain loyalty to *Chic*, especially since they've given me this European trip, but on the other hand . . ."

"I didn't know *Here and Now* had a fashion section."

"They don't—that's the point. I'd be moving right out of that area into quite a different sort of journalism. Paul wants me to travel around Europe—to look at Nazi Germany first hand, to go to Italy to see if Mussolini really is making the trains run on time and see what else he may be up to. He thinks that from here on out women are going to be more and more involved in political life and national life too, and that includes wars. Gone are the days when men must work and women must weep—well, the Great War proved that, especially for you folk over here. If there should be another war, which heaven forbid, women will be as much part of it as men, yet so far hardly any woman's voice has been heard reporting on what's happening in Europe."

She had forgotten her coffee and was sitting forward on her chair, her eyes bright with excitement.

"Just what is your problem?" I asked with some amusement. "You look like a young lady whose decision has already been made."

She sat back and sighed.

"I suppose you're right. I keep having these niggling feelings of guilt about leaving *Chic* in the lurch—foolish, of course, they can replace me ten times over—and also my parents won't like it one bit."

"Why not?"

"They want me to marry a highly respectable, up-and-coming Boston lawyer. He's nice and intelligent. He's rich and he's mad about me—"

"But you don't love him?"

"Mrs Leyton, what must you think of me? I'm a perfect

stranger, with no right to burden you with all these heart-searchings of mine."

"Drink your coffee while it's hot. Sometimes it's easier to talk to strangers."

"For some reason you don't seem like one."

Obediently she picked up her cup and began to drink.

"There's another thing," she said, as she set it down again. "I can't help wondering if I'm good enough for this new job—"

"Of *course* you are!"

I joined in her laughter at this, for naturally I had no evidence of this, never having read any of her work. I was, however, certain that I was right. It was at this moment of perfect accord between us that Philip walked in, unheralded and unannounced.

I introduced them and dispatched Philip for another coffee cup. He returned with it and sat down on the settee beside her.

"Miss Maybury is going to be a foreign correspondent," I said. She hastened to disclaim this.

"That's far too grand a name for it. I'm just going to be a sort of roving reporter."

"Good," Philip said. "Whatever's going on in Europe needs a commonsensical, down-to-earth eye upon it, and that, in my view, is more likely to be applied by a woman than a man."

Laura looked at him, almost open-mouthed in her amazement.

"I expected you to say that it would be interesting to have my view on French cooking or Spanish lace-work! You mean you really approve of a girl coming out of the kitchen?"

"You should meet my sisters," Philip said. "Any thoughts of male dominance have been beaten out of me long ago."

"You poor, downtrodden creature," I sympathised. "Was this a social visit, or was there some special reason for it?"

"I came for my golf clubs. I left them here the last time I came home, if you remember, and this being my day off I thought I'd have a practice round on my own this afternoon, Michael being weighed down with work. Last time we played I seemed to have acquired a ferocious slice, and my putting was abominable."

"You know what they say," Laura said. "Drive for show, putt for dough."

"Do you play?" He turned to her eagerly. "You wouldn't like a game this afternoon?"

"I don't have any clubs—"

"We have some for hire at the hotel. I'd let you have them free—now I can't say fairer than that, can I?"

"Well—" She was quite obviously wavering. "I guess it would be fun, at that."

"You really haven't lived until you've played golf with me!"

"I don't think Aunt Lydia has anything arranged for me."

"I'll give you a lift back to Watersmeet and we can find out, if you like."

We sat over our coffee for a while, telling her a little of the history of Priors and of Collingford in general.

"You must come again," I said, when at last she and Philip got to their feet.

"I'd love to," she replied, and I felt that she was sincere. I had taken an instant liking to her. I liked her air of toughness and self-confidence, and I was glad that she had not settled for the conventional life and married her worthy Bostonian suitor. Like Lucy, she would have been bored, I felt certain.

Philip bore her off to Watersmeet and in the afternoon I presume the game of golf took place as arranged. I heard no more from him for the rest of the week.

I had in the back of my mind the intention to write to Lydia Bollinger and invite them all to dinner, but that week was exceptionally busy and somehow the time went. I was busy in the garden cutting back the poor, dead summer flowers when Philip came again.

"Your day off always takes me by surprise," I said, as he bent and kissed me. "It's quite frightening how quickly the weeks fly."

"Some go quicker than others."

I gave him a searching glance. The remark seemed to be significant.

"How did the golf go?" I asked.

456

"The golf? Oh, the golf! Splendid, thanks."

"I've been meaning to ask the Bollingers and Miss Maybury to dinner—"

"She's gone."

"Oh dear—already? How awful of me."

"She asked me to say goodbye to you. She meant to come but—well, as you said yourself, a week goes so fast. She did phone on the day she was due to leave, but there was no reply."

"I see." I bent to my task again. "What an awfully nice girl she was. I gather you saw quite a bit more of her."

"Yes."

There was a bleak sound about the monosyllable and I was aware of him standing there hovering in an uncharacteristic way, undecided whether to go into the house or stay outside, to unburden himself or remain silent. I waited.

"She felt she had to get back to New York," he said.

"Yes, of course. She's definitely going to take the job with *Here and Now*?"

"Yes."

"Then presumably she'll be back."

"I don't know. She wasn't wildly enraptured with the Bollingers."

"As big a tribute to her common sense as we're likely to hear," I said, straightening up and smiling at him. He did not smile in return. "Philip? Is there something wrong?"

He sighed and shrugged and ruffled the back of his head.

"I don't know. I don't suppose so." He picked up a stone and hurled it the length of the lawn. "It's just maddening that the one time I meet a girl who makes me feel as if—as if—" he broke off. "Never mind, Mother. Forget it. I'm sure I shall. Is dad inside? I wanted a word with him about staff holidays."

I watched him go, feeling troubled. I had a horrid suspicion that once Laura Maybury captured a man's imagination, it would be a very hard task indeed for him to wrench it free.

During the winter that followed Philip seemed to retreat into work. The international news was bleak. Italy had marched into Abyssinia in October and while we all knew that we were letting that poor little country down, so recent was our memory of the loss and suffering of war that we stood shudderingly on the sidelines and connived with France to close our eyes and ignore the fact that Mussolini continued to storm into Africa.

Laura would have much to report on, I thought, if ever she got to Europe. So far she was still in New York, serving out her notice with *Chic*. I knew this, for Philip let slip the information that he had received several letters from her.

It was the week before Christmas when Philip's car drew up at Priors with a spurt of gravel, and I knew as soon as I saw him step out of it that something had happened to please him. There was an air of boyish excitement about him as he strode into the house.

"Well? Have you some good news?" I asked him.

"Laura's in London at last. Mother—is it all right if I ask her for Christmas?"

"Ask her here? What about the Bollingers? Surely they will think it odd!"

"They're going away, it seems."

"Well, in that case, of course she can come. Are you sure she'll want to be flung into the bosom of the family?"

"I'll ask her tonight. I'm dashing down to take her out to dinner."

"To *London*?"

"I'd dash a lot further than that, believe me."

I believed him.

"I thought he'd grown more sensible," Roger commented when I told him. "What's got into him?"

"I think he's in love."

"Huh!" Roger was sceptical. "I seem to have heard that story before. I don't suppose this girl will be any different from any of the others."

"You haven't seen her," I said.

And, of course, once she arrived he was impressed, just as I knew he would be.

I found it hard to judge how Laura felt about Philip. It was, after all, early days. I had no knowledge of how many times they had met during the week she had spent in Collingford, but even if they had met every day it could not have totalled many hours. But what difference does that make, I asked myself?

I tried not to watch them, but as the days of her visit went on they were so aware of each other that whenever I was in a room with them the very air seemed to crackle with tension.

By Christmas Eve, Clare, Ben and Ellie had arrived and I felt that the house was purring like a contented cat. It echoed to the children's excited laughter and when they were asleep, to the sound of the King's College choristers. We sat round the fire and listened—Ellie perched on the arm of her father's chair, half-leaning against him; Clare, large with child, sitting close to Ben. Laura looked diminutive in a winged, green-velvet arm chair, while Philip was sitting slightly in the shadows.

Laura was listening, her head resting on her hand, but I caught a movement from the corner of my eye and looked up to see her head turn a fraction to the right. Her expression was unreadable. There was a line between her brows as steadily she gazed towards Philip.

Imperceptibly I moved a little so that I included him in my line of vision. He was gazing at her with a look of equal intensity, his bottom lip caught between his teeth, and suddenly I was overwhelmed with shame because I was intruding on something that was strictly between Philip and Laura—something both private and painful. I looked away towards the fire where the ash logs were burning.

Lucy and Nick and the children arrived in time for Christmas dinner the following day. Nick's parents had been invited, but their visit had been cancelled at the last moment because of Mrs Marchant's ill health.

"It's nothing serious," Lucy assured me privately. "Just one of her turns. At last she's found a way of getting her own back on the colonel! She waits until they're almost leaving the house for some engagement or other, and then comes over all peculiar so that they have to stay at home."

"You shouldn't laugh at her. She may really be ill—"

"Nonsense! She's having the time of her life. Is Philip in love with that girl?"

I looked up at the sudden change of subject.

"I rather think he may be," I said.

459

"Good heavens! I wonder why? She's awfully plain, isn't she? Quiet, too."

Plain? Quiet? They were the last two words I should have used to describe Laura, yet now that Lucy mentioned it I realised that somehow the spirit had drained out of her, leaving her gaunt and colourless, ivory skin stretched tautly across her cheekbones. The red of her painted lips stood out like a clown's make-up and her eyes were huge, with deep purple shadows.

We ate and drank and laughed and were jolly, and all that day I was conscious of her. She did her best to join in. She spoke when she was spoken to and smiled a great deal but it occurred to me that it seemed her whole concern was to take up as little space in our lives as possible—to efface herself altogether if it could be managed.

Philip, too, was quiet. Late at night after Ben's boys had gone to bed and Lucy and Nick had borne their family off into the night, he went and stood over Laura where she sat narrowly in the corner of the settee. He sat down beside her and looked into her eyes for a long moment.

"Happy Christmas," he said miserably.

She turned her head away from him.

"Please, Philip!"

He looked at her for a little longer then leaned back with his eyes closed.

"Oh God, what now?" he asked of no one in particular.

Laura rose and gravely, politely, excused herself and said good night to us all.

"It's been a lovely day," she said to me. "Thank you so much for making me part of your family."

She left us and it was the signal for everyone else to make the move towards bed. Only Philip sat on, terribly alone.

The following day she came to see me in my bedroom and told me that she wanted to leave.

"This must seem dreadfully rude—"

"No," I said quickly. "I would never think that of you. Something's gone very wrong, hasn't it?"

She turned away from me and went to the window, arms wrapped round her body as if for warmth.

"It's my fault," she said. "I should never have come."

460

"Philip wanted you here so much."

"I should have recognised the danger. I did recognise the danger, but something made me keep in touch with him. I didn't expect him to roar down to London at the speed of light the moment I arrived there, with an invitation to his home for Christmas."

"That's Philip," I said with a smile. "He's always known exactly what he wants out of life."

"Lucky Philip," she said bleakly.

"Are you cold?" She was shivering, I noticed, her shoulders hunched.

"No, not really. Nervous tension always makes me this way. I'll be OK."

"Do you really have to go? Look—sit down for a moment. There's no immediate rush, is there?"

I propelled her gently towards the bed and unresistingly she sat down on it. I sat beside her.

"Whatever's happened between you and Philip, you're very welcome here, you know. You said yourself, that first time, that it felt like home, didn't you?"

"That's the really awful thing. It would be so easy!" She was silent for a moment, biting her lip, then seemed to make up her mind.

"Mrs Leyton, you've been so kind to me, I feel I owe you some sort of an explanation."

"You're on the brink of this new career—anyone would have doubts about relinquishing it."

"It's more than that. You'd have to know my mother to understand fully—and my father, too. I can't tell you how I've *burned* all my life, because of the way he has treated her. She has been a well-dressed, pampered, decorative chattel—so conditioned to accept the role that the best thing she could think of for me was that I should marry the same sort of man. I had to fight to leave home and fight to hold on to my career and fight to stay independent. Now, as you say, I'm on the brink of this new career, for the first time competing on equal terms with men." She broke off and picked nervously at a thread in the bedspread.

"Philip wants me to marry him. He says he's in love with me."

461

"I'm sure he is," I said.

"Yes. Well—maybe I'm in love with him, too, but it doesn't seem right to me that I should be the one to make sacrifices. Why should it be the man's God-given right to continue with his career, while his wife forgets hers and gives all her attention to taking care of a house and raising a family?"

I opened my mouth to speak, then closed it again. In all conscience I could not speak high-sounding words, vowing that a home and family meant perfect fulfilment for every woman. How could I? I had not found it so. I was merely lucky that my business and family life could be so harmoniously interwoven.

"Part of me *shouts* to give in," she went on. "It tears me apart to leave him right now." She closed her eyes and shook her head. "But it's no good—I know it wouldn't work! I went to a good school, I did well at college, I was trained to think. And my brain tells me that I would be hopeless in the role of wife and mother."

"Philip would be the last man on earth to expect to treat you like a chattel! He's always been used to a working mother. Is there no room for compromise?"

"How could there be? There's no work for me here, in Collingford. Besides which—I'm not at all sure that I'm in favour of marriage under any circumstances. The whole concept of binding oneself to one man for ever seems incredible. I question whether it's necessary, whether it's not an old, outworn convention."

"Oh, I'm sure it's not that!"

"My parents have nothing whatever to say to each other. They ran out of conversation about three months after they married, I think—not that I was around at the time, I'm just going on present form—yet presumably they thought themselves in love when they actually plighted their troth?"

"So what's the answer? No permanent relationship? A succession of men?"

"Perhaps—I don't know. I just know that I can't marry Philip, that I'd never be the sort of wife he wants." She put her hand on my arm. "I'm sorry, Mrs Leyton. I didn't mean to hurt him."

462

"I know." I took a deep breath, part of me sympathising with her and part of me hating her for making my son unhappy. "You go to your new job, Laura. See how it works out. You may find that your ideas change—"

"I doubt it. I really doubt it."

She left shortly after our talk, a white-faced Philip taking her to the train. Unhappily I watched them drive away.

There should have been something I could have said to make her change her mind, surely? All of my instincts told me that she was wrong about marriage; but because I was conscious that I had been luckier than most, I found it difficult to find the right words.

I turned, and there in the hall mirror I saw my reflection. I was a small, grey-haired woman with a sagging jaw-line and crows-feet around my eyes; my best friend could never describe me as anything else. Never again would I draw admiring glances from the opposite sex. Never again would handsome young guests at the hotel attempt to draw me into flirtatious conversation, or even try to arrange assignations. I was old.

Yet I knew that inside the room I was about to enter was a man to whom I was still attractive and desirable, who still liked to hold me in his arms, who was my husband, my lover, my friend.

Oh, Laura, I thought. Marriage still has a great deal to recommend it—don't write it off just yet!

"I'm sorry she's gone," Ellie said to me. "I liked her."

I nodded. "Still, her attitude is surely something that you can understand, Ellie. After all, you were of the same mind. You had the same goal in life."

"Yes, liberation! But from what, Mother? Sometimes I wonder. Bigotry and subservience and the assumption of inferiority, certainly, but who can liberate you from loneliness?"

"Are you lonely?"

"Only sometimes. There's always so much to do—and so little time, as someone or other once said."

"Cecil Rhodes. Are you staying for New Year?"

"There's a party in the constituency I said I'd go to."

We avoided parties that New Year. We went to the

midnight service at St Peters and returned in a rather sombre mood to listen to the wireless and hear the revellers at the Savoy ballroom in London. Roger reached to turn off the switch with an irritated gesture.

"I don't know what they've got to be so joyful about," he said. "The world's in a terrible state."

I laughed at him.

"You're just a crusty old curmudgeon who spends his time wondering what the younger generation is coming to."

"I daresay," he agreed, with a grin.

But although I laughed, I too felt that there was little to be joyful about. There was an uneasy feeling in the air. I was much more aware of events in Germany ever since Laura had been over there, sending back reports to *Here and Now*.

"How well she writes," I said to Philip one day when he was at Priors and I came across him reading an account of a Hitler Youth Rally. It was a chilling report, made even more so by the fact that at the outset one had the impression that she was describing a thoroughly wholesome jamboree of the type enjoyed by boy scouts. It was only as one read on that the sinister undertones became apparent.

"Yes," he agreed shortly, and threw the magazine on to a nearby table.

Shortly after the beginning of the year we listened to the news bulletin which told us that the King's life was moving peacefully to its close. There was something indescribably moving in the thought that he had gone. I had only seen him once and that but briefly, but I felt his loss more than that of any previous monarch, perhaps because we were contemporaries. It never occurred to Roger and me not to accept Ellie's offer to take us into Westminster Hall where the King's coffin was lying in state, in order to pay our last respects.

It was evening when we arrived at Westminster, for Ellie had been heavily engaged in parliamentary business all day. If we were moved before we arrived there, the sight of the two-mile queue, ten deep, waiting to file past the coffin underlined our feeling of loss. My vision blurred with tears as I saw them—ordinary people who waited patiently in the endless line, shuffling forward with agonising slowness, cold and tired after a day's work, but determined to show their love and respect for the dead sovereign.

He was dead, and was mourned and buried with all the appropriate pomp and ceremony; but everyone's darling, the Prince of Wales, was on the throne, and once the solemn funeral was over, it seemed that now Britain was in for a new kind of monarchy. For Edward was a man of the people. He had visited distressed areas and served in the forces. We all knew he had had to be restrained from joining the men in the worst of the battle areas. We had seen him in a safety helmet, going down a mine. Cinema newsreels had affirmed that he was one of us.

Until he fell in love with a twice-divorced American.

Everyone took sides over the Abdication. There were those who felt betrayed; those who said that it was a sin and a shame—why shouldn't he be allowed to marry the woman he loved? There were those who felt that hypocrisy had won the day. I happened to be shopping in Oxford the following day and saw glossy pictures of him in cheap frames turned face down on the counter of Woolworth's.

"It wouldn't have done," Roger said sadly. "One feels for him. But it wouldn't have done."

I was inclined to agree. Anyway, the Duke and Duchess of York were an attractive couple and had those two dear little princesses. Good old England would go on, weathering this and other storms as it had always done.

The whole episode had successfully taken everyone's mind off what was happening in Spain where civil war had broken out.

"Laura's staying in Berlin until after the Olympic Games and then she's going to Madrid," Philip told me.

"You write to each other?"

It was the first time he had given me an inkling of this.

"Oh, yes. Letters are strange things, aren't they? I feel in some ways the writing of them has advanced my cause—as if we've been able to state opinions and pursue arguments in a way we never could have done if we'd been face to face."

"What do you argue about?"

"Very little, when it boils down to it. I wouldn't want to tie her down—"

"But everyone is tied down, one way or another."

"You know what I mean! If she wants to be a journalist, she could be a journalist. If she wants to press on towards some personal, private goal, I'd cheer her on. If she wants to go away, I'd understand—just so long as she came back."

"But Philip, what kind of a marriage would that be? What about children? A stable home?"

He laughed bitterly.

"I wouldn't want a family or a stable home without Laura. Anyway, it's all academic—she appears to be perfectly happy with the job she's doing."

Which, I thought, was more than could be said for Philip. He still worked hard and efficiently, but there was no joy in it any more. He came home more often now. Most of his friends were married, many with growing families. I lost count of the number of times he had been asked to stand as best man at weddings and he was much in demand as a godfather. I worried about him.

And he worried about Laura, for the news from Spain was frightening. In spite of a declaration of neutrality which France and Britain upheld, Germany and Italy sent every material aid possible to the insurgents, and Franco's forces were advancing towards Madrid. We heard that tanks, aircraft and infantry were attacking San Sebastian, which fell at the end of September, but Madrid, it appeared, still held.

I was witness to the amazing spectacle of Ellie and Philip actually in agreement on current events for almost the first time in their lives, both vociferously supporting the Republicans in Spain and uttering dire warnings about Hitler's actions in the rest of Europe. When Lord Halifax was quoted as saying that Hitler's Germany was 'the bulwark of Europe against Bolshevism', their fury knew no bounds.

"The man's mad," Philip said. "Can't he see that the war in Spain is a curtain-raiser?"

"And Chamberlain assures us that Hitler is perfectly sincere in seeking a negotiated peace in the Rhineland," Ellie added disgustedly. "When has that man ever been sincere? Somebody has got to stop him, some time."

When we heard that the Nazis had marched into Austria and taken over without a shot being fired—enthusiastically greeted in fact, by a large proportion of the population—we did not know what to think.

Philip hardly registered it. He was obsessed with Laura's safety in Spain. Never before had there been such widespread bombing of towns and villages, and while she continued to file her stories and even managed to find time for the odd letter to him, he was desperately worried that she would come to some harm.

When letters did not arrive, he frequently phoned the offices of *Here and Now* for news of her. Always their reply was the same. Her reports were still coming through. They were invaluable—everyone was moved by them. There had been more letters to the magazine about them than ever before, on any other subject. The description of the bewilderment in Irun after the bombardment; the lost child, crying for his mother; and the bride, killed on her journey back from the church. Perhaps, said the editor, Laura was doing more than anyone to promote the future peace of the world. Who could tell?

There was a long period of silence. We heard that Madrid had fallen and that the Republicans had taken to the hills to continue the fight as guerrillas. Of Laura there was no news. Philip phoned everybody—the offices of the magazine, the Spanish Embassy, even her parents in New York. Nothing.

"I'm going over to look for her," he said.

"But the country's in chaos!"

"All the more reason. I'll get to Madrid somehow."

I had no doubt that he would.

He would go, he said, in three days' time. His assistant could cover for him; Michael Blanchard was in the office and could be called upon if necessary.

"Damn it, I'm here too," Roger said. "I'm not dead yet, you know."

"I didn't think for one moment that you were. A dead man wouldn't consume nearly so much of my best brandy. Still, I don't imagine there'll be any need to trouble you."

I thought Roger looked disappointed, but the fact could not be denied that rheumatism was making him increasingly lame. He exercised and ignored it as much as possible, but he tired more easily than of yore.

As I did too, of course. But I still kept my eye on the Ring of Bells for it was my pride and my joy and I loved every corner of it.

It was the day before Philip was due to leave for Spain that I was returning from it. I turned the bend in the road and she was there. A few years earlier I should have taken to my heels and run towards her. Now I stood stock still and whispered her name. Laura! How had she come here? Out of the blue like this, without a word to Philip or to anyone?

She seemed oblivious of my approach, rapt in her contemplation of Priors, but when I joined her at the wall she turned to me.

"It's so lovely," she said, as if we were continuing a conversation. "When I was out there, I thought of it often; I was afraid that when I saw it again I should be disappointed, but it's not so—I love it as much as ever!"

"Laura, what are you doing here? We've been out of our minds with worry! Philip—"

"I tried to call him from London and then again from Oxford, but no one could find him."

"He's preparing to leave for Spain tomorrow, to look for you."

"Let's go and stop him," she said.

30

It was a funny sort of marriage. Roger said so, frequently, with sadness in his voice, and I, too, felt that the fact that Laura lived by herself in a flat in London for the greater part of the time, coming back to Chantry Court and Philip's apartment there for weekends, seemed a strange way to conduct a life together.

"What made you change your mind?" I asked her, just before their quiet wedding.

"Europe," she had said, after a moment's thought. "All the unrest there. Death and uncertainty and families torn apart. Suddenly I felt that Philip represented everything that made life worth living—all the stability and happiness that most people long for."

"But you're not ready to settle for domesticity?"

"No. Not yet—perhaps not ever. Praise the Lord, Philip seems happy to settle for me as I am, not as everyone else thinks I ought to be. Paul's basing me in London for a while, so I shan't be far away."

The Bollingers regarded the match with total bewilderment. Marrying a Leyton was, perhaps, just acceptable in this strangely democratic age—especially for an American Bollinger who could be forgiven for not knowing quite what was expected of her; but to marry a man and then proceed to live apart from him was incomprehensible.

"I *simply* don't understand young people today," Lady Bollinger said to me after the wedding. "After all, there's all that business in the prayer book about *cleaving* only unto him—and how, I ask you, can anyone cleave when they're miles apart?"

"Spiritually, perhaps?" I suggested diffidently.

She looked at me in a bemused sort of a way, as if I were speaking in some strange tongue, and turned to Roger to talk of prospects for the Derby.

"We'll work it out," Laura said to me when we had a quiet moment together. "Don't worry about us. This is a marriage where my work and Philip's work are equally important to us. I know it must seem strange to you, but it makes sense to us. No one can possibly tell what the future will hold. Something's about to break in Europe, you know—something absolutely cataclysmic, and all I know is that when it breaks, Philip and I have got to be together." She smiled at me. "I'll make him happy, believe me. We'll make our own peculiar kind of intermittent heaven, I promise you."

"I'm sure you will," I said.

"And you know that Priors will always draw me back."

We must see that Philip gets Priors when we go, I thought. It's never been so important to Ben—he could be compensated in other ways.

"Are they going to be happy?" Charlotte asked me as we stood together, watching them from a distance.

"I think so," I said. "It's not everyone's sort of life, but it seems to be theirs. It's what we've always believed in, Charlotte. Equality."

She turned to me, smiling.

"It's been a long time coming," she said. "Is it really here?"

Although the wedding was quiet, it meant a full day for me and it was not until everyone had left and Roger and I were once more alone that I thought over Laura's words.

Something cataclysmic, she had said. Oh please, God— not another war, I prayed. Didn't mankind learn anything from one generation to the next?

It was later that year that we heard Hitler had invaded Czechoslovakia.

Ben and Clare were with us, with Roger and Christopher and Alan and, at last, Genevieve, already toddling; a sunny-natured, happy child, in grave danger of being spoiled to death.

"This must surely be the point where we stop him," Roger said, grim-faced.

Ben nodded, equally grim.

"I agree—but with what? Germany has been rearming for years."

"War," Clare said tonelessly, as if she was taking the word out of store and considering it, remembering what it had meant to her the last time. I looked at Ben and saw that he was remembering too. His skin had tightened about his bony face and there was misery in his eyes.

"There are worse things," he said, after a long pause.

"Are there?" Clare's voice was bitter.

"Certainly. Betrayal. Treachery. Cowardice."

I knew that he was right, yet when Chamberlain flew back from Munich with his piece of paper announcing 'peace in our time' every instinct I possessed made me sag back into my chair with relief.

"Thank God, thank God," I whispered.

"No!" Ben was on his feet and in one sudden movement had hurled a cushion to the floor. "No," he said again violently, then flung himself out of the room with an expression of the deepest despair on his face. Clare sat on the edge of her chair, her hands gripping the arms; then she, too, went outside.

Roger looked at me and for a moment his lips moved soundlessly.

"He's right," he said hoarsely at last. "For the first time in my life I'm ashamed of being British."

"But war, Roger!" I leaned forward towards him. "Think what it means. Think of Jamie and Nico."

"Think of others like them in Czechoslovakia and Austria. It's not to be borne, Jenny."

"No," I said, closing my eyes wearily. "It's not to be borne."

He came and sat on the arm of my chair and we clung together. Two sad old people, I thought—but together we could face what had to be faced.

More treachery. That's what had to be faced. Hitler broke the agreement by which he had been granted the Sudetenland and soon he was claiming Danzig in Poland. The weather was perfect, just as it had been in 1914.

Roger and I sat in the shade of the trees one afternoon watching Nico and Jamie play tennis. They had just completed their first year at Oxford. Just like Ben in 1914, I thought. How could I bear it?

Ben and Clare were to come again this summer, for on 3rd September we were to celebrate our Golden Wedding and a big family party was planned.

"We'll make it an anniversary to remember," Roger said. "Heaven knows when we'll all be together again. We shall have to make a list of guests."

I agreed that certainly we should; but lazily we sat there, enjoying the sun and the sound of the tennis ball and the voices of the twins.

"Remember our honeymoon?" Roger cocked an eyebrow at me.

"Vividly!" I turned to smile at him.

"We talked about our Golden Wedding then, didn't we? We worked it out, sitting there in the train on our way to Wales. 1939, we said. It seemed impossibly distant, and now, here we are."

"I wouldn't have missed a minute of it."

"Nor I."

For a while we sat in contented silence until I noticed that someone was coming down the track on a bicycle.

"Who can this be?" I asked, shading my eyes. "The post has been already."

"It's Jock McKay," Roger said after a moment. "What in the world can he want?"

"Money, I expect," I said with a laugh.

Jock was a small, wiry Scotsman who had turned up, apparently from nowhere, to live in Collingford some time during the last decade. He had been in the Army and he lived on his pension, but being brimful of energy he kept himself occupied with numerous voluntary activities. One week he would be collecting with dedicated vigour for the lifeboatmen, and the next would be organising a raffle for Homes for Retired Donkeys. People were inclined to make fun of him but Roger knew—none better—that if work needed to be done for the good of the community, Jock McKay would be the man to do it.

He disappeared from view where the trees and bushes hid the track from our sight, but reappeared a few moments later, minus his bicycle, whipping off his bicycle clips as he approached us, as if unable to waste a second.

His errand was soon made clear. He had been put in charge of arranging billets for schoolchildren who were likely to descend on us from London in the evacuation programme that was to take place the moment it seemed that war was inevitable.

"How many can I put you down for?" he asked, flipping over the pages of a notebook and licking a pencil with an air of brisk efficiency.

"We have plenty of room," I said. "How many do you want us to take?"

"Could you take an entire family? Say three or four?"

"If necessary."

"Jenny, Jenny—we have no staff worth speaking of!" Roger turned to me in an agitated way.

"We'd manage somehow."

"Well, that's kind of you, Mrs Leyton. Most kind. I'll be

in touch and let you know as soon as possible what our needs are."

"Won't you stay for some coffee?"

"No, thank you, though I'm obliged to you for the offer. I've a deal of cycling to do before the day is over. Good day, Mrs Leyton—and to you, Sir." He gave a smart military style salute and strode off.

"Well," Roger said heavily, watching his retreating form. "Now that you've calmly agreed to turning Priors into a home for heaven knows how many screeching children, I suppose you'll feel that we're doing our bit."

"I suppose I will," I agreed. I patted his arm. "Stop being such an old grouch! Priors was meant to be full of life, and you know it as well as I do."

He smiled and I knew his mind was going back through the years.

"You're right," he said. "As always. And there's been plenty of it, hasn't there, one way and another?" He frowned thoughtfully. "What happened to that train-set Ben and Philip used to have? It had enough rails to go right round the attic. If we get some boys here, we'll have to look it out."

"I know exactly where it is," I said. "It's in that brown trunk in the old nursery, next to the chest with the dressing-up clothes."

"*Really?*" He couldn't have been more delighted if I had announced the arrival of some old friend he had not seen for years. "I think I'll go and have a look at it—make sure it's all there."

He got to his feet and I looked up at him, laughing.

"Darling, there's no hurry! You don't have to go this minute."

"I've just taken the fancy," he said.

Shaking my head with rueful affection, I let him go. When, after all, had I ever been able to do anything else?

473

Epilogue

3rd September 1939

It was almost time to leave for church. The bells would soon change from their incongruously joyful carillon to the single tolling that meant there were only five more minutes left for the latecomers to scurry into their pews, yet Izzie could not resist one final journey through the green baize door from the kitchen.

She stood for a moment in her best coat and hat, her handbag clasped in front of her with tense, gloved hands, looking bleakly at the room before her, the graceful stairs leading from it, the high-mullioned windows at the end where the uncaring sunshine streamed through.

It had always been the heart of the house, this room. A log fire burned in the great hearth all winter and the family always gathered here to sit before it in the deep, comfortable, flower-patterned chairs. Fine old wood glowed, the smell of polish mingling with the scent of flowers. It had seen a lot of life, this room; had heard laughter and music and voices raised in anger and tears, as well as murmured expressions of love.

On this day—this terrible day—it had been arranged for a celebration. The long table from the dining room had been brought in and placed across the room under the windows at the far end, and two others were set at either side, forming three sides of a rectangle. All were prepared with the finest lace-edged cloths and napery, bright silver and gleaming crystal.

There were roses everywhere—golden roses. A huge bowl of them stood high in the curve of the stairs and each table bore its own decoration.

In the centre of the top table stood a three-tiered wedding

cake, not white, but a delicate gold, its icing intricately latticed and whorled, and this, too, was topped by a single perfect yellow rose in a slender golden vase.

You had to hand it to those people from Chantry Court, Izzie thought. They knew their job. It all looked beautiful.

And the tragedy was that it was all wasted!

Well—almost. Mr Ben and his wife had gone back to their school in Somerset, and Mr and Mrs Mark had never even arrived. And all the Hereford relations, they'd cried off, and Miss Ellie had gone rushing back to Whitehall the minute the word 'crisis' was mentioned.

"We're going to be late, Mrs Noakes." Doreen, the new kitchen maid, her face anxious under a frizz of red hair and a pert green hat with a scrap of veiling, looked round the door from the kitchen.

Izzie ignored the urgency in her voice and continued to look grimly at the display in front of her.

"I could forgive Hitler anything," she said at last, dismissing in a single phrase the concentration camps, the genocide, the rape of Poland and Czechoslovakia and Austria. "But not for this. Not for spoiling her day. She's been looking forward to it for months, all the family together again. It's a crying shame, it is really. I could kill him."

She turned to look at Doreen and noticed her attire for the first time.

"Is that what you're going to wear?" she asked.

The question was superfluous. There was now no time to change, even if she had the mind, and the girl's lips tightened at the implied criticism. She said nothing, but tossed her head defiantly, walking through the hall towards the front door.

"We might as well go this way now we're here," she said. "I don't want to be late, even if you do."

With disapproval expressed in every line of her face, Izzie followed her. There was, after all, much to disapprove of, from Doreen's unsuitable hat to the antics of the madman across the channel; from the celebration that had fallen so disastrously flat, to the effrontery of a kitchen maid who would use the front door as to the manner born.

It was time somebody turned round and told them,

Izzie thought—Hitler, Doreen, everybody. Times weren't what they used to be, and that was a fact nobody could deny.

The peal of bells came to an end and there was a second or two of silence, broken at last by the single bell. Izzie left the house and hurried up the track, her breath growing short as her pace quickened. And all the time the bell boomed on, tolling the death of an age.

There was a Bach prelude playing inside the church. It was dim there, except for the torrent of colours pouring through the east window, and the remnants of the Leyton family had already gathered and were sitting in the pew that Leytons had occupied for as long as anyone could remember.

Jenny groped for Roger's hand and turned to give him a brief, nervous smile as she felt its answering pressure, as warm and reassuring as always.

It was to have been such a joyful day. Family and friends were to have come from miles away to celebrate with them, and the service had been designed as a special thanksgiving for fifty years of happy marriage. Such irony! Who could feel joyful knowing that it was all to happen again; the misery of loss and separation; the waste of precious young lives.

It wasn't too late for Germany to draw back from the brink. Jenny could not suppress that small, flickering hope that Hitler would remove his troops from Poland and allow the world to breathe again. There was not long to wait now before everyone would know, one way or the other.

The processional hymn began and the congregation rose. There was comfort in the familiar ritual, in the unhurried observance of the traditional ceremony, but she hated the feeling that at this time the family was incomplete—that Ben and Clare and Ellie were missing, and Mark and Charlotte too. One could understand the caution of those who were to have travelled from a distance. Pray God their fears were unnecessary, and that life would return to normal.

That her prayers had not been answered she knew as soon as she saw Ned English come through the vestry door into the church. It had been his task to listen to the wireless and to bring the news, so that the congregation could be informed the moment the Prime Minister had spoken.

Surely she had read somewhere that a man in the dock always knew when he had been condemned to hang because the jury would never meet his eyes when they filed back into their box?

It was like that with Ned English. He plodded heavily down the transept, dragging the leg that had been wounded on the Somme, looking neither to right nor left, his grim gaze riveted to the worn stones beneath his feet. His appearance was greeted with a tangible silence; a communal abatement of breath. He handed a paper up to the Reverend Chalmers and turned to sit woodenly in a nearby pew.

The vicar, old and bent and white-haired now, held the paper in a trembling hand. He had as much reason as anyone to dread another war. He had lost a son in the last one; his grandsons were of an age to fight in this. Jenny found her attention fixed on that trembling piece of paper.

"My friends," he said at last in a voice that was surprisingly firm. "It is my sad duty to tell you that we are now at a state of war with Germany. The following is a summary of the Prime Minister's message to the nation."

Jenny bent her head. It was impossible to concentrate on the actual words; enough to know that it had happened.

She was still holding tight to Roger's hand, like a drowning man might cling to a safety raft. As long as they were together, she thought, they could withstand anything. For fifty years they had sustained each other and they would go on doing so.

And grandmother had said that he was the rackety sort.

From her seat at the high table Jenny looked around her. So many were missing. But Philip and Laura were there, and Lucy and Nicholas and the dear children, Beth and Jamie and Nico. And John and Angela had come with two of their daughters and their daughters' husbands and children. And Izzie was there, sitting down with the family as was her right, and other close friends; the Goodsons, the Fenwicks, the Chalmers.

The buzz of conversation was muted. There was only one

topic under discussion and that in quiet voices, for no one could quite believe that it had actually happened. Yet in a way there was a kind of relief that it had come at last. After so many months of uncertainty, they knew now what had to be done.

The food was served by the Chantry Court waiters—too much food and too many waiters. When the meal was over and the golden cake had been cut, Philip rose to his feet, first making sure that every glass was filled.

"My friends," he began. "Ben was to have proposed the toast to my parents, but he has had to go back to his school and I have had the honour thrust upon me. A poor substitute, I am sure you are thinking—and rightly so! I'm not clever with words the way Ben is. And even if I were—even if I could make jokes and deliver polished witticisms, I doubt very much whether any of you would feel like laughing today. So I'm not going to make a speech, but merely ask you to drink to this beloved pair."

He looked down at his mother by his side and rested his hand lightly on her shoulder. She smiled up at him and for a moment they exchanged a long look.

"On the other hand," Philip said. "Maybe I will make a speech after all."

Some of the guests had already risen, glasses in hand, but at this they sat down again with a laugh. It was the lightest moment so far.

"It won't be as good as the speech my academic brother would have made, but to the devil with it—not even Hitler can prevent me marking this occasion with a bit of a flourish even if, on the face of it, the news we've had today gives little reason to rejoice."

He faltered and looked down at the table, picked up his glass and nervously twisted the stem in his hands as if uncertain how to go on. Perhaps he should just propose the toast and shut up, he thought. Who cared about speeches on the opening day of the Second World War? But no! There was something he wanted to say, and say it he would, however clumsily.

"You might think," he went on, "that today we have little to cheer about and of course, you would be right. On the

478

other hand, fifty years of love and companionship, of caring for others, mustn't be allowed to go unrecognised."

There were a few 'hear, hears' from the guests.

"It struck me," Philip said, "back there in the church, that Priors has always been a sort of sanctuary—not only in the days when it was a Priory that succoured the poor and needy, but in a purely personal way, to the family and I hope to our friends. No matter what strains and stresses any of us have suffered in the big, cruel, outside world, and no matter what others have thought about us, we've always found sanctuary here. Mother and dad might not have approved of everything we've done"—and here he smiled down at his parents again—"but this was always home; always an oasis of love and acceptance where we could be ourselves. And for this, our eternal thanks, my dears."

Not far from tears, Jenny reached up and touched his arm.

"And during the next few days we're expecting a family of London children to be billeted on us here, so ladies and gentlemen, we are still in the sanctuary business. The tradition goes on.

"And that, perhaps, is the most important thing of all to remember today. No matter what happens in the years to come, Priors will last and the Ring of Bells will last, for the two have always been inextricably linked—and I hope that the values they represent will last too. I hope that after whatever is to come to us during the next few years, we shall be able to stand once again at peace in this incomparable countryside, knowing that we have not only survived, but survived with honour and without bitterness."

He laughed, a little embarrassed, and looked around him.

"So," he said, "having firmly stated that I was not going to make a speech, I proceed to drone on and on, which Laura would tell you was only to be expected. And having said so much, I'm damned if I remember what it was I wanted to ask you to drink to exactly."

"To mother and dad, of course, because it's their day and we love them. But what else? To courage, perhaps, because we're going to need it; and determination and humour, because we'll never get by without it.

"But when all's said and done, there's only one thing I am determined that we shan't forget. Please rise and raise your glasses—to love!"

Family and friends stood and smiled towards the white-haired couple at the top table.

"To love," they echoed.